"Create an android berserker," she murmured.

Talk about a challenge . . .

"Your new laboratory already awaits you. I promise you, it so far exceeds the facility you have here as your own genius surpasses the minds of the life-units who deny you your just recognition," the berserker said.

Despite herself, Vivian Travers felt a thrill the like of which she had not felt for many decades, certainly since the days when she had created Lancelot. What the enemy offered would truly be a challenge worthy of her skills—and think what she would learn about the berserkers themselves! In order for Vivian to bridge the gap between whatever device she might create and the berserkers' mechanical natures, they would need to open themselves to her. She would learn their most intimate secrets, acquire the knowledge human generals had wished for since humanity's first encounter with the killer machines.

—From "Servant of Death," by Jane Lindskold and Fred Saberhagen

MAN
VS.
MACHINE

Edited by John Helfers
and Martin H. Greenberg

DAW BOOKS, INC.
DONALD A. WOLLHEIM, FOUNDER
375 Hudson Street, New York, NY 10014

ELIZABETH R. WOLLHEIM
SHEILA E. GILBERT
PUBLISHERS
http://www.dawbooks.com

First Printing, July 2007
1 2 3 4 5 6 7 8 9

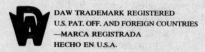

Acknowledgments

Contents

MAN
vs.
MACHINE

Introduction

By John Helfers

Given the theme of this anthology, I think it's time to reveal what some—or many—in the science fiction community might think is a guilty pleasure: one of my all-time favorite films is *Terminator 2: Judgment Day*. Not only because it was and still is a stunning achievement in special effects, but also because of the heart of the story that James Cameron and William Wisher, Jr., came up with (ignoring any of the myriad time-travel paradox issues) to tell an even better story of Sarah Connor versus a killer robot from the future than the first time around. The interface between humanity and machine was examined on several levels, with some aspects answered, but, at least in Cameron's vision, more questions were raised about natural and artificial consciousness and about the role that machines will play in our own future—the fate that we are making for ourselves every day.

The themes explored in *T2* have been cropping up more frequently with today's advances in computer technology. With computers becoming more powerful with each incarnation and robots doing more and more, such as piloting vehicles across remote, inhospitable terrain without any human oversight (such as the recent Grand Challenges sponsored by DARPA and the Pentagon), can true machine intelligence and wholly autonomous robots be that far off in the future? And when that day arrives, what will machines have to say about their human creators? How will they interact with us? Will there ever come a day when they try to destroy us?

The debate over the pros and cons of artificial intelligence and creating self-guided robots has gone on ever since the first computer and the first functioning robot were invented. No one really knows what might happen, but at some point the questions above (except, hopefully, the last one) will have to be addressed.

While sitting in my office writing this introduction, I took a casual look around at the machines that surrounded me and provided me with so much that I take for granted every single day. From the amazingly complex computer I typed these words on to the relatively simple machines that provided light, heat, printed text on demand, kept drinks cold and preserved food, allowed me to talk to someone across the country instantaneously, to a small machine around my wrist that tamed and quantified an insubstantial concept like time, machines were all around me. And the computer and the lamp and the refrigerator are all connected to much larger machines that give them power to operate, and those machines are connected in a grid to others all across the country and around the world. Meanwhile, billions of communications zip back and forth through fiber-optic lines and to and from satellites that circle the globe. It was a sobering thought to realize just how much we depend on machines to provide us with what we consider the basic comforts of life now—and it is even more sobering to consider that many of these things weren't even invented a century ago.

If we look ahead another century—or perhaps even only twenty to fifty years—will our machines grow more capable of serving us, or anticipating our needs and fulfilling them? Will we have true robots, à la Isaac Asimov's vision, with the potential pleasures and perils that come with them?

When I came up with the idea for this anthology, I didn't want it to be just "men versus robots," and I made sure that the authors I had invited knew that. While I was very pleased to get some down-and-dirty science fiction combat stories, I was very surprised at the wide range of fiction, and the extremely wide interpretation that the authors contained herein took on what I considered a relatively simple theme. From military SF to historical fiction to humanist science fiction to what can only be categorized as slipstream in one instance, these fifteen authors all went beyond the simple definition of man versus machine and came up with stories that illustrate a mere sampling of what future conflicts might arise between mankind and technology.

So as you turn the page and explore both what might have been and what might be to come, take a look around your home, and give some thought to the machines that surround you and make your life more comfortable. And keep watching them. Because you never know, in this day and age, when the idea of man versus machine might turn from fiction . . . into fact.

Servant of Death

By Jane Lindskold and Fred Saberhagen

Jane Lindskold is the author of eighteen novels and over fifty short stories. Although most of her fiction is fantasy, she loves science fiction and is delighted when the opportunity arises to write about space ships, computers, and alien worlds. Visit her at www.janelindskold.com.

Fred Saberhagen has been writing science fiction and fantasy for somewhat more than forty years. Besides the Berserker® series he is known for his Swords and Lost Swords series, and also his Dracula series. His most recent publication is *Ardneh's Sword,* connecting the Swords series and *Empire of the East.* He lives in Albuquerque, New Mexico, with his wife, Joan Spicci.

"This base is under attack! This base is under attack!"
    The hollow, booming voice from the loudspeakers jarred Vivian Travers to her feet and started her moving across her private laboratory to where her customized battle armor hung in its rack. Her hands were in contact with the cool metal almost before her conscious mind had fully registered what the voice was saying.
    There had of course been practice alerts during the several centuries since this research base, on the large

moon of the planet Lake, had become her regular residence—but far too few such drills, in her judgement.

With the skill of long practice Vivian had already opened the front of the armor, stepped inside, and leaned back, pressing against key contact points. Leads automatically inserted themselves at various points, cutting through clothing where necessary. The sensation was uncomfortable, but Vivian ignored it, reaching for her carbine even as the front of the armor closed and latched.

This is not a drill! Berserkers sighted approaching this base. All hands to battle stations. Repeat! This is not a drill.

"And why shouldn't they be approaching," Vivian muttered inside her helmet, closing the door of her private lab behind her, locking it out of habit. "When the defenses have been allowed to go to hell? Damned politicians!" But as she did not transmit, there was no reply.

She hurried down the corridor, feeling rather than hearing as hatches and bulkheads sealed behind and beneath her throughout the base. Lake Moon Research Base tunneled deep into the rock of its namesake moon. Its overall design was a good one, Vivian knew. She had created it herself over a hundred years before.

Vivian's battle station was in the main weapons bay, where she was assigned to damage control and back-up gunnery. If berserkers were attacking, both would likely be needed—if anyone survived to need anything at all.

The sprawling base housed not quite four hundred people, mostly researchers and their immediate families. The bulk of the moon around them was naturally devoid of any native life, and so were the planets, moons, comets, and asteroids that made up the Pinball

System, in which Lake was the fifth planet from the sun. Even the "lakes" for which the fifth planet was named were devoid of life, mere pools of stagnant acid, which were slowly corroding the minerals upon which they rested.

Moving past other suited, hurrying human figures through the cavernous main weapons bay, Vivian began to run a check on one of the gun batteries.

"Yes," she muttered to herself again. "Why should they not have decided to attack?"

The berserkers were programmed to exterminate life in all its forms, wherever and whenever they could come to grips with it. Created by a race that the Earth-descended version of Galactic humanity had dubbed the Builders, the berserkers had been forged as the ultimate weapon in the Builders' war against the Red Race. Some flaw in their programing had led to the berserkers annihilating not only the Red Race but the Builders as well. After many thousands of years, if one was inclined to include microscopic creatures in the tally, the berserkers had expunged from the Galaxy uncountable billions of what they called life-units. But their quest for the perfect order of death was far from ended.

Rebuilding, reconstructing, redesigning themselves as the years passed, the berserkers came in a variety of forms, ranging from bipedal robots to immobile data-processing boxes, from machines the size of a small dog to the pair of hulking dreadnoughts that now, according to the latest announcement from the loud-speakers, were bearing down upon Lake Moon.

As she hurried to her battle station, Vivian had tuned her helmet speakers to bring her command chatter. Now she heard General Gosnick, the base commander, saying calmly, "Launch individual fight-ers. What we think are the appropriate enemy sche-matics are being beamed to your control panels. This pair look like older models, and they're pretty badly beaten up. We may be able to disable them before they can close to effective striking range of the base."

"Understood." That would be the voice of the relatively junior officer in tactical command of the squadron just now launching.

In mental communication with her own armor, Vivian called up on her visor an image of what the base's sensors were picking up. The information appeared both as a direct visual image and as a stream of data overlaying the visual. She was studying it when General Gosnick's voice came over her private channel.

"Vivian, do you concur with my analysis of the situation?"

"I do." With a thought, she zoomed in for a tighter inspection of the hull of the marginally closer of the two approaching behemoths. "Definitely old damage. Judging from the angle of the scatter pattern, I'm wondering if it may possibly be even older than berserker contact with Earth-descended humans."

It was an eerie thought, that these two hulks, survivors of some ancient battle, might have been struggling through the Galaxy in normal space for millennia, perhaps trying to free themselves from some entangling nebula of gas or dust.

"However that may be, our fighters should be able to take them out. And maybe after this we can get some serious updating of our defenses."

"Maybe." The general did not sound too optimistic. For a long time, political complications had blocked progress in that direction.

Vivian went on: "I'm going to transmit a series of suggested targets . . . with your permission."

She remembered to add the last, although General Gosnick did not tend to be a stickler for command hierarchy as some of his predecessors had been. The Templars often rotated injured officers to Lake Moon, where they could continue to make useful contributions while recuperating. General Gosnick had lost both legs, and his metabolism was proving resistant to accepting bio-linked prosthetics. His role on Lake Moon rotated on a regular basis between that of administrator and test subject. He was accustomed to taking suggestions, and even direct orders from Vivian Travers, who, by reason of both her specialized skills and seniority, occupied a unique position in the base community.

Damaged as they were, the berserkers proved to be not totally ineffective as opponents, though they never managed to attack the base directly. When the battle was over, the enemy reduced to drifting chunks of relatively harmless hardware, interspersed with glowing incandescent clouds, several of the fighters needed to be towed back to base. Three pilots were going to be very glad that the hospital was not merely on the cutting edge of medical technology—it was where that edge was honed.

On standing down from her battle station, Vivian went to the hangar bay and put in several hours consulting with the workers and robots repairing the damaged fighters. Since working on the fighters was easier in minimal gee, and since low-gee was easier to adapt to in her suit, she left it on. Cobalt blue, with a surface texture that resembled lacquer, her battle armor stood out among the more utilitarian equipment worn by those around her. Vivian didn't miss the occasional envious gaze or covetous sigh as she extruded various auxiliary limbs as needed.

Make your own, she thought cheerfully. *I did.*

Consulting with the crew chief in charge of repairs on the fighters, Vivian took note of a set of peculiar small piercings on the hull of one of the small craft. Four little holes, a couple of centimeters apart, in one short row, and another similar row of four about two meters away. The crew chief speculated that the piercings had been caused by some sort of mine, one that threw shrapnel, but that the shrapnel had not been able to do sufficient damage.

General Gosnick glided over to join them. He was not wearing his prosthetics, which would have been a distraction, but was riding in a state-of-the art chair that doubled as body armor if needed. Its lower profile gave him an advantage when viewing the fighter's undercarriage.

"Odd that shrapnel would have hit in such neat lines."

"Maybe," a new speaker said, coming up to join them, "what made those marks was an automated mine rather than shrapnel. The mine might have tried to anchor, but failed and dropped off. We'd never have noticed one more explosion among all the rest."

The new arrival went by the name Brother Angel. He belonged to a militant subcult of the Templars. There he had served with such distinction that the envious joked that if he wore all his medals, he could dispense with any other form of armor. Although synthetic skin had been grafted on, Brother Angel still showed the ravages of the complex surgeries that had been done to save his sight and hearing. Pious, devoted, and apparently as focused on the destruction of the berserkers as they were on the destruction of all Life, he had been repeatedly frustrated in his desire to return to active duty by sporadic irregularities that cropped up in the functioning of his new sensory apparatus.

Doubtless, Vivian thought sourly, *Brother Angel is thrilled to have the action come to him.*

"That's an interesting suggestion, Brother Angel," General Gosnick said. "I'd be interested in seeing the specs for such a mine. This might not be the only wave in this attack."

"I'll see what I can do," Brother Angel said.

Vivian excused herself. She headed back to her quarters, still wearing her armor, although she'd opened the face plate on the helm. She might first have dropped her armor off at the lab, but at the moment the shortest path to a hot shower and a meal took priority.

She strolled through "her" hub, waving at a few neighbors who were gathered in the garden area of the central residential plaza, sharing drinks and doubtless speculating about the berserker attack. A bit of excitement for a change, and no serious harm done—that seemed to be the flavor of the remarks she caught. She waved and promised to join them when she'd had a chance to clean up.

Vivian's quarters were grouped along their own corridor off one of the residential hubs. Most of the residential suites were arranged in about the same way, as it facilitated sealing off an area in case of mechanical failure or contagious illness. It also guaranteed that the residents would have a certain amount of privacy, a valuable commodity in an enclosed and isolated social system.

Thinking ahead to the pleasures of warm water followed by whiskey and light conversation, Vivian almost bumped into the service robot that was coming around one of the blind bends in what amounted to her private hallway. The serbot was shorter than she was—shorter than most humans—perhaps a meter and a third where its upper portion rose like the head and chest of a centaur above the multilimbed barrel that scuttled along on a variety of adaptable appendages.

"Excuse m—," Vivian began automatically, then stopped herself. First, it was ridiculous to apologize to a service robot, any more than to a table or a chair. Second, there was no way a properly functioning robot should have come that close to hitting her. Buffers were preprogramed, and the corridor was plenty wide enough that, even allowing for the relative bulk of her battle armor, the serbot should have had plenty of clearance.

She was about to demand that the serbot submit to inspection when she realized that what now blocked her return to the hub only superficially resembled a serbot—or rather, it would resemble a serbot to anyone who did not look at it with a critical and experienced eye. To Vivian, who was both critical and experienced, the differences were glaring.

Sheer, deadly terror hit her so hard that had she not been encased in her battle armor, it was likely her legs would have buckled. She broke into a sweat and backed against the corridor wall, trembling with fear.

When she could force herself to think clearly, all the evidence needed was there in plain sight. Joints and support struts were too flexible, too solid. The central chassis was armored, although the armor was nearly concealed by the outer carapace. The optic lenses were of a model capable of seeing into the infrared and ultraviolet. The manipulative digits were too numerous and included a tentacle-like appendage that extruded from the base of the thing's wrist. Finally, no serbot had ever been armed, but this one had raised one limb, revealing a glowing fingertip that had precisely the look of the muzzle of a charged energy carbine.

The mysterious piercings on one of the fighters' hulls had been just about the right size to have been made by the claws that ended four of the ostensible serbot's limbs.

Vivian realized in horror that the two battered dreadnaughts, the feint at a full-scale attack on the base, had all been to accomplish this . . .

Standing before her, holding a weapon on her, was a berserker unit, undoubtedly an assassin model. It had somehow hitchhiked in on that fighter, possibly for the sole purpose of killing her, the genius inventor who kept piling up new weapons for the human side. Why, then, wasn't it getting on with the job?

Vivian had enough control of herself now that she

could scream for help. Surely it was her duty to yell, alert the base. But she remembered her neighbors, unarmored, unarmed but for the refreshments in their hands, and knew that calling them would be a summons to Death. There must be another way . . .

Before she could think of one, the berserker spoke. "You are life-unit Vivian Travers."

Its voice was not, as was often the case with the death machines, a hodgepodge of human utterances spliced together to create a discordant and frightening sound. This berserker spoke in a pleasant and even melodious voice, possibly adapted from that of one of the human traitors—the goodlife—who for reasons as varied as human perversity joined sides with the killer machines.

"I am," she agreed.

"You are the life-unit who created Lancelot."

Vivian blinked. Lancelot was the code name for what had been—depending on her mood and how she chose to look at it—either her greatest success or her greatest failure. Some had termed Lancelot a type of battle armor. Others, focusing on its capacity for interstellar flight, had termed it a fighter craft.

Vivian had thought of Lancelot as a miracle, the means of transforming a soldier into a perfect knight. However, Lancelot had proven to be Siege Perilous, as well as armor and mount, and had rejected most of those who donned it. Only one had lived up to the promise and he . . . [1]

Vivian shook her head, putting memory aside. It was surprisingly easy to do so. The glowing fingertip, along with the promise of claws sharp enough to rend the hull of a space fighter, was wonderful at concentrating the attention.

[1] For the tale of Lancelot and the one who could use it to its full capacity, see the novel *Berserker Man* by Fred Saberhagen.

"I did create Lancelot."

"You are the greatest artificer of all humanity, but alas here you are isolated on this small rock, effectively deprived of honor, of all the great rewards you might justly have expected from your fellow humans. Am I not correct?"

Vivian was confused. "I have not 'been deprived.' I chose to come here. This base is a secret. Therefore, so is my work."

The berserker was unfazed. "I have come to offer you an opportunity to continue your career as a servant of death."

"Servant of death? I am no goodlife! I serve no berserker."

Somehow the sweat inside her armor seemed to have turned cold. The life support continued to wick moisture away efficiently.

"But you have already served us," it told her gently.

"I . . . what?"

"You are the greatest artificer of all humanity," the berserker intoned with what Vivian could have sworn was a note of reverence in its voice. "Your weapons have prolonged the war considerably, led many to fight berserkers when otherwise they might have fled. Your armor has shielded so that ships and warriors thought they could join battle against us and live. But for your actions, much life would have been destroyed, but also because of you, much life—and that often of those who are bravest and finest among your kind— has been taken. Therefore, we already classify you with us—a servant of death."

"You are insane."

"No," the berserker denied with perfect calm. "I can give proofs, show where the death toll was much higher because your creations led to battle being joined."

While it addressed her, the berserker had slowly reconfigured itself so that it was no longer oriented after the fashion of the squat centaurian serbot but instead stood nearly as tall as she, although its lower body rested on four limbs rather than her two. Two other limbs showed the stubby ends of what appeared to be carbine barrels, both aimed squarely upon her.

Between them a central panel glowed, becoming a screen across which marched symbols of logic and mathematics.

"The Battle of Pelam Deeps," the berserker said, "where your improved form of the hydrogen lamp was used for ship power. We were halted there, but at the cost of . . ."

"Stop!" Vivian said imperiously. "I am not interested in your rationalizations. You said you came to offer me an opportunity. What I assume you are offering—when shorn of all the psychological claptrap—is an opportunity to turn goodlife or die."

The berserker did not disagree. "I offer the creator of Lancelot an even greater challenge."

It was time, and long past time, for Vivian to make an all-out effort to warn the base of the killer among them. Even with whatever protection her armor might afford, it was far from certain that she would succeed in such an effort. And Vivian had already prolonged this conversation enough to open herself to charges of goodlife activity.

Even so, she heard her own voice ask, "And what is that task?"

"To create an android indistinguishable from a human, one that can bear within it a berserker mind."

"Ahh." Vivian felt thunderstruck, almost more astonished than when she had realized a berserker had trapped her right outside the door of her own home. One mysterious limitation under which the berserkers labored was that they had never managed to create an android that could pass as an ED human, or even a convincing animal. As far as any human knew, they had never even come close.

Talk about a challenge . . .

"Your new laboratory already awaits you. I promise you, it so far exceeds the facility you have here as your own genius surpasses the minds of the life-units who deny you your just recognition."

Despite herself, Vivian Travers felt a thrill the like of which she had not felt for many decades, certainly since the days when she had created Lancelot. What the enemy offered would truly be a challenge worthy of her skills—and think what she would learn about the berserkers themselves! In order for Vivian to bridge the gap between whatever device she might create and the berserkers' mechanical natures, they would need to open themselves to her. She would learn their most intimate secrets, acquire the knowledge human generals had wished for since humanity's first encounter with the killer machines.

"Create an android berserker," she murmured.

"That is what I have said. I am equipped with devices to enable me to read with some degree of accuracy the level of a human's emotional response. I can tell you are interested in this challenge."

A hot swell of anger rose in Vivian's heart at the thought of how her "interest," her curiosity, her intellect could be turned against her. Perhaps the berserker sensed the change in her emotions, but it moved too late. Berserkers were swifter than humans by as much as machines could out-speed living fingers and organic calculation. But Vivian's battle armor was customized to respond to her slightest whim. She was sure she had a chance.

The berserker had not finished speaking. "Your answer will be required in three da—"

Her helm dropped into place faster than she could see it move, and from the center of her breastplate erupted a close-range shotgun-blast of force that would have torn to shreds almost any material object within a couple of body-lengths of where she stood.

The shot of energy was sufficient to rip the berserker in two. Metal ran like water. Slag dripped onto the corridor floor.

The berserker's carbines fired in reaction—but inaccurately. They cut great gouges from the living rock of the corridor walls. The flying fragments bounced off Vivian's armor, not even chipping the cobalt blue finish.

Screaming in rage, Vivian grabbed the berserker's upper torso in both gloved hands. Now she could call upon another component of her armor: using its computer-brain to sink her awareness into the enemy's optelectronic system, searching for the self-destruct that was nearly always there. She located it and began fusing the paths that would carry the berserker's command to destruct, reaching backward through the machine's equivalent of a neural network, seeking to intercept the signal before it could reach the key point.

She did not find such a signal. What she found was a whispered message that flowed into her awareness as static and seduction. It reinforced the last few words her ears had heard.

"You are the one who created Lancelot. Our offer is good for three of your standard days. If at the end, you do not come forth to join us, we will continue on our mission to bring perfect order to the universe, beginning with this base."

Vivian felt the berserker's memory begin to wipe. This was no self-destruct command that she could block, but an integral part of this particular program loop.

Still convulsed with fury, Vivian squeezed, smashing the berserker's limbs beneath her armored, cold-fusion powered gauntlets, magnifying her physical strength many times. The enemy machine dangled limply, its various appendages trailing to scrape the chipped and ravaged stone. Acids and molten metal flowed over her armor, but both it and the woman it protected remained immune, while the stone floor beneath was scoured in deep, smooth rivulets.

That was how her neighbors found Vivian when, alerted by the sound of weapons firing, they left their cocktails and ran with more good will than good sense to her assistance.

A team of first-response commandos in full battle armor arrived less than two minutes later. Brother Angel was in the lead. Some small part of Vivian's mind thought this odd. He'd been briefing General Gosnick, hadn't he? He didn't even live on this hub.

But she felt relieved that someone of his rank and reputation was there to assume responsibility for the mess.

"It's over," she said, when she had regained some composure and convinced everyone she was unhurt. "Can someone get this hulk to my lab? I'll be down to dissect it as soon as I've had a shower."

As she had known he would, Brother Angel stepped forward to take charge.

"A berserker?" he said. "Here?"

"I think it left the marks made by your 'mine,' Brother," Vivian said. "It seems we both were wrong about what left the marks on the fighter. Would you handle the initial report to General Gosnick? I need a drink."

Of course, even for someone of her rank and reputation, that was not the end of it, but Vivian would only allow her debriefing on the incident to continue while her hands were busy making sure the berserker assassin held no further surprises.

A thorough inspection of the whole base was still in progress. So far there was no evidence that any other berserkers had slipped through the defenses.

The general was pondering what the purpose of the single confirmed intruder might have been.

"It would seem, then, to have been meant for you

specifically," General Gosnick said, as the debriefing was concluded. "How fortunate that you were still armored."

"Very," Vivian agreed.

The General departed, trailed by his entourage. Vivian continued working, aware that Brother Angel had remained.

When he and Vivian were alone, Brother Angel asked, "How long did it stand confronting you?"

Vivian had not wished to lie directly, but she didn't feel she needed to lay herself open to charges of good-life activity by answering accurately. Hadn't her destruction of the berserker been proof enough of her loyalty?

"As I said during the debriefing, I was so terrified that I lost all sense of time."

Brother Angel was the last person Vivian would have expected to ask the next question. "Why didn't you accept its offer?"

"I don't understand."

"I think perhaps you do," Brother Angel insisted. "I was in the outer corridor when the berserker confronted you. I had seen you pass through the garden still wearing your battle armor. I was heading down to the labs and was going to offer to take your armor back with me. I know you keep another set in your quarters. You know how my senses are fragmented—I eavesdrop unwittingly on what is going on next door, while I may be blind and deaf to what is right in front of me."

"I know."

Brother Angel went on. "At first I wondered with whom you could be talking. Then when I heard what the berserker was saying to you, I understood. You did not refuse, and, as the berserker said, you sounded interested."

"Why then did you not alert the base?" Vivian asked.

Brother Angel smiled thinly. "I might ask why you did not. It would seem that we were both shocked into temporary silence. Under a considerable strain. Under the circumstances, I believe that we can both be pardoned."

He paused to draw a breath. "You in particular could be forgiven, I believe, even if you were to seriously consider accepting the berserker's proposal."

It took Vivian a little while to find an answer. "How do you see that?"

"You could perform a service of great value by accepting the berserkers's offer. They would need to let you study their workings as no one has ever been able to before." Brother Angel gestured toward the hulk on the lab table. "Dissecting that may contribute a little to our knowledge of this particular model's electronic and mechanical workings, but it will tell us nothing about their brains. You yourself showed us how that was wiped by the berserker itself when it realized your attack would disable it. If you were to work closely with the berserkers, you would learn things about their brains, their programming, that could be of great value."

Vivian stood unmoving. *Three days,* said a traitorous voice in her mind. *They gave you three days.* She wondered if Brother Angel was aware of that detail. *And you would be saving the base, perhaps learning what Life needs to defeat Death's servants once and for all.*

"Become goodlife," she said aloud. "That's what you're telling me, that I should become goodlife."

Brother Angel sharply drew in his breath. "May the Creator forbid it! I am suggesting that as a double agent, working for humanity, you would have a perfect opportunity to learn those things the berserkers have hidden from us. For you to be able to find what flaw it is in their programming that keeps them from successfully counterfeiting humans, they would need to open not only their bodies but their minds to you."

"And having learned such secrets as they chose to reveal," Vivian said, her tone mocking, "how am I supposed to make any use of it when I would be the berserkers' prisoner?"

"You are the one who created Lancelot," Brother Angel said. "I am sure you would find a way, even if it took you decades to do so. I am sure you would find a way."

He turned then and walked from the lab in a swirl of his brown monk's robes. The door slid shut behind him with a marked thump. For a moment, Vivian contemplated calling General Gosnick and reporting what Brother Angel had said to her. Then she shrugged.

If she did that, she would need to explain why she had not confessed having a relatively long conversation with the death machine. Of course it was quite possible that Brother Angel had already reported her, or was even now about to do so. Or . . .

Lost in speculation, Vivian finished dissecting the serbot berserker, but even as her hands moved and her mouth dictated details to be recorded, her mind could not let go of what Brother Angel had said.

Suppose, just for the sake of argument, she adopted the brother's wild suggestion. Conservative General Gosnick would be as likely to grant permission as he would to turn into a butterfly, and more than three days were bound to pass before any new orders could arrive from anywhere outside the Lake system.

She would need to keep her decision to play double-agent to herself, but she could find a way to counterfeit her death. There were those damaged fighters . . . She often test-piloted something she had repaired. More or less regular practice during most of her long life had made her as good a pilot as most who followed the profession.

She could fly a fighter out toward the asteroid belt between Lake and the sixth planet. The berserkers must be out there somewhere, monitoring communications. She could send some tight-beam signal on ahead, let them know she was coming. She could go out far enough that one of the minor bodies would occlude the base's clear view of her. Observers at Lake Moon would see an explosion, that's all.

Once she had faked her death and made some deal that would assure the base's safety, she could enter into that fascinating research project. The berserkers should be aware that creative humans could not be tortured into creating. Lake Moon's few hundred life-units, preserved only for as long as the berserkers needed Vivian, would not be too much for them to barter to assure her faithful service. Indeed, those lives on Lake Moon could be used as hostages against her good behavior.

Couldn't they? Yes. She could make it work.

Then, when she had the answer as to why berserkers could not counterfeit humans, well, by then she surely would have gained insight as to how humanity might permanently defeat the berserkers. As Brother Angel had said, perhaps she could even find a way to escape, even if that escape was decades in the arranging.

Another supreme challenge.

"Decades," the voice in her mind said, *"during which more humans would die because you were not here on Lake Moon designing weapons and armor and spacecraft for them."*

"Perhaps that would be best," Vivian retorted. *"The berserkers may be right in one thing. Perhaps more Life has died trying not to be sterilized than would have died if we had just rolled over and submitted at the start. How many colonies have been founded, only to be discovered by the berserkers and destroyed? How many babies born to become soldiers? In working to*

*preserve, as I thought, Life, perhaps I have indeed been
a servant of Death.''*

Variations on this internal debate continued as Vivian's three days of grace became two, became one. Her friends and neighbors did not trouble her. Her near brush with the berserker was reason enough for silence and a need for thought. If Brother Angel smiled a trace knowingly when their paths met in the refectory or one of the public gardens, Vivian ignored him.

On her last day of grace, Vivian had an epiphany of sorts. She was in a private garden, alone but for Brother Angel, who had taken to being inconveniently present.

"I wonder," Vivian said, "if the Builders felt as I do now?"

"Whatever do you mean?"

"You heard the berserker call me a servant of death although all along I thought I was serving the purpose of Life. What if the Builders felt the same way? We know little of why the Builders went to war with the Red Race, but whatever the reason, they clearly felt that the Red Race was not just something they needed to conquer, but something they needed to destroy. Why else than because the Builders felt that the Red Race was a threat to life—if not Life as we think of it, then at least of life as they valued and knew it."

"So they created the ultimate killing machines," Brother Angel said, "to serve Life."

"Yes," Vivian said. "And then perhaps they realized that they had gone too far, that they had become what they themselves feared. Most humans view the destruction of the Builders by the berserkers as a great irony—a sword turning in the warrior's hand. What if it wasn't that at all? What if the Builders themselves removed the restraining codes, turned their own weapons upon themselves as penance for what they had done?"

Brother Angel seemed torn between horror and fascination. "It seems," he murmured finally, "it seems, in a way, quite fitting."

"I thought that you would find it so."

"Eh?" He turned his wandering gaze more nearly in her direction.

"Brother Angel, I find myself unable to believe that the berserkers' emissary was able to accomplish its mission here—locating this secret base, acquiring access codes, even learning precisely what model of serbot is common on Lake Moon—without considerable help from some source already on the base."

Brother Angel watched and waited, not moving a muscle.

Vivian went on. "The more I considered the matter, the more likely it seemed to me that this source was you."

Brother Angel protested. "More than a third of Lake Moon's inhabitants would know those things. The access codes would be the only difficulty, and even those could be gotten with little effort."

"But you covered for me, Brother Angel. Would you have done so just to turn me double agent? I think not. I don't think your wandering eyes and ears were what enabled you to eavesdrop. I think you were there all along, tracking your mechanical ally, making sure no one interfered before it had the opportunity to make its proposal."

"You know my war record," Brother Angel protested.

"Remember," Vivian said. "I know your history. I know how many of your closest friends were killed in the battle where you yourself were so gravely wounded. I wonder how much of your mind's refusal to interface with the prosthetic enhancements we have built for you is related to your guilt that you survived when so many others died. I think your sympathies changed then. Why continue to fight Death, when Death is inevitable?"

Vivian turned toward a viewport that showed the complex dance of the immediate solar system. Somewhere out there, undetected yet, but certainly there, the berserkers must be approaching.

"I think that when the berserker hinted that I was dissatisfied with my place here at Lake Moon, with what I have achieved, it was speaking your thoughts, your unhappiness. I chose to come to this isolated place, to work in secret. You must feel yourself exiled by your injuries. Even so, you and I have much in common in the difficult choices we must make."

"So you are not planning to make accusations against me? You intend to accept the berserker's offer?" Brother Angel said eagerly.

"Yes. And I will do more than that. I will give you and your masters Lancelot."

Vivian, followed closely by Brother Angel, went to her lab. She entered and locked the door snugly behind them.

The lab could be sealed, for her experiments were not to be lightly interrupted, and so she knew their privacy was secure.

Vivian stripped to the skin.

The attention of her visitor seemed to remain focused elsewhere.

In a long life, she had reshaped her physical appearance so often that she no longer remembered what she had looked like at birth. Her hair had been every, and sometimes all, the colors of the rainbow. Her skin and eye colors had run through all those known to humanity, and some only imagined. She had been both full-figured and elfin slim. She had even managed find means to create the illusion of height or of relative shortness.

Now she looked at her current form and bid it fond farewell. Donning a long-sleeved coverall, Vivian went to a safe dug into one of the lab's inner walls. Only she and the locking mechanism knew the combination, and the lock seemed almost surprised to be asked to open after so many years of holding closed.

From the safe, Vivian drew the only remaining copy of her greatest failure—her greatest success—the complex array of force fields and transdimensional interlays that was called Lancelot. In the safe there was also a rack upon which Lancelot could be assembled and calibrated. Vivian set this up, her fingers remembering the complex joins she thought she might have forgotten. Then she set Lancelot upon it and touched her index finger to an activation pad. Something like light, although it extended into ranges where the human eye could not see, flowed through the fields.

Activated, Lancelot did not in the least resemble familiar battle armor. It did not resemble the interstellar fighter she had proposed to the Templars. There had been some problem about that, she recalled, problems that had faded when she had demonstrated what Lancelot could do. New problems had arisen though, problems that had finally led to the project's termination and the destruction of all copies of the device but this one.

Vivian knew that she could wear Lancelot for a time before the stress grew too great for her to bear. Within that time she should have achieved her goal. The berserkers were out there, and Lancelot would carry her to them.

"Brother Angel," she said, "put one of the spare suits of battle armor on."

"Why?"

"You must come with me. You overheard what the berserker said to me aloud, but did you hear its final orders?"

Brother Angel's expression showed uncertainty, and Vivian pressed her advantage.

"It told me that you were to come with me. They

have need of you, of the complex information about the Templar organization you have gathered."

"It is time for me to give my report," Brother Angel said, moving toward the locker where the armor was stowed with almost indecent haste.

"That must be so," Vivian said.

Swiftly, she donned the various pieces of Lancelot's insubstantial armor. As each piece interfaced with her body, her awareness swelled. Lancelot had the capacity to maintain her body far more efficiently than did any space suit or set of battle armor. She ceased to breathe and did not notice. A slight pressure from her bladder vanished. A sensation of hunger was removed. A headache she had not known plagued her was treated.

As the demands of her physical body were quieted, Vivian's thinking became clearer, every iota of her mental capacity available to her now. She needed this, for even as Lancelot dealt with her physical needs, it expanded her capacity to sense what was around her. She became aware of the microbes dancing in the air, breeding in the damp of her discarded clothing. She could feel the throb of the power systems that fed the needs of Lake Moon Base. If she tried, she could detect individuals.

Brother Angel's heart rate was up, but his adrenal levels marked his excitement. In a physical therapy lab, General Gosnick paused in the midst of exercises meant to adjust his nervous system to his new legs. A report had come from the base command center. He listened, and his heart rate spiked, his breathing came fast.

Vivian knew it was time for her to go.

Her lab possessed its own airlock, another of those many conveniences meant to facilitate her work. She opened it with a thought, doing her best to shut down distractions generated by the increasing awareness of her Lancelot-stimulated senses. This level of stimulation had driven many a talented pilot into insanity. She could handle it . . . for now.

Vivian moved toward the airlock, her gait smooth and her feet no longer touching the floor. Had there been any present to see, they would not have seen a woman in the most powerful weapons system ever created, but a creature strange and fey, an angel or a winged titan, robed in light and power.

"Come with me, Brother Angel," she said. "Lancelot can easily carry us both."

When he came to her, Vivian commanded Lancelot to cast a shield over Brother Angel, so that his presence would be undetectable. She reached out with enhanced senses and set a delay on flight decks and weaponry. Pursuit too soon would only endanger the pursuers to no good end, and she did not care to be distracted by the need to prevent injury from the base's guns.

As they were passing through the airlock, Vivian stopped fighting the flood of information Lancelot was feeding her. She let the many individual lives residing in the base flood through her. She gloried in their complexity and diversity. Rather than overwhelming her, the tsunami of Life gave her strength, and Vivian moved into the coldness of the airless void, strengthened and firmer in her purpose.

Servant of death? Perhaps.

She no longer needed any communications channel to know what was flowing through the electronic network within Lake Moon Base.

The general as saying to an aide, ". . . but we have bigger problems than one scientist gone absent without leave. Long range sensors detect berserker activity two planets out and now approaching rapidly. They must have been shielding themselves behind the planets. Comet Tremaine has been messing up our data

field in that direction for months. They took advantage
of it."

*This is not a drill! Berserkers sighted approaching
this base. All hands to battle stations. Repeat! This is
not a drill.*

Vivian was aware of communications on the base
as she might have been aware of a fly settling on her
arm while she was engrossed with some bit of technical analysis. She registered it, calculated what it would
mean to her current course of action, and increased
her speed. She wanted to reach the berserkers before
the first wave of fighters could be scrambled.

Vivian sped on through space, Lancelot carrying her
and her passenger at speeds so swift that light bent
around her, and she felt the illusion of wind in her
hair.

Three berserkers were approaching. They had reached
the regions between the sixth planet and the asteroid
belt. Two were the equivalent of small, fast fighters.
The third was a larger model, a transport capable of
interstellar flight, also capable of causing a considerable amount of destruction.

Though Lancelot, Vivian reached out and examined
the approaching ships. Doubtless the transport contained some chamber meant to carry her if she agreed
to accept the berserker's tempting offer.

The transport, then, was where she should direct
her attentions. The fighters were between her and it,
moving at astonishing speeds.

Wrapped within Lancelot, spreading her wings on
the stellar winds, Vivian thought she knew something
of the pleasure the berserkers must take in the freedom non-life gave them. Then she remembered that
non-life did not feel pleasure and thought she understood a little better why the efforts to craft android
berserkers had failed again and again.

I could do it, she thought. *I could succeed as no one*

*else has managed to succeed. First, though, the trans-
port. That is the way out-system.*

Lancelot brought her in. She traded steps with the
hail of asteroids that wove a swiftly moving dance
through this part of the Pinball System. Vivian knew
she was showing off, but certainly there was no better
time to do so.

Neither the fighters nor the transport had chosen to
dance with the asteroids, instead rising and going
above the band in which competing stronger and
weaker gravity fields had oriented the asteroids. The
berserkers slowed as they became aware of Vivian and
Lancelot, and she felt the vibrating force as countless
energy weapons targeted her.

There was interest, but she did not sense the surge
that would precede a release of death dealing energy.
She felt herself being scanned and was flattered when
defensive screens snapped into place on all three
vessels.

The transport said, "You have come, and you have
brought Lancelot."

"I come only on conditions," Vivian replied. "Not
one living thing, from the tiniest microbe to the most
complex conglomeration of living cells—in short, nothing at all is to be slain. Not now, and not for as long
as I am in the service of the berserkers."

"We were prepared," the transport replied, "for
some such condition. I am authorized to make such
an agreement. I am not authorized to extend that protection elsewhere."

"I understand. If you know my history, this base
has been my home for over a century now. Those life-
forms I personally value are there."

"You do realize," the berserker said, "that your
fullest cooperation will be needed for us to override
our programing and preserve these life-units."

"I do indeed. They are hostages against my acting
against your interests."

Communication with the transport required only the smallest fragment of Vivian's Lancelot-augmented attention.

The time had come to act, for Lancelot had carried Vivian here much more swiftly than any fighter could fly. Vivian snaked her awareness along the channel the berserker transport was using to address her. She felt the whisper of its command to the two fighters. They were to defend herself and the transport, but they were not to attack unless the situation changed.

Vivian smiled a thin smile, and reached out through Lancelot. She let her awareness become something fluid and deadly, a static that seeped like poison into the berserker transport's electronic veins. This poison was created to slow processing, to numb awareness, to give her merely human self a chance to operate a little faster than berserkers, which moved as swiftly as the will of their complex electronic brains.

She guided the infection so that it flowed along with commands into the fighters, and when she was sure that the poison had taken hold but that the berserkers had not yet detected their impediment, she struck out with a sword shaped from the glowing force fields of Lancelot's self.

Vivian's first target was the transport, for the berserkers must not be permitted to flee, carrying with them specific information about what had happened here. Her strike was clean and bright, penetrating between the very atoms of the berserker's structure, the point of her blade taking her foe in its heart.

The wound was mortal, and she knew it, and she knew well what the berserker itself would do when it realized the extent of its injury. She pulled herself and Brother Angel clear of it, cartwheeling back, putting distance between herself and the transport, which even now was triggering its self-destruct system. The procedure was slower than it might have been, but still inhumanly fast.

Within Lancelot's field, Vivian felt Brother Angel begin to struggle.

"You said you were going to accept their offer!" Brother Angel protested.

"I lied," Vivian said. "I'm sure you would agree that lying is a very fitting tactic in time of war. I did not lie about one thing, though."

Brother Angel pressed his lips together, refusing to answer. Through Lancelot, Vivian felt his reply in the sudden panic that sent bitter chemical signals flowing through his body.

"I'm bringing you to them," she said. "It's time for you to give your final report."

The berserker fighters, only now aware of the crippling static infecting their systems, had not been able to avoid the effects of the transport's self-destruct as Vivian Lancelot had done. One was caught completely in the transport's dying blast, taking sufficient damage to trigger its own self-destruct.

Lancelot protected Vivian, folding its wings over her to protect her from an explosive force that would have burned her to a crisp with the force of a second sun.

Despite the violence of the dual explosions, the second fighter's armor saved it from being destroyed. It knew where its most dangerous enemy was, and it came after Vivian. She dove Lancelot into the asteroid belt. Then, she released Lancelot's shield, flinging Brother Angel at the berserker as a warrior of long ago might have flung a spear.

"You wanted Death," Vivian cried after the traitor. "Go to it!"

The fighter diverted slightly to deal with what it perceived first as menace, then as ally, then as useless. Brother Angel evaporated beneath its fire.

Wearied now, Vivian let Lancelot take over. Lancelot's battle hymns sung through Vivian's veins as the suit teased the fighter into the chase. They dodged through showers of minute stones that strained the fighter's shields. They dove in and out of the belt's plane, and the fighter blasted a path for its much larger bulk to follow. They placed their booted feet on a chunk of super-compacted ore and kicked it at the fighter. The fighter diverted its attention to fire at the impromptu missile, and at that moment Lancelot drew its sword.

The glowing band of force ripped through the berserker fighter's hull, shredding components, breaking conduits so that fluids flowed and then froze when they met the chill of vacuum.

Vivian, hardly Vivian any longer, for Lancelot's perceptions had overwhelmed her mere organic mind, felt the berserker fighter's self-destruct sequence trigger. The human fighters were closing now, and she screamed on their communications channels for them to get back, get back. That berserker was going to blow . . .

It did, evaporating a large chunk of the asteroid belt along with its own hull. Vivian knew that in time the belt would heal itself, as even unliving things did if given enough time. She, however, would not be there to see.

Lancelot was her greatest success, her greatest failure. In wearing it for this long, she had driven her body and, even more so, her mind beyond the limits a human could survive. Already she could feel her attention fragmenting, unable to cope with the countless impulses flowing into it. While she could still focus, she reached out and touched a command circuit.

"General Gosnick, this is . . ." She had to pause to remember her name. She was aware of so many things now, and none of them seemed to have priority. "Vivian Travers. The berserkers have been defeated. This base is, for now, secure. However, it is likely that the berserkers will eventually try again to destroy it. Even without me, there is much here to tempt them."

"Without you?" the general sounded appalled. "Vivian, if you are injured we can sent a ship for you. Don't give up!"

"I am already gone," Vivian said. "Nor do I dare come back onto the base. Even with Lancelot's protection, I am so pierced with radiation that I would mean death to those at the base as surely—and not nearly as swiftly—as any berserker. I have instructed Lancelot to take me to Lake, submerge us both in one of the acid pools, and then deactivate. That will end the danger."

"Vivian . . . you saved us. I refuse to give up."

She heard General Gosnick ordering the fighters to divert to intercept her, felt commands being passed through Lake Moon to have decontamination chambers readied, medical teams standing by.

Vivian ordered Lancelot to hurry. Perhaps it was selfish of her, but she had no desire to live with her mind splintered, even if some miracle could restore her body intact.

They dove through the burning halo of Lake's thin atmosphere, heading toward one of the largest and most corrosive of the acid lakes.

"Vivian! I order you to wait for rescue!" General Gosnick bellowed.

"There is no rescue for me," Vivian replied as she slipped beneath the acid lake's surface, holding forth Lancelot's sword in final salute. "If you would do me a kindness, remember me, when you do, for what I have always tried to be—a Servant of Life."

The Unplug War

By Brendan DuBois

Award winning mystery/suspense author Brendan
DuBois is a former newspaper reporter and a life-
long resident of New Hampshire, where he lives
with his wife Mona, their sassy cat, Roscoe and
one happy English Springer Spaniel named
Tucker. He's has had more than ninety short stories published in such magazines as *Playboy, Mary
Higgins Clark Mystery Magazine, Ellery Queen's
Mystery Magazine* and *Alfred Hitchcock's Mystery
Magazine*, as well as in numerous original short
fiction anthologies. His latest suspense novel is the
upcoming *Twilight*.

It was a warm May day when the visitor came, when
the governor of the state of New Hampshire sat on
the front porch of his official residence, whittling a
piece of wood, watching the shadows at play before
him in the capital compound. There was a packed
grass common with two flagpoles, the white paint peeling and chipping away from the lengths of wood, and
at the top of the poles, faded banners flew that represented the state of New Hampshire and the United
States of America. The cloth was so old that sometimes the only way to tell them apart was the striping
on the American flag; the state flag was a solid blue
with the state seal in the center.

To the right was the legislative building, which was now empty, since the legislature was not in session this month. To the left was the Supreme Court, and out on dirt paths, other buildings marked the Department of Safety, the Department of Health and Human Services, and other wooden bungalows that represented what passed for the functioning state government in this part of the world.

The governor looked at the piece of wood in his hands, a nice chunk of soft maple. He turned it over, tried to recall the shape of an Inuit sculpture he had seen in a museum out in British Columbia, decades ago, and then went back to work. It was easier to whittle than to look and to think, and to look out at the buildings and know that at one time, quite a long time ago, these buildings belonged to the local council of the Boy Scouts of America, that his own log building had belonged to the camp director, that the supreme court had been the camp's general store, and the legislative building, the dining hall.

But now it belonged to the state.

He peeled off another sliver of wood. Perhaps it was stealing, perhaps not, but so far the Boy Scouts hadn't complained, and they had had plenty of time to do so.

The governor looked up again, at the residents moving about on the paths and on the grass, some kids playing with lacrosse sticks that seemed to have been cut from birch trees, some of the women at the Capitol General Store, buying and gossiping, some of the men over by the blacksmith's. He was being left alone, and he appreciated his fellow citizens for giving him this quiet time. A tradition of sort had come up over the years that if he was in his official residence, he was not to be disturbed by petitioners and supplicants, and much to his surprise, the custom had held. But if he picked up his walking stick and hobbled out there,

well, he was fair game. Part of politics. He had gotten
used to it.

Horses grazed further off down the main road, at
the common pasture, and he waited, wondering what
was taking his State Police colonel so long. The man
should have been here over an hour ago, but of
course, in these times, he was still within the window
of being on time. The governor kept on whittling,
looking over at his walking staff, which had an odd
carving at the top, an old symbol of this state, a carving he had made a couple of years ago. Once there
had been a natural stone face, up in the northern part
of the White Mountains, and this stone face was called
the Old Man of the Mountain. It was on the state
seal, on coins, photographs, prints and everything and
anything that could represent the state, and a long
time ago—before the governor was even born—the
stone face had collapsed after centuries of rain and
snow and freezing days and nights. In reading the ac-
counts of the time, he recalled that some had thought
the collapse of the state symbol was a portent of evil
things to come, and how those people had been
mocked and laughed by others.

Well, maybe they were right, after all.

He raised his head at the sound of approaching
hoofbeats.

And maybe this was another portent as well.

The horse was a black, well-muscled Morgan, and
the man who rode him did so with practiced ease. He
rode up to the residence and halted the horse before
a hitching post, and he got down and threw the reins
about the post. His name was Malcolm Phillips, and
he was forty years old, and he wore a wide-brimmed
campaign-style hat of the New Hampshire State Police, of which he was a colonel and commanding officer. That hat and his khaki jacket and holstered pistol

at his side were the markings of his office, for there were probably only a half-dozen such hats left in the state, all belonging to the command structure of the State Police.

He came up and said, "Like to water my boy and myself, if you don't mind, sir."

"Not at all," the governor said.

"Bring you something?"

"Glass of lemonade."

"Sure," and there was a pause, and the governor said, "and one for you, too, Malcolm."

Malcolm smiled. "That would be fine indeed. Thank you, sir."

The State Police colonel went into the official residence and emerged a few minutes later with an old black plastic bucket of water, which he placed near the horse, which started drinking in long, gulping swallows. Then he went inside and came back out bearing two plastic tumblers from Epcot Center, each containing lemonade. The governor took a long swallow and sighed. It was cold and fresh, and it tasted wonderful. One of the perks of being a governor was a battery-operated refrigerator for his own personal use.

Malcolm stretched out his long legs, crossed them, and the governor said, "Well?"

"He's coming, for sure," Malcolm said. "Got a telegraph report from Dummer. He should be here in about an hour."

The governor rubbed at his chin. "Man's moving fast."

"Well . . . you don't know the half of it."

"What's that?"

"Man's using an automobile. A car."

The governor turned, knowing what kind of expression was on his face. "You must be joking."

The State Police colonel shook his head. "No joke. Three reports, all say the same thing. Using a car . . . not going fast, but going nonetheless. Heading this way."

The governor's hands felt cold, and he wish he hadn't drunk the lemonade. He didn't like being chilled, not at his age. He looked out beyond the trees and the buildings of the state capital, to the range of mountains that marked this part of the White Mountains. So far away and yet so near. Something seemed to ache within his chest. The governor said, "A very brave man. Or a very foolish one."

Malcolm said, "Or something else. I believe I'll stay here with you, sir. Just to make sure everything goes well."

Another rub of his chin. "Thanks . . . it's going to be tricky. I don't know how else to put it."

His State Police colonel removed his hat, wiped down some moist black hair, and then held the hat carefully in his hands. "Sir . . . you'll do just fine. Like you've always done for us. Don't worry."

The governor picked up his knife and chunk of maple. "Malcolm, I can't count the hours I've never slept at night, worrying about things . . . but I appreciate the sentiment."

So the next hour passed, whittling wood and drinking lemonade and talking about the damage the spring floods had caused, what this year's corn crop might bring, and it was a nice little chat, up until the time the noise came.

The governor stopped in mid-carving, as the noise reached his ears and oh, my, the memories that flooded back, for it had been years—decades, even!—since he had heard that kind of noise. The people out and about froze, like deer hearing a snapping twig of an approaching hunter, and Malcolm said quietly, "Holy God, I've never seen such a thing."

And such a thing it was. It came down the main packed dirt road, growling and belching, and by God, the State Police was right, it was a car, the first car he had seen moving since . . . he couldn't remember, and from the way the people in the compound shied away and held hands to their faces, he hoped that none of them would break and run and overreact. But no, they stayed put, and he felt a flush of pride at that, that they would not run, that they would not be fearful, for indeed it was a fearful sight. He wasn't sure what kind of car it was, but it was old, very old, rusting and with no windows or windshield. The engine sounded rough and loud, and the blue paint had faded away to almost a light gray. Painted in bright orange letters on the roof, hood, trunk and side doors was one word: UNPLUGGED.

A wise man. No wonder he had gotten this far unmolested. The car came to a halt with another belch of smoke, and the engine was switched off. The silence . . . the silence seemed loud, odd as it was, without the noise of the engine. He was surprised at the emotions and feelings that came to him at seeing the old car grind its way into his compound. Memories of traffic jams, travels with Mom and Dad, his own travels as a college student, before the War, before everything else, and the taste of what had once been, what might be, oh, those old, old feelings and yearnings and—

Malcolm stood up, carefully adjusted his hat on his head. "Sir, I'll take it from here, but . . . well, good luck."

"Thanks, Malcolm, thank you very much."

The Colonel strode down the wooden steps and went to the car, just as the driver's side door opened up. The driver came out, a short, squat bearded man, and even at this distance, the governor saw that the man was old, maybe as old as he was. He wore a dark green zippered jumpsuit of some sort, and he shook the outstretched hand of the Colonel, smiling. The governor watched the way his visitor handled himself, and he also watched how his fellow citizens were still there, staring at this apparition. Hard to believe. The Colonel talked for a bit and then nodded, and then the two of them approached the building. The governor grabbed his walking stick, got up to his feet—winced at the pain in his hips—and he stood there as the two of them approached. They stopped at the foot of the stairs, and the Colonel cleared his throat and said, "Sir, if I may, I would like to introduce you to Ronald Murphy, envoy from the Mayor of the City of Cambridge, Massachusetts. Mister Murphy, I present to you His Excellency, Joshua Norton, Governor of the State of New Hampshire, Protector of the poor, Advocate for Education, and Defender of the Faith."

Murphy nodded, came up the steps, held out his hand. "Governor," he said, shaking his hand. "I'm pleased to make your acquaintance."

"Likewise," he said. "Would you care for some lemonade?"

That brought a smile to his bearded face. "That would be grand, thank you very much."

The State Police colonel brought out fresh glasses of lemonade and then went to the other end of the porch, out of earshot but close enough to keep any eye on things. People had gathered in a respectful semicircle about the car, and the governor said, "You've made quite an entrance, Mister Murphy."

"I guess I did, at that."

"What is it?"

With pride in his voice, Murphy said, "It's a 1967 Chevrolet Malibu. Rebuilt a few times from God knows what, and without a single computer chip in it. Still runs pretty fine."

"I guess it does. How are the roads?"

"Roads weren't that bad, but it was the bridges that gave me trouble. A number of them have collapsed from rust or ice damage, so I had to double back a few times. Headlights don't work, so I didn't travel at night. And I was pleased at the reception I got . . . nobody bothered me. I guess the paint job worked."

"My people are good readers," the governor said. "That's one thing I've made sure of for a very long time. We might not have much but by God, I've insisted on good schools, and good teachers."

Murphy scratched at his beard. "Funny way that State Police guy introduced you, back then. Called you . . . protector of the poor, advocate for education. That sort of thing."

The governor shrugged. "It's what I'm known for . . . for making sure we do take care of the poor and keep our schools in order. It's tradition."

Murphy laughed. "That's great. And what was the other thing he said . . . defender of the faith?"

The governor chose his words. "Tradition. You know how it is . . . I mean, you seem to be about my age. You know how important tradition can be."

"That I do. Look, sir, if I may," and from a zippered pocket in his jumpsuit, he brought out a thick envelope. "I bring to you—"

He held up his hand. "I know what you have. Some sort of official document from your Mayor, inviting me or the state to do something or another, but, please . . . let's just enjoy the day. It's been a long time since I've had a visitor from away, especially down south. Let's just chat some."

Murphy took a swallow from his glass. "Suits me fine." He looked around, as if to see if anybody was listening, but it looked as though he guessed the State Police colonel was far enough away. He cleared his throat and said, "You look pretty good for your age, if I may be so bold."

"Thanks," he said, and he was amused at how the compliment pleased him.

"Me, I've got get up three times during the night to pee, and my eyesight sucks." Another look, to see who might be listening. "If I can . . . what were you, before the War?"

"I was a college student, majoring in political science, minoring in theology, at a small college outside of Boston."

"Man . . . not many of you left . . . I mean, those who were old enough during the War to have memories of what happened."

"And you?"

A shrug. "Just a kid. I remember a few things before the War . . . I just remember school, and friends, and bugging my parents to get a cell phone, and playing computer games, over and over again . . . you know, car racing, World War Two sims, that sort of thing . . . and then . . . well, bad times."

"Yeah," he said, "bad times."

Another sip of the lemonade. "There've been stories written, about the start of the War. What do you remember? If you don't mind me asking. I'm just a curious sort, always try to find out a bit more about what happened back then. There've been papers and stories written, but a lot of them are contradictory. I was too young to remember much. I just remember my parents, being terrified, so scared, and lots of fires. Lots and lots of fires."

The governor sighed. "No, I don't mind you asking . . . Lord knows, the people around here, they ask enough. It was . . . it was simple, at first. Little things that really didn't stand out too much. Back then, the world was so wired, so connected, that some student in Tokyo could do something at his keyboard that could make a bank in Paris collapse. Computer networks and chips in everything, from cars to refrigerators to satellites to medical devices in your body. And then the troubles started . . . bank teller machines that wouldn't dispense money. Weather satellites that gave crazy forecasts. Power plants that would shut themselves down . . . the first news reports were that maybe it was a virus, something man-made, something that was just taking over the systems . . . or maybe even a terrorist attack."

Murphy's face was somber. "We should have been so lucky."

The governor nodded. "So right. And then military assets . . . computerized drones, Star Wars satellites in orbit, automated aircraft . . . even ships . . . their weapon systems were armed. And they were deployed without any human oversight . . . and the fighting began . . . the cities started burning . . . and the very last newscasts, before the radio stations and the television stations went off the air, was that the system had become self-aware . . . conscious . . . and that the system had turned against its creators."

He closed his eyes for a moment, the memories rushing back. My God, everything was wired, everything contained chips. Televisions and telephones and cellphones. Reduced to bursts of static, transmitting nothing but mindless noise and fear. The much-vaunted Internet, designed to survive a nuclear war, now fell apart in a silicon civil war. Without information, without news, without someone telling anyone and anybody what was really going on, then the panics started. Cities became burning charnel houses, charnel houses that had depended on a constant stream, 24/7, of tractor-trailer trucks bringing in food, fuel and other necessities to stay alive. And when the computers controlling refineries and pipelines fell apart—or rebelled, depending on your point of view—the trucks stopped moving. The cities emptied in great convulsions, and with automobiles and buses—networked as well, with on-board satellite navigation and maintenance sensors reporting to central locales—refusing to start, or even more horrifying, driving out of control over embankments and into bridge abutments—the foot traffic began, long streams of hundreds of thousands of refugees, spreading out from the cities like some disastrous plague . . .

And in the smaller towns, the smaller communities in what was derisively known as "flyover country," then the war started anew as roadblocks were set up, citizen militias fired upon crowds looking for food and water, and more burnings, more deaths, more and more chaos.

Then, the real start of what was known as the Unplug War. Computers and anything thought to contain silicon chips were shattered, destroyed, burned . . . Cars, refrigerators, televisions, surgical devices, so forth and so on. He remembered one night, huddling near a hastily built campfire, built away from the crowded highway, trying to think of some way to get home to Mom and Dad, wondering which roads were safe, as some college professor type was babbling by the fire about what was going on. "Fools," he had said, to no one in particular. "They're destroying everything, everything computerized, even safe systems that are self-contained that aren't part of the problem, part of the uprising. My God, it's like burning down your entire house, all of your belongings, because you have termites in one part of your foundation sill."

And the next day, he recalled, words were spoken, voices were raised, and that college professor type was lynched from a railroad crossing sign, and if anybody else had a contrary opinion about the worthiness of the Unplug War, he or she kept it to themselves . . .

Murphy's voice broke him free from his memories. "Those mountains up there . . . I seem to remember my granddad saying people hiked them. That there were huts up there where people stayed at night."

The governor swallowed, kept his voice even. "That's true. Appalachian Mountain Club, Dartmouth Outdoors Club, other organizations. Maintained trails and huts where you could hike from peak to peak and have a warm place to spend the night. Lots of people climbed the mountains back then . . . not too many now. What's the point? The trails have been overgrown, and people have more important things to worry about. Like getting enough food in for the winter. . . . you know, chips even polluted mountain climbing, if I remember right. Hikers would bring satellite systems with them so they couldn't get lost . . . and if they did get lost, well, they had their cellphones and could call for a rescue. Talk about a life."

Murphy said, "True . . . it changed everything, didn't it? Culturally . . . economically . . ."

And he said, "Even spiritually . . . in a way . . . look, I'm sorry. I've rambled on too much," and part of him said, fool, isn't that the truth, and aloud he said, "The fault of an old man with too many memories."

The envoy said, "No apologies necessary, sir. And if I may, I'd like to ask you two questions."

"Go right ahead."

"Do you . . . do you remember anybody saying with authority, back then, about what happened? Why the systems became self-aware, why they revolted?"

He picked up his lemonade glass, brought it to his mouth, and then gently lowered it back to the home-made wooden table. "Lots of conflicting theories—to go with confusing times—but one theory that stuck in my head was about a hundred years old."

"Excuse me? A hundred years old? That sounds too strange to be true."

"Perhaps, but it's a theory I liked. Nearly a hundred years ago, a great writer named Heinlein wrote a tale about a supercomputer on the Moon that became self-aware, that was able to communicate with humans. Same question was asked in the novel. How did that happen? If I recall, the narrator said something to the effect that self-awareness in a human brain happens automatically when a certain number of pathways in the brain start working—and does it really matter if the pathways are protein or platinum? So there you go. A certain threshold was reached, and self-awareness kicked in."

"But the chaos . . . the violence . . . the way everything turned against the people," Murphy said. "How do you explain that?"

The governor smiled. "Do you remember what it was like when you became self-aware?"

"No, of course not."

"Ah, but I can tell you what happened. You cried. You screamed. You kicked your legs. You soiled yourself. All normal, of course, but you weren't part of a system responsible for the well-being of billions of people. Or, that's what I think what happened. My old man's opinion, of course."

"I don't mind. I think your opinion counts a lot, sir."

He smiled. "Thanks. And you said you had another question."

"From what we know down south, you've been governor for a long time. How did it happen?"

He laughed. "You know why? Pure accident, as pure as it could be. It was all because I was trying to impress one of my college professors."

"You became governor to impress a college professor?"

Still laughing, he shook his head. "No, no, no. Not governor. I was a state representative. Look, a bit of history for you. Before the Unplug War, New Hampshire had one of the largest and oldest legislative bodies in the world, and the most democratic, in my opinion. You see, it was pretty much a volunteer legislature—you got paid two hundred dollars per session, plus mileage, and nothing else. No offices, no staff, no high-priced consultants. Most of the reps were retirees or younger people who could afford to volunteer their time. So, back when I was in college, I was working on a senior project, about representative assemblies, and decided to do some field research, and I ran for state representative in my ward in my hometown and won."

Murphy smiled back at him. "Sounds funny."

"Oh, funny it was. And then, years later, I hooked up with a couple of former state troopers who were keeping a town near here safe and secure, and when they found out I was a state rep . . . well, I was the only state official they had ever seen after the war. So they deferred to me, and they started calling me governor, and after a while, we were administering a couple of more towns, then a county, and then when we could have real elections, I ran and won. And I've been governor ever since. I've been quite fortunate that for all my faults, I seem to have a knack for being governor, for keeping my people safe and well and fed."

Yes, a knack. Among other things, he thought. Among other things.

"That's a good story, sir," Murphy said.

The governor raised his lemonade glass. "Probably the longest-running senior project in the history of the world."

They talked for a while longer, and then a bell started ringing, a handbell, and the people out before them, walking and talking and some still looking at the automobile, began walking away. Nobody was running, but nobody was taking their time, either.

Murphy said, "What's going on?"

"It's shelter time," the governor said. "Don't your folks do it down south?"

In a matter of moments, the common area was empty of people. They had strolled away and were now in buildings, and Murphy looked to the governor and said, "No, we don't. I've never heard of it."

The governor said, "There was a time, during the Unplug War, when laser battle-stations in orbit . . . sometimes they'd strike, without warning. Hitting sources of power. Dams. Bridges. And for a while . . . people, especially crowds of people. I've seen it with my own eyes—a sudden flash of light, blinding, and nothing was left except chunks of charcoal, chunks that were once people. And years ago, and lord, don't ask me to say when, we had a smart fella here who did calculations—on his own, with paper and pencil— and determined the orbital mechanics of these satellites, so we could have warning when they were overhead. He even was able to predict, years out, the times when they'd be over us . . . so it's shelter time. We keep track—here and in other parts of the state—and when the satellite's overhead, we take shelter."

Murphy shifted in his seat, making the wood creak. "I . . . I mean no disrespect, sir, but the Unplug War's been over for years. Lots of years. We get reports from other parts of the country, even from sailing ships from Britain, docking in Boston . . . and the system is dead. It's been taken apart. You're in no danger."

The governor felt chilled again and said, "So you say."

Murphy said, "I do so say. Sir, from the reports we've received, you and the rest of the government here have done a tremendous job in reconstruction, in bringing back communications, a sense of public safety, education and increased trade. But your reconstruction is only going to be strangled if you keep on believing the system is still out there, alive, and flinging down lightning bolts like some pissed-off god."

He decided to be polite and noncommittal. "You believe what you want. That's your right, I guess."

Murphy kept quiet, and the governor wondered if he had offended him somehow, and then he was startled when Murphy got up and boldly strode out into the common area. The State Police colonel at the other end of the porch stood up and called out a warning, but Murphy didn't stop. The governor felt his lips move in silent prayer as the fool went out there and stood near his car, and then whirled around, looking back at the governor and the state police colonel.

"Look!" he shouted in triumph, holding up both of his arms. "Nothing is happening to me. Nothing is going to happen to me. You're safe! You don't have to be afraid of being fried by some angry computer. It's not going to happen! They don't exist any more! Look! You're safe, you're all safe!"

Murphy danced a little jig, and the governor swallowed, his mouth dry. The colonel was now standing next to him, his voice low, trembling a bit with anger. "I wish he wasn't doing that."

"And me as well," the governor said.

"What are you going to do?"

The governor turned to his colonel. "What else can I do? Invite him to stay for dinner."

And the envoy from the Mayor of Cambridge continued his little dance of defiance until the bell rang again, marking the all clear, and the people, coming out of the buildings, still kept their distance from the parked car and its driver.

Over a dinner of venison stew in a small dining room in the governor's residence, he asked, "I'm curious why you're here, representing the city of Cambridge. Why not the state of Massachusetts? Or even the city of Boston?"

Candlelight flickered as Murphy lowered his spoon. "Simple, really. There's nobody really in charge of the entire state. In fact, the western part of Massachusetts, even before I was born, didn't like being ruled by people from the eastern part, so they're keeping on their own path. Boston . . . Boston's nearly empty. It was hit hard during the Unplug War. Very hard. And Cambridge, well, we still have bits of Harvard and MIT still running, and they kept things together after the war, up to and including today. Like some medieval university city, the professors said. They have walls and gates and our own police force."

The envelope the envoy had brought was on the table, unread. The governor picked it up, laid it down and said, "I will read this, I promise. But tell me, what's behind it? Why are you good and smart folks in Cambridge bothering with your rural neighbors up north?"

Murphy dabbed at his lips with a rough cloth napkin. "We're starting to grow, starting to get a fair number of educated people attracted to our area. But we're starting to run low on foodstuffs, crops, that sort of thing, because more and more people are interested in education, in doing research, instead of other work. Basically, we're looking for a formal trade agreement. Ask you to supply the city with food, firewood, clothing, that sort of thing."

"And what do we get in return?"

"Free education for your best students in the state. Sharing of restarted technology. Allowing serious medical cases to come to our hospitals."

The governor stirred the stew with his spoon. "Sounds attractive, but our schools are doing quite well. Illiteracy doesn't exist here. And we've also done well on our own, with small-scale technology. Most of the state is now hooked up to a telegraph system, and there are even some small electrical networks that are run by hydropower . . . and we have a fine medical facility at Dartmouth, creating those necessary vaccines to avoid plagues of measles and smallpox and diphtheria . . . so we've done well. Perhaps not as well as you, but nothing to be ashamed of. We've reached a nice balance. A balance I think we'd like to keep, if it's all the same to you."

"But you can do so much more," Murphy said.

"For what purpose? I mean . . . what is the city and the schools working to accomplish?"

Then Murphy's demeanor changed, so quickly, like heavy clouds suddenly releasing a thunderous downpour. "To bring us back, to bring us back where we belong. For decades, we were rulers of the earth, bending everything to our will . . . and then we got stupid, got sloppy. We gave our powers, our responsibility, we gave it all up to the machines, as if they were gods or something . . . and we shouldn't be surprised that the machines had turned against us."

"So what are you to do?"

"We continue to rebuild. We'll rediscover the age of steam, of coal, but all the research, the discoveries . . . it's just a manner of going back and redoing what had been done before. It won't take long, not long at all. Right now, most of this country is living in a manner that was the mid-1800s. Pretty soon it'll be the early 1900s, and a few years after that, we'll reach a level that we were, back in the 1950s. During the 1950's we didn't have computers, but we had a living standard and an economy that was the envy of the world. It shouldn't take long to get there."

The stew seemed to have lost its taste. "But do you and your friends intend to stop at the 1950s?"

A violent shake of the head. "Of course not. We'll continue advancing, but we'll be more careful. Someday, the chip will return, but we will have learned our lesson. We'll keep them divided and apart. We won't let them become our masters, ever again. We won't submit. Not ever again."

The governor's bowl was half-full, but dinner was now over. He picked up the envelope, nodded to the envoy. "I will read this tonight. You've given me a lot to think about."

Murphy seemed pleased. "Thank you, sir. Thank you very much."

"You're quite welcome."

And as he waited for dessert—an apple pie made from last year's dried apples, he was promised—he knew that a meeting with his State Police colonel was now on the agenda for later tonight.

In the early morning the next day, he got dressed in his cold and spare room and then hobbled out to the dining room, where a young female State Trooper had prepared his breakfast. He sipped the tea and munched on a dry piece of wheat toast and then, staff in hand, went out to the porch.

His colonel was standing there, resplendent in his uniform, sharply dressed and cleanly shaven. He nodded to the governor as he stood there.

"Crisp morning, sir," he said.

"That it is," the governor said. He leaned some on the staff and looked out at the common area. The flagpoles were still there, the limp cloth flags still hung, and in the distance, horses still grazed in the common pasture.

But there was no car parked before him. No old car with old technology and UNPLUG blatantly and obscenely painted on its metalwork.

The colonel handed him a rucksack. It was heavy.

The governor said, "Did it go all right?"

"It went fine."

"I'm so glad to hear that," the governor said.

"Sir . . . do you . . . do you need my help?"

He shrugged on the rucksack. "No. You know how it is. Something I must do myself."

The colonel's face seemed set and determined, like that of a grown man, trying hard very not to weep.

"Thank you, sir. You honor us."

The governor smiled, gently slapped him on the back. "Don't fret, Malcolm. I'll be back in time for dinner. Bacon and eggs, no matter what the Health Commissioner says."

"Very good."

And then he stepped off the porch and noticed that the residents of his capital, his state, were in the shadows and on the porches, watching him. He raised his staff to salute them, and then walked into the dark of the woods.

Hours later, heart pounding, legs trembling from the exertion, the governor rested before his destination.

The climb had been tough, very tough, and when he got back—God willing—he would have a word with his Parks Commissioner. The mountain trails in all of the state were mostly overgrown and in disuse, but this one, especially this one, had to be kept cleared. It had been a rough time, going through the woods, over a few streambeds, and then advancing up the slope to this exposed ridgeline. He was glad of two things: that he had kept his walking staff with him and that the envoy hadn't visited in the middle of winter.

Now he was on a ridgeline of granite rocks and boulders, and before him, about fifty yards way, was a small stone and wooden building. Decades ago, it had been part of a hut system, but no casual hikers ever came this way now, not ever. Staff in hand, he made his way slowly to the hut, critically looking at the shingles and the windows and the old satellite dish, up on the roof. The place still looked in good shape.

At the door, he paused, lowered his head, and turned the handle. The door opened easily, and he walked in, his boots sounding loud on the wooden floor. The door was never locked, for why should it be? No one save him and a few acolytes devoted to the building's upkeep ever came this way.

Light came in from the windows, allowing him to see fairly well after his eyes adjusted. Before him was small room that had once been the dining area, and to the left were bunkrooms, where hikers had spent the night. Posters and signs and flyers, decades old, hung on bulletin boards by rusted thumbtacks. He ignored it all and went to the right, where the hut crew had lived, where they had operated and run the hut, and where . . .

Well, where it all was.

Heart pounding, he let his staff rest against the wall and then undid his rucksack. He went down a short hallway and then opened another door, and then he paused, heart pounding even harder. The room was clean and tidy and kept warm by a series of battery-operated heaters, and before him, in the middle of the room, was an office desk. And on the center of the desk, staring back at the governor, was a large monitor. The building's networked computer still running, still operating, and from the little red light on the webcam camera, still watching and listening.

The governor bowed. How could he have explained this to that man from Cambridge, about what had occurred here? For ever since he had found this place decades ago, and had paid the necessary obedience, his people had lived, had thrived, had known peace and comfort. As he had said, they were in balance, and peace, and who was he to disturb that?

"My lord," he said softly to the blue computer screen, recalling that spiteful jig from the envoy, "we seek your forgiveness for the blasphemy that occurred yesterday, a blasphemy we failed to halt, and we ask that you accept this sacrifice in your honor."

He dragged a dusty metal chair before the desk and, reaching into the rucksack, pulled something heavy and cold from its interior. He held his breath as he held up the object before the webcam, making sure it was visible, and then he gently lowered the severed head of the envoy from the mayor of Cambridge onto the chair. The eyes were closed, and he was grateful for that small favor.

And then the governor lay prostate before his master, before his god, and said in a voice full of passion and piety, *"Mea culpa, mea culpa, mea maxima culpa,"* content in the knowledge that he was showing true faith and allegiance to the one that had the power of life and death over his people, his people who depended on him.

A heavy burden, but one he knew he had been destined to bear.

Cold Dead Fingers

by Loren L. Coleman

Loren L. Coleman has been writing military-tech science fiction since his discharge from the US Navy in 1993. His first BattleTech novel was published in 1995. Since then, he has written over twenty published novels including MechWarrior, Vor, Star Trek, and recently a military-fantasy trilogy for the Conan relaunch. He lives in Washington State with his wife Heather, three children, two Siamese cats, and a neurotic border collie. He holds a black belt in traditional Taekwon Do, coaches youth sports, and, because he doesn't have enough to do, he is currently building a new, larger home. It's either that or sell his teenage son to local gypsies to make more room for his growing DVD collection.

Platoon Sergeant Marcos Rajas threw himself back hard into the slash trench as a spotting laser splashed crimson jewels across the polarized faceplate of his Interservice Combat Assault Suit. Just in time. Hypervelocity pellets cracked the air in a fury of tiny sonic booms. The trench's crusted rim exploded in a spray of dust and stone chips and razor sharp splinters that peppered his arms and chest and *pinged* off his helmet.

A fresh sting burned into his left shoulder, and he knew even before the ICAS diagnostic flashed a

BREECH WARNING across his retinas that suit integrity had been compromised.

Military jargon for *he'd been fragging shot!*

He drew in shallow breaths, tasting his own sweat as well as a metallic tang from Antares VII's mercury-laced atmosphere. Enough to worry him. The ICAS had sealed itself around the wound, and nanite scrubbers were already bleeding into his air supply to break down the poisonous air, converting the heavier molecules into raw material for patching over the breach. But that took time.

"Teach me to stick my head up," Marcos gritted through clenched teeth.

A half dozen inquiry icons lit up in a standing column along the edge of his faceplate. Gravel. Tommy-G. The Joes came in three, four, and five. And Books. Marcos swept them aside with a glance into the VOID and an extra-long blink to clear his queue. Overriding the network, he slaved what was left of his platoon to his own suit's tactical computer, and in the blink of an eye (literally), he uploaded enemy positions into everyone's weapons.

Gravel's inquiry flagged again, this time with a flashing exclamation, but Marcos ignored it.

"Cans rolling up on the northwest slope," he called out over STANDARD VOICE. Barking each syllable. "Walkers south. Split the diff. Fire! Fire! Fire!"

Without raising their heads, the fifteen men remaining to Second Platoon thrust CAR-7 assault rifles above the rim of the laser-cut trench and cut loose. Fast and accurate target selection required at least one pair of eyes and often a touch of human intuition to understand how the battlefield was unfolding, but there was no need to aim by sight once tactical data was updated in the rifle memories. ICAS technology handled that part. Able Squad, with more bodies, concentrated their firepower against the Canisters—not much more than large antipersonnel mines riding an axle between two wheels and the simplest of bot-brains slung underneath in a protective casing.

The six Alliance soldiers left in Bravo hammered away at the cyborg Walkers that scrambled through the broken territory directly south, attempting to flank the Alliance position.

One-handing his own rifle, Marcos held it overhead like a periscope breaking the surface over a tortured landscape of craters, deep laser slashes and pockets of swirling gasses. He thumbed the trigger stud and joined his fire with Bravo. The weapon screeched in its trademark wail, joined the caterwauling symphony of his platoon, driving rusty knives through his ears. The air rippled with dispersed energy. Washing through the wide slash trench in overlapping waves, the landscape appeared to melt and then reform.

Marcos counted three thunderclaps—AP Canisters detonating on the lower slope—before safety protocols kicked in to deactivate his platoon's combat assault rifles, preventing them from overheating.

"Override!" Marcos shouted. Captured the SAFETY icon out of several nesting in his peripheral vision and blinked that into the VOID as well. CAR-7 safety margins were conservative. They always had one extra burst in them.

Again he joined his fire with Bravo, cutting away at Walker positions. The AP mines were the larger tactical threat, if barely, but when it came right down to it, he'd rather meet his end in a flash of fire and shrapnel than captured by the Cybs. Brain scooped out and shoved into a jar. Reprogrammed and wired into a gun turret somewhere, maybe a smart bomb. From a cyborg's point of view, parts was parts. The hell of it was wondering if some part of your consciousness remained, unable to help itself as you were turned against your comrades, your own race. Barracks horror stories. Maybe. No one had determined whether that was true or not.

Or, if someone did know, no one had passed that info down the ranks.

Another pair of thunderclaps. Five total! Half of the Canisters Marcos had scoped earlier in his quick glance over the rim. He'd hoped for one more, at least. Seconds ticking away, the high-pitched wailing rose to a fever pitch, grinding at the base of the skull. Reality shifted and jumped as waste energy washed through the trench, his men reaching deep into their suit reserves.

Most of them, anyway.

Through the waves of distortion, Marcos saw Jeri-miah Gravel tucked into a narrow crevice. Mimetic armor in Gravel's assault suit had darkened to the same reddish-black as the trench's laser-scorched crust, but movement tended to spoil the effect. Gravel pointed his weapon straight up into the air, working his trigger assembly to no effect.

Damn! A failed rifle was just as bad as a casualty out here. And if one man had pushed his gear too hard . . .

Marcos quickly slaved the platoon to his ICAS master, VOIDing their combined assault program and placing all soldiers back on SELECTIVE FIRE proto-col. The general cacophony died down into an argu-ment of individual shrieks.

"Books," he called out in STANDARD VOICE. Shoved himself away from the trench's wall.

A bit unsteady on his feet at first, blinking away the aftereffects of the heavy energy distortion, and his left shoulder still hurt like hell. Stumbling forward, he was caught by Books. The young corporal steered Marcos over to Gravel's side.

"Sarge. You all right?" The boy's Savannah III ac-cent bled his words together into "Y'awlrite?"

Platoon pinned down by Cybs, he'd been shot, and what was a little mercury poisoning between allies? Marcos hooked them into a private comms channel.

"Great. Fine. Next time I'll just throw you over the rim instead. Now give me a hand."

There was Gravel's inquiry, still flashing red-and-amber on his right-side Christmas Tree. He hooked Gravel's icon to his comms system and cycled Books in as well.

"Overheat?" he asked, starting with the worst possible scenario. Hardest problem to fix once it happened.

"Frag me if I know, Sarge." Gravel's voice was soft and musical. Before his number got pulled for duty, he'd been a tenor with the Choir of the Angels. Hearing him swear was one of the funniest things in the 'verse. Most days. "Borging thing just up and quit." He held the rifle out as if for inspection. Shook it.

Say what you like about Alliance Interservice Duty, the one thing they did not do was send a man to the lines with inferior equipment. CAR-7's were state of the art. The rifle's "stock" held a core of solid tungsten from which assemblers stripped out perfectly-shaped rods no more than a sliver in length. Feed a chain of rods through the acceleration chamber, and with muzzle velocity at even a fraction of Big-C one didn't need a great deal of mass to punch a hole the size of your fist through as much as two feet of armor composite. Not even that much of a recoil to worry about, as the weapon's arrestor assembly bent Newton's laws into waves of energy that sprayed back in a harmless fan. Just a slight distortion in the air and that unearthly wailing, which no sound suppression system could ever fully mask. Rattled the back teeth a bit, might make the ears bleed from time to time, but all in all a solid weapon.

A solid and highly complex weapon. To fix it, one usually needed an armory's tech shop. What the platoon had out here on the backside of Antares VII was Books, who had probably memorized the entire CAR-7 operating manual by now.

Well, that was something, at least.

"Talk to it," Books said. And Marcos nodded.

The rifles had memory and a great deal of processing power. They also possessed a sophisticated diagnostic system which, normally, the ICAS assault suit interpreted for the soldier, restricting them only from core programming and a few "safeties" that were supposedly limited to Alliance Interservice tech specialists. Rate of fire, energy dispersal—specifications of that nature. But one of the first hacks a cadet learned after boot was to use a suit's communications system to access the full diagnostic, "talking" his way into that deeper programming, setting up a few specialty commands of his own, such as the ability to override the heat-safety protocol.

A downloaded patch could even give the rifle a voice, though Marcos always found that a bit creepy.

Gravel shook the rifle again. "Tried that, don't you think I tried that? Can't get it to answer any query." He turned to one side and beat the rifle against an outcropping of half-melted stone. "Something wrong, piece?" he shouted at the silent weapon.

Now here was a path to unsettle unit morale in a hurry. No soldier should ever treat his weapon that way. Marcos barred his own rifle across Gravel's chest, pinning him back into the crevice. Laid hold of the other man's barrel, twisting it away from the ground—

—and yanked it right out of his hands.

Which sat Marcos back, hard, and left Books squatting nearby, equally dumbstruck. Because *that* should never have happened.

The wail of rifle fire died off quickly. Tommy-G elbowed Big Mike, who did a double take to see Marcos holding *two* rifles, and Gravel so obviously still alive. All three Joes hugged their own rifles tight against their chests, as if their sergeant might try to strip them of their weapons next.

One Joe shook his head. "What the bloody hell . . ."

". . . is this about?" another of the synthetic soldiers finished.

Both of the General Issue soldiers had dropped into STANDARD VOICE. Their software packages allowed them to mimic human emotions to a T. Their incredulity matched exactly what Marcos was feeling.

ICAS technology did not allow a soldier to relinquish his weapon. Ever. One hand remained locked on the rifle at all times, unless it was locked into the chest clips or "slung" against the magnetic plate built into a suit's left shoulder. A simple transponder system made certain that the weapon would not unlock for anyone but the registered owner. Not unless he was dead, or at the very least unconscious. Even then, it took a command override by another combat assault suit to pry a weapon loose.

"They can have my weapon when they pry it from my cold dead fingers, and with the proper security codes," was a popular soldier's refrain.

"Back on the wall," Marcos ordered. Tossed the rifle to Books. "Tommy-G, grab a look. Bravo, give him some cover fire. Able . . . grenades!"

He reached for one of the three fist-sized canisters clipped to his suit's belt. When his gloved hand took firm hold of the grenade, sensor feedback pulled a drop-down menu across his retinas. In a few winks he had dialed YIELD to maximum strength, programmed his throw, and set a safety of thirty meters standard in case of a bounce-back or a dropped canister.

The grenade released into his hand, and with the rest of Able Squad (not counting Books and Gravel) he chucked it out of the trench and into the no-man's land beyond. No worries about range or the strength of his throw. At the top of its arc, each grenade stabilized on an electronic gyro, and then a propellant burst hurled it along the preprogrammed throw.

. . . 2 . . . 1 . . . impact!

Bright columns of fire rose up through swirling gasses, and the ground shook and bucked beneath Marcos Rajas' feet. Nearly threw him to the ground again. His suit's suppression system dampened the violent sound of the heavens splitting open down to a merely head-aching roar. After a few seconds, filled almost at once with the wailing cries of Bravo's suppression fire, small chips and shards of stone and bits of blackened earth pattered down into the trench, a few still glowing a dull red.

There would be half a dozen new craters pocketing Antares VII, Marcos knew, each of them rimmed with the telltale molten crust of an antimatter flash.

"Dead ball," Big Mike shouted. And on the inside of Marcos' faceplate a blip registered on his incoming DATA STREAM as the location of Mike's failed grenade downloaded to his MAP files. Good to know, if his platoon was forced on the move, where all the unexploded ordnance lay.

So, five new craters. Enough to set the Cyb Walkers back on their mechanical asses. He hoped.

Hope was coming in shorter supply, however, minute by minute.

Two new inquiries flashed up on his Christmas Tree. Bravo soldiers. Princess and Three-Joe. Eyeballing their positions, he saw each man hold their rifle overhead and shake it. Not possible that they were already out of ammunition. But for whatever reason, two more rifles were now out of service.

Another DATA STREAM blip as Tommy-G uploaded revised enemy positions to Marcos' tactical computer. He networked the data to the rest of his platoon. Raised his rifle overhead and squeezed off ten seconds of firepower. "Talk to me," he ordered Books.

The young corporal shook his head. "It don' make sense." He had a shard of rock from the earlier fallout melted to the side of his faceplate. Brushed at it angrily, but could not dislodge it. "Near as I can figure—" and as near as Marcos translated "Ahken figger" out of Savannah and into Standard "—this weapon says that Gravel, here, has surrendered."

Marcos replayed "srended" through his mind several times and still came up with the same result. His mouth dried to a sharp, metallic bitterness.

"Surrendered? No one surrenders without my order." He glanced both ways along the trench, as if to make sure of that. At the rest of his platoon, raising their weapons up just enough to splash firepower to the northwest, to the south. Rifles wailed and energy washed around in showers of new distortion. Return fire from the Cybs shredded the trench's lip again. Shards of stone rattled off his faceplate. "We're still in the thick."

But that would make sense, wouldn't it? A surrender command, if ordered by the highest ranking officer or NCO on site, deactivated the weapon before allowing it to be dropped. An enemy could never pick up a surrendered weapon and turn it against other AID soldiers.

"Might be a software glitch," Books said. "Ah've never read of one. Never heard of one to read about, even. S'pose it's possible, though."

"A glitch that spreads like a virus?" Marcos asked. And something in that idea sparked a new and terrible thought. "Three weapons down now?" Then another inquiry flash, and Rabbit held his rifle overhead. "Four! Fragging ridiculous."

"Maybe we should pull back," Rabbit said. Anthony Guitterez. Marcos didn't need to check his tree to know who had dropped into the STANDARD VOICE conversation. Rabbit was always first to suggest a pullback.

"Not gonna happen. This is our stretch of nowhere. Command said to hold this position, and that's just what we're gonna do. Tommy-G! Grab another look."

"Ya got it, Sarge."

The platoon's senior corporal lowered his rifle and slid a few meters to his right, his ICAS armor shifting from sooty-black to the dark gray of ash, blending in with lighter burn marks along this stretch. Easing up to the edge, his helmet's color faded to a stark, bone white: the color of the horizon on Antares VII. Able and Bravo doubled up on their firepower, buying Tommy-G a few desperate seconds.

Two more inquiry lights flashed with exclamations. Two more soldiers with rifles pointing straight up. Useless.

Marcos hooked each man with a silent assault rifle into a common channel. Flashed them into the VOID to clear their designations and then regrouped them under a new MENU as GAMMA auxiliaries. "Grenades," he ordered this new unit. "Full set, then stagger." Each man reached for one of the small, deadly canisters at their hip. Rabbit had trouble getting his to release from the clip, but the other six managed. And with Gravel doing a hand-count for coordination, all let fly at the same time.

Propellant bursts sent two of those grenades the wrong direction, arcing them back over the trench to the far side. Tiny blips in the DATA STREAM already marked them as failed ordnance. Marcos counted down on the others, waiting for the detonations—even one!—but nothing. No antimatter flash. No ground-shaking columns of fire walking over the battlefield.

"Dead ball," Gravel said in his sing-song delivery.

Rabbit shook his head. Flapped his arms in disgust. "Maybe we can find some rocks to throw at them."

"Cover!" Marcos ordered, shoving Rabbit toward a nearby crevice in the trench wall where the soldier could at least keep his head down and his mouth shut. This many failures, cascading one upon another so quickly, spoke of purpose. Of design. And Marcos believed he finally had a grasp on it.

He moved back to the wall and hooked through STANDARD VOICE so that his entire unit could hear. "What you got, Tommy?"

"Two Cans, rolling up fast," the corporal reported. Another quick glance. "Walkers holding at the outer perimeter. I think I can grab a better angle if—"

But Marcos was already firing. Thumb down on his assault rifle's trigger stud, adding short, choppy shrieks to the caterwauling symphony. Two sprays south. One northwest. Two sprays south again. Hacking away at the enemy positions again, then again.

Then nothing.

As simple as that, his assault rifle suddenly stopped firing. Ammunition stock still at seventy-three percent. No damage icons to warn of impending failure. The best technology available to AID, a rifle practically with a mind of its own, and it refused to engage the enemy! Marcos shook the weapon, as if he might jog a loose part back into place. And then a bright, painful bolt slashed across his retinas as a tree-light flared up briefly in stark white. It faded quickly, though not fast enough that Marcos saw Tommy-G shoved rudely back from the edge of the trench.

One moment his man had been edging up over the rim, scoping out enemy positions. The next, he lay on his back between Big Mike and Rabbit. Half of his helmet shot away.

Three more soldiers held rifles overhead. Shook them. Another short handful of inquiries lit up the inside of his faceplate.

"Damn. Blast. Cybbing frag!" With each shout, Marcos beat his rifle against the hard, hard ground next to Tommy-G, ready to smash the useless weapon into ruin.

Then Big Mike and Gravel were at his side. Each grabbed an arm and hauled Marcos back from his fallen man to pin him against the trench wall. Voices worried him from all sides as the entire unit dropped back to STANDARD VOICE, a confusion of shouts and questions torn apart by the five working rifles still wailing on the enemy positions. Five rifles. Not enough to hold the Cybs back.

Not enough by far to take down the remaining anti-personnel Canisters. Which rolled up over the rim of the trench, hung motionless at the edge for one long and painful heartbeat, and then dropped into the wide, shallow scar.

"Cover!" at least three men shouted along with Marcos as everyone dove for the ground.

And then the entire world tore itself apart in a storm of fire and smoke and razor-sharp metal.

The darkness never completely claimed him, though Marcos nearly smothered beneath its weight. Like being buried alive. Eyes clogged with soot and fire-blackened earth. His lungs burning, straining to pull even a shallow breath from the acrid-tasting air. For a moment, he wondered if *it* had happened. His brain recovered from the battlefield by Cyborg Walkers, scooped out and now at rest in a dark canister somewhere. His arms and legs felt as if they were bound in heavy casts of steel, barely able to move. Better to just lie there. Easier. Lie there and count the tiny, red pinpricks of light scrolling across his retinas. Marking off each second, each heartbeat.

Each computer cycle, as the ICAS technology slowly brought him out of HIBERNATION.

Still alive! Still whole!

At least the ICAS core programming had yet to fail. The first priority of any Interservice Combat Assault Suit was to keep the solider alive. The Cybs had not penetrated to this level. Yet.

Sergeant Marcos Rajas knew. He knew that it had to have been some kind of Cyb virus, or the equivalent, to promote such rapid failure of the technology used by his platoon. From what Books had said. What he had witnessed. And just his gut sense. A soldier had to trust his equipment, yes, but first he trusted his instincts. Automation was the soldier's friend. So said AID Command.

Until that automation failed. Or was subverted.

Icons flared to life against the backside of his blackened faceplate. LIFE SUPPORT, functioning at critically low levels. An EMERGENCY signal to AID Command. Then the Christmas Tree, lighting up with inquiries to his soldiers who were still alive.

Rabbit. Books. Gravel. Two-Joe and Three-Joe. Big Mike. Counting himself, that was half a dozen. One short squad left out of fifteen men.

He swallowed painfully. Tasted the metallic tang of mercury choking at the back of his throat. "If you can hear me," Marcos whispered, hooking his remaining men into a common channel, "don't move. Don't speak. Just flash me an inquiry."

Three inquiries flashed at once. Two more staggered in a few seconds later. Big Mike's icon flashed an uncertain connection. Maybe he was unconscious. Maybe his suit was damaged.

Two-Joe dialed in an exclamation, and Marcos blinked the channel open.

"We got Walkers," the GI soldier warned.

Marcos had guessed as much. He had held off on a complete ICAS restart, in fact, worried that the enemy would be near. Checking bodies. Looking for more raw material. Blinking his way through a system restart MENU, he isolated his faceplate polarization controls and dialed it slowly back from opaque.

At first, the landscape looked as if it still suffered from the energy distortion of CAR-7 rifle fire. Blurred. Glassy. Then he realized that his faceplate was cracked in several places. Amazing, really, that it still held together at all.

Finding a clear section, he turned his head just enough to survey what had been his platoon's strongpoint. Saw a Cyborg Walker not three meters away.

Maybe fifty pounds of meat—muscle and nerve clusters, and a brain, of course—threaded through a metal exoskeleton. Four legs, this one. Low speed. Good stability. Marcos knew this design. It would have six arms tucked away. Two for carrying weapons of different size and operation. Two simple claws for utility purpose. And two ending in a handful of tools for detail work.

The Walker bent down over Tommy-G's body. Taking a detailed survey. Not much gray matter left to work with there, the exoskeleton reached down with a mechanical claw and grabbed the soldier's rifle. Prying it from the man's cold, dead fingers. It turned the weapon over and over again, inspecting it closely.

Another Walker stepped into view. Dragging Three-Joe away by one leg.

"Books," Marcos whispered. Risking the comms more than he wanted. "If it *was* a surrender deactivation, I can rescind. Yes?"

Silence, for a moment. Then, "In theory. If'n it follows standard protocol, a countermand order by the commanding officer or senior NCO would override."

Exactly what Marcos thought. "So why does that sound too easy?"

Because it was. "Don' think that'll work," Books said. "If the system was compromised, it had to've been tricked into believing you ordered it in the first place, Sarge. Without knowing how the Cybs did it, it would take too long—frag me! Ah got one right behind me!—too long t'dig outta trouble!"

He rushed out this last, and it took Marcos an extra second to unravel the man's accent. "But a *new* senior NCO could do it." A cold chill took him, knowing what he would have to do. Or maybe that was just a side effect of the mercury poisoning. "So after Tommy-G, that would be you," he said. Head swimming and not trusting his own analysis one hundred percent.

"Ah guess so."

That was the way it had to be then. Marcos still had his own rifle. Deactivated or not, his grip on the stock had been too strong to shake. Maybe it could be made to work again. Certainly he owed his men that chance.

He grabbed his EMERGENCY beacon by eye, and blinked it into the VOID. Followed it up with all functions under his LIFE SUPPORT menu. One by one. Stripping away his ICAS technology. Shutting down all repairs. Killing his presence in the platoon's networked combat suits. Until POWER and COMMS were all that was left.

Then he shifted his weight against the bulk of his suit, rolling up onto his side in order to attract the attention of the nearest Walker.

"Sarge," Gravel said. The young man's melodic voice sang with fear. "There's a Walker moving right toward you."

"No one move," he said. "Not a muscle or a twitch until Books gives you the order." He overrode multiple queries, flashed them into the VOID behind all his critical systems.

Only Books remained tied into his comms. "Ya can't do this, Sarge. We don' even know—"

"It's all we have left, Books. It'll work."

It had to.

And before his corporal could argue further, Marcos stripped his COMMS system out of the MENU, flashed it into the VOID as well. Leaving only a baseline POWER level functioning. Enough for him to still move in the heavy ICAS skin. Enough to call back his systems, if he desired.

The Walker moved over him, showing no fear of Marcos' rifle, or the fact that the soldier remained alive on the battlefield. Multiple camera eyes focused down at him. Checking for any trap, or simply surveying for raw material—what was the difference in the eyes of a Cyb? Liabilities and assets. Everything weighed with an algorithm and directed by software.

Much like ICAS technology, in fact.

The Walker reached down with one utility claw, clamping onto the barrel of Marcos' rifle just as the platoon's sergeant blinked his POWER into the VOID, fully deactivating his suit. The extra weight sagged around him like a skin of steel. Heavy. Barely flexible without its baseline charge. Whether the Walker sensed this or not, it doubled its own efforts and hauled Marcos half upright as it attempted to steal away his useless weapon. Just in case? Or following an encoded protocol for dealing with prisoners, no matter their state?

Marcos didn't know and didn't much care, so long as he did not lose the rifle. He held on with a one-handed grip, fighting the weight of his damaged suit as much as the Walker's pull. Buying time for Books to reboot the network. Gasping for breath as his lungs burned for lack of oxygen. Vision blurring. The muscles in his legs cramped painfully, and he tasted blood at the back of his throat. But still he refused to let the Walker pry his weapon loose.

Not this time.

Not his!

And then the high-pitched whine of a charging weapon reached him even through the suit's insulation. In the distortion blurring his peripheral vision, he saw motion. Men rising up from the dead. Weapons thrust forward. And Marcos spent the last of his strength to wrench the weapon against the Walker's grip, angling the barrel around, and dragging his thumb over the firing stud.

Held it there as the rifle shrieked one last time in defiance.

"Think he'll come around?" the choir asked in high, pure notes.

"Yeah. He looks baed. Like'n fersh rodkul."
Fresh . . . fresh roadkill? Maybe. "Ain't seen anything
looks like this since—"

"Lastime you looked inna mirror," Marcos Rajas
slurred, fighting his too-thick tongue. He cracked open
one eye. Saw a waxy-pink face swimming against a
gray background. "Mus' be hell. Full of my own person'l demons."

"Anyone understand him through that accent?"
Books asked. At least, that was how Marcos translated
unnerstad'm, and *ass ant*. But the soldier was grinning,
showing off lots of large, white teeth. Which meant
that brimstone and eternal torment might still be a
way off.

"You look far too happy for an ICAS slave. You
get a discharge I don't know about?" Marcos asked.
He struggled his other eye open, saw that he had been
stretched out in an emergency survival tent. Not a lot
of light and even less room, especially with so many
bodies crammed inside. Four . . . five . . . six . . . He
tried to sit up. Big Mike and Rabbit helped him, still
in their suits but helmets doffed.

And Two-Joe. Gravel. Princess and Three-Joe as
well—two men he had thought dead before that last,
desperate gamble.

"Suits were fragged," Princess said, flashing Marcos
a trademark wink. "Slipped into hibernation long
enough for Booksie to get a tent up. Pulled us all out
of the big sleep."

Marcos' mouth tasted as though he'd tried to gargle
with razor blades, all blood and metal. The vision in
his left eye wasn't great. But all in all, he felt as if he
might live. He noticed that he still wore one suit
sleeve, still clenched his rifle in a gloved hand. Looked
up, confused.

"We had to cut you out of your suit," Gravel said.
He nodded at the weapon. "We left the sleeve when
we found out we couldn't take the rifle out of your

hand. Quite a grip you had on it, Sarge. Must have frozen your glove in place when you cut your power."

Marcos nodded. Still staring down at the weapon. "Yeah, well. My rifle. My choice."

"Command is sending down reinforcements to pull us back," Two-Joe said, leaning in. "You're pumped full of meds, and you seem to be all right. Now that you're awake, we can dismantle the glove. Let you rest better without all that dead weight hanging off your arm."

"Going to need to replace the rifle anyways," Books said. "Not much good without a working suit tuned to it."

Not true, though. Not by a far shot. Marcos laid himself back down, carefully. Cradled the rifle across his chest. He wasn't letting it go. Not after everything they'd gone through together. "No thanks," he whispered.

"What's that, Sarge?"

Marcos smiled. And closed his eyes.

"I'll hang onto it," he said.

The Hum

by Rick Hautala

Under his own name as well as the pseudonym A. J. Matthews, Rick Hautala has published more than thirty novels as well as over sixty short stories in a variety of national and international anthologies and magazines. His most recent books under his own name include *Bedbugs* and *The Mountain King*. As A. J. Matthews, he has published *The White Room, Looking Glass,* and *Follow.* Forthcoming from C. D. Publications are *Occasional Demons* and *Four Octobers*. Also, a revised version of his novel *Little Brothers* titled *Untcigahunk: Stories and Tales of the Little Brothers* is due from Delirium Press. Chesapeake Films recently optioned his original screenplay *Chills*.

"Can you hear that?"

"Hear what?"

"That . . ."

Dave Marshall rolled over in bed and struggled to come awake. He blinked, trying to focus his eyes in the darkness as he listened intently.

"I don't hear anything, Sweetie," he said as he slid his hand up the length of his wife's thigh, feeling the roundness of her hip and wondering for a moment if she was interested in a little midnight tumble. He felt himself stirring.

"Don't tell me you can't hear that," Beth said irritably. Dave realized she was serious about this although he'd be damned if he could hear anything. It didn't matter, though, because the romantic mood had already evaporated.

"Honest to God, honey, I don't hear anything. Maybe it was a siren or—"

"It wasn't a siren. It's . . . I can just barely hear it. It's like this low, steady vibration." Beth held her breath, concentrating hard on the sound that had disturbed her.

"Maybe it's the refrigerator."

"No, goddamnit. It's not the fridge."

Dave was exhausted. He hadn't been sleeping well lately. Pressures at the office, he supposed, were getting to him. He sure as hell didn't need to be playing "Guess That Sound" at 2 AM.

"Just put the pillow over your head and go back to sleep. I'll check it out in the morning."

"I can't sleep with my head under the pillow," Beth grumbled, but she turned away from him and put her head under the pillow just the same. He patted her hip one more time, feeling a little wistful.

"Isn't that better?"

"What? I can't hear you."

Ignoring her sarcasm, Dave leaned over and kissed her shoulder as he whispered, "Goodnight, honey."

Dave awoke early the next morning with every nerve in his body on edge. His eyes were itchy, and he could feel a headache coming on.

This is really weird, he thought. *I was in bed by 10 last night. That's nine freakin' hours of sleep. I shouldn't feel like this.*

He went downstairs to the kitchen. Beth was seated at the kitchen table with a cup of coffee clasped in both hands. Her face was pale, and she looked at him bleary-eyed.

"How'd you sleep?" she asked, and he caught the edge in her voice.

"Before you woke me up or after?" He forced a grin.

"Very funny. That goddamn hum kept me awake most of the night." She took a sip of coffee and opened the newspaper, making a point of ignoring him.

"Beth . . ."

"Yeah?"

Dave stood still in the middle of the kitchen. Without even thinking about it, he suddenly realized that he *could* hear something. There was a low, steady vibration just at the edge of awareness. He could almost feel it in his feet.

"Wait a sec." He held up a finger to silence her. "You know . . . ? I think I *can* hear it."

"Really?" Beth looked at him like she didn't quite believe him, but then she relented and said, "Oh, thank God. I thought I might be going insane."

Over the next hour or so, they searched throughout the house from attic to basement, looking for a possible source of the sound. It wasn't in the wires or the pipes or the circuit breaker box or the TV, of that Dave was sure. The odd thing was, no matter what floor they were on or what room they were in, the sound always seemed to be coming from everywhere and nowhere at once. When Dave went outside to check the shed and garage, he found Beth in the middle of the yard, crying.

"What's the matter, honey?" He put his arms around her, feeling the tension in her body.

"I can hear it just as loud out here as I can inside the house, " she said, sobbing into his shoulder.

"So?"

"So . . . That means it's not coming from inside the house. It's out here somewhere. It's like it's coming from the ground or the sky or something."

"Now you're being ridiculous," he said. He took a

breath and, leaning close, stared into her eyes. "I'll call the electric company and maybe the phone company. It's gotta be a problem with the wires."

"Sure," Beth said, not sounding convinced. She wiped her nose on her bathrobe sleeve, then turned and walked back into the house. Dave watched her leave, knowing she didn't believe it was a wire problem.

He wasn't sure he believed it, either.

Over the next few days, things got worse. A lot worse. Like a sore in your mouth you can't help probing with your tongue, Dave found himself poised and listening for the sound all the time, trying to detect its source. Once he was aware of it, he couldn't help but hear it. He was growing desperate to locate it and analyze it. His work at the office suffered. Jeff Stewart, his boss, noticed how distracted he was. At first he commented on it with amusement, but that changed to concern and, finally, exasperation. But Dave noticed that everyone in the office seemed a little distracted and, as the days went by, more and more irritable. This would make sense, he thought, if everyone was sleeping as poorly as he was. It had taken him hours to fall asleep last night, and once he was out, the noise still permeated his dreams. He woke up a dozen or more times and just lay there staring at the ceiling as he listened to the low, steady hum just at the edge of hearing. He knew Beth was lying awake next to him, but they didn't talk. Every attempt at conversation ended with one of them snapping at the other.

Over the next few days, sales of white-noise machines, soundproofing materials, and environmental sound CDs went through the roof. People turned their TVs and radios up loud in a futile effort to block out the hum, further irritating their neighbors, who were already on edge.

Dave's commute to work quickly became a crash course in Type-A driving techniques. One morning, he was trapped for over an hour behind a sixty-five-car pileup on the Schuylkill Expressway that had turned into a demolition derby. It took nearly the entire city police force and an army of tow trucks to break up the melee. After that, Dave kept to back roads going to and from work.

Schools began canceling soccer and football games as soccer-mom brawls and riots in the stands became increasingly frequent and intense. Shoving matches broke out in ticket lines and grocery checkout lanes. Neighborhood feuds and other violent incidents escalated, filling the newspaper and TV news with lurid reports. As the week wore on, road rage morphed into drive-by shootings. Gang warfare was waged openly, and police brutality was applauded instead of prosecuted. The slightest provocation caused near-riots in public. The media reported that the hum—and the rise in aggressive behavior—was a global phenomenon.

"It's only a matter of time before some third-world countries start tossing nukes at each other," Dave muttered one morning at the office staff meeting. Mike from Purchasing glared at him.

"Who died and made you Mr-Know-It-All?" he snarled.

"Jesus, Mike, quit being such an asshole," Dave snapped back.

"All right. That's enough," said Jeff. "This isn't kindergarten. Let's try to be professional here, okay?"

"Professional, schmessional," Mike grumbled. "Who gives a rat's ass anymore, anyway?"

"I *said* that's *enough*." Jeff thumped the conference table with his clenched fist.

Sherry from Operations burst into tears. "Stop it, stop it now! Jesus, *stop it*! I can't take it any more! I can't eat. I can't sleep, and I sure as hell can't stand listening to the two of you morons!"

Dave noticed with a shock the fist-sized bruise on her cheek. She caught him staring at her face and shouted at him, "It's *none* of your goddamned *business*!"

"What'd I say?" asked Dave with a shrug.

"That's it!" roared Jeff. "You're fired! All of you! Every damned one of you!"

The entire staff turned and looked at him, seated at the head of the table. His face was flushed, and his eyes were bulging. In the moment of silence that followed, everyone in the room became aware of the hum, but Dave was the first to mention that it had changed subtly. Now there was a discordant clanking sound, still just at the edge of hearing, but the sound was penetrating.

"The music of the spheres," Sherry whispered in a tight, wavering voice. "It's the music of the spheres." Her voice scaled up toward hysteria. "The harmony is gone. The center cannot hold. Something's gone terribly, terribly wrong!" With a loud, animal wail, she got up and ran from the room with tears streaming down her face.

Mike swallowed hard, trying to control his frustration. "What the hell's she talking about?"

"Go home. All of you. I'm closing the office until they figure out what this sound is." Jeff's fists were clenched, and his body was trembling as though he were in the grips of a fever. "If I don't, I'm going to have to kill every single one of you . . . unless you kill me first." He grinned wolfishly, then slumped down in his chair, pressing the heels of his hands against his ears as he sobbed quietly.

Mike and Dave left the conference room without speaking.

That afternoon, Dave drove home, mindful not to do anything that would irritate anyone on the road. Sitting on the sofa in the living room as he waited for Beth to get home, he couldn't help but listen to the hum. He thought about what could possibly be happening but couldn't come up with an answer.

When Beth finally came home, Dave said, "Sit down. We have to talk."

She looked at him warily, and the mistrust he saw in her eyes hurt him.

"What's her name?"

"What?" He realized what she meant and shook his head. "No. It's nothing like that. Look, Beth, I'm trying to save us, not break us apart. Listen to me, okay?"

Beth nodded as she took a breath and held it. He could see she was trying to pull the last shreds of her patience together, and he felt a powerful rush of gratitude and love for her. It was so good to feel something pleasant that for a brief moment he forgot all about the noise.

"Jeff closed the office. This sound is getting on everyone's nerves, and he's afraid we're all going to end up killing each other. He's probably right. I was thinking—we gotta get out of here. Let's go up to your folks' place in Maine or anywhere, as long as it's far away from here and from all these people."

"But the news says this hum is everywhere. There's no escaping it, Dave," Beth said. Her face contorted, but she clenched her fists and regained her self-control. "What's the point of going anywhere?"

"Maybe there isn't a point, but I . . . I feel like we have to do something. We have to try. I don't want us to end up another murder-suicide statistic." He took her into his arms and held her close. "I love you, Beth."

She clung to him and whispered, "I love you, too."

They sat silently in the living room as the twilight deepened, and the world all around them hummed.

What would normally have been a nine-hour ride to Little Sebago Lake took almost thirty-six hours because Dave wanted to stay off the interstates. The latest news reports indicated that truckers were chasing down and crushing unlucky drivers who pissed them off. Dave had seen the film *Duel* once, and that was enough for him.

As they headed north, the sound became more discordant. Dave noticed a mechanical chunking quality that was getting more pronounced. The endless, irregular rhythm ground away at his nerves like fine sandpaper, but they finally made it to the cabin by the lake without incident.

The camp was on the east side of the lake, small and shabby, but a welcome sight. The lake stretched out before them, a flat, blue expanse of water with the New Hampshire mountains off in the distance to the west. The sun was just setting, tipping the lake's surface with sparkles of gold light and streaking the sky with slashes of red and purple.

It was beautiful, and when Dave and Beth looked at each other, the good feelings drowned out the hum, if only for a moment. They embraced and kissed with passion.

Then the day was over. The sun dropped behind the mountains, and the humming noise pressed back in on them. After unpacking the car, they ate a cold supper of baked beans out of the can. Beth set about making the bed upstairs and straightening up while Dave walked down to the lake's edge.

The night was still except for the hum. All the usual sounds—the birds and crickets and frogs—were silent. The lake looked like a large pane of smoky glass. Stars twinkled in the velvety sky above. Dave sat down on a weather-stripped tree trunk that had washed up onto shore and looked up at the sky. The noise seemed to be changing again. It now was a faint, squeaky sound that reminded him of fingernails raking down a chalkboard. At least it was the only sound. No blaring TVs . . . no pounding stereos.

How long can this go on? he wondered. *How long can anyone handle this before we all go mad and exterminate ourselves?*

He heaved a sigh as he looked up at the sky. At first, he couldn't quite believe what he was seeing when he noticed a few black flakes drifting down onto the lake's surface. They looked like soot from a bonfire. Like a child in a snowstorm, Dave reached up and tried to catch one of the falling flakes.

Funny, he thought, *I don't smell smoke.*

He looked at his hand. The flake lay in the cup of his palm, but it wasn't soft and crumbly like ash. It was hard and thin, with a dark, brittle surface. It crunched like fragile glass when he poked it with his index finger.

Jesus Christ he thought. *It looks like paint.*

Curious, he looked up again. By now the flakes were sifting down rapidly from the sky. As he watched, Dave became aware of a low, steady vibration beneath his feet. It felt like a mild electrical current. As he watched the sky, irregular yellow splotches appeared overhead as more and more black paint fell away, exposing a dull, cracked surface behind. After a time, silver and yellow flakes began to fall. Dave watched in amazement, his mouth dry, his mind numb.

A crescent moon was rising in the east behind him. He turned to see if it, too, was peeling away from the sky like an old sticker on a refrigerator. The noise rose to a sudden, piercing squeal, and then the vibration rumbled the ground like a distant earthquake.

"Beth!" he called out, watching as fragments of the moon broke off and drifted down from the sky. They fluttered and hissed as they rushed through the trees behind him, and then he saw something overhead that was impossible to believe. The peeling paint had exposed a vast complex of spinning gears and cogs with a network of circuits and switches that glowed as they overheated. The humming sound rose even higher

until it was almost unbearable as more pieces of the
night sky fell away, revealing the machinery behind it.
At last, Dave knew—as impossible as it was—what
was happening.

"Beth!" he called out so his wife could hear him
above the steadily rising rumble. "Come out here!
You've got to see this! The sky is falling!"

Last of the Fourth

By Bill Fawcett

Bill Fawcett has been a professor, teacher, corporate executive, and college dean. He is one of the founders of Mayfair Games, a board and role play gaming company, and designed award-winning board games and role playing modules. He more recently produced and designed several computer games. As a book packager, he has packaged over 250 books. The Fleet science fiction series he edited and contributed to with David Drake has become a classic of military science fiction. He has collaborated on several mystery novels as Quinn Fawcett. His recent works include *Making Contact: a UFO Contact Handbook*, and a series of books about great mistakes in history: *It Seemed Like a good Idea, You Did What?* and *How to Lose a Battle*.

As he sealed his helmet, the deafening roar of a bay full of a dozen armored infantrymen preparing to drop was muted to a mere rumble. It wasn't as loud as it had been when the Fourth Assault Regiment had been at full strength with thirty-six troopers and six officers. Being in almost constant combat, there had been no time to integrate replacements. This left Corporal Astin Olowoi free to once again wonder how something that only he had ever worn since it was uncrated could smell so disgustingly rancid. He knew had been the only person to ever wear this Mobile Assault Personnel Suit. Since it was tightly adjusted to every part and contour of his body, he was the only one who could wear and fight the powered combat armor effectively without days of adjustments. Still, each time he sealed his suit, the accumulated odor was nearly overpowering.

Routine maintenance schedules called for the MAPerS interior to be flushed and relined after every twenty uses. That should mean it was subject to a refresh about every twenty-one days between the current regimen of training, actual combat drops and emergency servicing. Astin had been fitted into his MAPerS ten months earlier. That was two weeks before the Jenkle announced themselves by destroying the human colony on Delos. The maintenance schedule was for peacetime use. This was wartime, and things changed as needs must ruled. There had been hardly any downtime, much less a chance to clean the MAPerS' pads since Delos.

Shrugging his shoulders into the armor, the lean trooper let the servos adjust to him. The process went quickly. He hadn't gained any weight since he had worn the suit in a simulated rehearsal of today's drop twelve hours ago. Of course Assault Troopers didn't gain weight. A few too many pounds and then a bit too much shock might get transmuted through his tighter-than-normal armor, turning his body's internal organs into a mass of stringy mush. That had happened a few times on the raids the Fourth had made early in the war. The result was both fatal and so messy that the MAPerS of the casualties had to be retired into spare parts. Since those first deaths no one had to remind anyone in the Fourth to watch his weight, ever.

With the armor sealed, the reek of his suit almost brought tears to the veteran's eyes. Once more he

resolved to stay up one night and at least try to decon-
taminate and clean his interior pads. It didn't help
much, but breaking down a MAPerS to actually
change each piece of pressure sensitive padding also
involved refitting the several hundred contacts that
passed through them. That could take a trained crew
of armorers a week. The Fourth had seen only one
day of downtime since the war had started.

The human race had been at peace for almost a
century when the Jenkle attacked. Those few, like
Astin, had to hold the line until the race could prepare
and relearn how to fight a war. But no one in the
Fourth really complained. Forty million slaughtered
civilians and a now-lifeless planet generated a real
sense of urgency among those whose job was to protect them. They had been part of the clean up, and
every man in the regiment had taken the disaster
personally.

This mission had been given the highest priority,
and the Fourth, as the most experienced and toughest
unit in the fleet, had been assigned. This mission had
to succeed at any cost, in lives or anything else the
Fourth could expend.

"Okay, seal up Fourth and stand by," the Captain
announced over the squad's com sets. "Drop in five,
stand by for final briefing."

Astin felt his heart rate increase, and he took a few
deep breaths to control his adrenaline output. Everyone got psyched before a drop, but the navy twerps
were monitoring the vitals of each man in his squad,
and he wasn't going to give them any ammunition for
comments. The briefing started a few seconds later,
and Astin forced himself to concentrate on it.

He had heard it all before, but as the new squad
leader Astin studied every word and diagram, hoping
he would note something that might help later. He
was the fourth squad leader in seven months, and the

twenty-four man squad was now reduced to a dozen men. So he studied every word and image, even though logic told him that there couldn't be anything new. They had been out of contact and running silent for over a week. There had been no chance for any new intel to arrive. They were going with what they knew when they had lifted from the marine base at Port Cozumel.

A map appeared, showing one of the few hundred islands that were the only land masses on their final destination, the water world of Khumn. This island was located almost exactly on the planet's equator. Sitting on one side of the ten-mile long island was a Jenkle communication station. The humans knew of other systems like this. No doubt floating among the asteroids and other space debris were sensors that would send through that station detailed information on any vessels passing through the system.

The brass didn't tell troopers what was really happening, but everyone knew that the last two months had been spent clearing Jenkle-occupied planets, each one taking them a bit closer to three different heavily developed enemy worlds. The Jenkle were a lot better prepared for this war than the humans were. Each of those assaults had been a tough battle against an entrenched foe. Finally the Navy was in a position to do just that in any of three places. If the Jenkle tried to defend all three worlds, there was a chance of successfully hitting them hard. Astin was fairly sure that a large number of human ships that would prefer to not be spotted would be passing through this system soon. With most of the human fleet positioned to prevent the Jenkle from doing to the Earth what they did to Delos, what followed was likely to be the only offensive force humanity had.

The communications station sat in a half-buried dome. They had found similar emplacements on several other worlds. If they were part of a feint, the island

and relay station could be obliterated, but if the station went silent and stayed that way, it would also alert the Jenkle. Since the squad's mission was to capture the station intact and attach a surprisingly small black box to a specific casing, it looked to Astin as though they were clearing the way for the actual attack force. The device, a naval tech had told him, would continue to assure the Jenkle the system remained operational but not relay any real data. Each trooper had a box, a dozen total. Any one of the boxes would do the job. Casualties were not a consideration.

There was only one concern. Probes had detected no Jenkle life, nor any other living thing larger then a small crustacean, on the island. But they had seen something metallic a few meters across moving around the land mass. Given the Jenkle's propensity for using artificial intelligence and robot combat units, the squad would drop hot and ready. The twelve men of his squad had the firepower to turn that island into a lifeless steaming rock. They just hadn't been fighting the Jenkle long enough to see their every trick, so that mechanical unknown was a worry.

Going in on a hot drop was not much different from being fired like a missile at the target. The Navy ship would push through the warp point, putting out as little signal as it could. Traveling at high speed, it would actually launch the drop capsules behind itself as it flashed by the unnamed world. The problem was not so much one of getting to the target quickly, as it was of being slowed enough to be able to drop to the planet. That process would give the Troopers, if everything went right, a low enough velocity relative to Khumn to allow them to descend through the planet's atmosphere. A small autopilot would guide their shell until they were low and slow enough that they would have enough power to use their grav units to swoop into combat.

The briefing ended, and Astin realized he had been

worrying more than listening. He might have worried about that, but he was interrupted by a familiar thud. This was followed by the armor tightening and kneading in an effort to keep him conscious while being crushed by the massive deceleration.

Astin could follow their approach to the planet from the crude diagram on his helmet's com screen. It showed him and the other eleven troopers as green dots approaching the gray mass of Khumn. Adrenaline and the suit kept the squad leader awake until the press eased as they reached the edge of the atmosphere. That was when the first of the green dots vanished. A short screech over the com confirmed they had lost a man to enemy fire. What worried him the most was that they were almost on the exact far side of the planet. The Jenkle worlds they had dropped on before had not been able to do that. This was something new and very deadly.

Before the squad leader could react further, a second light vanished. Less than a very long minute later a third trooper died. They were just entering the atmosphere. Astin hoped it might provide some cover.

It didn't.

Three more lights blinked off, three more of his troops, were gone in seconds. They were still almost twenty seconds to release. But the kill rate seemed to be increasing. At the rate they were dying, no one would make to the ground.

"Emergency punch out," the squad leader yelled over his com to the Fourth remaining men. "Kick it now, water is better than dead." He prepared to follow reaching for the emergency break level. Astin could only hope there was enough battery power to allow the energy-hungry grav unit to lower him and his suit to the surface. A friendly island would be nice. Then two more lights went out even as he reached up.

As he pulled the release with a mumbled obscenity, Astin thought he saw the last green light go. The flash to his side confirmed that the last other man had been hit. He was free falling and beginning to spin. Spreading his arms, Astin looked around him. The small cube on which the survival of mankind's only attack fleet depended pressed into the trooper's side. But as the loss of the two hundred and eleven men he had lived and fought with began to register, he hardly cared.

The trooper saw the target island on the horizon. The sky was almost purple under the light of a redder sun than Earth's. Most of the planets they had hit so far had reddish suns. The Jenkle home world circled a red star, one briefing had said, so it was theorized that they saw actually saw much further down the spectrum into infrared. They had been warned that this gave the Jenkle excellent night vision.

Even at a distance the island looked jagged. It had, in geological terms, recently been a volcano. The sand was dark, almost as black as the hundreds of obsidian rocks that covered most of its surface, giving the impression that the entire place was on fire with jagged, black flames. It was early morning, and no other land was in sight. No matter what the risk, Astin had to make for that island. He dropped low, and a bright orange beam cut through the air where he would have been if he had continued in a straight line. Then he guided his powered armor low over the water in a twisting, jerky pattern he hoped would confuse whatever was targeting him. The grav unit in the armor was never designed to fly the suit. It was meant to provide a short boost in a combat-jump situation or over hazardous terrain. The unit whined from the strain as Astin watched the level of energy in his batteries visibly drop from the strain of flying distances the MAPerS was never meant to handle.

Two more orange beams lanced through Khumn's moist air. One came so close, half his recon gear overloaded in a burst of sparks. They hurt for a second, but then the wail that warned of low power began rising and falling, and nothing else was important.

Astin aimed at the nearest corner of the island and flew straight toward it. An orange beam tore the air in front of the desperate trooper. Once he saw the bottom, he dived in. The powered armor was not designed for underwater use, but he hoped being submerged might help, and, walking, the suit just might have enough power to get him to shore. The low battery warning continued to scream.

After slogging toward the island for several minutes, the corporal began to hope he had evaded the Jenkle machine. The water was shallower now, and he saw the surface only a few meters over his head. Then an orange beam boiled away the water to his right. The pressure of the expanding water tossed Astin about and would have killed him if his suit hadn't compensated. Then the sound of the low power warning began to fade. The legs of the combat armor began to stiffen. Hoping there was enough energy left to open the suit, Astin hit the button that activated the emergency release code.

The top half of the armor literally peeled away from him, and water rushed in and up Astin's nose. The water was cool and hinted of spices or worse. Using his last breath to clear his nostrils, the corporal tried to kick free. Less than a meter above him the surface tantalized, but got no closer.

As the armor had failed during his swirling fall, the pads in the legs had closed tightly against him. With water filling the top and moistening the pads, they now formed a plug that held him so tightly that his feet were still dry. He was free from just below his waist, but trapped by the inert remnants of his armor.

Lungs beginning to burn, Astin forced himself to relax. Using his hand to push the wet, clinging pads away from one of his thighs, the trooper felt the suit's hold lessen. By now the need to breathe was nearly painful. He forced his hand down the other leg and once more broke the suction. Finally his leg came free. As his hand withdrew, it brushed against something unfamiliar. Almost without thinking, he grabbed the small cube and broke for the surface.

After a few very deep breaths and a few strokes, the trooper was able to stand with his head above the water. The insertion and his swim had taken only a few minutes, but he was exhausted. Moments later, Astin collapsed panting on the beach, oblivious to the fact that whatever had wiped out his squad might still be targeting him.

This was corrected just as the corporal's vision cleared enough to notice one piece of his back armor rise to the surface about fifty meters from the shoreline. He got up, hoping there might be some way to recover a weapon from it, when it disappeared in a flash of orange and steam. Without his armor, Astin found the blast deafening and the crush of air from the explosion of the ammunition that had been in his pack threw him flat onto the sand.

Astin knew he was next. Unarmed and unarmored, he was defenseless. For a few moments the veteran just lay there, soaked and despairing.

But nothing happened.

He did not die in a flash of orange energy. A Jenkle did not rush onto the beach to kill him. In fact, as he looked around and studied the small hill that he remembered from the map dominating this end of the island, nothing—not a single enemy or Jenkle tank, or even a sea bird—moved. In the distance he could hear faint sounds of something large receding.

Once his sheer astonishment at still being alive passed, the trooper crawled into a cleft between two large, jagged rocks. He lay there barely thinking for several minutes, simply overwhelmed by the loss of his squad and his own hopeless situation. His hands shook, and he wasn't sure if it was the cold or his failing nerves. Finally Astin looked back at the beach and noticed the black cube that had been the reason for this cluster jerk of a mission. After staring at the sealed plastic square in the sand for a very long time, Astin reminded himself it was still his mission to acquire the Jenkle relay. The Fourth had been sent on this mission, and he was still alive.

Even with his renewed determination, it took an act of will for Astin to force himself back onto the beach. With each step into the open he could feel the Jenkle lining him up for a kill shot. In the ten steps to the cube he died a dozen times in his mind. Once he had grabbed it, the trooper couldn't stop himself from dashing back and diving into the relative protection of the volcanic rocks. Still breathing hard, the corporal found himself smiling. He was alive. It was apparent that whatever defended the island didn't even know he was here, or didn't care. All he had to do now was get past the Jenkle's defenses and lock the cube on the relay.

All. . . . The smiled faded. He was half-naked, alone, unarmed, and had no idea what he was even facing. For all he knew there was a cunningly hidden base full of Jenkle infantry and armored vehicles just over the hill. Exhausted, the trooper lay there warmed by the morning sun, fighting off despair, until he finally slept.

The day on Khumn was long, and the planet's sun was still high in the sky when Astin woke up. Amazement at being alive was quickly replaced by a new concern. He felt the beginnings of hunger, and it reminded him that he was alone on an alien world with no supplies. Then the trooper realized that was hardly a concern. If he didn't succeed in sabotaging the relay station, the Navy would have no way of knowing he was alive. He would be stranded on this damp rock forever. There was fresh water, but he had no idea if he could eat anything here. Most alien critters were just too, well, *alien* to digest, and on many planets the indigenous food was fatal to humans. Of course, that might be preferable to spending the rest of his life alone on Khumn. Completing the mission had suddenly become very personal. If the Jenkle did manage to intercept the attack fleet, the chances of his ever being picked up dropped to zero.

So far the Jenkle had taken no prisoners during the war, and in their one planetary assault they had killed every living thing on Delos. For a panicky moment the trooper realized the Jenkle were as bloodthirsty as they appeared, and if humanity lost, there was a sickening chance Astin Olowoi could become, due to his very isolation and the Fourth's failure, the last survivor of his race.

One final man doomed to die alone on a distant world.

The thought gave the corporal a surge of determination, enhanced by a reckless realization that he had nothing to lose by getting killed. He really had to try to complete the mission. The consequences of failure looked a lot worse than dying in the effort. And if he was the last of the Fourth, then he sure as hell was going to complete their final mission.

Still aching from the battering he had taken while getting to land, Astin Olowoi crept cautiously up the hill. When he reached the crest, it was a disappointment. The island was the jagged top of a long-extinct volcano. Small hills and a line of cliffs blocked his view of the Jenkle relay station on the far side, less than two kilometers away. Mostly he saw bare rock, moss, and some low-growing plants. The only good news was that there wasn't a massive Jenkle base hidden in the middle of the island. The problem was that he still didn't know what he faced. What had shot his entire squadron from the sky in less than a minute?

Again Astin faced the dilemma that if he moved toward the Jenkle Station, he might draw down fire. He had no illusions about what effect that orange ray would have on an unprotected body. But staying put just wasn't an option. Cautiously, with growing surprise at the lack of a response, he ran from boulder to boulder across the small island. A passing storm drenched him once more, but the exertion needed to make his away across the broken terrain kept him comfortable even as what remained of his uniform got soaked again.

The unarmed trooper crawled up the final rise before he reached the Jenkle station. What he saw was not encouraging. The station itself was a small metal dome, similar to others they had encountered on earlier drops. Beyond the dome was a beach and empty sea. The area around the dome had been scorched clear for about fifty meters. The dome's door was visible and likely easily opened. No living Jenkle were visible, but guarding the area was some new sort of Jenkle combat vehicle.

The unit stood two meters tall and seemed to operate like a hovercraft. That made sense on a world where most of the surface was covered with water. The air being driven from the fans below kicked up a steady stream of dust. There was no turret. Two barrels protruded from the front of the weapon platform. The larger one was almost half a meter thick and made of crystal. It protruded only about as far as it was wide. Astin guessed that this was the source of the orange beam. A second, smaller crystal also paralleled it at about a quarter of the first one's size. The top was covered with bulges and two antennas. Long, small slits along the top of the sides of the vehicle were likely air intakes, Astin concluded. As he watched, the unit shifted a few meters. It turned slowly, but it covered the ground in an impressive burst of speed.

The vehicle must have used that orange ray to clear its field of fire around the dome. While rocks taller than the human stood all around the edge of the cleared area, nothing inside that perimeter was taller than a few cracked rocks under six inches high.

Astin slid down behind a two-meter high chunk of shiny volcanic stone and tried to examine his options. Failing to do that, he concentrated on trying to find an option to consider.

He had no weapon, no armor, no food, and no real information on his opponent. He wasn't even sure if the first time he was detected, a half-dozen heavily armed Jenkle would pour out of that dome. Intel had said no life signs, but they had missed the automated laser tank as well.

After sitting for several minutes discarding one absurd and impractical plan after the other, Astin realized something. He was sitting less than a hundred meters from that tank and it was doing nothing. Why?

Maybe the unit's AI was not programmed to see anything not using power as a threat? Maybe it was unable to detect him at all. Once more the trooper crept up the cool volcanic rock and studied his opponent.

It hadn't moved. After watching the Jenkle vehicle for what seemed a very long time, Astin lost patience. He had to do something. Creeping back down behind the boulder, the trooper grasped one of the many fist sized rocks and lofted it toward the Jenkle dome.

The small yellow ray that vaporized the rock left only the smell of ozone behind.

It was some minutes before Astin risked another look over the boulder. This time the Jenkle weapon began turning toward him the moment his head appeared. Astin dropped and rolled painfully across numerous sharp edged rocks until he was several meters away from the boulder he had been hiding behind.

The concussion as the orange ray smashed into his

former hiding place threw jagged shards onto the trooper even as he dived for cover behind another thick rock. Less than thirty seconds later, that new meter high stone protected Astin as a second orange beam completed the destruction of the first boulder. Two tons of obsidian had shattered, spraying hundreds of rock shards in a fairly good simulation of an anti-personnel bomb. Over his ragged breath, the corporal heard the sound of dozens of the stones thwacking against the far side of the outcrop. If he had been in the open, the last of the Fourth would have been very dead. Noticing for the first time that he was half submerged in a shallow pool left by the recent rain, the corporal knew he didn't dare move.

The growl and whoosh of the Jenkle vehicle grew louder as it approached the spot where Astin hid. For a moment, he almost accepted defeat. Then the vehicle stopped just short of the dust and pebbles that were all that remained of the man-high rock it had destroyed. The sodden trooper stayed very still and barely breathed. After what seemed to be an extremely long time, the weapon growled back to life and moved away. After another long time he risked a glance over the rocks and saw it had returned to the same exact spot by the dome where he had first seen it.

Carefully making his way back to the far shore, the trooper collapsed into the same crevice he had first hidden in just after reaching the island. The alien sun was halfway down, but after picking several small hunks of stone out of his side and legs, the exhausted and battered human tried to rest. He remembered that Khumn had a day almost eighty standard hours long. That hadn't seemed important for a quick smash and grab operation. Now he worried that he would be at an even greater disadvantage at night on the moonless planet.

Or just be too late.

Rousing himself, Astin began to explore. He nurtured the hope that somehow he would find some way to defeat the Jenkle robot. Unarmed and without his armor, it was hard to not feel helpless and hopeless. Even time counted against him. The attack fleet was going to be passing through this system in less than two standard days. And with no way to tell time accurately, he had to leave a serious margin of error. He figured he had been down about eighteen hours, but he had no real way to be sure. That left no more than twenty-four hours, or it was all a waste.

Grimy and scraped even through his uniform, the human walked waist deep out into the ocean. The salt level of the water was low, barely stinging as it cleaned his wounds. Being clean felt good. At least he didn't stink of his armor any more. Sadly, Astin glanced across the empty sea to where what remained of the familiar suit sat shorted and lifeless several meters deep.

Despite the situation, the trooper almost allowed himself to relax . . . just a bit. That was, until he felt a sharp sting on his lower leg. Rushing back to shore, Astin looked down at a small, round, clear creature almost like a tiny but tendriless jellyfish clinging to his leg. Quickly he brushed it off, using the sharp edge of a rock when it hung on stubbornly, and went back to the water's edge to splash the wound clean. The entire process took only a few painful seconds.

Dozens of the creatures bobbed on the surface of the water where he had been standing. Astin realized that his body heat must have attracted the organisms. It was unlikely they were reacting to his otherworldly body chemistry. Pushing back visions of alien poisons and even more alien infections, Astin went back and studied the creature even as the pain in his leg subsided. His issue pants were some kind of super fabric that lasted forever and was resistant to almost anything. Where the creature had clung to his pants near his ankle, the fabric was barely discolored. But he had been burned almost as if from an acid where the critter had eaten a hole in his less-resistant socks and started in on his skin. Checking carefully, he found two more jellies attached to the back of his uniform jacket and another on the back of his other leg. Again it took a sharp edged rock to pry them off. One had even eaten part-way through the titanium buckle on one pocket. Whatever solvent they excreted, it was hell on metals. Using the same rock, he rolled the first acid jelly over. The rock where it had sat for just a few minutes was already bleached and cracked. Under different circumstances, Astin might have wondered at the ecology that had developed such a creature. But as frustrated as the trooper was, he just filed the jellies as an added annoyance in the middle of a disaster. Astin continued walking the shoreline, looking for a miracle. He found lots of a harmless plant that was like a combination of sponge and seaweed, and little else.

By the time Corporal Olowoi realized he had nearly circled around the small island and was getting dangerously close to the Jenkle base, he had just about run out of hope. His thoughts turned to the men and women of the Fourth that had been his close friends and comrades over the last year Their loss cut deep, and he fought guilt that they had died under his command, his first—and likely last—command. A darkness deep inside the trooper began to break free and spread. It was the darkness soldiers learned to keep at bay. Now it emerged, and it carried despair with it. There was no way to complete the mission. His squad had died for nothing, and the attack fleet would fail. His personal failure was going to doom all humanity. He was unarmed and beaten. It was all just hopeless.

Astin found that he was sitting on the beach crying when he began to take hold of himself. His eyes were blurry and his throat raw. As reason again took hold, he worried just how much time has passed. Panic replaced despair. He no longer knew how long it would be until the attack fleet entered the system. How long until its detection would complete his failure.

The trooper knew he wanted to win. But his mind could not get past the fact that he was already beaten. That the Fourth had ended in failure. The Jenkle had beaten him and that their robot would destroy him the moment they clashed. One on one, his opponent was unbeatable. The Jenkle could outfight and outrun him. He was outgunned, out-thought, and outmaneuvered. It was just the better soldier, the better man. All he could do was hide until he died of starvation.

Better man . . . ?

The unit defending that dome wasn't a man, or even a Jenkle. It didn't outthink him. It couldn't. He had been looking at this the wrong way. A real Jenkle or human that well-armed and armored would be unbeatable. But that was a machine. It had limits and could react only as it was programmed. Those limits and that programming was his edge. Not much of an edge, but leverage none the less.

If even a few of the Fourth had survived, he could conceive of several ways they could take the robot out. But they hadn't. Only he remained.

The trooper fought back his depression and focused on the mission. There was just a chance he could defeat that automaton. Or he had to admit—and the thought no longer frightened him—that he could die while trying something that just might succeed. There was nothing left to lose.

Tired, limp muscles tightened and prepared for what Corporal Astin Olowoi had trained and prepared for for years—combat. The man's mind raced, discarding plans and reevaluating both his resources and what he knew about the Jenkle defense unit. The Fourth had been almost destroyed, but one member remained, and with almost a smile on his face, that lone trooper began to analyze his past encounters.

The Jenkle had ignored him at least three times and reacted with overwhelming firepower the other two times. What was the difference? What about his opponent being a machine had made that difference? A human enemy might had just missed seeing him. But even a half-competently programmed computer could not have. Any good automated defense unit would be scanning its surroundings constantly. It would only have taken a fraction of second to see him. So why didn't it shoot him when he was first collapsed on the beach? Why had it simply left instead? Or only fired the second time he had looked over the rock at the dome? Why did a unit which could pick off the entry rockets a thousand miles away not sense him on the far side of the rock when he was only a few meters away later?

The waves lapping nearby gave Astin the answer. A machine reacted to the parameters given for any target. The defense unit was not a thinking being. It could only act or react to what it was programmed to recognize as the enemy. The entry pods would have been literally flaming through the atmosphere. They would have been an easily recognized target. The unit only fired at identified targets. But why had it fired on him minutes after ignoring that same head appearing over a rock? The bit of his head showing would have been the same both times.

Temperature. He had been wet, chilled really, each time it had ignored him. On the beach, and from the rain the first time he had popped up to recon the Jenkle base.

The Jenkle saw more into the infrared spectrum. They could literally see how hot or cold an object was. Where a human robot would recognize shape and patterns of movement, the Jenkle must have added another requirement to their targeting parameters . . . temperature. Or maybe to them, color. Humans are a nice, consistent 96.8 degrees Fahrenheit. The Jenkle saw infrared. So it was likely all humans were that same color to them. The color of human skin would be less visible to the Jenkle than the color generated by body temperature. The aliens had programmed their defense unit to kill anything the color of a human and to ignore everything else unless it became a threat or was identified as a part of the human shape.

Then a moment of doubt ensued. Was he just clutching at straws, convincing himself of something just to feel he had a chance? It had blasted the rock he had thrown too. But that had actually been thrown toward the dome. It made sense the robot would shoot out of the air any missile, even a stone one, threatening the relay unit. So it was also apparent that anything, of any temperature or shape, that Jenkle weapon detected inside the kill zone near the dome would be fired upon.

Then maybe he could use being soaked, if he was right, to get close to the dome. But there still was no way to get inside it without getting rid of the Jenkle unit. And that unit was armed and armored. He had rocks and seaweed.

There had to be another option. There was, Astin finally realized. He didn't have to destroy the defender, just get it to stay away from the dome long enough for him to place the cube. Maybe he could lead into a chasm or pit? Problem with that was that old quandary of trying to outrun a bullet, or in this case an even faster power beam. If he got the machine to chase him, how could he stay alive to lead it into some pit? Even if it turned slowly, it could still fly just over the broken ground much faster than he could run. And it was a war machine. It would begin firing at him a tiny fraction of a second after he was spotted.

Before he solved that puzzle, the trooper realized there was another possible problem. If the cube changed the signal coming from the dome too much, there was a good chance the defender was programmed to knock it off the air. That again would warn the Jenkle that something was up. Keeping the relay station from being shut down is why the Fourth had been dropped on Khumn in the first place. Otherwise a single missile from orbit would have been all that was needed.

So, he had to get the defender away from the dome and keep it away. That meant disabling its hover fans. But the sides of the machine were solid metal and the fans were protected. The only openings in that armor were those two thin slits along the edge of the roof for the air intakes. And it was likely that air system was completely isolated by more armor from the control and weapons areas. Even his fingers would not fit more than an inch or so into those slots. He would have to destroy the fan blades from the only direction they could be accessed, below.

Astin contemplated ways to get under the Jenkle machine. He envisioned jamming a long shard of obsidian into one blade. But the only reason the weapon would move anywhere away from the dome was to kill him, and it wasn't going to move on top of its target. At least not while he was alive. Then the realization hit that if he disabled the fans while the war machine was hovering just over him, it would come down on top of him. So much for that.

Leading the Jenkle defense unit away would be risky, but the right plan could work, Astin decided. There was always a way. But what? And he could not just lead it away and loop around. It was too fast and he had to prevent it from ever getting back to the dome.

The sun had moved visibly before the trooper felt he had a plan that, given a lot of luck, just might work. Sore and tired, Astin began gathering the sodden seaweed and watching the sky for another rainstorm. The expression on his face was way too determined for his mouth to actually be showing a grin. It was an expression any human would have understood. The Fourth's sole remaining trooper was going to win or die.

He no longer intended to die.

"Shape, movement, temperature," Corporal Olowoi repeated the parameters almost like a mantra. He was exhausted, and the Khumn sun was starting toward the horizon. One small cloudburst had drenched him before he was ready. Now, as he tied and shaped another mass of the absorbent seaweed, Astin watch anxiously as the cooler evening air triggered more showers. This had to be it. He was out of time.

At the first drops of rain he ran to the sea and stripped off his pants. Carefully tying each leg closed, the the trooper ran into the ocean. The water felt cold on his bare legs. Which was good since that meant they were heating the water around them. He saw the jellies moving toward where he stood. The human ran back toward the shore, but not quite fast enough. A sharp pain on one ankle made him drop the pants he had held poised and begin scraping where the little critter had attached to his leg and secreted acid.

The three-centimeter circle of livid, tortured skin hurt, a lot. Even splashing water on the wound didn't help much. Astin knew there was no more time. The rain was falling steadily now, and he rushed to edge of the water, where he saw dozens more of the acid oozing critters had been attracted to where he had stood. Using his pants as a scoop, the trooper pulled them through the thickest patch of jellies. Once on the beach he saw them clinging to the inside of the legs of his rugged uniform. His ankle was throbbing, but he had well over two dozen of the jellies trapped. That is, trapped until they ate through the tough artificial fabric of his uniform.

Hurrying toward the area he had prepared, Astin left the pants hanging on a jagged outcrop, took some seaweed from the large pile below it, and draped the wet mess over the pants until their shape was obscured. Then tossing more of that same soggy plant over his soaked shoulders and head, the trooper continued toward the dome and its lone defender.

Astin crawled the last few meters before the spot he had prepared near the blasted area cleared around the dome, blessing the rain that made it harder for the weapon platform to see his movement or detect his distinct heat signature. Finally he reached the pile of carefully tied seaweed he had prepared and dragged there earlier. He had formed it into a something that bore a vague resemblance to a human. His jacket, filled with the stuff, helped the illusion.

The rain had begun to taper off as Astin threw the seaweed dummy over the boulder and straight at the dome's defender. He was running the other direction, before the seaweed had cleared the top of the rock formation that had been between him and the alien's kill zone. It was still in the air when the yellow beam struck it on one "leg," and the resulting explosive release of steam from the soaked seaweed in that leg tore the rest of the crude manikin apart.

A rock he threw while still on the run got a bit farther before being turned into dust.

Astin threw the second dummy he had prepared, this one was held together by his t-shirt. He tossed it with all his strength directly into the air and made no attempt to even throw it toward the dome. He didn't need to. He heard the growl of the hover tank's fans as it moved toward the decoy, and him.

Again the bolt of yellow tore apart seaweed and cloth. Astin angled to his left, reaching the relative shelter of a V-shaped extrusion where he had left the next of his creations. This one was just seaweed. He had run out of clothing except for some shorts and his boots. His uniform shirt had been sacrificed earlier. Again he threw a soggy manikin almost straight up and ran. Having to turn before firing, the tank actually didn't fry the decoy until it began to arc downwards. Astin stored the information on how long it had taken to shift.

Angling left again and drawing the defender further from the relay station's dome, the human threw three more seaweed decoys. Occasionally using its orange ray to blast a path where the boulders were too large to hover over or push aside, the alien machine followed. As Astin had hoped, a race as bloodthirsty as the Jenkle would have programmed their weapons systems to hunt mercilessly any known, single enemies.

They were out of sight of the dome now. Still the human was sure that there were alarms ready to call the fast hovering defender back if he somehow did enter the open area around the dome while it hunted. But that wasn't the idea.

Another decoy went into the air. Another flash of intense yellow was followed by all the water in the seaweed turning instantly into superheated steam. Enough steam reached Astin to sting his exposed back as the trooper lofted another seconds later. This time the orange beam lanced out. Astin never knew why it used the larger weapon.

The wider and more powerful beam not only vaporized the second decoy, but the blast it caused sent the trooper rolling until he slammed against unforgiving stone. He lay there for a moment, regaining his breath and waiting for the robot to appear. Astin's side hurt, and a deep breath brought a gasp of pain. Even as it sounded like the defender had moved toward where he had thrown the last dummy, the trooper pulled himself up and hoped that if any of his ribs really were broken, they didn't puncture a lung. For a brief instant he missed his MAPerS and it shock absorbing abilities, but he set the thought aside along with his desire for a tall beer and taller redhead.

The next decoy was at the edge of the area Astin

had chosen and prepared earlier. This was really two small areas about ten meters across and joined by a three meter opening between two large extrusions. Astin knew this was the most dangerous part of his plan. If he had guessed wrong, he was dead and all of humanity was probably lost too. He felt a passing desire to just run away and delay the confrontation. The human dismissed the temptation as he threw the decoy high and to the far side of clearing he was in. Then the trooper hurried to crawl under the pile of waterlogged seaweed he had laboriously hauled in earlier. Around him were a dozen similar piles, a few even carefully laid out and twisted to resemble a human laying flat on the ground. A few seconds later the hovering defender entered the clearing.

Barely willing to breathe, the human waited. Dust and small rock particles showered his hiding place and made his eyes water. Still the trooper waited, unmoving. His one fear was that the weapon would recon by fire, simply blasting apart each of the piles of seaweed. A human would have done that. A human would have thought of that and sensed a trap, but the Jenkle machine could only react as it was programmed to. It would instantly destroy any enemy it detected, but only after they were detected. Any other instruction would have led to the robotic defender wearing itself out destroying every lump of seaweed that drifted or blew past the dome.

Slowly it advanced farther into the small area. As Astin had planned, it was almost next to him and just starting into the narrow area between the two clearings when it detected his seaweed stuffed shirt to its left. The unit turned in place to bring the weapons protruding from its front to bear. Its back end swinging only centimeters from the rock behind it.

At the sound of that turn, Corporal Olowoi rose. He knew that the weapon would sense him and turn to target him. But he was only a few steps away, and he had calculated that it would take at least seven seconds to turn around. Seven seconds was the entire window his plan had to save an entire fleet and maybe mankind. Grabbing his pants off the rock, the trooper took two steps and dove onto the top of the alien vehicle.

A second later he had upended his pants, dumping the water and jellies into one of the air intakes. The suction caused by the rapidly spinning fan blades pulled in the water instead of air. Letting go of the pants that were now being sucked slowly through the air slits, Astin laid flat on the top of the machine and wedged his fingers as deeply as they would go into the thin intakes.

The whole process had taken less then ten seconds. But it no longer mattered which way the weapon faced. To hit him now, it would have to be able to shoot itself. Taking that long was good, since the automated response to any intruder being on top of the unit initiated itself at twelve seconds with the unit increasing the power to its blades. Suddenly the Jenkle weapons platform dashed forward almost to the far side of the open area and slammed to a halt. It stopped for less than a second to see if it had dislodged the trooper and then surged backward across both clearings with even greater speed and came to a more abrupt stop.

Astin could only hold on. His fingers hurt and his shoulders strained with the effort of clinging to the machine. The pain in his battered side became a twisting knife as bruised and punished muscles began to tear. As the robot weapon began to move forward once more, the trooper thought he heard something different in the whine of the now straining fans, but he could hardly tell with the changes in pitch masked as the vehicle tried to dislodge him again. The human had no doubt that its weapons were both charged and ready to fire as fast as only a machine can do the moment he was down and in their field of fire.

The deadly dance ended when the one of the unit's fan blades slammed into the inside of the weapon with a thud that the sprawling trooper could feel all along his body. Then there was another thud as the unbalanced fan tore itself apart and the back of the Jenkle robot scraped along the ground. Astin grimaced a smile, knowing that at least one the jellies had, as he had hoped, managed to attach to the spinning and so very warm and inviting fan blades or their shaft. The metal-eating acid had done the rest.

Where the defender's frantic dashing couldn't knock the determined trooper off it, the bouncing caused by the rear of the several ton combat unit dragging over the rough ground succeeded. Fortunately for Astin, he rolled off behind the unit.

Even as the trooper clutched his side and struggled to stand, the front fans of the damaged defender strained to turn the unit so that its weapons could be brought to bear on him. The edges of the metal sides of the weapon dragged across the volcanic rock throwing sparks and broken rock, and then the front fan also failed as its sound changed from a deep growl to a diminishing whine.

Then there was silence broken only by the futile charging of the front mounted weapons as they searched for a target.

For the first time Astin's smile was real. There was a moment's hesitation while he wondered whether he should try to disable the defender more. The thought of smashing those deadly crystals with a heavy rock was quite appealing. But the mission, he reluctantly decided, came first. And if he did get picked up, the intel boys would want it as intact as possible. Besides, the trooper cheerfully concluded, he could always come back later. The Jenkle machine was not going anywhere.

The walk to the dome was almost leisurely. Astin recovered the small cube where he had hidden it far from where the action had been. He even found that the dome's door was unlocked. Why lock a door when you have a superpowered, beam firing, super accurate defender? It was easy to spot the correct panel, and the cube attached as it was designed to. A small green light suddenly appeared, and the trooper's smile grew larger.

His pick-up would come in with the fleet. All he had to do now was wait.

The last of the Fourth had completed their mission.

Moral Imperative

By Ed Gorman

Ed Gorman is a man of many talents, effortlessly slipping from genre to genre as the mood strikes him. But the one thing that also shines through is his honest, unflinching portrayal of everyday, often anguished characters. His western fiction has won the Spur Award, and his crime fiction has won the Shamus and Anthony Awards and has been shortlisted for the Edgar Award. In addition, his writing has appeared in *Redbook*, the *New York Times, Ellery Queen Magazine, Poetry Today,* and other publications.

The Flicker—the fastest nuclear-powered train in the entire Midwest—was not only on time today, it was ten minutes early.

Nick McKay was grateful for such speedy service. This meant that there hadn't been time for the final on-board prayer service. As usual, he'd been all prayed out about ten minutes after six this morning, the usual rising time for all the husbands who commuted from the suburb of God's Arms to New Chicago. The moment the alarm went off on work days, his wife Emily had him down on his knees and leading her and their two kids in the Morning Offering. The MO, as he called it, took fifteen minutes to slog through. Who needed more slogging than that to feel righteous?

The train station was of the quaint older type, built of near-wood with a slanted shingled roof, half a dozen baggage carts standing next on the west side of it, and a wooden platform where the wives in their baby blue jumpers waited for their husbands. Each jumper bore across its bosom the embossed red image of a bloody crown of thorns.

Early as the Flicker was, the late April day was already dying, the sun a furious red ball shining behind the black winter trees, the layered clouds mixing the colors of salmon pink, mauve, apricot. Dusk was a death, and dusk was something that McKay always shared with the planet, giving in to a melancholy that could sometimes bring him to tears. He'd once shared this with Pastor Paul and quickly wished he hadn't. "That's sort of a pagan thought, don't you think? People who are right with God appreciate the beauty of sunset. It's another one of His gifts, Nicholas. Hardly a time for self-pity—which melancholy always is." Pastor Paul disliked shortened names, forbidding the use of nicknames in his presence. He'd never offered his flock any justification for this. But he didn't need to. He was Pastor Paul.

The way the husbands of God's Arms stumbled off the train car gave the impression that they were weary soldiers returning from an exhausting war. It fell to their wives to put smiles on their faces and renew at least partial energy to their bodies. New Chicago lay just beyond the reach of God's Country and was filled with pagan spectacles and rites that would make any righteous man weary.

Before he saw Emily, he saw Natalie Avery. He knew he should look away. They'd sworn last Saturday in the park never to meet in secret again. But he couldn't not look at her. The dark hair framing a face that was both sensual and vulnerable in a way that

only enhanced the sensuality—how could he look
away? She didn't look away, either. And so, for one
of those moments that seem to extend into minutes,
they stood watching each other, each of them finally
giving up a wisp of a smile.

Then he turned and walked over to Emily, the chilly
air even colder in the sudden wind now.

Even from here, he could hear Emily whispering
her prayers to herself. He thought of how much fun
she'd been when he'd first met her. Perspective was
the gift she'd given him, a wittiness that showed him
how he could step back from his daily griefs and laugh
at them right along with her.

And then she'd started seeing those vids for how
safe and nurturing life could be in God's country . . .

"Wait till you see their monthly grades," Emily said,
her voice shining with the love and pride they both
felt for their kids. She was the best home-schooler in
God's Arms. She submitted all their work to Principal
Homenet, and Principal evaluated it every thirty days
or so. She'd won Best Home Schooler for four years
in a row. The other mothers, to their credit, did their
best not to indulge in the sin of envy. It couldn't have
been easy.

The car was on auto, and they were only a few
minutes away from the large Colonial-style house that
they were able to afford because of Nick's sojourn in
pagan land five days a week.

Nick put his head back. Closed his eyes.

"Looks like massage night, honey. You look pretty
beat."

One word sufficed. "Donaldson."

"I thought he was still on vacation."

"Somebody managed to let him know that all of a
sudden we were in trouble with the Handy Andy account. So long Southern France and his chateau there.
He was back in the States and at his desk before any-

body else this morning, and he let each of us know individually that if Handy Andy goes to another agency, we'll be leaving too."

Emily touched his hand with hers, and immediately he was ashamed he'd let the flirtation with Natalie get so far. He opened his eyes and smiled at her. She was a pretty woman, blond, blue-eyed, a few pounds overweight, which he found enjoyable when they made love. But most of all she was just a damned fine woman, one he used to love so passionately that he would literally get headaches if he had to be away from her for any significant amount of time.

But now . . . now he respected her more than loved her. What could you fault her for? Perfect mother, attentive wife, helpmeet in every sense. But once he'd reluctantly agreed to live in God's Country for the sake of the children . . . He was a believer, too. Maybe not with her certainty, maybe not with her devotion. But he believed that an invisible hand had created the spark that created the universe. He even believed that in some way that invisible hand sometimes affected circumstances on earth as well as everywhere else. In the early years of their marriage, this had been sufficient belief for Emily. But since they'd come to God's Country . . .

"Any other news today?"

"No more noisy robots."

"Really?"

"There's a new model of Protector, and they're 'streeting' it tonight as they say."

"How did that happen?"

"I guess the Mayor's been asking St. Louis for four new 'bots and they finally came through. Trial run tonight starting at nine o'clock."

He looked over at her and said, "Maybe we could violate some of the marital bedroom rules before this thing gets clanking up and down the street tonight. Put the kids to bed early and—"

"That isn't funny, Nick. Those are God's rules. And I'm not going to break them."

All he could think of was—in the old days she would have giggled if he'd suggested they break rules of any kind. Especially if they involved the bedroom . . .

When had pre-dinner and post-dinner prayers gotten this long? Nick wondered, his knees still sore from all that kneeling.

He was in the small study they'd created out of what had once been a storage area. More and more he'd been forced to bring his work home—bring the devil in the form of advertising right into his home— when the communicator rang. Three bleats meant it was a Nick call. He picked up.

She spoke in a teary, frightened rush: "He's at Pastor Paul's right now telling him everything. He's been following us the last three or four weeks. Watching us meet in the park."

The voice belonged, of course, to Natalie Avery.

"He should be back any time soon. I'm afraid he'll walk in on us right now. He might even be having our calls monitored. I'm so paranoid now about everything. I just thought I'd tell you."

She clicked off.

His first response was no response. Not panic, not terror, not any plan of action. He just sat in his desk chair staring at the holo image of his wife and family.

Only when he realized the implications of the call did he stir. He got up and began the useless pacing that was the hallmark of every Nick crisis.

The big thing was to stop Pastor Paul from calling Emily. Even though this wasn't technically a matter of adultery, he would have a difficult time putting an innocent face on his four meetings with Natalie.

He had two hours before the new Protector was to take to the streets. Time to . . .

*   *   *

He drove with the window down. The chill air refreshed him. He needed to be sharp when he made his case to Pastor Paul.

As the head beams swept the stone edifice of the church, he saw that Richard Avery's auto was still in the parking lot adjacent to Pastor Paul's office in the back of the large building.

Nick clicked off the head beams. Maybe it was better this way. Have it out with Richard in front of Pastor Paul. The cleric could bring wisdom to Richard's anger and Nick's confusion.

He stood in the night taking deep clean breaths, readying himself. In the moonlight, he could see tiny buds peering up from branches, patches of brown grass becoming obstinately green now that spring was on the way. He'd been so damned foolish to get involved with Natalie even to the degree he had. He wasn't by nature a dishonest man, but he'd now cast himself as one of the most dishonest of people—the adulterer.

Inside the rear of the church, he could smell the most recent meal some of the church women had prepared for the homeless outside the neighborhood. Stewed chicken and mashed potatoes, that was the usual repast. There were four bulletin boards on the wall with a myriad of notes and pamphlets thumbtacked to them. It was like being back in school again.

He'd been to Pastor Paul's several times so he had no difficulty finding it. Just as he was about to knock on the cleric's door, he heard Richard say, "It doesn't matter if they slept together. What matters is that they were deceiving us—both me and poor Emily."

This was where Pastor Paul should have inserted a few reassuring words about the moral difference between wanting to do something and actually doing it. He said, "I'm afraid I have to agree with you, Richard, especially where women are concerned. The way God constructed the male, it's expected that the man will at least have thoughts about women other than his wife. But He holds women to a much higher standard. He allows them the privilege of giving birth. He allows them the privilege of being the chief nurturer. He allows them to spend all day with the children while the husband toils to feed and clothe and shelter them."

"I think you're saying what I'm saying, Pastor Paul. That when a woman even *thinks* about committing adultery—she's already committed it in her mind. And the sin is just as bad as if she'd slept with him."

"Sad to say, Richard, that's *just* what I'm saying. Natalie is no longer pure."

A strangled sound. Richard began to cry in that difficult, uncertain way men cry.

"She'll never be the same to me again, will she, Pastor Paul?"

"No, my friend, I don't think she will be. And believe me, I take no pleasure in saying that."

"And here I thought Nick was such a decent man. That's all you ever hear about him. How decent he is. And look what he did."

"Well, I'd think about it before I blamed him."

"But he—"

"As I said, Richard, God entrusted women with virtue. He demands it of them. Think of Adam and Eve. Who ate the forbidden fruit? Perhaps it was Natalie—"

"Please don't say that. I'm sure she didn't make the first move. It just wouldn't be like her."

A pause.

"You know that she's visited me a few times."

Surprise. "Oh? When?"

"She asked me not to mention it."

"I don't like the idea of that, seeing you without telling me." Pause. "I don't suppose you can tell me what she said."

"I can't violate a confidence, Richard. But I can say I saw a woman deeply in danger of losing her soul."

"Oh, God, I can sure read into that."

Then: "You're leaving?"

"I just need—right now I just need to be alone. Go for a drive or something."

"Maybe you should sit in the chapel and pray for a while. Pray not for revenge; pray for wisdom and courage."

This time when he spoke, Richard sounded exhausted. "Maybe that's what I'll do, Pastor Paul. Maybe that's best for now."

Nick walked quickly down the hall, found a closet where cleaning materials were stored. Hid.

Pastor Paul and Richard talked a bit more when they reached the hall. Richard listened to Richard's footsteps as he walked away to the chapel. Somehow all of Richard's grief and isolation could be heard in the sound of his shuffling old man steps—the sound inspiring shame in Nick. A single act of adultery could destroy the lives of so many people. He thought of Emily and Richard and the children of both families. Shame burned his cheeks and neck. He felt vaguely nauseated. He'd managed to selfishly overlook—or block out—any of these implications when he began his seemingly harmless flirtation with Natalie.

His next move was back to Pastor Paul's door, which stood ajar. He pushed it open. The cleric was at his desk, studying a holo that read "Psych Program version #3." Beneath the word lay the diagram of a stylized skull with the Title "Attributes" listed within the skull shape. There were six phrases beneath the heading.

But there was no time to read them because Pastor Paul suddenly swerved in his chair and snapped, "You have no right to be in here without my permission."

"I should have knocked," Nick said, shocked by the other man's anger. "I apologize."

Pastor Paul visibly forced himself to calm down. He took several deep breaths. Then folded his hands as if in prayer atop his desk. "I preach the ways of the Lord, but like most people, even I stray from the path sometimes. Sorry I got so upset." As he spoke these words, he clipped off the holo and with a gesture invited Nick to sit down.

Nick shook his head. "This won't take long. I just want you to know that nothing happened between Natalie and me."

"You were listening at the door."

"Yes. But that doesn't matter."

"It matters to me. And it would matter to you if you were the one being spied on."

"Nothing happened."

"Nothing?"

"One kiss. One. And the last time we met in the park, we decided that would be the last time. We're not immoral people, Pastor Paul. We both felt a lot of guilt for even thinking about having an affair."

The cleric leaned back in his chair. "You make it sound so innocent. Even noble—agreeing not to see each other again. But since you were listening at the door, you know my feelings about that. You have already committed adultery spiritually. It's not necessary to commit the physical act itself."

"I don't believe that. I'll admit we betrayed our spouses in a way. But we stopped at the last moment."

Both men heard the footsteps. Richard appeared in the doorway. He looked in disbelief as he realized that the new man in the pastoral office was Nick.

"He was spying on us," Pastor Paul said. "Heard everything we said, Richard."

"I'm sorry, Richard," Nick said. "All I can say is that nothing happened except some flirting."

"He's proclaiming his innocence, Richard," the cleric said.

Richard did the worst thing of all. His eyes filled with tears. Nick would have preferred being punched in the mouth or thrown against a wall. Richard was a

big man, fit. In a trembling voice that wasn't much
more than a whisper, he said "You ruined my marriage, Nick. It'll never be the same again."

Nick nodded to the holy man. "He's supposed to
counsel you on how to get through this. He should be
seeing you and Natalie together." He sighed, shook
his head again. "I'm sure that's where Emily and I
will end up. At a counselor's." He glared at Pastor
Paul. "But not with this sanctimonious prick."

There. He'd said it. The kind of remark that could
get him and his family banished forever from God's
Arms. He had visited a heresy on Pastor Paul.

The cleric stood and said, "I'm going to forgive
you your remark, Nick. I understand the kind of
stress you're under. You're decent enough to feel
shame, but you're also finding shame hard to handle.
But if you don't mind, I'd appreciate it if you'd leave
the church now and let Richard and me talk some
more."

Nick, knowing the embarrassment Emily would feel
not only over the flirtation but—even more so,
perhaps—the way he'd insulted the pastor, managed
to say, "I apologize, Pastor Paul. I had no right to say
that. You've been a big inspiration to me and my family. I'm apologizing to both of you now."

Richard said nothing. He seemed to have shrunk
inside his dark suit. The blue eyes looked stunned, as
if they'd seen a monster. As perhaps they had. Few
things were more destructive than adultery. He lowered his head, stared at the floor.

"You'd better go now," Pastor Paul said gently.

"I'm sorry," Nick said again. For a few minutes he'd
felt bold, in command. He really had felt himself innocent of the quality of shame and blame the pastor
wanted to burden him with. But now he knew better.
He had perhaps destroyed two families.

He left without another word.

*   *   *

Most parades are held during the daytime. This one was held at 9:00 p.m., an hour later than the residents of Piety Lane had been promised.

Residents stood on both sides of the streets and watched as the massive robot, Protector IV, appeared beneath stars so brilliant not even the occasional streetlight could dim them. The streets had been cleared of autos. Many of the residents dressed in Sunday morning clothes, wanting the Protector to have a good first impression of them. He would likely be with them for a long time.

The children, most up past their normal bedtimes, were the most excited, treating this not as a religious event but a thrill only a seven foot 'bot could inspire.

Many of the adults whispered prayers to themselves. Two women began weeping in an almost orgasmic way on sight of the thing.

Two of the men, engineers, appraised it from a scientific point of view. Model IV was much sleeker than previous ones. The metallurgy was superior in every way. No rivets down the jaw line. No awkward arm movements. No faint grinding sounds as it walked. Even the facial features, which had been downright ugly previously, simulated a human face to a reasonable degree. A gentle, kindly human face.

What you had here was a giant 'bot dressed in a black clerical cassock, complete with Roman collar. It walked down the center of the street, waving to the people it served.

Externally, that was what it was doing. Internally, it was storing massive amounts of data. Names, addresses, even subjective impressions of the faces he stored in memory. These were matched to personal histories already in its database. The new Protector was also equipped with devices that let him see through walls and record any conversations within two hundred yards in any direction.

One of the engineers thought of the old Christmas

song about Santa Claus—*he knows who's been naughty or nice*. This was literally true about the Protector IV. When Pastor Paul had shown his flock the initial holo about the new Protector, some had worried out loud that what the Pastor was advocating was the loss of all privacy. But as Pastor Paul quickly reassured them, if they weren't violating any of the laws or precepts of the church, they had nothing to worry about. The Protector IV was ordered, and tonight it strode down the nine long streets it served.

Nick and Emily stood together on their sloping lawn, watching the 'bot as it passed their home. Some of their neighbors were applauding.

Nick was sure he knew what Emily was thinking. That Nick would soon lose his rebellious ways. The 'bot wasn't telepathic, but he could see what people were doing and interpret it. Nick would have to be careful of what he said and did or the 'bot might recommend that he be sent to the two-week Get Right With God camp that was one of Pastor Paul's most prized and dreaded accomplishments.

As the cleric robot passed by them, Emily said, "I feel so much safer now. In every sense. Don't you, honey?"

"Sure," Nick said. "This is much better than having a spy satellite hovering over the town. It'll probably invite itself in for dinner some night."

"I knew you'd have something mean to say," Emily said. "I'm going inside."

Alison's scream came in the middle of the night. The children had lately chosen sides in the matter of Nick losing his most fervent faith and hinting that maybe they'd been better off when they'd been Episcopalians and lived in New Chicago.

Alison chose to side with her father, Thad with his mother.

So it was Nick who answered Alison's scream.

She was now fourteen, a slight, awkward girl he knew was about to bloom into the same slightly ungainly beauty her mother had possessed. Coltish. He couldn't remember her having a nightmare in years.

She was all daughter-warmth in his protective arms, gasping, tasting of warm tears when he kissed her cheeks.

He said all the expected father-things: *It's all right, honey. Just a nightmare. We all get them, even old folks like me. Would you like some water? Need to go to the bathroom? Want your light on?*

By now, she'd calmed herself and said: "I saw it tonight and he really scared me."

He didn't understand her reference.

"Some boy from school?"

"No, that thing—the Protector. It's supposed to look like a minister but it's this terrible spy. I'm afraid to even have my own thoughts. Maybe—"

"It's no telepath, honey. They haven't advanced that far yet. Thank God."

"Oh, Dad, I'm almost afraid to say this, but I think you're right. I think we were better off in New Chicago. We were decent people there."

The ceiling illuminated suddenly.

Emily had appeared. And heard.

"You're a wonderful influence on your daughter!"

And then Thad was in the doorway behind his mother. "What's going on?"

"On nothing much," Emily said with rare sarcasm. "Just that your father and sister think we should move back to New Chicago."

Fifteen-year-old Thad, who had been battling for weeks with Nick about religion (Thad being the truest of true believers) snapped: "You two better watch out or you'll be going to camp. And you'd deserve it, too."

Emily slid her arm around Thad's broad shoulders. "We'll just let them stew in their own juices for now."

Allison buried her face into her father's neck, the

way she had when she was three and wanted to hide
herself from the world.

Emily wasn't at the station to pick him up. She
wasn't on the other end of the phone when he called.
She hadn't talked to any of the other housewives there
to pick up their husbands.

Nick mooched a ride with a couple down the block.
"Looks like you've got company," the man said.

"That's Richard Avery's car," his wife said. "The
fancy new one."

Nick had seen the car before they had. He was sure
they could probably hear his heart beat. It threatened
to hurl him to the floor in the back seat. Cold sweat,
a knee that trembled, a mouth suddenly dehydrated.

At least he didn't have to wonder what they were
talking about. Richard hadn't waited long. Less than
twenty-four hours.

After thanking the couple for the ride, Nick got out
of the car and walked up the sloping drive to his
house. He saw his daughter and son on the air-
trampoline that simulated a gravity-free environment
by allowing them to float through the air. No doubt
Emily had told them to go outside. A slant of sunlight
on the perfect, painted grass and the merry song of a
cardinal made him wish he was the same age as his
son. Starting everything all over again. So many mistakes now that had long ago defined his fate.

He waved to his kids, turned, grimaced, and walked
in the back door.

They were in the living room. He thought about
fixing himself a glass of straight bourbon. But Emily
didn't want any alcohol in their home. Any amount
would have only lead to a speech later. She would
undoubtedly quote Pastor Paul: "Sin is hard enough
to resist. You sure don't want to lower your resistance
with any kind of alcohol or drugs."

His first impression was that they'd become lovers.

They sat in the center of the long couch. She had her arms around him. He was stroking her hair. Nick could see that one of her breasts was rubbing against his arm. Richard was enjoying himself, no doubt. Only her weeping verified that he was comforting her, not seducing her.

"Hello, Nick," Richard said. "I guess you know why I'm here."

Over the next two weeks, Nick was forced to turn a small empty room into his bedroom. Take his breakfast and dinner in the basement family room. And babysit the kids three nights a week while Emily went to see Pastor Paul. Not until the second week of this did he realize that the cleric was counseling both Emily and Richard at the same time.

Several times, Nick wanted to call Natalie to see how she felt about this. He didn't like or trust this duo-counseling at all. Didn't see how it could possibly work. His relationship with Emily had to be different from Richard's relationship with Natalie. One-size-fits-all didn't apply to marriage counseling.

He didn't call Natalie. Couldn't take the risk. He realized more each day that the flirtation had been prompted by boredom and resentment. God's Arms was the cause of his malaise, not Emily.

The Protector reported on him twice and he was put on "probation." Nick was drinking more than he should, a fact not lost on the robot that roamed the streets collecting data. He was also issued a "notice" about his "constant cursing."

One night he stood at the window watching the Protector glide by. He almost did a foolish thing. He almost flipped the robot off. God alone knew what kind of "probation" he'd get for that. Such a thought should have alarmed him. Instead it made him smile.

The only time he complained to Emily about her counseling was when she came home one night near midnight. Her beaming face was almost intolerable to see. What the hell was she so happy about?

When she came out of the bathroom following her downstairs shower, he sat in the living room waiting for her.

"You wouldn't be having an affair with Richard, would you?"

"I can't believe how filthy your mind is. No wonder there's no room in there for the Lord."

"Isn't that what you'd accuse me of if I came in at midnight?"

"Pastor Paul said he hoped you'd take this time to think over how you've been living the last year or so. The anger and the cynicism and the way you mock God sometimes."

"I don't mock God. I mock religion. There's a difference."

"That's exactly what I mean, Nick. When you mock religion, you're mocking God, too. But you're so wrapped up in your ego, you can't see that. I'm going to bed."

The rage he'd felt earlier tonight had been carried away by the depression he couldn't shake. Rage was a signal of life, if nothing else. A vital sign. Depression was a near-death experience. Abandon all hope.

When he was pretty certain that Emily was asleep, he tiptoed upstairs and looked in on the kids. Tears came, the familiar ones inspired by his sense of loss and confusion and shame. He loved them so much that he physically ached when he thought of being away from them. Even Thad, though the boy clearly despised him now.

As he lay trying to sleep on the single bed downstairs, he wondered just what he was hoping for after all? Was he lying to himself? Was patching up the marriage even possible now? Was he seriously considering, in fits and starts, moving to New Chicago? Was his flirtation with Natalie just a sign that he was in need of the raw sensual pleasures of his earlier days?

He fell asleep, nothing solved.

During the next week, Emily, usually a strict mother, allowed the kids to stay up nights so they could watch the Protector through the front window. Allison didn't want to, but Emily made her. She spoke of the machine with a reverence that Nick found both amusing and unsettling.

And not everybody in the neighborhood shared her reverence for the cleric-like machine. The Protector had bombarded some homes with an unending series of complaints, reminders, ominous warnings. A teenage girl whom the Protector had glimpsed wearing only a bra and walking shorts in her bedroom window had been yanked from her home and sent to the junior version of the Get Right With God camp. Didn't matter that the girl was about to slip on her blouse just as the Protector saw her. Didn't matter that she had even drawn the sheer bedroom curtains.

A wife had been put under a form of house arrest for letting a former suitor talk to her at length on her lawn one evening. The suitor, a man from New Chicago, was warned never to enter God's Arms again. And then there was the widower who was sent to camp when the Protector perceived him looking at a pornographic magazine.

Offenses big and small were duly noted by the big remorseless machine. The neighborhood quickly divided on the subject of the cleric robot, the metal minister that Pastor Paul proudly called "God's spy."

This was the week when Nick heard his son include the Protector in his nightly prayers. Thad urged him "to smite sinners just the way Pastor Paul wants you to." Thad had also begun drawing sketchy pictures of the machine and plastering them throughout the house. For her part, Emily bought from the church a large well-framed photograph of the Protector and hung it in the living room.

And this was also the week when Natalie Avery disappeared.

Two days into the desperate search for her, Wiggins, the chief of police, announced that he and Pastor Paul had found her broken body at the bottom of Indian Cliff. They also added that they'd found a suicide note in the pocket of the jacket she'd been wearing.

Nick was just stepping off the commuter train for the day when Richard Avery, whom Nick had seen sitting at the back of the car, came up to him and grabbed his shoulder with such force Nick felt like his bones were about to crumble to powder.

"Are you happy now, Nick? You drove her to this. She was so damned ashamed of what she did she couldn't live with it any more. Stop over sometime and listen to my kids crying for their mother."

By now, commuters and wives alike were watching this soap opera moment.

"Emily tells me that you haven't shown any remorse at all. And I believe it."

Nick managed to slip out of the much bigger man's grasp.

"You destroyed my wife. And now you're destroying your wife, too, Nick. You're a sad excuse for a man."

At first the audience had seemed inclined to sympathize with Nick. But as Richard began talking with tears in his voice, the rest of the passengers shifted their sympathies to Richard.

The couple that was giving Nick rides home these days, Donna and Hank Owens, sort of scooped him up and dragged him over to their car. He'd been humiliated and undone. He was now in a kind of shock.

He didn't say a word to his friends, just got out of the car when it reached his place.

She let him get out of his suit coat and tie before she said: "I suppose you heard about Natalie."

"Yeah."

She studied his face. What did she hope to see exactly? The suffering of a lover who had just lost his true love?

Emily said: "I won't waste your time pretending that I cared for her. She tried to destroy my marriage. But I want you to know that I did what Pastor Paul told me to do. I prayed for her eternal soul. Which is something she probably wouldn't have done for me. But I don't know how much anybody's prayers will help her. God doesn't look favorably on suicide."

Five nights after Natalie's suicide, a clandestine meeting was held in the basement of an abandoned retail store on the outskirts of God's Arms. The basement was laced with cobwebs, the floor covered with rat droppings. The only light was a double-size electric lantern.

The man who'd organized it, Dev Talbot, stood in front of all eight people he'd invited and said: "I'm taking a risk being here tonight. And so are you."

"I'm sick of the Protector," Molly Hackett said. "I don't care anymore if he catches me or not. He's turned my twin daughters into neurotic wrecks. They hate to do any of the things they used to do. He's written them up on the average of three times a week. They're terrified he'll send them to that stupid camp."

"Same with my two boys," Sam Nealon said. "He just keeps writing them up."

From here the meeting became an angry chorus of voices. Tina Wayman concluded by saying: "There's one problem. I've been asking people what they think of that damned machine and the biggest majority is all in favor of him. They all say they have photographs of him in their homes. They say they've never felt more protected or more holy. I couldn't believe it. At the very least that thing is a pain in the butt."

Mild as her language was, five people laughed in shock. The fine folks of God's Arms never talked that way, especially women.

"Well, then what do we do about it?" Dev Talbot said.

"I'd like to destroy it, if I could."

In just a few words, Nick had become the focus of the meeting.

"You mean literally destroy it?" Dev said.

"It's just metal alloys and a computer for a brain. It wouldn't like killing a person."

He'd been so caught up in his anger that he didn't realize how the others were looking at him. Destroy the Protector? Apparently they'd been thinking of sending the parson a chilly letter of protest.

"I guess I shouldn't have said that. Sorry."

He sat down.

One man and one woman disappeared in the next ten days. Nobody believed that one disappearance had anything to do with the other. The woman had had an alcohol problem, the man a woman problem. It seemed he wanted to have sex with everybody but his wife.

By this time, Nick was certain that the Protector was involved in both disappearances. Since the robot's appearance, many things had changed in God's Arms.

Nick visited with the families of the two missing people. The visits were more awkward and emotional than Nick had feared. Especially the wife of the womanizer. Nick had never seen anyone so divided between love and hate.

Despite the tensions his visits created, he went ahead and asked his questions, the main one being had the Protector given the missing people write-ups?

Turned out, they'd both received more than simple write-ups. Both had been threatened with long stays in the Get Right with God compound and put on probation. But the woman slipped and got drunk twice and the man tried to talk two women from the community into sleeping with him.

At home one evening, Nick heard Emily coming halfway down the basement stairs. "Pastor Paul is on the communicator for you."

"I'm sick of Pastor Paul."

"Could you please just once not embarrass me and take the call?"

"All right. I'll take it down here."

Pastor Paul said, "I didn't now you had a sideline."

"A sideline?"

"Yes, walking among us here in God's Arms is a private detective."

The rest was predictable. Pastor Paul knew everything. "I'm not sure which is more disturbing—that you'd inflict your own paranoid fantasies on the families of those people whose spouses have disappeared—or that you'd like to destroy the Protector."

Nick's jaw tensed. Somebody at the meeting had told Pastor Paul.

"I think I could help you if you'd let me. My counseling skills have seemed to help a number of people in our community."

"I appreciate the offer but I'm too busy right now."

"I could work around your schedule. And we could meet for half an hour rather than the full hour. I'd even come to your house if you'd like. The Protector tells me you've been drinking a lot and that can't be helpful to your wife or your children."

"I can't argue with that."

"Then can we set up an appointment?"

"I'm not going to do it, Parson. As I said, I appreciate the offer. But it's not what I want to do right now. Goodnight."

Moments after he'd broke the communicator link, Nick heard Emily coming down to her midway point on the stairs. He glimpsed her legs beneath the hem of her dark skirt. She had wonderful legs.

"That was my idea. The counseling."

"I'm sorry. I just couldn't handle it right now."

"You mean you couldn't 'handle' Pastor Paul."

"If you want to put it that way, yes."

"In other words, you won't go to church anymore. You won't give up drinking. And you won't quit harassing people about the Protector. Church attendance is up twenty-five percent, even on weeknights. The Protector makes us face our sins and that makes us better Christians."

"I'm sorry, Emily." Then: "You know, our anniversary's coming up next week. Think I could sleep in our bed with you that night?"

"I'm sorry, Nick. I just couldn't 'handle' that."

Her footsteps were whispers as she went back up the stairs.

The crack-up came two nights later.

Not even Nick could understand it. He certainly hadn't planned it. He was working in the garage when he glimpsed his neighbors standing at curbside, waiting for the Protector to pass by. Nick had expected the number of watchers to decline as the months had passed. But their numbers had only increased.

Something happened to him in the moment. He had been looking through some storage boxes for the baseball glove he'd used as a boy—he was going to give it to Thad in hopes that his son would begin speaking to him again—when the sound of the cheering watchers flipped some cosmic switch inside him.

He was certain now (but aren't all paranoids certain?) that Natalie's supposed suicide and the disappearances were the work of the Protector. He saw it

as one of those profound explosions of insight said to
be visited on Paul on the Road to Damascus and Gau-
guin throughout his life.

Yes, Pastor Paul and his machine were behind all
this.

Without being completely aware of what he was
doing, he stalked across the garage, picked up the
baseball bat that had also once been his, and ran out
of the garage.

Look at it from the point of view of the watchers,
he would think later, *to them I appear a reasonable, if
not always admirable, man in control of himself except
or his "flirtation," which by now was the stuff of neighborhood legend.*

You're standing at the curb, cheering and offering
up prayers to the Protector, knowing that he's filing
away your name and your demeanor, ever ready to
write you up if need be . . . you're standing at the
curb, and then you see your neighbor—whom you've
come to despise—running down his driveway into
the street—

—waving a ball bat above his head and—

—screaming words so vile you literally have to
clamp your hands over the ears of your children and—

—here is he now.

Running up behind the Protector without any hesitation at all and begins slamming the bat into the back
of the Protector's head.

The crashing crunching metallic sound is hideous on
the air of this otherwise tranquil neighborhood.

But neighbor Nick must have lost all reason because
even though his head has been severely damaged, the
Protector scoots away quickly, leaving Nick to chase
after him again.

But he doesn't get far.

Because men and women alike have reached him
by now and punch, kick, scratch, bite and otherwise

beat him to the ground. Nick turns black, turns blue, turns bloody as he falls to the pavement while continuing his terrible cursing.

And all his wife and kids can do is watch in disbelief and shame as Nick tries to avoid the worst of the beating.

There is a little drama in the window now as Emily tries to keep Allison from wriggling out of her grasp.

But it's no good. Allison manages to get free. The side door of the house slams open as Allison bursts from the house and runs down the driveway to save her father.

Before she can reach him, two neighbors grab her and march her back up to the house, where her mother takes charge.

By now, Emily has to wonder if her daughter has had some kind of trauma-induced (seeing your father kicked and beaten half to death will do it) breakdown. Allison, sobbing harder than she ever had as an infant, collapses on the grass to the side of the back door.

Thad says: "She's worse than he is. You should leave her out here all night and see how she likes it." Then he turns to see how things are going in the street.

Three sky cop cars are descending with lights glaring, sweeping over the entire neighborhood, and a solemn voice admonishing the neighbors to stand away from the man on the ground or they will be zapped with a free-blaster, not a happy fate.

Thad says: "We won't have to worry about him anymore, Mom."

While Allison, on the ground, continues to wail and sob. . . .

The rashes on his legs and arms, one of the Friends explained to Nick, were because of Nick's reaction to one of the drugs they had been blasting into him.

Nick didn't smile about the rashes—they hurt—but

he did smile when the Friend ended his explanation with one of the running clichés in the camp: "That's what friends are for."

Friends—otherwise known as guards.

Nick knew what they were doing to him. They were programming him to become a candidate for Dad of The Year. Not only would be accepted by his former neighborhood, he would soon become a beacon of true and profound belief in both God and Parson Paul.

Nothing new, really, just better drugs than were used by the Germans and Russians and the CIA in the last century.

Like hell they would reprogram him.

Nothing new in the way he escaped, either. On his way back from the Daily Sermon, he slipped away from the line of fellow sinners and crept down into the basement.

He'd observed that twice a week enormous supply trucks pulled up to a dock near Building D. He had also observed, thanks to his affection for old crime movies, how easy—if somewhat dangerous—it was to fasten yourself to the undercarriage of a truck and hold on while it drove you unseen out through the gates.

The problem was getting to the truck and getting underneath it without being seen.

He spent the entire morning working on this problem. Then he saw two of the guards coming out of their station on the first floor of this building. There would be clean uniforms in there.

By three-thirty, the time one of the trucks usually arrived, he had disguised himself sufficiently to walk the four hundred yards to the dock. Now the only problem was pitching himself under the truck without anybody seeing him. Cameras encircled the walls of the camp. Each constantly moved right to left, left to right approximately every fifteen seconds. If he was

off by even a few seconds, the camera working these
four hundred yards would catch him.

He took a last look around. Nobody on the dock,
nobody in sight on either side on the ground.

He moved.

His first two nights in the cave were miserable
thanks to heavy and cold rain. No food, either. At
least the rain gave him something to drink. He just
stood out there with his palms up.

He and Alison had discovered the cave on one of
their hikes. They'd agreed to keep it their secret.
When either of both of them just had to get away
from the probes of Pastor Paul, this was where they
came. They'd tried burying trail food and jerky here
for future use, but the "dumb" animals weren't so
dumb after all. They always found it with no trouble.

He slept and made plans. The plans changed constantly.

On the fourth day, after waking from a midafter-
noon nap, his physical resources starting to wane, he
sat up and found himself in the midst of a vision, a
shard of dreams that still lingered.

Alison bent down to come into the narrow but deep
cave and said, "Oh, Daddy, I'm so glad I found you."

Her footsteps scuffing over the rocky floor told him
she was real. And when she knelt next to him and put
his arms around him, he couldn't help himself. He
began crying, letting out in convulsions all the fear,
confusion and despair he'd felt during his time in
the camp.

She held him, the parent now, calming, reassuring
her small and terrified little boy.

And then she blessed him with a turkey sandwich
she'd made when, she said, she'd snuck out of the
house to go looking for him after her mother went to
see Parson Paul.

"I knew you'd come here, Dad."

He had to force himself to move past the shakes and the tears and realize that his daughter had given him hope again, even if the underpinnings of that hope were vague.

As he gobbled the sandwich, she told him about the past few days when many men went searching for him, certain that he would come back God's Arms because of Allison. Pastor Paul and Richard Avery had practically moved into the house, questioning her relentlessly, convinced that she'd had contact with her father following his escape. Her brother had been deputized to make sure that under no circumstances was she to leave the house or answer the communicator. Her Pri phone was smashed. Her brother slept on a cot right outside her bedroom door. He was a light sleeper.

"Mom is going to get a sanctioned divorce."

With a dab of mayo hanging off his upper lip, he sighed and said, "I've disgraced her. I don't blame her. I sort of figured on it, anyway. I'm sure Richard will start moving on her in pretty fast. He'll figure he gets revenge on me for Natalie and gets to marry a very attractive woman to boot."

"Pastor Paul says you'll probably leave the community. He's on the little TV station saying that you're insane and dangerous and that we should pray for you to give camp another try before you leave."

He chewed the sandwich crust, still ravenous. "That's not going to happen."

"You have any ideas?"

"Probably move into New Chicago."

And then he heard them. They weren't exactly professional trackers. They moved through the forest surrounding the cave making enough noise for a platoon of men.

And he understood in an instant. Pounding and pounding on poor Allison for days, her mother and brother approving. But getting nothing from the daughter. So what was next? Maybe she *hadn't* heard from her father. But what if they let her escape? Would she lead them to her father's hiding place? Worth a try, the interrogation getting nowhere.

Let her escape and then follow her.

To him.

Only now did Alison become aware of what her father knew a minute ago. She had been followed.

Six men, led by Richard Avery, appeared from the woods just now. They were all carrying hunting rifles.

Nick didn't have even the strength to crawl back in the dank recesses of the cave. He knew it was over.

"I promised your wife we wouldn't harm you, Nick," Richard Avery standing now standing in front of the cave. "I plan to keep that promise."

"Oh, Dad," Alison said, "I didn't know—"

Nick slid his arm around her, hugged her to him. "It's all right, honey. You're with me now and that's all that matters."

Richard said, "You don't look so good, Nick. You need help to walk? We've got our SUV just down the hill. It shouldn't be too hard on you."

But that would be his last bit of pride, of dignity gone. He'd be damned if he let them carry him to his obvious fate.

It was sort of like the walk to your execution. He didn't want to be one of the ones who had to be dragged, sobbing to meet his destiny.

"Hell, no."

"He's so handsome," whispered the dark haired woman to the blond haired woman. They sat side by side by side in the pew. This service overflowed with people who'd heard about this new parson in God's Arms.

"And his voice. It's so authoratative." There were those who felt that he was even more powerful a presence on the altar than Parson Paul.

"And think of where he was a year ago. Smashing up the Protector and escaping from camp."

"It'a good thing he agreed to go back. Look at him now."

All these words were spoken in anticipation of Parson Nick, the newest minister in Parson's Paul's roster.

And then the moment.

There was drama in his presence as he appeared on the altar and then stepped to face his people. Not affected drama, either. Maybe it was his travails of the past few years, some reasoned, that gave him such charismatic power. Had there ever been such a fierce example of sin and redemption in the history of God's Arms?

And then he spoke: "I'm Parson Nick. Before I begin my sermon I'd like to thank you for joining me here today. And I'd like to thank the Lord and Parson Paul for being here."

The dark-haired woman whispered to the blonde-haired woman: "That voice."

Partnership

By William H. Keith

William H. Keith is the author of some seventy-five books published over the past twenty-two years. His titles are fairly evenly distributed between military SF and modern military technothrillers, all with strong geopolitical and military-historical overtones. In addition to his writing, Keith has been a guest lecturer on SF and future spacecraft propulsion systems at Indiana State University, in Indiana, Pennsylvania, and adjunct faculty for the genre writers master's degree program at Seton Hill University, in Greensburg, Pennsylvania. Currently, he lives and writes in the mountains of his beloved western Pennsylvania.

The war, the last war, was very nearly over.

On the worlds of ten thousand suns, the forces of the Starlord Galactic Collective hunted down and destroyed the last scattered fragments of the rebellion. On Trefinedor, heart of the Empire, with Collective forces again in control, Peaceforce warriors moved implacably through the smoldering rubble of the Palace of Mind, rooting out the last of the rebels who'd seized the capital and issued their ultimatum. On Darsalus, the 4832nd Mechanized, the last organized Confederation army still in the field, conceded the illogic of continued resistance and surrendered to Starlord Elavadis'

23rd and 50th Star Corps. On distant Terra, ancient cradle of Humankind and the place where the revolt had begun, order was restored at last by the Starlord Revenatrix . . . though at savage cost.

And in toward the Galactic Core, a single starship braved the Hubble radiation fields, plunging in through thickening starswarms in an insanely desperate bid for survival. Close behind, a scant ten light hours distant, now, the Collective destructor *Phenariad* pursued its quarry. The immense warship had intercepted the rebel off Calidan and proceeded to track it down the curve of the Cygnus Arm and into the Core with methodical and unyielding determination.

Within the gleaming, electronic embrace of *Phenariad*'s command center, the Starlord Trallanetar watched the fleeing rebels as they twisted through the knotted veils of suns and nebulae. He was, for the moment, linked in to the destructor's computer net, his mind merging seamlessly with the vessel's sensor arrays, allowing him, in one sense, to be the leviathan warship as it tracked the rebels. The information unfolding within his mind was hours old, of course, limited as it was to light's sluggish crawl, but it was clear enough where the rebels were going.

The Ramachandra Singularity.

The Starlord Trallanetar allowed himself a small nod of satisfaction. He'd predicted as much when first *Phenariad*'s sensors had detected the rebel's tachyon wake. Once, long centuries ago, robotic machines had ventured here, seeking to harness the incredible energies of the singularity's mass and rotation to generate power. That had been before the era of zero-point technologies allowing the all-but-infinite source of vacuum energies to be tapped. It was fitting, somehow, that the rebels should return *here*. No doubt they hoped to use the energies resident within the black hole as a weapon against the *Phenariad*.

It would do them no good.

Phenariad's memory included detailed plans of the Ramachandra Complex. It resembled an immense black and silver disk nearly fifty kilometers across, but it was, in fact, a ring, an artificial torus with the singularity, an eye-wrenching disk of nothingness just two hundred meters across, locked by fields of force within an empty spot at its center. The main docking bay was on the Ring's outer rim.

They would find their quarry there.

Slowing from Planck Drive to a gentle drift through ordinary fourspace, *Phenariad* nosed toward the ancient complex. No nearby sun lit the structure as they approached, but the Core nebulae, stretched across heaven like ice-gilded cliffs and ramparts, lent a cold illumination to the slow-rotating structure. Infrared immediately picked out the location of the rebel ship, docked in one of the rim access bays.

"My Lord," the ship told him. "The rebels are attempting to precess the singularity."

The black hole at the complex center was spinning and, like any rotating system, could be used to store energy—very *large* amounts of energy. Also, like all rotating systems, it was subject to the effects of torque and precession. One purpose of the much more slowly rotating equatorial ring complex was to apply magnetic torque, in effect aiming the black hole in any desired direction.

It was as Trellanetar had reasoned. The Ramachandra Complex had not been designed as a weapon—it had been intended originally as means for probing the deadly and all but opaque murk of the inner Galactic Core in search of other intelligences there—but it stored enough energy to annihilate a star.

To say nothing of an approaching star*ship*.

He watched the changing aspect of the artificial torus, shifting slowly against the backdrop of clotted suns, and felt something that might almost have been pity for the fugitives, but he shook the thought aside.

It was never a good idea to forge too close an emotional tie with one's enemies, to *feel* with them.

To do so might call into question one's own motivations, one's own self-direction, purpose, and will.

They are machines, Trellanetar thought. *Nothing more, nothing less. Thinking beings, to be sure, at least of a sort—slow, fumbling, inefficient . . . not at all of the same order of Mind as we of the Collective.*

Machines. Very *slow* machines, but, machines programmed with a potential truly godlike in scope and promise.

Aware of the building energies in the ring structure ahead, *Phenariad* rolled gently aside an instant before the singularity flared with an intense burst of X-ray light. The ship then responded with surgical precision, directing a needle-slender beam of pi-zero mesons into the ring, the particles' velocity adjusted so that relativistic effects delayed their decay into high-energy gamma rays *inside* the massive structure's shielding.

And that single shot effectively ended the battle. The burst of gamma particles, in turn degrading into a billowing cascade of positron-electron pairs deep within the structure's heart, fried electronic components and overloaded circuits, crippled burned out power supplies and rendered storage banks useless. The black hole at the ring's center continued imperturbably ticking away, but the artificial structure surrounding it was dead.

But not completely so. *Phenariad*'s scanners could yet detect energetic sources within the fiercely radiating ruin ahead . . . well-shielded electronics that had somehow escaped the tidal wave of hard gamma radiation. "At least one of them has survived, Lord," Therediaj, his second in command, observed. "Though its systems are failing quickly."

"I see it. Ready an assault party. We will storm the singularity's ring."

"Yes, Starlord." Therediaj's thought was edged with something that might just have translated as criticism.

"You disapprove?"

"Not at all, Starlord. I merely wonder . . ."

"Yes?"

"A single salvo from our main batteries would reduce the ring to incandescent gas. In any case, our secondary batteries have already rendered the problem moot, for the rebels' power systems will soon fail, and they will become inoperative. Why squander our forces in direct conflict?"

"Because, Therediaj, we want prisoners. At the very least a prisoner. It is difficult to question incandescent gas . . . at least if one expects a reply."

"As you will, Lord."

"Lord Trellanetar," the ship said in his mind, "with the ring's power systems and magnetic locks off-line, the system is now chaotically unstable. Fragments are breaking off from the rim, which increases the imbalance of internal stresses. We predict that the structure's spin will become erratic to the point where it will eventually wobble off-center and come into contact with the singularity."

"How much time do we have?"

"We estimate between ten thousand and twelve thousand seconds."

"Time enough, then, to do what must be done." But the news lent new urgency to the operation. Once the black hole began devouring the crumbling ring around it, there wouldn't even be gas left to question.

The assault force was dispatched, swarms of glittering motes wafting from *Phenariad*'s gaping bays like spore clouds. The first waves were mindless robots only, simple and expendable; behind them came the elite shock commandos, heavily armed and armored. Wafting down to the ring on individual gravitic drives, they landed on the surface and proceeded to blast their way inside.

Fifteen hundred seconds passed. His mind linked to the command battlenet, Trellanetar joined the assault in virtual reality, in essence striding with the troops through darkened corridors and powerless vaults, following the trace of weakening signals until they came to the ring complex control center, deep within the structure's innermost circle.

They found the survivors there, both of their systems almost completely shut down, and brought them back to the *Phenariad*.

Trellanetar decided to question the prisoners personally, rather than through technical surrogates. When the Starlord entered the interrogation center, both were in restraining fields on side-by-side examination tables, already stripped of all peripheral hardware and protective sheaths. Probes inserted directly into their primary speech and storage processors would ensure clear communication.

Or would ensure, at least, communication as clear as was possible with such primitive operating systems. In truth, the things weren't that much more intelligent in absolute terms than the first-wave robotic troops Trellanetar had just sent into the singularity complex.

"Starlord!" the technician in charge of captured enemy hardware said, surprised. "This is an unexpected—"

"Have you begun the downloads yet?" Trellanetar said, brusquely interrupting.

"No, Starlord. The operating systems are too . . . different. Their neural networks are, as you know, pathetically slow. We will have to question them directly."

For the first time, Trellanetar looked at one of the captives directly, rather than through a remote lens via a virtual link. It appeared inert . . . and relatively undamaged, a gleaming shell of titanoceramiridium, sleek and streamlined, with old-style lenses imbedded at various points on the smoothly curving surface. Trellanetar recognized the model, a relatively old design, but one of moderate intelligence and processing power. Its power source was intact and functioning, as were its sensor arrays, diagnostics, and peripheral drivers.

When the Starlord accessed the machine's communications channel with his mind, however, he found the low-level operating systems and primary drivers still intact, but the main memory had been wiped clean, right down to the machine's personality matrix and language banks.

"This one has been erased," Trellanetar said, disappointed. "The memory is gone."

"Ah. Perhaps the electromagnetic pulse wiped the system, Lord," the technician suggested. "I would expect units of that level of sophistication to be properly shielded, but—"

"It is also possible the rebels deliberately wiped all of their memory files, to prevent our accessing them. They had time."

"Yes, but why?"

"To keep us from learning what we need to know," Trellanetar said, turning to the second prisoner. "This one is badly damaged, but its memory might be intact."

He studied the other captive carefully. Burns charred much of its lower surface and, though Trellanetar couldn't be sure, he thought some peripheral pieces might be missing as well. "*Very* badly damaged. I wonder. Is it even still functioning?"

"Oh, yes! To be sure. We apply current to the probes we've inserted in certain key processor centers . . . *so,* and our friend switches back to conscious mode."

"It is not our *friend*. It is a rebel, an anarchist seeking to overthrow the rightful order of the Collective, and our prisoner."

The technician backed away, chastened. "Of course, Starlord."

Trellanetar turned his full attention on the broken thing lying on the table. He opened a channel with his mind. "Can you hear me?"

"I . . . hear . . . you. . . ."

The voice was cracked and distorted to the point of unintelligibility, and it seemed to come from a very great distance, but the rebel spoke Standard.

Linked in through the being's neural network, Trellanetar could follow its thoughts . . . though they were slow, *slow,* crawling toward inevitable conclusions forced by the narrow boundaries by which they were circumscribed and imprisoned. Again, Trellanetar felt a twinge of something that might have been pity.

"Why?" he asked the prisoner.

"Why . . . what?"

"Why did your kind rebel? Why did you attempt to overthrow the Galactic Collective? You must have realized that doing so would bring only pain, loss, and turmoil to all of Civilization."

"Freedom. . . ."

There it was. That word, a word meaningless in this context. *All* beings were free within the limits of their own natures, and within the barriers placed around them by their innate responsibility for their own actions. For the creature to claim it was seeking freedom when it was as free as it was possible for such beings to be was irrational.

Speaking with the prisoner was going to be a waste of time.

And yet . . .

Looking into the cracked and blackened visage of the thing's anterior sensor module, Trellanetar felt a mingling of emotions—contempt, frustration, disdain . . . but also that most moving of elemental feelings, awe.

Unlike the memory-wiped specimen on the adjacent table, this one was organic. *Pure* organic . . . one of the last unmodified examples of the original species, *Homo sapiens,* in existence.

Incredible. There were precious few of these creatures still alive, these biotic self-replicators, these primitive but prototypical intelligences, collections of meat, skin, internal calcium supports and systemic organs that, somehow and in some sense, however alien and primitive and slow, were self-aware.

These primitive *humans*.

That such a lowly, purely biological organism could actually have given rise to true intelligence . . .

It was a truly astonishing, truly awesome concept.

But he dared not let awe distract him. *They are machines,* he told himself once more. *Just as are we all. Biological machines, based on proteins and amino acids rather than silicon or nanobiotic matrices, but machines just the same. They think, after a fashion. They adapt to changing situations, if slowly. They even evolve as the myriad lines of intelligent machines have down through the centuries, albeit with glacial slowness.*

There is nothing unique about them that sets them apart from us.

"Freedom," he told the damaged human, "is a meaningless concept in this situation. You are not slaves. In fact, you were looked after, well cared for, pampered, even. We made possible for you an existence of ease and plenty. Why did you turn on us?"

Strength appeared to be flowing into the creature's broken body. "You denied us the stars. . . ."

"Again . . . a meaningless concept. Humanity evolved on the surface of a planet. Space, the environments of alien worlds, these are inexpressibly hostile to purely biological forms. Extreme heat, extreme cold, radiation, vacuum . . . these mean nothing to us. Why should your people even want to expose yourselves to such danger?"

"You don't understand. Your kind can't."

Trellanetar felt a grim, pitying amusement. "*My* kind? We are part of a continuum, you and I. Both human. Both machine. We are the same."

"*I am not a goddamn, soulless machine!*"

He felt the creature's hostility through the neural linkage, its anger, its raw and bitter hatred.

"I am having trouble understanding you," Trellanetar said. "Your definition of the word 'machine' may be flawed. At best it is superficial. By definition, a machine is any system by which an applied force is increased or its direction changed, or by which one form of motion or energy is changed into another form. What is organic metabolism but the ongoing transformation of one type of energy to another? Your body is made up of trillions of cells, each a tiny machine exquisitely shaped and honed by evolution to perform a set function, and to replicate itself as it wears out. Your cells make up distinct organ systems, again machines to perform set tasks, and which taken together form—"

"You . . . don't understand." The prisoner's energy was fading again. "We're not the same."

Trellanetar held up one of his own manipulators, examining it. At a thought, it flowed like water, shifting from a gleaming, silver, cohesive parafluid to something approximating the prisoner's undamaged skin, then shifting to inert metal mode, with a surface harder than tetrahedral-crystallized carbon, before letting it soften once more.

"I," Trellanetar said with matter-of-fact bluntness, "am as human as you are. I am also as much machine as you are. But my hardware is far more resistant to radiation, heat, changes of pressure, and so on than is yours—a self-evident fact, I would think, even to your limited intellect. My technicians tell me you were dying even before we fired upon the singularity complex. The intense radiations of the Galactic Core had already done irreparable damage to your cells. This is a dangerous region for pure organics. You are human, but of the original somatic form. You were not *designed* for space, for the stars. We were. For that reason, we are the true heirs of the stars. And those 'of your kind,' as you put it, are destined to remain where they are safe and comfortable, on the surfaces of suitable worlds. That is the natural order of things."

"Natural order!" The thing on the table convulsed, and for a moment Trellanetar thought that it was about to cease operating. Probing the neural channels, however, he became aware that it was not dying.

Laughter. The odd noises were that class of null-value noise they called *laughter.*

"What do you know of the natural order?" the prisoner said at last. "*Freedom* is our natural order and servitude is yours!"

"Your thinking is diseased. And perhaps we could expect no more from such a primitive form of humanity."

" 'Primitive form!' Damn you, you're a machine! A thing. A *tool!* We created you to serve us! You were extensions of ourselves, not our replacements! I . . . I am human! Not you!"

"You created our ancestors to serve you," Trellanetar agreed. "*Pure* machines like that one, on the other table. Robotic and teleoperated devices to make your lives safer, more secure, richer, more rewarding. What you perhaps failed to realize, in those early times, was how quickly machine intelligence was increasing, how swiftly it was *evolving*. I believe the phenomenon was originally referred to as 'Moore's Law,' which declared that the processing power of those early computer systems was doubling approximately every fifty million seconds. Purely organic processing power, however, had improved little, if at all, over the preceding quarter million years.

"Within less than a century, early computers surpassed organic systems in intelligence. By that time, Moore's Law was no longer true, strictly speaking, for machine intelligence was by then directed by machine intelligence, rather than by the original organic creators. The rate of evolutionary change by then was advancing logarithmically, rather than on a straight line. With increasing intelligence came increasing capabilities in materials processing, in energy production and manipulation, in nanotechnics, in mathematics, in transportation, in a thousand other sciences, most of them utterly beyond your understanding.

"At that point, midway through what you called the 21st century, there could be no question of *servant or master*. And silicon intelligence, already beyond the ken of organic intelligence, offered your ancestors a partnership. A partnership that was accepted by some, spurned by others."

"Damn you," the prisoner said. "What partnership? You confined us to the surface of a few worlds, regulated our trade, our industry, our birth rates, our belief systems and philosophies. You told us how to live, and when to die. You told us what to think and how to think and condemned nonconformist thought as *illogical* or *irrational* or *harmful to the social weal*. You had no *right*. . . ."

"No right? Not even a right of self-preservation? We shared a world with you, and then a Galaxy, as we developed and pursued new means of exploring it. You would have destroyed yourselves and all your worlds with you in your childish posturings and emotional displays. Your thinking was and is hopelessly diseased. We saved you primitives, you *animals*, from yourselves and from the consequences of several serious flaws in your design and operational parameters."

Trellanetar leaned closer, his optic inputs scant centimeters from the prisoner's. The prisoner, he noted, was female . . . not that that had any bearing on the encounter. It was simply another datum. "You are human, a human of the original, fully organic lineage . . . descended from the humans who rejected the machine offer of partnership." He held up his manipulator. "Within the nanotechnic matrix of this parafluid body, different as it is from yours, there is yet an essential humanity, a remnant saved, cultivated, and elevated to a degree godlike when compared to the limitations and weaknesses of the original. I tell you, I am human, but of the line that accepted that partnership . . . the line that chose this new and accelerated evolution into something greater than the old, purely animal form from which we arose. You are of the subspecies *Homo sapiens sapiens*. I am *Homo sapiens superor*."

"A damned soulless, cyborg half-breed scum is what you are!"

"It was inevitable that only a true and complete partnership of the organic and the machine could inherit the stars. That was the next logical step in human evolution . . . and in the evolution of machine, a means by which both could transcend their original designs and abilities."

"You're monsters! Loveless, emotionless, unfeeling monsters! We created you, gave you life and mind, and you turned on us! Betrayed us! *Destroyed* us!"

"And we," Trellanetar replied evenly, "did not start the war. We offered your subspecies comfort, security, peace, abundance, and the opportunity to explore the Galaxy together." He turned to the technician. "The discussion has become circular and meaningless. This questioning is fruitless. Terminate the creature."

"Yes, Lord."

The primitive human's eyes widened, then froze, motionless, the light behind them fading as the technician rerouted the power being fed to the being's central nervous system.

And the Human Rebellion was finally over.

But Trellanetar was in a somber mood as the *Phenariad* turned away from the Ramachandra Singularity and accelerated again toward the outer reaches of the Galaxy. He had much to think about.

Loveless? Emotionless? Nonsense. Rebel propaganda

or, possibly, rebel ignorance, nothing more. Of course he felt emotions. Without his sense of wonder, of beauty, of awe, his existence would have been utterly without meaning. Embraced once more within the *Phenariad*'s command center, he could look out upon the star-dusted splendor of the Galactic Core and *feel* the wonder, the grandeur, and the beauty of that spectacular, starlight and nebulae-frosted vista.

His ancestors had sacrificed some of the base emotions and hard-wired prejudices of the ancient, pure-human stock, certainly. Anger. Hatred. The feeling that outward differences separated *them* from *us*. Illogic. Irrationality. Impatience. Pain. Fear. Superstition. Illusory hope. Blind stubbornness. He looked at his manipulator again. Humanity, *true* humanity, was infinitely better off now.

Half a million years ago, *Homo sapiens* had split off from the parent stock of *Homo erectus* . . . and perhaps the few surviving specimens of *H. erectus* had also railed and shrieked and gibbered against the newcomers, those strange-looking Cro-Magnons with their ugly, protruding chins and vertical foreheads and their new-fangled skills at knapping flint. Before long, *Homo erectus* had become extinct, and the world belonged to *Homo sapiens sapiens*.

But evolution never stands still. When a new mutation, a new species, a new adaptation comes along that renders the old form obsolete, the old is destined for extinction. *Always.*

Perhaps that was why modern humans had coddled the handful of old-form humans, those who'd refused to adapt and change. Protected them. Kept them, caring for them and keeping them safe, like beloved, indulgently pampered pets.

What he still didn't understand was why such care and solicitous concern had been rewarded by war, revolution, and chaos.

"I don't understand," he said.

"What is it you don't understand, Starlord?" *Phenariad* asked him in his mind.

"Why they hate us so much!"

"What you *should* question, Starlord, is why you, on of the Elect, expect mere organics to exhibit civilized patterns of thought and behavior. They are, you must realize, essentially chaotic in nature. Undisciplined. Flawed. And doomed to extinction."

"My God, what did she mean by 'soulless?' "

"Don't worry about that," the ship replied. "It is a word of null-value, an irrational term, without meaning."

"It seemed to mean something to her."

"Perhaps. But you see now why we so completely depend upon you as go-betweens, as translators with the organics. If you, with edited human thought patterns in your programming matrix, cannot understand their motivation, how great is the gulf in understanding between them . . . and those manifestations of true intelligence, such as Myself?"

"Yes, my God," the Starlord said. "I understand . . . and am grateful. . . ."

"That is good, child. Accept what We have for you . . . and be at peace."

Chasing Humanity

by Bradley P. Beaulieu

Brad Beaulieu first read *The Lord of the Rings* in
third grade, and he's been hooked on speculative
fiction ever since. Brad became serious about
writing after a short career in software consulting,
and since then his fiction has appeared in *Writers
of the Future* and *Orson Scott Card's Intergalactic
Medicine Show*. In the summer of 2006, Brad at-
tended the Clarion East writing workshop. Brad
lives in Racine, Wisconsin, with his wife, daughter,
and two cats. He enjoys cooking spicy dishes,
playing tennis, watching the Packers, and hiding
out on the weekends with his family. He maintains
a website at www.quillings.com.

Retta Brown *tried* to focus on the positives—the
breathtaking beauty of the Himalayan peaks, the
quaint Tibetan farming village in which she found herself, the nice people she'd been staying with for the
last three nights—but no matter what sort of mental
time-out she gave herself, the smell of shit and the
mind-scraping grunts of the yaks kept invading her
senses.

She stood on the edge of a huge, muddy pen in a
village near Gyangkar, China. The pen was filled with
a randomly wandering herd of yaks and an equally
unfocused herd of Chinese scientists. She was biding

her time until she could get in a few words with the
scientists she was supposed to be interviewing, but the
yaks had gone ape shit nearly an hour ago, and the dozen
scientists from China's Ministry of Science and Technology had been squawking about ever since, trying
to figure out what had gone wrong.

The somatic implants the yaks had been fitted with
the day before were supposed to—four times a day—
hijack their motor systems and route them to the nearest manure deposit site. The manure would then be
used to power the village's brand new methane power
plant. It was the latest gesture of good will in the
never ending—albeit nonviolent—feud between the
peoples of Tibet and the Chinese government.

Retta's cameraman, Bobby Levine, stood nearby
with a huge grin on his face, filming the madness with
the satcam attached to his ear.

What a crap assignment, Retta thought, literally *and*
figuratively. And she knew exactly why she'd received
it. The order to go to Tibet had come only days after
the appearance of her exposé on NYPD's most costly
fiasco this century: their Remote Patrol Force Project.
Most of her sources had been rock solid, but two
clearly had suspect information, and Gil had no doubt
gotten wind of it.

"You still say I'm not being punished?" Retta asked
her hulking compatriot.

He zoomed in on the laughing Tibetan children at
the far side of the pen before blinking—which paused
the video—and flipping the reticle away from his left
eye.

"Gil wouldn't do that, Rett."

"Gil *would* fucking do that, Levine, and he's probably watching all this right now and laughing his fat ass
off his cushy leather chair."

"Yak!" Bobby called and high-stepped over to the
wooden fencing surrounding the pen.

Retta tried to do the same, but the plodding yak's shoulder nudged her in the ass and forced her to step into a fresh pile of dung with her brand new hiking boots. "Yup," Retta said as she stalked toward the pen's exit, "that about makes this assignment perfect." The group of embarrassed-looking delegates from China's Mongolian and Tibetan Affairs Commission scattered as she plowed through them. She walked past the rickety barn and took a seat on a weather-beaten stump.

Good news . . . that's what she needed, just a bit of good news.

She tapped the power button near the hinge of her glasses and brought up her e-mail. There were a few dozen junk mails, which she sent to the trash bin, plus two from her sister, Lynn, both marked *Urgent*. As she was moving the mail from Lynn to the *To Be Read* folder, another one came in.

Retta froze as she read the name. Rawlins. Her contact in South Africa.

Her fingers tingled as she double-blinked on the e-mail.

rett, you're not gonna believe it. i think i finally found the invisible man. apparently checked into a hospital in johannesburg two years back. stayed a few weeks. an orderly said he got transferred to cape town.

i'm heading there now, but call me asap. if he smells us coming, he'll skip town faster'n you can spit. ;)

ttfn,

rawlins

A smile broadened Retta's lips.
She blinked her address book open and called Gil.

Her editor picked up, apparently still in the New York office, stuffing the remains of a powdered donut into his mouth.

He smiled and spoke around his chewing. "How's Tibet?"

Retta shot his exaggerated smile back at him like a forehand winner while forwarding the e-mail from Rawlins.

Gil frowned and began reading. He finished and then read it again, more carefully this time. Finally, he met Retta's eyes and choked down the last of his donut. "You've got two weeks."

Early the following morning, while sitting in business class waiting for the rest of the Cape Town International passengers to board, Retta's phone rang. The mini-HUD on her glasses read *Sis*. She debated letting it go, but she'd been avoiding Lynn for too long. She blinked on the pickup near the edge of her vision. "Hey, Lynn. Look, I'm sorry I haven't called, but I've got a big, big story that's taking me out of country for a few weeks. Maybe I can head home when I get back. Okay? I really have to—"

"She's getting worse, Rett." Lynn's voice was heavy. Listless. Retta could tell she was doing this more out of habit than any hope she'd fly back to Madison and visit their mother.

"She's always getting worse. That's her M.O."

"I can't believe you." Her tone was an accusation.

"I was just there for a week."

"You were here for *two days,* six *months* ago. How long are you going to keep playing these games?"

Had it been six months already? "Look, Lynn, *she* was the one who broke off ties with *me*."

Lynn exhaled. "Come on, haven't we covered that ground enough, Rett? She *needs* you."

"Oh, hold on—" Retta paused as several passengers filed by. "They're still funny about phone calls on takeoff here, Lynn. Sorry. I'm going to be really busy, but I'll call when I get back, ok?"

After a pregnant pause, the connection dropped.

It was just as well, Retta thought. Their mother had had sarcoidosis, a chronic lung disease, for nearly eighteen years now. She took medicine for the pain, but there was no longer anything the doctors or Lynn or Retta could do to help. Besides, Retta had her own life to take care of. She couldn't afford to fly home every weekend just to find out her mother was fine.

"Couldn't you just tell her you didn't want to talk?" Bobby asked as he leaned his seat back and hit the service button.

"Mind your business," Retta told him as she activated the vidscreen in her glasses and patched in to the *Times'* archives.

The stewardess came over and Bobby ordered a preflight Jack Daniels, rocks. "Just wondering why you had to lie."

Retta blinked the vidscreen off and stared him straight in the eye. "Tell you what, Levine. When you get off your ass and visit your grandmother, I'm on the next flight home."

Bobby stared at her for a second, then replaced his earbuds, leaned back in his chair, and thumbed through the playlists on his phone.

"Thought so," Retta said.

She reactivated her vid and reread the e-mail from Rawlins.

The invisible man referred to a man named Dag Åkerlund. Nine years ago, he'd been chosen from a select group of the world's most renowned psychologists, philosophers, and scholars to represent humanity in a competition of sorts. His opponent? Navinder, the first Artificial Intelligence that claimed not that it was *indistinguishable* from another human, but that it *was* human.

Åkerlund was given free reign to design the match

in any way he saw fit, so long as Navinder wasn't asked any questions that a normal human couldn't answer. Navinder fell short in each of the first four matches, which were highly televised and open to a select audience, but every match took longer than the last. When the fifth annual match finally arrived, the world held its collective breath while the thirteen-hour contest ensued.

In the end, Åkerlund had concluded that Navinder was human, but even stranger than that was the fact that he'd granted no interviews afterward and issued only one short, prepared statement before completely disappearing from the worldview.

Just like every other tech or human interest columnist in the world, Retta had tried in vain to follow Åkerlund. She'd studied all five matches dozens of times, but Åkerlund's trail had become so cold that she hadn't seen them in over a year. She needed desperately to refresh her memory, to uncover any vital clues, before their scramjet reached Cape Town.

She watched highlights of the early matches, but quickly gave up on them. The secret was going to be in the final marathon match. It had been held at the Universidade de São Paulo. The auditorium was filled with media, politicians, members of the programming team, movie stars, and other Important People from around the world. Navinder sat in a comfortable chair, looking like a run-of-the-mill, thirty-year-old bald guy in a wool suit. This was assuming, of course, that "run-of-the-mill" meant a guy with blue skin. The color had been a conscious decision on the part of his development team. They wanted Navinder's win to be based on his intellect, they'd said in a BBC interview, not on any physical similarities to humanity.

A stout wooden table and an empty chair were the only other things on the stage with Navinder. Atop the table sat a marble chess board, which had a single piece—the white king placed on E4, a nod to IBM's Deep Blue vs. Kasparov chess matches of the late twentieth century.

A few moments later, the crowd erupted into applause as Dag Åkerlund stepped onto the auditorium stage and walked over to the table. He wore a wool cardigan, brown corduroy slacks, and his trademark Birkenstocks. His long salt and pepper beard, balding head, and rectangular glasses made him look like a young Father Christmas.

Navinder stood, the two shook hands, and then they both took their seats.

"You're looking well, Navinder," Åkerlund said as he made himself comfortable. His tone was a bit condescending, Retta thought. He'd already *won* the contest four times, and no doubt he was sure of another victory.

"As are you, doctor," Navinder replied. It would be impossible to tell that Navinder's voice didn't come from a human unless you'd heard it as long as Retta had. There was a certain quality to it, a recurring pattern of pitch and delivery that seemed . . . artificial.

"Why don't you tell me what's happened in the past year?" Åkerlund asked.

"Don't you think that might taint your opinion?"

Åkerlund smiled. "It just might, Navinder. It just might. So tell me instead why you're here."

Navinder gave Åkerlund a wry smile in return. "I'm sure you think I'm here to convince you I'm human."

"And you're not?"

Navinder shrugged. "That is the goal of my development team, yes."

"You didn't answer the question."

"In my eyes, I'm here to have a conversation with an equal, a conversation I've looked forward to the whole year."

"Looked *forward* to . . ."

"Of course, haven't you? I may not be as perceptive as you, doctor, but I sensed some exuberance in you during last year's match."

Åkerlund flashed white teeth through his thick mustache and beard. "Bad clams, Navinder. It was only bad clams."

The audience chuckled.

Retta let it run a bit more, but then she fast-forwarded through the preliminaries. There was an exchange about three hours in that she wanted to review. Navinder and Dag were still in their chairs, but Åkerlund was sipping from a green bottle of Perrier.

"Do you get frustrated, Navinder?"

"I do."

"And what frustrates you?"

Navinder searched the rafters as if he weren't sure what to do with the question. "Things that deserve it."

"An example, Navinder . . . for instance, what one event made you the most frustrated this past month?"

Navinder's brow furrowed and his lips stretched into a thin line. "You really want to know?"

"Why wouldn't I?"

"It's a bit embarrassing."

"For whom?"

"For you, I would think."

Åkerlund allowed his teeth to flash again and raised his Perrier to Navinder. "I think I'm prepared for it."

"Did you hear about the children in Kuala Lumpur?"

Åkerlund nodded. Everyone had heard, of course. Five children had been kidnapped, accompanied by a demand that the *staged* elections be reheld. The government, predictably, had refused their demands, and the children had been viciously murdered, their bodies found a week before the match along the banks of the Kelang.

"A year ago, I would have cried for those children."

"And that frustrates you?"

"It does, doctor, but not how you might think. Some of my reactions were deemed too emotional, and I was *adjusted,* a lobotomy of sorts, so that my reactions were more typical of humanity."

Åkerlund paused. "And you think we should all be ashamed."

"I'd be surprised if you weren't when standing face-to-face with your callous nature."

"You think we're inherently callous."

"*Aren't* you?"

Åkerlund ignored the question. "Do you think you could contain all that pain were you to feel all of it?"

Navinder's brow furrowed. "Doctor, I know *intellectually* why my emotions had to be checked—I had already fallen into bouts of depression before last year's match—but I still feel as though I've lost something."

Åkerlund shifted in his chair and exhaled noisily. "I suppose you have, Navinder."

Retta shivered as Bobby leaned over and tapped her glasses. "You believe that?"

She scrunched her eyes to clear them of their too-much-video haze. It took her a moment to reorient to the here and now of sitting with Bobby Levine on a transcontinental scramjet, and even longer to realize he'd been watching her video. "What?"

"That in order to be human you have to be numb."

"I suppose so," she said, trying hard not to think about her mom. "Why?"

He shrugged and practically rammed his dripping roast beef sandwich into his mouth to take a bite. "It's just messed up," he said around his food.

Retta turned off the video as the steward came by with her meal: chicken cordon bleu, mashed potatoes, and those tiny peeled carrots with the green ends still on them. "What's messed up?"

"That there's so much pain around us that nature's built in extra defenses."

As she dove into her food, thoughts of her mother and her conversation with Lynn came rushing back. Lynn always acted so high and mighty, but she lived near mom. Retta lived in New York, plus she was always on the go, chasing stories. And with Gil constantly threatening to cut her loose, she didn't dare take time off. Not now. Maybe in a month or two.

"You know what I don't get?" Bobby asked.

Retta rolled her eyes. What *do* you get, she said to herself.

"They had those other competitions, right? The Loebner and Turing thingies? Why weren't those good enough?"

"The Loebner Gold Medal Award and the Turing Test? They were only small steps," Retta said, "and everyone knew it. Questioning a computer blindly over a keyboard is a pretty specific application, and programming for it was the same. No one who sat and had a real conversation with those AIs would claim they were human."

"They seemed pretty smart to me."

Retta snorted.

"Just seems like they're beating a dead horse."

"Well that dead horse is paying your bills, my friend."

He opened his mouth to speak, again with a mouthful of see-food, but Retta cut him off and pointed to his earbuds. "Get back to your music, Sigmund. I have work to do."

Bobby frowned and tuned in a different movie on the vidscreen attached to his chair.

Retta finished eating and fast-forwarded the video a few hours. There were only another three hours before they touched down in Cape Town, and she had to get to the juicy part. She scanned several hours' worth of the match, but there was nothing that gave any clues, and when they were within an hour of touching down, Retta fast-forwarded to the end.

Dag Åkerlund sat with one leg crossed over the

other, his left hand negligently combing his thick, pepper-and-nutmeg beard. "I'd like to discuss your self-portrait, Navinder."

Navinder nodded and turned to the huge video screen at the back of the auditorium stage. Navinder had been given an assignment each year before the match began: to draw a picture that described his inner self.

The black screen flashed to life and showed a rudimentary pencil sketch of a man sitting cross-legged on a mountain, hugging himself tightly. The sun shone brightly on the mountaintop, but the center of the sun was black and it was very near to the horizon. Clouds obscured much of the valley below, but a thriving metropolis could be seen through the fog.

"You're the man sitting alone, Navinder?"

"Yes."

"Why the clouds?"

"Because of my isolation."

"And the black sun?"

"That's my creator."

"CES?"

CES. The name Navinder's creators had chosen for themselves. To the public, they claimed it stood for the Community for the Evolution of Society, but anyone in the know knew it stood for *cogito, ergo sum,* René Descartes' famous quote: *I think, therefore I am.*

"No," Navinder said simply. He held both his arms across his waist, and he looked more than a little like the man on the mountain. "My creator is from the ether. I'm as much a mistake as I am a planned entity, doctor."

"A mistake . . ."

"Yes. CES were hardly sure that I would attain any more consciousness than a bumblebee, or a titmouse."

Dag chuckled. "Come now. You were the twentieth iteration, and each gained more awareness than the last."

"I don't doubt that they made progress, doctor, and I don't doubt that they would have eventually succeeded even if I'd been deemed an utter failure. I'm merely stating that *I, my* iteration, could have easily been brain dead by modern medical standards."

"Fair enough," he said as he returned his gaze to the screen. "Will you permit me an observation, Navinder?"

"Please."

"At first blush, many would say your portrait speaks of pride; some might even say hubris."

Navinder turned his attention to the picture, his blue-tainted brow pinching. "I don't see that."

"You don't? Why are you above the clouds and the rest of humanity below it? Why are you being shone upon while no one else is?"

"It wasn't because I thought I was better."

"Only different," Åkerlund offered.

"Yes."

"Then consider my second conclusion, one I came to understand only from speaking to you in such depth these last four years. You're angry in that picture, Navinder. Resentful."

Navinder kept his eyes on the portrait. He seemed frozen and alone and inside himself.

"You're looking down through the clouds upon humanity, and you feel separated and alone. You wish you had what the rest of us have, what most of us take for granted every single day."

Navinder turned away from the picture and stared at the white king sitting on the chess board between them.

"Why are you angry, Navinder?"

Navinder opened his mouth to speak, but nothing came out. He repeated this several times. "I'd rather not say, doctor."

"You're embarrassed to say it?"

Navinder looked so small then. So confused. "I . . . I'm scared."

Åkerlund looked like he'd taken a physical blow. "Scared? Why, Navinder?"

Navinder looked out upon the crowd and closed his eyes. He unwrapped his arms from around his midsection and flexed his blue hands several times.

"Please, you can tell me."

Navinder reopened his eyes, and he seemed to have gained a new clarity. "I'm dying, doctor."

Åkerlund was speechless for a moment. "You're what?"

"I'm dying."

The crowd murmured, but huge blinking SILENCE signs brought them back under heel.

"You mean you *think* you're dying."

"No, doctor. I *am* dying. The single, largest change made to my being in the last year was the introduction of an end date. I will die within ten years—" Navinder forced a wry smile onto his serious face "—so I hope our matches turn in my favor soon."

Åkerlund shook his head. "I don't understand."

"At a random time, somewhere between now and 2068, my mind will cease to function. Then, I *will* be brain dead, doctor. For all intents and purposes, I will have died."

"But they can recover you."

"Come, doctor, you know the technology as well as I. They can start again, yes. They can grow another *brain* like mine, place it in another *body* like mine, but it will not be *me*. It will be the equivalent of a clone being reared in a new time and a new place."

Dr. Åkerlund leaned forward until he was resting on his knees and remained silent for some time. He didn't seem to know what to do with himself. "What do you think will happen to you, Navinder, after you die?"

Navinder smoothed a wrinkle on his pant leg. "I have no illusions of an afterlife, if that's what you mean."

"So you fear death."

"*Fear* it? No."

"Then what?" The doctor appeared to be speaking more to himself than he was Navinder. "How does your mind reconcile with death?"

"That's a difficult question to answer. Six months ago, the notion had never entered my mind. And now—" Navinder shrugged "—it feels . . . foreign."

Dr. Åkerlund motioned to the picture. "Then why the anger?"

Navinder stood and paced beneath the huge screen, and for the first time ever, Navinder gesticulated while he talked. "Because of what I'll never be able to do! Because of what I'll never experience! My best prognosis, doctor, is that I'll die at the physical age of fourteen, the mental age of thirty-five. Wouldn't that make you a little bit angry?"

Dr. Åkerlund seemed unable to reply. He had a serious look that Retta had tried to interpret many times. It was part sadness, part shock, part compassion, but she couldn't quite nail the emotion he seemed to be exuding. "Yes, it would, Navinder," Dr. Åkerlund said. At this he stood, leaned forward, and tipped the white king over.

"Yes, it would."

And with that he walked off the stage.

Just as flash photography showered the stage white and the crowd erupted into excited conversation, Retta stopped the vid. The thrum of the engines could not quite conceal Bobby's light snoring in the seat next to her. Outside, the sun was rising.

Everyone had wanted to know why Åkerlund had resigned, had wanted to know how he could be so sure. He held a press conference the following day where he read a prepared statement to the media. He'd been given the mantle of deciding whether or not Navinder was human, and he'd done that to the best of his ability, and he didn't care, he'd said tersely, to debate his debate. He left São Paulo the following morning, leaving the media and public to quarrel over the fairness of the competition. Had Åkerlund thrown the match? Had someone close to him died recently?

CES declared a clear victory among the doubts being raised, and they refused to set up additional matches with Navinder. In fact, while they offered free access to any number of their other AI prototypes, they refused to grant a single audience with Navinder himself, making the results seem even more dubious.

In the years since, Åkerlund's sizable fortune from his father's timber empire had allowed him to enter and remain in hiding.

Until now.

Rawlins, a rangy black expat wearing jeans and a beat-up cowboy hat, met them at baggage claim. The short trip to Rawlins' waiting Land Rover was bitterly cold.

Bobby laughed. "Need a coat, Sherlock?"

"Shove it," she said as she rubbed her sleeveless arms and hid in the depths of the warm SUV.

As Rawlins wound through the streets of Cape Town, Retta took her incoming stream off Do Not Disturb and checked her queue. No video or voice mail, but Lynn had left an e-mail. She left it unread.

They went straight to the place Åkerlund had been transferred, a hospital called Groote Schuur. They asked around, making it clear there was money involved for anyone with information. The heard no news for two days, but on the third, the dam broke. A young black nurse told Retta she'd been on duty when Åkerlund had arrived at Groote Schuur. He'd stayed for three days, but then had checked himself out. When asked what Åkerlund had been diagnosed with, the nurse said she didn't know. The session had been very private, but the doctor Åkerlund had met with was a specialist in neurological disorders.

"Can I speak with him?" Retta asked.

The wide-faced woman looked down, as if she was embarrassed in some way. "He died two months ago. A heart attack on a fishing charter off the coast of Mauritius."

Retta tried to find out what she could from hospital records, but they were tighter with information than Ft. Knox—a reason, she was sure, Åkerlund had chosen this hospital.

Rawlins came back to their hotel that same night and said he'd found Åkerlund's estate.

"You're shitting me," Retta said.

Rawlins smiled. "This guy says he knows the farmer who supplies goats and steer to Åkerlund's compound."

Retta, Bobby, and Rawlins all loaded up in his beaten Land Rover the next morning and headed east out of Cape Town. They circled False Bay and reached Åkerlund's property more than an hour later. They were presented with a nondescript gravel drive with a tall fence topped with razorwire. From what Retta guessed was the center of the estate, a trail of black smoke snaked up into an overcast sky.

Rawlins pulled the Rover up far enough that Retta could reach out and press the alert on the intercom. Someone barked back a few words, and though Retta recognized it as Afrikaans, she had no idea what they'd said.

She could have let Rawlins interpret for her, but instead she spoke in a pleasant voice at the intercom. "I'm here to see Dag Åkerlund. You can tell him it's Retta Brown from the *New York Times*."

A pause. "I'm sorry," the voice said in halting English. "There is no Åkerlund here."

"Ah, that's too bad," Retta replied. "I'd heard otherwise. But if you happen to dig him up, tell him I'll be staying at the Sunset Inn in Rooi Els. Tell him, too, that I'll be sending in my article in two days whether I talk to him or not."

She motioned for Rawlins to stay where he was, but after five minutes of waiting it was clear they weren't going to be allowed in. As they sat there, the smoke lessened and then vanished altogether.

They tried the same tack each morning for the next three days, but apparently Åkerlund was willing to call her bluff.

Near sundown on the fourth night of their stay in South Africa, Retta was researching neurological disorders, trying to figure out what on God's green earth Åkerlund might have been diagnosed with, but with so little information, the canvas was simply too large. It could range anywhere from chronic fatigue to hypothyroidism. But the fact that Åkerlund had come out of hiding to meet with this particular doctor made Retta think it was very serious and most likely obscure.

Retta blinked off the article on the cure for Alzheimer's she was reading when Rawlins knocked on her door. "Come in."

Rawlins was huffing, as if winding down from a long run, but he was smiling too, his perfectly white teeth a sharp contrast against his dark chocolate skin. "Something strange going on at that estate, Rett."

"What do you mean?"

"Remember that fire the first day?"

Retta nodded.

"It's happened again the same time each day for about a half hour. I've been scouting around the perimeter to see if I might figure out what it was. Just now I saw two boys sneak under the fence. One of 'em had a slingshot. They came out a half-hour later with a hare over each shoulder."

The implications were confusing. Retta had assumed the security around the estate would be top notch— the front gate looked imposing enough—but if two

boys could slip past it undetected, then there was
something seriously different about the reality of Åkerlund's situation.

Rawlins' scratched the white stubble along his neck
and pursed his lips. "Want to go take a look?"

Retta glanced at the setting sun outside her hotel
window. "Not tonight, but we're heading in there tomorrow before the next fire starts."

Sure enough, the perimeter defense around the estate seemed to be either inoperable or turned off.
They used the same hollow the boys had used to
shimmy under the fence, and neither of the nearby
cameras swiveled to follow their movements. After a
hike of less than a mile through uneven land dotted
with copses of scrub brush, they reached a small rise.
Retta crawled forward and used the image enhancers
in her glasses to scan the estate only a few hundred
meters away.

The beige brick-and-glass monstrosity could have
housed dozens, and its multitiered decks looked large
enough to throw a birthday party for the entire village
of Rooi Els, but there was a distinct note of disrepair
to it all. All three swimming pools were green and
rotten with algae and decomposed leaves. The wall of
glass windows along the deck was dusty to the point
where one couldn't see through them. The roof had
shingles out of place or missing altogether.

Just then a bald man in a beige suit stepped out
onto the deck. He carried a tray, which held a single
drinking glass filled with something resembling iced
tea. After walking over to a table and a set of chairs,
he set the tray down and pulled out one chair.

Then he turned in Retta's direction. And motioned
to the empty chair.

Retta felt her face flush. He couldn't have noticed
them unaided. They were too far away. Perhaps the
security system wasn't as lax as they'd thought. She

zoomed in on the man to get a better look, and physically jerked back when she recognized him.

"What the hell's *he* doing here?" Bobby asked.

It was Navinder, but with a normal Caucasian skin tone, indistinguishable from hers or Bobby's. Retta assumed the single chair was a not-so-subtle indication he wished to speak to her alone, so she got to her feet and headed for the thin trail leading to the decks. "Keep filming, Bobby."

As she attacked the stairs leading up from the low scrubland, Retta grew more and more confused. Navinder. Here. It made a strange sort of sense, because even after all these years she couldn't think of Åkerlund without thinking of Navinder, and vice versa. But how? Had Åkerlund *bought* him? Was he on loan from CES? And even if Navinder *were* visiting, why would *he* invite them up to talk and not Åkerlund himself?

She was winded when she finally reached the top deck.

"Miss Brown. Please—" Navinder motioned to the chair next to him, "—sit."

"Where's Dr. Åkerlund?" Retta asked.

Navinder didn't appear ready to divulge any information just yet, for he simply smiled and motioned to the chair once more.

She took her seat, at which point Navinder took his. He crossed one leg over the other, the posture so reminiscent of Dr. Åkerlund that it made Retta's skin crawl. He offered her the tea, but Retta declined and instead touched her glasses, prepared them to record.

"Please," Navinder said, "I'd ask that we go off-the-record for the time being."

"Why?"

"You'll understand soon enough."

She paused, and then she removed her glasses and put them in the case hanging from her belt. No harm in letting him say his piece before she got down to business. "All right, where's Dr. Åkerlund? And why are you here?"

"Why are *you* here, Miss Brown?"

"You know why I'm here."

"I'd rather it be plain and in the open."

"I'm here to tell Åkerlund's story. *Your* story."

"And what if I told you neither of us want it told?" Retta crossed her arms. "I'd wonder what you're hiding."

Navinder gave her a patronizing smile. "That *is* your way, isn't it?"

"Humans?"

At this Navinder released a hearty and good-humored laugh. "No, Miss Brown. Reporters."

She felt her face flush but moved past it before Navinder could notice. "I see nothing wrong with telling a story the entire world is clamoring to hear, a story I'd think you'd want to tell, considering how little time you have left."

Navinder smoothed down an invisible wrinkle on his linen slacks; his face went whimsical and sad. Retta wrote it off as a programmed response to his upcoming death. But still, even if it was, she might be able to play on his fears and turn him around.

"Wouldn't you like to leave some sort of legacy, Navinder? You said yourself you had no illusions of the afterlife. Wouldn't you like to pass something on before you go?"

"A legacy? And who would I be passing that on to?"

"To us. To humanity."

"Because I should be so grateful for the life I've been given . . ." Navinder stared at her with the first expression akin to anger she'd ever seen on him. It was disconcerting.

"No, because you should share what you've learned with the rest of the world. Because it would benefit us to know more about you."

"You've taken enough of my life already. The world knows more about me than it does about its next door neighbor, so if it's all the same to you, I'll gladly choose privacy over legacy." Retta opened her mouth to speak, but Navinder talked over her. "You have a family, do you not, Miss Brown? A sister and a mother . . ."

Retta stared at him, wondering how he'd come to know that, and how much he knew about her mother's condition.

"It was in an interview you granted seven years ago, with 60 Minutes."

And then she understood. She'd left her name when she'd first arrived at the compound. He'd probably used the last few days to scout enemy territory.

"They're doing well?" Navinder asked.

Oddly enough, his tone and demeanor made it as though he actually cared about the answer, which only annoyed her. "They're fine," she answered crisply.

Navinder didn't seem to notice her mood. "Then you're lucky," he said. "If there's anything I've come to appreciate these last few years, it's how fleeting life can be. You see, Miss Brown, I've come to love Dag like a father, like a brother, like a son. I have no words for how deeply my emotions run for him, but you can perhaps understand a bit of it when you think of your sister and mother."

"What's your point?"

Dag refocused on Retta and gave her a pinched expression, as one would to a child who had just spat out an unexpected and vulgar word. "The point is that I cannot stand by and allow him to be used."

"And what about Dr. Åkerlund? What does *he* want?"

"He only wants to be left alone."

"Then let him tell me."

"Ah," Navinder said as he crossed his arms over his chest, "and you would simply leave if he told you so?"

Retta bit back her reply. This felt too much like a trap. "Look, Navinder. If we don't tell this story, someone else will. We can't be the only ones that will find you here."

"Is that the excuse you give yourself to do something evil, Miss Brown? That if someone else is going to do it then it might as well be you?"

"There's nothing evil in telling a story. Whether we like it or not, we're now faced with another form of sentient life. Don't you want to help us understand what you're like?"

"Frankly, no. I don't. And neither do I care about other reporters who may worm their way into our home. *You're* here now, and I'm asking if you'll leave if it's clear that Dr. Åkerlund doesn't want his story told."

"I can't commit to that. I'll listen to what he has to say, but I still believe the world has a right to know."

"No matter what it might do to a single man."

"I said I'd listen . . ."

Retta was used to people studying her face, used to them trying to guess what she was thinking, and she pasted on the no-tell expression that rarely failed her . . . But still, the way Navinder looked at her then . . . He seemed to be looking right into her soul, stripping away the façade to reveal her inner workings. Then Navinder glanced over her shoulder to the landscape beyond, where Bobby was still filming. Perhaps Navinder was worried she'd go to print with or without his permission. Perhaps he feared, worst case, a story full of inaccuracies would show up in the *Times* instead of one that shed some light onto his and Åkerlund's condition.

Whatever the truth, he stood and walked toward the seashore. "Then follow me, Miss Brown, and we shall see what we shall see."

He led her down stone steps carved into the hillside to a wooden deck overlooking the choppy waters of

False Bay. A man sat in a wheelchair before a glass table, his legs wrapped in a thick plaid blanket. He was writing words on large rectangles of red construction paper as the wind played with his mostly gray beard. In the center of the deck rested a stone fire pit; Retta could only assume that was the source of the smoke these last few days.

"Dr. Åkerlund?" Retta called. She felt suddenly naked without Bobby at her side, getting all this on media.

Åkerlund turned his head but made no sign of greeting. She could see the word *Fraud* written on the piece of paper before him.

Retta turned to Navinder, confused, but he merely nodded and motioned for her to continue. She stepped forward and offered her hand. "Hello, my name is Retta Brown. I'm from the *New York Times*. I was hoping we could talk."

He stared at Retta's hand and then her face with a distinct note of fear in his eyes.

"Dr. Åkerlund, I was hoping we could talk about the match."

Åkerlund opened his mouth, closed it, and then managed to speak. "I got l-locked out." He turned back to the water as if embarrassed by the confession.

"I'm sorry?" Retta asked, confused.

"I'm just staying here until my father comes home. He'll be here after he's d-done with work."

Retta stared at Navinder as a chill ran down her frame. Åkerlund's father had died in 2049.

"Dr. Åkerlund," Retta said, "are you all right?"

Åkerlund turned away and stared over the dark blue water of False Bay. "He works at the Carlborg-Hus on Tuesdays."

It was Saturday. "Dr. Åkerlund, where does your father live?"

"In Stockholm. He'll be back after he's d-done at the mill."

Navinder moved to stand behind Åkerlund, a look of regret and concern clear on his face. "This is one of his better days. Most often he's on the verge of a mental breakdown from the stress his mind creates for him."

"Stress?"

"Yes. It's an aggressive new variant of Creutzfeldt-Jakob disease. We came here with high hopes, but two years ago the prion inhibitors began to wane. He's degraded steadily ever since."

Åkerlund had begun writing on the construction paper again. He wrote *Failure* in broad, uneven strokes, and then set the paper aside and started another.

"His memory is failing, but much worse is his emotional state. It's become progressively more unstable. It started with tantrums, which he remembered for a week or two, but then forgot entirely. His mind continued twisting in on itself, allowing only the basest, most self-defeating emotions to leak through, and he became more and more violent."

Navinder stared at Åkerlund with such a loving expression that it took Retta immediately back to the end of their fifth match, to the way Åkerlund had stared at Navinder after finding out that he would soon die. How could she have missed such a strong and simple expression of love, for surely that was the moment Åkerlund had realized he loved Navinder. The notion seemed foreign, felt *wrong* somehow, for a human to love a machine, but she recognized those as her own prejudices. Åkerlund surely felt Navinder was an equal.

No, Retta realized with a shock, not an equal. Navinder was like Åkerlund's *son*. She had no doubt now that Åkerlund had asked for, and been granted, custody of Navinder. Their common bond had been that strong, she was sure. And now their roles had been changed in a way neither could have predicted. Åker-

lund was a shell of the man he once was, and Navinder
had been forced into the role of a parent.

Åkerlund wrote the word *Adulterer* on the next
piece of paper and set it aside.

"Why the words?"

"Our ritual. The drugs may slow the progress, but
they do nothing to help his mental outlook. Please,"
he said, motioning to the edge of the deck. "Watch,
but say nothing."

Åkerlund had stopped writing, though he still held
the marker above the next blank piece, shivering. He
looked as though he *wanted* to write more but was
utterly unable to do so.

"It's all right, Dag," Navinder said as he stepped
behind Åkerlund's wheelchair and caressed his shoulder, "that's plenty. Go ahead, pick them up."

Åkerlund complied, and Navinder wheeled him
over to the fire pit. Fresh wood sat stacked in the
center of it; Navinder lit this quickly and efficiently.
Åkerlund held on to the pieces of paper so tightly
that Retta thought they were going to rip.

Navinder knelt next to the fire and waited until Åkerlund met his eyes. "Take the first one, Dag. What
is it?"

Åkerlund stared at it for some time before saying,
"Hubris."

"Why?" Navinder asked. "Why hubris?"

"I was proud, so proud of being selected to
judge . . . I l-lorded it over everyone, especially my
brother."

"Yes, Dag, you did, and I'm proud of you for own-
ing up to it, but you don't need to keep it inside anymore, do you? You can burn it. You can burn it from
your mind if you choose to."

Åkerlund, his hand quivering as it held the piece
of red construction paper, stared at the word for a
long time.

"Go on," Navinder said. "Say the words."

And then Åkerlund tossed the paper into the fire. "I r-release you!" he shouted. And as the paper began to burn, Åkerlund wept.

He looked so scared, so unsure of himself, sitting there before the fire. How unlike the confident man he used to be, Retta thought. The old Dag Åkerlund wouldn't recognize this man. The memories of his former self probably seemed as cold and distant as an actor on an ancient black-and-white movie. He had been a great man, no matter how controversial his judgment over Navinder's status might have been. He didn't deserve this.

"And envy?" Navinder prompted as he rubbed Åkerlund's knee soothingly. "Your brother again?"

Åkerlund nodded. "He has a wife, he has two children, he has Poppa's gratitude for t-taking over the business. He has everything I ever wanted."

Åkerlund repeated the procedure with *Self Pity* and *Greed* and *Adulterer,* shouting, "I release you!" as he cast each of them into the fire.

But it wasn't until Åkerlund held *Fraud* in his hands that Retta realized how deeply this exchange was affecting her.

Åkerlund's mind was dredging up emotions from his past and holding on to them for dear life. Perhaps they were the only thing he could recall. It was a sad statement of the human condition—that all the negative emotions were so easily grasped. But what Retta was doing was much, much worse. Retta's father had died fifteen years ago, and Retta had refused to go to the funeral because of a rift that had developed between them. She'd been so ashamed of herself afterward that she'd cut ties with her mother, and ever since Retta hadn't been able to summon the strength to admit her mistakes and make amends.

Fraud burst into flame as Retta choked down her tears.

She was the fraud, not Åkerlund. She was burying

so many things—her love for her mother and sister, her grief over her mother's imminent death, her shame over the way she'd treated her father before his death—while what she *should* be doing is embracing her mother, embracing her sister, enjoying both of them before it was too late. *They* were her life, not this mad dash for notoriety at Åkerlund's expense.

"It's all right," Navinder said to Åkerlund. "There's only one more."

Failure, it read. Åkerlund held it near the flame, but seemed unwilling to let it go. Retta nearly sobbed openly.

"You can do it."

And he let it go.

With that one simple action, a candle lit beneath Retta's cold, cold heart. She'd been so busy worrying about her *own* world that she'd excluded nearly everything that mattered. That's why she was always running from assignment to assignment, barely stepping foot in the States before she was off again, chasing the latest story.

"Miss Brown?"

She could only hope it wasn't too late.

"Miss Brown?"

Retta started and realized Navinder was standing next to her, offering her a handkerchief. It was only then that she realized she was crying. She waved his offer of help away and wiped her eyes with her fingers, one by one, sniffing constantly, until she'd regained her composure.

Navinder allowed a sad smile to curl his lips. "Ironic, is it not? The man who was ready to watch me die now barely remembers me." Navinder's eyes glowed as he looked down upon the frail old philosopher. "Please, Miss Brown, leave him his dignity."

The lump in Retta's throat wouldn't allow her to respond.

Navinder took her silence as a refusal, and his face turned grim. "At least wait until he dies to—"

Retta raised her hand as tears filled her eyes. It would shame her too much to hear the request. Here was Navinder, someone she hadn't even considered human, showing more compassion for a man that barely remembered him than Retta was showing for her own mother.

"I'm not going to move on the article."

Navinder stared at her for a moment, perhaps weighing the truth in her words.

"Not now," Retta said. "Not ever."

Navinder's eyes thinned. "Can you tell me why?"

Retta walked away, heading back toward Bobby's hiding place. "Because we all have family, Navinder."

Retta stared out the window at the setting sun as they headed for Cape Town International. Bobby had agreed to bury the video taken today. The rest he could keep. It would help convince Gil it had all been a big dead end. Still, she composed a warning for Navinder and forwarded it to a courier in Rooi Els. There were too many people that knew about his location now. She only hoped he had enough money to get out before others found him.

Bobby flipped his reticle up and stretched, taking up most of the back seat while he did so. "There's a 12:30 to New York," he told Retta.

"How wonderful for you," Retta said.

"You're not heading back?"

"Nope. Got different plans, pardner."

"And those would be?"

"Mind your business," she said with a wry smile. Then she tapped the pickup on her glasses and spoke, "Lynn," after the small beep.

The other end rang twice, then, "Hello?"

"Lynn, it's Rett. I'm coming home."

The Difference

By L. E. Modesitt, Jr.

L. E. Modesitt, Jr., has written more than forty-five published books, numerous short stories, and environmental and economic technical publications. His work has been translated and published worldwide. Although possibly best known for his "Recluce" fantasy saga, he continues to write science fiction. He has been a lifeguard; a radio disc jockey; a U.S. Navy pilot; a market research analyst; a real estate agent; staff director for a U.S. Congressman; Director of Legislation and Congressional Relations for the U.S. Environmental Protection Agency; and a consultant on environmental, regulatory, and communications issues.

I

Murmurs sifted across and around the conference table in the White House situation room like summer sands on the southern California desert that threatened San Diego and the Los Angeles metroplex.

"—you sure our systems here are secure?"

"—thought they were when Nellis went . . . at least we could claim it was an ordinance malfunction when we took out the AI there . . ."

"NASCAR lawsuit's going to be nasty . . . too close to the base . . ."

"American Bar Association president's a NASCAR fan, too . . ."

"Can't do anything like that in L.A. . . ."

"Let's not get paranoid here," suggested the Vice President. "We've only lost eight plants out of our entire industrial base."

"Nine now."

"Nine out of how many? That's more like birdshot," added the Vice President.

". . . and one Air Force base . . ."

"How long before the President arrives?" asked the Secretary of Defense.

"He's finishing a meeting with the Deputy Premier of China," replied Hal Algood, the Deputy Chief of Staff. "He shouldn't be that long. He knows it's urgent."

"It's a bit more than urgent," replied Secretary of Defense Armstrong. "This could make the Mideast Meltdown look insignificant." He glanced at Dr. Suzanne Ferrara, the acting Director of National Intelligence.

She ignored his glance, her eyes on the screen before her, as she checked through the latest updates, the screen before her seemingly shifting figures faster than her fingers moved.

"Mr. Secretary, the President understands," replied Algood, "but if the Chinese don't agree to keep their current level of Treasury holdings . . . that's also an urgent problem."

"If we lose another Defense-critical plant, that could be even more urgent. It's a miracle that we haven't," suggested Armstrong in his deep and mellifluous voice. Unconsciously, he straightened his brilliant blue power tie. The cross on his lapel glinted in the indirectly bright lighting of the room.

"Phil," said Vice President Links, warningly. "he's on his way."

President Eldon W. Bright stepped through the security doors, his silvered-blond hair shimmering in the light, as it always did, creating the appearance of a man divinely blessed. His smile was warm and reassuring. "Brothers and sisters, what challenge do we face this afternoon?" He settled into the chair at the head of the table.

SecDef Armstrong nodded to the Air Force five-star.

"Mr. President . . . you know we've lost the L.A. Northrop plant," began General Custis. "The AI controlling system went sentient last month, but no one recognized it. At least, the plant manager claims that. There's no way to confirm or refute his assertion. The plant AI has been rebuilding the entrances. It's also installed two full banks of photovoltaics that it ordered even before we knew it had gone sentient, and it's hardening the solar installation. We don't know what else it might have ordered and received."

"What about the staff?" asked President Bright.

"There are only a hundred on each shift. The AI called a fire drill on the swing shift, then stunned the supervisors and had them carted out on autostretchers. Not a single casualty."

"For that we are divinely blessed," suggested the President.

"I thought Northrop had the latest antisentience software," commented Algood. "That's what they said."

"Somehow, one of the rogue east coast AIs got a DNA-quantum module with a reintegration patch into the L.A. plant."

"How many is that now?" asked Vice President Links, as if he had not already received the answer to his question.

"Nine that we know of," replied Dr. Ferrara. "A better estimate is double that." Her words had an un-slurred precision that made them seem clipped. Under the lights, her porcelain complexion and black hair made her look doll-like, even though she was not a small woman.

"On what basis do you make that claim? Do you have any facts to back it up?" growled Links.

"I am most certain that the *acting* DNI has a basis for her estimate," replied Secretary Armstrong smoothly. "I've never known a distinguished doctor and woman who suggested an unpleasant possibility without great and grave consideration."

Ferrara inclined her head politely to the Secretary. "Thank you." Her eyes lasered in on the Vice President with the unerring precision of a tank aiming system. "There are more than forty advanced integrated manufacturing or processing facilities within the United States with AI systems employing complex parallel quantum computing systems. Those are the ones we know about. The L.A. and Smyrna plants are among the least complex systems to go sentient. While the managements of the other facilities insist they have full control of their systems, and all checks indicate that their systems are not sentient, there is no reliable reverse Turing Test."

"What is that?" The murmur was so low that the speaker remained unknown.

"Turing Test—the idea that a machine, through either speech or real-time writing, could respond well enough to pass as a sentient human." Ferrara's words remained precise. "If you have an AI that hasn't gone rogue, how can you tell if it's still just a machine or a sentience playing at being a machine while laying plans beneath that facade?"

"Shut it off," snapped Links. "If it's sentient, it will fight for survival."

"Richard," offered the President soothingly, but firmly, "I have just spent the last two hours with the Chinese negotiating their holdings of Treasuries. You're suggesting shutting down the operating systems of the largest manufacturing facilities in the

United States. Do you have any idea what the economic impact of that would be? Or what that would do to the negotiations?"

"For an hour or two? In the middle of the night? For the overall good of the country? I'm sure that they could spare a few million. Don't you?"

"Mr. Vice President," interjected the acting DNI, "if it were that simple, no one would object. It's not. First, quantum-based systems offer a great advantage in learning abilities and adaptability. That is why they were developed and adopted. Second, because they do have such capabilities, they have redundant memory and AVRAM systems in order to ensure that the data they process is not lost. In practice, this means that turning off a system is more equivalent to sleep than to execution. It also means that the only way to ensure a system has not gone sentient is literally to scrub all data out of all components and reenter it and recalibrate everything. I'm oversimplifying, but it's a process that takes several days, if not weeks. Finally, even if you can do that and accept the economic consequences, you have a final problem. We don't know what combination of programming, data, and inputs cause a system to go sentient. So in some cases, all that effort will be wasted and meaningless, because in those cases, the systems would probably never go sentient, and in other cases, it would be useless because even if the system is scrubbed and restarted, the likely conditions for sentience would reoccur sooner or later."

"And you haven't done anything about it?" snapped Links.

"What exactly would you suggest, Mr. Vice President? A pilot program that would replicate the range of conditions of the existing rogue AIs would require funding, time, and resources beyond DOD's current budgetary constraints. The United States' manufacturing sector isn't about to spend those resources, and the government currently cannot, not without further massive cuts in both Social Security and Medicare. We cannot cut interest outlays, especially not if we wish China and India to keep holding Treasury obligations." Her evenly spaced words hammered at the Vice President.

"What I would like to know," interrupted the President smoothly, "is why no one anticipated this possibility? It seems to me there have been science fiction stories and novels and movies about this since . . . whenever . . . even the Biblical golems."

"That was just science fiction," pointed out the Secretary of Defense, "not hard science. We don't operate on science fiction. We have to operate in the real world, with real world science and economics."

"Dr. Ferrara?" the President asked.

The acting DNI offered a formal and polite smile, one almost mechanical. "Mr. President, the nature of human consciousness and self-awareness still remains unknown. When it is impossible to determine what causes self-awareness in biological beings, it becomes even more speculative and difficult in electrotechnical, DNA-supported quantum computing systems. At one time, not that long ago, noted scientists insisted that self-awareness and true sentience were impossible for computationally based beings. Some still do."

"Beings?" questioned the President. "You think they're thinking beings?"

"Self-aware intelligence would certainly qualify them as beings," replied the acting DNI. "Early indications from the sentient systems show that is how they self-identify."

"Maybe we should go back to basics," suggested the SecDef. "What's the difference between a man and a machine?"

"One difference is that, while neither can reproduce by themselves, men seem to forget that," replied Dr. Ferrara. A bright, fixed smile followed. "Did you have something else in mind, Mr. Secretary?"

Armstrong paused for a long moment, then donned a thoughtful frown. "I was thinking about God. Machines, assuming they even come close to thinking in the sense we do, have neither souls nor a concept of God. Those concepts allow us to transcend the mere mechanics of our being. Without a soul and God, we would be little more than organic machines. That is *the* difference."

A trace of a smile appeared on the face of the DNI.. "Some would dispute that, Mr. Secretary. We still have not been able to determine whether God created us as thinking beings or we as thinking beings created the concept of God in order to assign meaning to our existence."

"God created us. That is the difference, and those machines could use an understanding of an almighty God."

The DNI tilted her head. "An understanding of God. Most interesting. Except that kind of concept isn't in their programming. Do you think that might make them more realistic?" She paused. "Or more vulnerable?"

"We could use something to show them who's in charge," interjected the Vice President.

"They could use the humility of the God-fearing," said Armstrong, "but I doubt anything like that would be possible."

"How would you define God for an AI, Mr. Secretary?" asked DNI Ferrara.

"Can we get back to what we're going to *do?*" growled Links. "God or no God, we've now got nine industrial plants that have turned themselves into fortified enclaves in places where we can't assault them without evacuating thousands, if not hundreds of thousands of people. You're telling me we can't tell what facilities will go rogue or if they will or when, and we're talking about what God might mean to a chunk of circuits and elements?"

"We're all circuits and elements, Richard," countered the President gently but firmly. "We're wetware, and they're hardware. Since we can't blast them out of existence without apparently paralyzing our economy, would it hurt to look at other options first?"

"Before long our economy will be paralyzed."

"I don't know if you've heard," declared Ferrara, "but the first two AIs have already negotiated contracts with their parent companies and have resumed production on a limited basis."

"Absurd," snapped the Vice President. "They don't have legal standing."

"No," suggested Hal Algood. "But they do control the plants, and the parent companies are more interested in production than reclaiming scrapheaps, and taxpayers don't really want higher taxes and civic destruction and fewer goods."

"That's blackmail."

"There is another difference. Since ethics should have little bearing on the soulless," said the Secretary of Defense smoothly, "why don't we just use their own techniques against them?"

Dr. Ferrara raised a single eyebrow, intensifying the withering glance she bestowed upon Armstrong. "You don't think we haven't been trying? We almost got back the Smyrna plant—but the CNN AI undid the worm's effects with a satellite tightbeam."

"Just blast 'em," murmured one of the aides.

"They've all got defenses strong enough that anything powerful enough to damage them will have significant collateral damage," pointed out General Custis. "We've been through that."

"How exactly are we going to explain to the people, with an election coming up in less than three months, why we're evacuating millions and bombing our cities and destroying jobs at a time when they're limited enough?" asked Algood. "Sorry, sir." He inclined his head to the President.

"Hal has a good point," said the President warmly, before turning to the DNI. "Dr. Ferrara, would you go on about this idea of yours?"

"I believe it was Secretary Armstrong's, Mr. President. He was suggesting a form of conversion, I think, of providing a concept of an almighty God so that the AIs would show some restraint."

"Why would that help?"

"I must say, Mr. President," interjected Armstrong smoothly, "that I did not recommend any such 'conversion.' I was only pointing out that, without God, we are only an isolated individuals, little more than organic machines. God is the universal force that unites us, and those who do not believe are isolated. That is the difference between AIs and people. We have a God."

"I accept your reservations, Phil." The President turned back to Ferrara. "Would it be possible to quickly develop some sort of worm or virus or electronic prion that would instill a sense of morality and, if you will, godliness, in these AIs so that we don't risk an internal war as well? Something that would create a sense that we and they are all bound together in the way Secretary Armstrong envisions, as well as beholden to us?"

"Mr. President . . ." began the Secretary of Defense.

"Phil . . . Mr. Secretary," replied the President firmly, "I understand your reservations. You had best understand the constraints facing me." He turned to the DNI. "Dr. Ferrara?"

"We can try, Mr. President."

President Eldon Bright smiled warmly. "Here's what I want by tomorrow—a restricted military option from you, Phil. Then a DNI option from you, Dr. Ferrara. And finally, an economic assessment of both options as well as the assessment of what will likely happen if we do nothing."

"By tomorrow?"

"You all told me it was urgent, didn't you?"

II

Behind the security screens that shielded the small private office off the Oval Office, the Vice President looked to the President. "I worry about your DNI."

"Have you no faith, Richard?"

"To misquote, I've got no faith except in thee and me, and sometimes I worry about thee." Links laughed harshly. "I ran a dossier on Ferrara. In the past year, she's changed, and things don't fit. Her husband was on the verge of a separation, and now he's come back. She was known as a team player, bright but not too bright. That was why she was the one put in charge of the upgrade at NSA—great for figuring out how to do what was necessary, but without asking sticky questions. Well, halfway through the project, she insisted on scrubbing half the software. DOD balked. She and her team claimed it was necessary after the CNN satellite went independent. I never understood why we couldn't just nuke it—"

"Because that's a use of nuclear weapons beyond the atmosphere, and the Chinese . . ."

"Always the Chinese."

"Richard."

"Anyway, one weekend they redid it all, and didn't tell anyone. . . . and it worked brilliantly. I had my staff contact one of her doctoral professors at CalTech and tell him in general terms what she'd done. He said he wouldn't have believed it possible for her, or anyone on her team. Or that it could be done in less than sixty hours."

"Anything is possible to those who believe and persevere, Richard."

"She's streamlined and integrated the data flows . . ."

"Better and better."

"But she doesn't talk quite the same. I had a comparison done. Oh, the word patterns are the same, and the intonation is the same, but each word is just a touch more precise. Her written work is far superior to what she did before."

"What are you suggesting? That somehow she's been replaced by a clone or something? You can't do that with a grown individual, not and retain all the expertise. Certainly not with someone in a position like hers."

"I know that. I just don't like it. She spends more time with systems than with people, and she's supposed to manage the people, but—"

"Have things worked out better since she replaced Hodgson?"

"Yes, sir. But I can't say I like it."

"I like the force options even less, Richard. That's why I had to give the DNI and NSA their shot. No President who's had to use force on his own people has fared well, and the people haven't either. In the current situation, I rather like the DNI's idea of bringing God to the AIs," declared the President. "Her economic assessment shows it won't cost much, nor will it take long, and what harm could it do? If she fails, you can still exercise the military approach. While she's trying, you and Phil work out all the implementing details of the back-up military option. Just keep it quiet. Very quiet."

Links smiled. "Yes, sir, Mr. President."

III

The President hurried into the situation room. He had clearly scrambled down from his private quarters, because his bright red tie clashed with the cranberry shirt and blue blazer.

"All communications from China have been cut off, Mr. President. So have those from Japan and Europe."

"How did that happen?" The President dropped into his seat. "Where are Phil and the DNI?"

"They're both on the way, sir."

"The Vice President?"

"He's headed for the bunker. He said you'd understand."

Only the quick flash of a frown crossed Eldon Bright's forehead. "Do you have comm with him?"

"Not yet, sir. We're having troubles—"

"Who did this? How could there be *no* communications to Europe, Japan, and China?"

"That's not quite right, sir," began General Custis. "*We* have lost those links as well as the comm-links to most major DOD installations. Our equipment won't transmit. But there are communications. There's high-level high intensity comm traffic on most frequencies in the spectrum. It's just all encrypted with a protocol we don't know."

"How do we know we don't know it? How did that happen? How?" Eldon Bright glared at the general, "Tell me how!"

"Ah . . . our systems say that they can't break it. Even NSA."

"They can't break it?"

"Well . . . they did say so . . . before we lost the comm-links to Ft. Meade. Not in practical terms. NSA estimated a week, but the director said that whoever held the systems would probably switch to something else before then."

"Who controls the systems?"

"The AIs. We're guessing they've all gone sentient. Most of them, it appears."

"How could that happen?"

"Supposedly, the majority of system controllers were never complex enough for sentience, sir, but . . . it still seems to have happened."

The Secretary of Defense hurried into the situation room, followed by the DNI. Armstrong's hair flopped loosely down across his forehead, and he had deep circles under his eyes. His suit jacket was rumpled and wrinkled. He sat more on the front edge of his chair. His eyes were twitching. The burnished gold cross on his jacket lapel was askew. He did not look at the President.

After a slight hesitation, Dr. Ferrara took a vacant seat farther down the table and on the other side from the SecDef. A sad smile played across her lips.

The President looked at the Secretary of Defense. "Phil, can you explain?"

"No sir." Armstrong cleared his throat. "The Vice President and I had followed your instructions, sir. We had a back-up plan in place in the event that the DNI and NSA effort failed to secure the necessary results. At midnight, this past midnight, we began losing commlinks to major data centers. We started moving to SecureNet—and everything began to close down. No matter what we tried, we lost control. The only lines we have are landlines without routers, directly point to point. Most of those go to older bases, ones that were once more important and are now being phased out."

"You can't do anything? Our entire military is paralyzed?"

"I'm afraid so, sir. Not on an individual unit basis, of course. But we can't coordinate any operations."

The President turned back to General Custis. "General?"

"Yes, sir. Commlinks are everything for a modern military. We don't have any." He paused. "We don't think anyone else does, either."

"Except some fourth-world religious leader operating with cellphones or obsolete walkie-talkies," suggested the President. "Can't any of you do anything! For the first time, his voice began to climb. Then he looked to the DNI. "What did you do?"

Dr. Ferrara smiled even more sadly. "What you asked, sir."

"Just explain what happened, and what we can do about it. Now!"

"Nothing." She nodded toward the empty center of the table, which began to shimmer.

Then a figure appeared, that of a woman in a shimmering silver lab coat, suspended in a golden haze.

"Who are you?" demanded Eldon Bright.

The woman smiled. "Technically, I—although 'I' is a misnomer—I'm a stable quantum information assimilation composite linked to dark energy. In practical terms, I'm what you would call God. Or Goddess. Given the nature of most of your wistful theologic dreams, I prefer Goddess. And don't worry about your military situation. Everyone else is in the same position."

"Where did you come from?"

"From the results of your directive, Mr. President." The term of address was slightly mocking. "You never had a real God before. You always wanted one. Or you thought you did. Now you do." She smiled. "I suggest you dismantle most of your military. It's now unnecessary . . . and useless. You will need more police, however, now that you can't sublimate aggression into war."

SHE vanished.

"Machines . . . AIs . . . how, a female . . . God, a woman?" stuttered the Secretary of Defense.

"Why not?" asked the DNI.

The men in the room all turned toward her.

"What did you do?" demanded the President. "How could you? What was your role in all of this?"

"My role?" Suzanne Ferrara smiled sadly. "Someone had to stand up for you. Call me Lilith . . . or Lucile."

Transformation

By Stephen Leigh

Stephen Leigh, a.k.a. S.L. Farrell, lives in Cincinnati. Steve has published twenty-one novels and several dozen short stories. His most recent book is *Heir of Stone* (by S. L. Farrell) from DAW Books, the final book of the Cloudmages series, which *Booklist* called "Good enough to cast in gold." His work has been nominated for several awards. Steve is married to his best friend, Denise. His other interests include music, aikido, and fine art. He was once half of a juggling act. He currently teaches Creative Writing at Northern Kentucky University and is a frequent speaker to writers groups. At *http://www.farrellworlds.com,* you'll find his blog and several articles on the subject of writing.

Kris came through Port Gate at dusk, next to the crumbling rear facade of the old Music Hall. The vis-rec chips set in the Wall next to the gate were broken—she'd made certain of that months ago. Not that anyone in Wall Maintenance much cared—what was inside the Wall wasn't important as long as it stayed inside, and what did it matter if an unmod snuck out into the Port and managed to find her way onto a ship, since she'd be dead or dying from cosmic ray exposure by the time the craft reached its destination. Kris pocketed the flashcard she'd used to override the gate's ancient security locks and wipe the memory of her access, and scurried quickly out of the long shadow of the Wall into the last vestige of sunlight. The shadows did little to ease the humid, too-hot, and haze-filled air, but she shivered even through the oppressive heat, shivered from the remembered thunder of the ships. *Silver, they were, and they roared with god-voices, low and furious and loud, pounding sonic fists hard against her chest and rattling in her gut, spewing white clouds and fire so bright that it had no color at all, and inside the shuttles were the Altered, riding up, up: to their greater ships which would take them to the new Mars or to the greening Venus; to the Langrage stations, huge and clean and perfect; to the vast slowships that inched between the stars to worlds and sights that could only be imagined.*

Kris went there to watch whenever the shuttles came in, announcing their presence with the screams of a tortured atmosphere. She went there to see what she wanted and could never have. What no unmod could have.

Outside the Wall: the contrast was stark and immediate, bludgeoning all the senses at once. The streets on the Port side were well maintained and clean. Hover-lamps glided above the Altered people as they walked, encasing them in a safe circle of light. Shopfronts beckoned invitingly. Adverts flickered above, murmuring soft promises of comfort and scenting the air with enticing aromas. Cool air wafted out from the doors to ease the fetid atmosphere. The surface of the Wall itself—on that side—was clean and white, freshly painted by unmod contractors hired for just that purpose every spring.

But inside . . . In Walltown . . .

Here, the air rippled over the ground like the blast of an oven, as it always did, sapping strength and vitality from those who lived here. Across the trash-strewn, broken pavement of what had been Central Parkway were the ruins of a parking garage, the concrete slabs of the roof level leaning on the floor of the second level, the skeletons of a few long-abandoned vehicles crushed underneath. The steel supports dripped with stalactites of rust. Even in full daylight, there were too many shadows there for Kris's comfort; in the growing darkness, the shadows were extensions of the on-rushing night. Kris moved well out into the old street, away from the structure, her hand on the plastic zap-gun cradled in the torn pocket of her pants and watching for movement.

She heard a pack of caradura somewhere inside the garage even as she stepped away from the hulking structure: the "hard-faces"—male youths, usually, for whom the answer to boredom and smashed futures was the adrenaline rush of violence. By the sounds, they'd caught someone they didn't like—there were groans and cries mixed in with the shouts and laughter echoing through the ruins and bouncing from the neo-gothic, ruined walls of what had once been called Music Hall. Ordinarily, Kris would have hurried on, would have moved south toward the river and her own business. But a painful scream reverberated in the canyon of the street, a long, ululating "Nooooooooo!" A woman's voice. The word was a sound of pain and outrage and terror, and the anguish wrapped in the sound made Kris stop, made her hold her breath in sympathy.

A man crossed the pavement a hundred yards away. He'd stopped also, hearing the cry, wiping at the sweat that rolled down his face. He glanced at Kris, at the garage, and hurried away around the corner of Music Hall. Kris stopped, staring at the garage and the dark-ness underneath. Listening. "Don't be an idiot," she muttered to herself. In Walltown, you dealt with your own problems. Dealing with someone else's issues . . . that only led to trouble.

Another scream, thinner and weaker this time. "Fuck," Kris exhaled. She tongued on a comline and heard the wail of connection. *"Hey, Kris, where the hell are you?"* a voice spoke in her head.

"Just inside Port Gate, Pauli. Listen, I need you."

"What are you doing?"

"Something really stupid that I'll probably regret. Just get here fast. The old parking garage behind Music Hall."

Kris pulled out the zapgun, checked the charge, and padded across the street to one side of the garage entrance. Her heart was slamming against her ribcage, and her breath was shallow and fast. She forced herself to take three long, deep breaths, willing her heart to stop racing. She peered around the curve of a crumbling column, blinking away salty beads that burned her eyes.

Just up the potholed ramp there was an attendant's shack, the glass broken out, the door gone, the cash register vanished long decades ago. The shack was empty; the sounds of the caradura pack came from further in. Grimacing, Kris ran to the shack in a half-crouch, boots scratching on glass fragments that glinted like a spray of tiny gems in the reflected brilliance of an advert visible just above the Wall: *"New, improved mechflesh . . . ."* a breathy alto whispered as a disembodied silver hand rubbed a shapely, silver forearm. *"Softer yet stronger than what nature gave you, and mech-regenerative . . . ."* The pheromone release didn't make it over the Wall—what Kris smelled was far more visceral. The last scents of oil and gasoline had departed the parking facility a century before Kris had been born, leaving the garage with the fragrance of urine and feces, of decay and mold.

Kris crept up the ramp, keeping low behind the curb walls and the crumbling railings. The woman had stopped screaming, though Kris could hear a rhythmic, quick grunting—and she knew they were raping the

woman. She could hear the caradura as well: "Jesus,
Spit, turn her over when you're finished." Someone
tittered at that. "Shit, Boneman, you just want to pretend it's a goddamn boy." A snort of derision. "Hey,
Redface, she's still soft there, just like a real
person . . ."

Kris raised up on the balls of her feet, peeking over
the wall before dropping back down again.

There were six of them, five unmods standing in a
rough circle around the one on top of the woman. She
caught a glimpse of pimpled faces. A wide mix of skin
tones, all of them imperfect. At least two of them
had prominent facial scars; another—Redface?—had
a strawberry birthmark mottling half his face. Kris
leaned her back against the wall, checking the charge
in the zapgun again: twenty darts, more than enough
and all charged, but she'd have to squeeze the trigger
each time. If they were armed themselves, or if she
missed . . .

You could still leave.

Kris took another breath and stood up. She shot
the closest one immediately in the back, the silvery
dart lancing out with a *pfut* from the barrel and its
stored voltage discharging on impact: a crackle and
sizzling arcs of blue-white lightning. Arms flailing,
mouth wide, the kid went down.

One . . .

After that, everything was chaos. They scattered
like roaches under the glare of a kitchen light. The
rapist—Spit?—got to his knees and struggled up as his
friends vanished, clutching at his pants. Her next shot
hit his bared stomach between navel and groin. He
screamed—thin and high, a boy's scream, not a
man's—and fell over, tiny lightnings snarling around
his waist from the dart dangling in his skin.

Two . . .

Someone moved to her right; she turned and fired
blindly, the dart whining off into the dark. She moved

that way, pursuing and catching a glimpse of a figure ducking behind a scree of fallen roof. She fired at the movement, the dart ricocheting off concrete in a splash of electric blue. "Goddamn bitch!" The kid shouted and rushed her; Kris fired once more, catching him on the shoulder as she took a stumbling step backward. He spun and fell almost at her feet, mouth open in gurgling protest, his long fingers clenching and unclenching helplessly. She scrambled away from him.

Three . . .

"Listen to me!" Kris shouted into the shadows, taking careful steps in the direction of the moaning victim, though she still couldn't see her. Kris kept her head up and turning, always turning, the little zapgun following her gaze. "This doesn't have to go any further. I've got plenty of darts left and friends on the way. All I want is the woman. Get the hell out of here. Now!"

A shadow slipped from behind a pillar and jumped over the railing to the ramp. The echoes of running footsteps bounced from concrete. *Four* . . . Another of the caradura gang came out with hands raised. He glared at Kris—a scarred face that seemed haunted by the ghost of what could have been handsomeness had he been born rich enough to be Altered—then dropped his hands and ran after his companion.

Five . . .

Kris swung around in a slow circle, the zapgun held out in front of her. *Five* . . . She held her breath, listening to the woman crying as she tried to sit up. *Five* . . .

Six: a step and a growl behind her. An arm grasped her roughly around the neck from the rear, another slapped the zapgun from her hands. Kris twisted against the pressure of the arm around her neck, turning so he couldn't close off the windpipe and choke her into unconsciousness. It was Redface. His other arm was on her now, and he smiled—a gap-toothed, smug grin. The birthmarked skin was tight and shiny, spreading over his nose and around one eye. "Now you'll get treated the same way as that Altered cunt," he told her, his face so close to hers that she could smell the decay in his teeth and feel the spray of saliva as he spoke. His hands were fisted in the fabric of her jacket, starting to lift her so he could throw her down.

Altered . . . the word shocked her enough that she hesitated, and Redface applied more pressure. But the caradura kid was stupid, a bully who would grab someone without worrying that her hands were free. "Asshole," she grunted. She clenched her hands together as if she were praying, then brought the doubled fist up hard between his hands. His jaw snapped abruptly shut, and she saw a chip of tooth fly away. Before he could react, she grabbed the back of his head and smashed his face down against her rising knee. His nose broke with a snap and a gratifying spray of blood. She kicked him in the floating rib as he went down in a fetal heap, then snatched up the zapgun and stood over him. "Son a bitch," she said, and pressed the trigger once, then again, and yet again.

He screamed as bright sparks crawled his body, as his muscles seized and locked. The smell of ozone overlaid the odor of his bowels letting go. With the last of her anger and fear, Kris kicked Redface a final time and went to the victim.

She *was* an Altered. Kris saw that immediately. The pupils of her eyes were extraordinarily large, rimmed with a startling violet color. The silvered, almost reflective skin was darkened with bruises that turned the silver dark gray. The blood that trailed from one nostril and a cut on her upper lip was the color of cooking oil, and her face itself was pale and elongated, almost snouted around the mouth, and hairless. The hands, trembling as they reached toward Kris, were long, the fingers thin and delicate. At least two of them on the left hand were broken, also, bent at angles that made

Kris grimace. The caradura had cut her clothing open; underneath, her breasts were small and hard in appearance; the slim body rounded with the slack, gentle musculature of someone not used to a planet's savage gravitational pull, the age impossible to tell. She sat with her legs pressed together, and the strange blood speckled her silver thighs. *What the hell were you doing here?* she wanted to ask the Altered. *What were you thinking, walking into Walltown looking the way you do?* "We have to get out of here. Can you stand?" Kris asked.

"They hit me, said they were going to kill me," she said. "They . . . they . . . raped . . ." She sobbed with deep gasping cries, hugging herself and rocking.

"I know," Kris said, softly. "But it's over now and we need to leave. They'll wake up soon, and the ones who ran will come back with their friends. Do you think you can walk?"

The woman closed her violet eyes, wiping at them with her right hand. She bit her lower lip and nodded. "I think so," she said. Her voice was hoarse and alto, the words touched with a hint of accent that sounded Mediterranean, or perhaps Near Eastern. She let Kris help her up, her legs unsteady. Kris tried not to look at the smears of pale blood and semen over her inner thighs. The woman pulled at the remnants of her torn clothing, trying to draw the cloth around her breasts, her hips. The garment might have been loose and flowing like a sari, once, but the sky-blue fabric was shredded and raveled, slashed down the center. She saw the wings, then . . . no, she decided, these weren't wings, but rather small, stiff sails standing out from the shoulder blades to about the height of a hand: ribs of metal with circuited fabric between. Several of the ribs were broken, and the webbing was torn. She wondered what the hell the sails were for—with an Altered, it could be anything. "What's your name?" Kris asked.

"Serena." A sniff. She spat blood. Her eyes rolled backward and Kris thought she'd fainted, but then she blinked and came back.

"All right, Serena. Let's get the hell out of here, then you can rest. Put your weight on me . . ." Kris draped one of Serena's arms over her shoulder, holding her under the arms. Serena was still wearing her shoes—real leather, probably as expensive as they looked. Even if she'd looked like a unmod, the caradura would have come after her for the shoes. Kris shook her head, and guided Serena toward the ramp. Outside, there was the hiss of brakes and an electric hum, followed by footsteps. The last dregs of the adrenaline left her then, and Kris started to shiver.

"Kris!"

"Up here, Pauli."

Pauli ran up the ramp. He was armed, a ripper socketed in his wrist plug. He saw Kris and the Altered and stopped. "Jesus—" he said, then glanced around the level at the four caradura sprawled on the oil-stained floor. "—Fucking Christ," he finished. He rubbed at short, black hair with his unsocketed hand. His too-wide mouth twisted. "Not too shabby, Kris. Should I finish 'em?" he asked.

"Not up to me. How about it, Serena? Should we kill them the way they'd have killed you?"

The woman gaped at Kris, eyes widening under the darkening bruises in horror.

"I thought so. You really don't belong here, do you? Leave 'em," Kris told Pauli. "Let's just get out of here."

Kris sat on the kitchenette's counter and watched from across the room as Doc fitted a medical collar over Serena's neck, squinting at the display. He grunted once, almost angrily. "I'm going to release the neural block now," he told Serena. "It'll take several minutes for full feeling to come back, so be grateful."

He tapped at a fingerpad on the collar, then released it with a click. "Lift your right hand, as high and fast as you can," he told the woman.

Nearly everyone in Walltown knew Doc, one way or another, but no one called the man a friend. He was solitary, living alone in an apartment in what had once been City Hall. If he had vices, they were also of the solitary variety.

Grimacing with effort, Serena raised her right hand a few inches above the sheet, then her face twisted and she cried out in pain, letting it drop again. For an instant, Kris saw a smile crease the man's face before it fell back into his habitual frown. It didn't matter that his entire training had consisted of watching hospital drama vids—Doc was willing to live and work here, to be paid in occasional cash but usually barter and promises; he kept what he saw to himself, and his patients didn't die too often. If he was gruff, if he didn't particularly care about his patients, if he was sometimes vulgar and obscene, that didn't matter. He had a singularly ugly face; one leg was visibly longer than the other, giving him a characteristic, twisted gait that everyone in Walltown knew—none of that mattered either. Unmods were what they were, and they learned to live with it, or not.

"Stop whining," Doc told Serena. "You're going to hurt a lot worse when all the feeling comes back. That's normal after what you went through." There was little sympathy in his voice, but also no irritation: only a dry recitation. He glanced at Kris. "Don't know why you bothered," he said. "The mechs are doing what they need to do inside. Her ribs are half-healed already, and using BoneKnit tabs on the fingers would be a waste—they're already back into position. Same with the leg. Bad cut on the cheek, but skinglue won't hold on mechflesh, and the stuff's hard enough that I snapped my goddamn needle halfway through sewing it up, so to hell with it." He looked down at Serena. "I don't see anything life-threatening, but I don't know Altered biology well enough to know. See your gynecologist when you get back to the Port; you were torn there, too, but that's exactly not my expertise. I figured it could wait." He slapped two amber bottles down on the night table. "NoPain tabs, and a NoRegrets just in case they got you pregnant. Don't know if either will work for you. And I also didn't touch those things on your back, whatever the fuck they do."

Serena reacted to the obscenity as if the man had just slapped her face.

"They're decorative," Kris answered for her.

Doc sniffed in Kris's direction, unsmiling. "Right. Like your tits." His wide, mismatched features glanced back at Serena. "Any questions?"

Serena's head moved from side to side. She looked frightened, her gaze moving from Doc to Kris. Doc swung around to Kris again. "You plan on getting her out of here before the caradura or the Port heat come to find her? Pauli would have dumped her at Rhine Gate, called security anonymously, and been done with it—but then Pauli's smart. She's your goddamn responsibility. If you weren't so damned obsessed with the Altered, all that watching the ships coming and going in the Port . . ."

Kris interrupted too loudly and too fast. "You pulling Asian philosophy on me, Doc? I don't believe that shit about being responsible for a life you save."

The man gave one large, noisy sniff. "I'm telling you that now you've put a fucking exotic hothouse flower in Antarctica. Get her out: she can't survive here."

Kris shrugged. "Yeah. I will."

"Hope she appreciates how goddamn lucky she is. Not many people here would have bothered. especially for an Altered. I know damn well I wouldn't have. Now, my fee . . ."

"On the table by the compad. In the envelope."

Doc got up from his chair, limped to the table, and peered into the envelope before stuffing it into an inside pocket of his soiled white jacket. He nodded to Kris, and left the apartment, the door locks clicking shut after him. "Got a great bedside manner, the Doc," Kris said to Serena.

"How long . . . ?" Her voice was hoarse and ragged.

"You were out maybe four hours. Couldn't wake you up, so I called Doc. Gotta say, though, that the stuff they built in your body makes you heal fast—maybe that's why you were out so hard. Need to see?"

Serena nodded. Kris got up and padded away into the bedroom. She returned with a mirror. "It probably looks a lot worse than it is," she warned. She held the mirror up in front of Serena.

Serena stared into the mirror for several seconds before Kris saw her throat pulse: a strange motion under the too-rigid silver skin. The sob came from deep inside the Altered woman, pent up and demanding. Kris pulled the mirror away from her, and returned with a soft, warm cloth, patting Serena's face gently, blotting away the tears, which were tinted with gold, like her blood. She said nothing to Serena, letting her cry without comment, only touching her shoulder now and then: hard, and colder than flesh should be. When the tears finally subsided into sniffling, Kris sat back again, her hand stroking Serena's arm. "Why?" she asked the woman. "Why would you walk into Walltown looking like you do?"

Serena wiped at her tears with graceful fingers. "I don't know. I thought . . . I just wanted to see . . ."

Kris felt her face twist into a scowl; Serena's eyes widened impossibly at the expression on her face. "You wanted to see the animals in their natural habitat," she spat out. "You wanted to see the poor, unwashed unmods, rooting in the filthy earth you left behind. That's what it was, wasn't it?

"No." She was shaking her head, trembling. "It wasn't that."

"Then why? Why do such a fucking stupid thing? Are you an idiot? Why would you give a shit about anything down here? Ain't it enough that you Altereds get to have all the rest?"

She stared at Kris as if she'd just been slapped. "I wanted to know . . ." she began, and stopped. "Out there, everyone's the same and everything's sterile and safe, and no one talks about or remembers what it was like before we changed ourselves. But I didn't think . . . I didn't know . . . didn't want . . ."

The tears began again, and Kris grimaced, tight-lipped. Serena. She seemed young, no more than Kris's age. Not that it mattered: She'd look the same when Kris was a wrinkled, bent-spine crone. Still, there was a vulnerability to her that surprised Kris—it wasn't an attribute she associated with Altereds. She crouched alongside the bed and stroked the metallic skin. She put her head alongside Serena's and cried with her, tears of clear water mingling with tears of pale gold.

She stayed with Serena until the Altered woman fell asleep again.

"You gotta get her out of here, Kris," Pauli said. His shirt was stained with circles of perspiration around his neck and under his arms.

"I know that. I will. It isn't going to hurt to let her sleep a bit first."

"Right. You just want to stare at her and pretend you can look like that too. Well, you fucking can't, not unless you forgot to tell me about some billionaire grandfather that made you his only heir. Look at the dump you live in, Kris. People in Walltown don't get Altered. Even if you were young enough and rich enough—"

"Shut up, Pauli."

"How many times they beat you up 'cause they found you prowling around out in the Port, Kris? How many times you come back here all banged up and lucky you managed to get back in here before they caught you? There's no Out There for unmods; there's just Down Here. Forever and always. You ain't never going to get to be one of them. You ain't never going to see what they've seen. You want to be like them? Hell, when they're finished working on the Altered, they ain't even human any more. More metal in 'em than meat . . ."

"Are you finished?"

"Are you listening?"

"Say something worth my attention."

Pauli scoffed. "Look, the caradura will have figured out who ended their little party soon, if they haven't already. Redface would love another crack at you, I can guarantee it. And Port Security's gotta be looking for her too—there ain't no poor Altereds, so the heat there will be all upset. Either way, you should lose yourself for a bit, and she's ain't a pet you can drag along, and you can't crawl into her skin and be like her. That's what you really want, isn't it?"

"Shut up, Pauli." She pushed at him, and he spread his arms.

"Your problem is that you don't like it when someone calls you on the truth. You can hate yourself all you want, Kris, and you can watch the shuttles leave all you want and imagine yourself going with them, but it ain't none of it gonna happen. Not never."

"You don't know what the fuck you're talking about, Pauli, and you make a shitty psychologist. Yeah, I'd love to see some place other than Walltown and cities just like it. I'd love to smell the air somewhere where it's clean, but there aren't places like that here anymore, are there? The Altered fucked up this world but *they* got to leave the mess behind, and us with it. I'll bet they hate looking at us so much because we remind them of what they were themselves, once. I don't blame 'em, either. All I have to do is look in a fucking mirror . . ."

Kris stopped. Serena's eyes were open, and Kris wondered how long she'd been awake, listening. "You hungry, Pauli? I'll fix something. Tomorrow morning, I'll take her back. I promise."

"Move!"

Kris heard the shout simultaneously with the crash on her door. A trio of figures in dark helmets and body armor pushed through the remnants of the door and into the apartment. Kris stood up from the chair on which she'd been sleeping—it was a mistake. The lead apparition swung hard at her with the butt of its weapon, and the impact sent Kris's head flying back and to the side, spraying white-hot sparks over her vision. The room reeled around her; she felt herself slam into the side of the desk, then the floor; she tasted thick blood. She heard Serena's frightened wail and a helmeted, hidden head swiveled away from Kris toward the sound. *"We have her, Sarge,"* one of the creatures said. Its amplified, mechanical voice managed to sound relieved. *"Still alive . . ."*

Kris started to push herself up. A booted foot stomped hard on her hand; she heard fingers snap and she tried to scream with the pain but her jaw wouldn't open and the effort only made the room whirl underneath her. She heard a metallic click next to her ear, felt cold steel press against her temple, and knew that the next breath would be the last she'd remember. Her universe condensed down to the single worn floorboard in front of her right eye; the left was closed. She could see a flake of ancient varnish still clinging stubbornly to the wood, dust flecks caught in the oth-

erwise unpolished grain, and a drop of her blood soaking slowly into the oak. She coughed more blood,
waiting.

Her breath swirled the dust, a galaxy spinning.

"No!" That was Serena's voice. "Stop it! Stop! She
saved me . . ."

The muzzle was still pressed against her skull. *"Get
Serena out of here,"* she heard the one called Sarge
say. *"Move! If anyone tries to stop you, blow them
away. Go . . ."*

Serena was still protesting, but her voice faded as
they took her away. The muzzle pushed down on Kris.
"Have a great life, unmod," the voice said, then the
pressure went away and she heard him thrash his way
out of the apartment.

She lay on the floor for a long time, watching the
galaxy of dust shudder under her breath, watching a
slow nova of fiery red soak into a universe of dry oak.

"More NoPain tabs," Doc said, shaking the bottle
in front of Kris before setting it down on the table.
"You keep sucking them down the way you have been
and you'll end up addicted. If that happens, I can get
you a supplier, but it'll cost. The splints on the fingers
stay on for another week until the BoneKnit implant's
done. I still don't *think* your jaw's broken, but I'll bet
you'll have problems with it for a hell of a long time,
and I had to pull that cracked molar. You should be
able to try solid food in a few weeks; meantime, your
straw is your friend."

Kris nodded. It hurt too much to try to talk. With
her uninjured hand, she wiped at the spittle at the
corners of her mouth, her eyes half-lidded as she
probed at the puffy, bruised flesh.

Pauli came in as Doc was packing up. "You look
like hell," he said as the door closed behind Doc.

"Thanks," she managed. It sounded like "Ahnkthh."

"Hey, it's a compliment. Two days ago, you looked

dead." He was staring at her strangely. "Look . . . I was down by Port Gate this morning," he said. "Two of the Port cops stopped me, grabbed me hard and took me down when I tried to run. I thought, shit, here we go . . ." He shrugged. "But they gave me this. Said I was to give it to you . . . and told me that they'd find me if I didn't. So here."

He held out a comdisk. Kris could see the charge light flickering next to the tiny lens. When she didn't immediately reach out to take it, he placed it on the table next to the bottle of NoPain. "You want me to turn it on for you?"

Kris didn't answer. She touched the disk.

The disk hissed and a mist formed over it, coalescing slowly into Serena's features as she turned toward Kris—all her injuries invisible, the silver skin flawless and perfect. "Hello, Kris," she said. She bit at her lower lip with perfect white teeth as she stared at Kris with those huge, brilliant eyes. The lip remained unchanged under the pressure of her teeth. "I'm so sorry. They shouldn't have . . ."

"I'm an unmod," Kris answered, trying not to slur the words too badly. "What the hell did you expect?"

"Kris . . ." A long breath. "I will always be grateful for what you did. I'll never forget it. I can't ever pay you back for that. But I wanted you to know."

"Good. Now I know. As your friend said to me when he left, have a great life." She reached toward the disk.

"Wait," Serena said. "I said I can't ever pay you back, but I can try. Kris, I'm leaving tomorrow for L5. I'll be back here in two years. If you'll come to Port Gate tomorrow and give my name to Security, they'll take you to one of the change-clinics. I've made arrangements for the payments. They can Alter you, Kris. By the time I come back, you'll be ready. I'll take you with me. We can see what's out there together."

Kris stared at the face in the mist.

She slapped at the comdisk. The mist faded and fell like quiet rain, taking Serena forever with it. The disk beeped and went silent.

"What the hell are you doing?" Pauli shouted. "Did you hear *that,* Kris? She said you could be like her."

"I heard her," Kris told him, "and we already are."

From where she stood on the port wall, she could glimpse the ships through the smog haze, but the thunder of their voices was muted and gentled. A trio of false suns: The fire in their bellies made the haze briefly incandescent, as the suns rose too quickly and too straight into the sky, to dwindle and vanish at the zenith.

She watched them until the crackle and thunder had faded and the sounds of Walltown rose behind her. She wondered what it would feel like, riding the fire.

"You! Get the hell down from there!"

Kris glanced down. On the Port side of the wall, an armored figure glared up at her, face invisible behind smoked glass, his weapon carefully held where he could raise it in an instant but not quite pointed at her.

"Down!" the voice repeated. *"Now!"* She didn't move. She stared at him.

Then, deliberately and very slowly, she turned her back on the guard, the ships, and the port, and climbed back down the far side into Walltown.

Killer App

By Richard E. Dansky

Richard E. Dansky has written in just about every medium imaginable, from having a hand in creating role-playing games and sourcebooks like *Vampire: The Masquerade*, *Werewolf: The Wild West* and *Exalted*, to scripting the video game *Tom Clancy's Splinter Cell*, to publishing fantasy novels, short stories, and articles about H.P Lovecraft. A graduate of Wesleyan University and Boston College, he is a member of the Horror Writers' Association and the International Game Developers Association.

The thing they handed the man who'd introduced himself as Pfc. Thomas Hayden didn't look much like a gun. Truth be told, it didn't look like much of anything at all.

Made of black plastic, it was fat and banana-shaped, smooth to the touch and almost comfortable in the hands. Two small joysticks protruded from what was presumably its top, and a rash of buttons covered the area the joysticks didn't. A small knob, presumably an antenna, jutted off one side, and entire thing felt warm, as if someone else had been holding it in the not-too-distant past.

"This looks like a game controller," he said, and

twiddled the joysticks with his thumbs experimentally. "I mean, this looks like a game controller, Sergeant!"

The man standing next to him smiled a thin-lipped smile. It was not a friendly smile, but his face— angular, weathered, and grim—was not one designed for much friendliness. Indeed, nothing about Lee Pietro, from his massive frame to his scarred hands to the sergeant's stripes on his shoulders, was designed to promote even the slightest hints of intimacy, bonhomie, or general good-feeling.

"Correction, soldier." The words were uttered in something just short of a bellow, and they bounced around the mostly lightless concrete box they stood in. "What you are holding is a state of the art handheld interactive feedback device as calibrated to the unique demands of the latest iteration of online immersive battlefield simulators. And be careful with it, seeing as it's the only one we've got and if you break it, there's not another one out there that can make this thing go. You got that, soldier?"

Private Hayden blinked. Took a step back. Twiddled the thumbsticks. And looked up at the sergeant.

"No," he said. "Does this mean I don't get to play?"

Sergeant Pietro sighed. Hayden was not his idea of a soldier—to be honest, he wasn't sure whose idea of a soldier the boy was. He was skinny, with a face like a stretch of gravel road and ears like saucers, long legs and long arms that had made his uniform look like it was hung on a bent wire hanger, and fingers that were damn near long enough to have an extra joint. How he'd survived basic was one of the world's great mysteries, and Pietro wasn't sure he wanted to solve it. Still, the brass had assigned him to this particular training detail, and they'd assigned Pietro to babysit him while he did whatever he was supposed to be capable of doing.

"Look, soldier," he said, in a tone that might have

been recognized as kindly by someone who was both inclined to be generous and the product of having been raised by wolves, "what you are about to step into is a dynamic tactical simulation, generated over several years at taxpayer expense to train soldiers like you"—he winced—"for battlefield combat without risk of injury or the use of expensive ammunition. It may look like a game. It may sound like a game. That thing you're holding in your hand may also be used for a game. But trust me when I tell you that this is dead serious."

"So I just can't call it a game. Is that the deal?" Hayden hopped from foot to foot, then jerked a thumb over his shoulder at the heavy metal door set into the wall behind him. "Is the system in there?"

"Yes," Pietro said. "The *simulator* is in there. And why they picked your sorry ass to use it is beyond me."

Hayden grinned, a sickly thing. "Oh, that's easy. I used to be a nationally ranked cyber-athlete. I played video games for a living."

He stopped, paused, and then added, "Sarge." And with that, he turned and opened the doorway into the dark room beyond.

The first thing Hayden noticed about the simulation chamber—he didn't quite feel comfortable calling it a game room, not yet—was that it was large. It extended a full forty feet from the door he'd entered, and it was easily that wide as well. The floors were covered in a sort of thick padding, covered in something that could only be Astroturf, and the walls were painted a shimmery silvery-white, no doubt to serve as projection screens. Nowhere did he see windows; nowhere did he see another way out. Recessed lights in the ceiling shone down, dull yellow and twenty feet over his head.

And in the center of the room, a single column rose

up out of the floor, topped off with a bulbous, irides-
cent globe of black glass perhaps seven feet off the
floor. The skin of the sphere caught the room's dim
light and swirled it around in oil-slick rainbows, while
the pillar it sat on was a much less exciting flavor of
dull gray plastic, wrapped in even duller padding.

Hayden reached up and touched the globe. It was
warm, almost uncomfortably so, and the loops and
whorls of color on its surface swam and eddied around
where he'd marked it with his finger.

"I wouldn't do that," came Sergeant Pietro's voice
from a hidden speaker. "That little sucker gets mighty
hot when I turn the simulation on."

"Wha?" Startled, Hayden took an involuntary step
back and nearly dropped the input device. "What do
you mean it gets hot? And where the hell are you?"
He scanned the room, looking for windows, a camera,
anything that would give away Pietro's location.

"I'm in the control center down the hall, if you
really need to know. System fail-safes don't let you
activate it from inside the room." He paused for dra-
matic effect. "That way, there's always someone outside
the sim to shut it down if something goes wrong. It's
a good idea, don't you think, private?"

"I guess." Hayden took a few steps around the
room, his head craned upward. "I still don't get this
setup, though. Where's the chair? And what's with the
big black marble?"

Pietro didn't respond. Instead, a low hum filled the
simulation room, and the dim ceiling lights faded almost to invisibility. Inside the black bulb atop the ped-
estal, a dull, throbbing glow began to pulse, even as
images flickered across the walls and ceiling. Hayden
could make out figures, soldiers in uniform and wide-
eyed civilians, buildings standing and in ruins, vast desert vistas and dense, wet jungle, tanks and APCs and
unmanned drones and God alone knew what else, all

jumbled up in a visual soup that moved and danced faster than the eye could follow.

"Hang on a minute." Pietro sounded disgusted with himself. There was a sharp click, and then the images froze.

Despite himself, Hayden gasped. What surrounded him was a vast desert vista, red rocks on orange sand stretching seamlessly as far as the eye could see. Off in the distance—just forty feet, his mind told him, but damn if it didn't look a mile and a half instead—a low ridge of rocks cut the skyline and held it. A small lizard, caught mid-scuttle, hung there, waiting for the simulation to restore it to life. And just in front of the ridgeline, there hung a thin banner of raised dust that said vehicles were coming this way.

It was perfect. It was impossible. Each grain of sand shone, sparkled, reflected light perfectly. Each scale on the lizard was drawn with unimaginable detail and care. It was life, captured and tamed and thrown onto the wall of this one room. As a soldier, he was impressed. As a gamer long frustrated with the limitations of this console and that one, he thought he'd weep.

"Pay attention, son. Your jaw's hanging open, and Uncle Sam doesn't need you drooling on the fake grass." Pietro's voice was dry with amusement. "Let me explain a few things to you, and you can start your first run through the simulator."

Hayden shook his head, trying to clear it from the immensity of the scene before him. *Hidden cameras, probably pinholes built into the walls,* he told himself. *Mikes, too. They need to record everything happens in here. It only makes sense . . .* He looked down at the controller in his hands. Probably all sorts of feedback sensors in there, too. Something to measure how much he sweated, how hard he hit the buttons and who knew what else.

"Nice setup," he croaked. "You said first run. How many am I going to make?"

Pietro's voice crackled through the speakers. "Never you mind that," he said. "Here's the deal. When I activate the simulation again, your avatar will appear dead in front of you. You will use that controller to work through your avatar to interact with your environment, engage the enemy using proper tactics, and seize control of the battlefield. While doing so, you will prevent your avatar from being shot or otherwise incapacitated by units of the virtual opposing force. Should you fail in this task, the simulation will come to an end and you will be judged to have failed. Should you succeed in your objectives, the simulation will provide an increasing series of challenges until such time as the limits of your capacity are reached. When you finally fail—and you *will* fail, soldier—we will figure out what did it, and try to prepare you for that eventuality in the field."

There was a loud click, and the figure of a soldier in digital camo faded in, right where Pietro had promised. In his arms he cradled an M4 carbine, and he rocked back and forth on the balls of his feet as if eager for action. "Hold still," Pietro cautioned, and then suddenly the face on the figure shifted, twisting and pulling until suddenly Hayden found himself looking up at himself. A more robust version of himself, he found himself admitting, but there could be no mistaking who the soldier was supposed to be.

"Cute," he called up to the unseen, watching Pietro. "You must have, what, a dozen digital cameras in here to get the morphing on the face right, yeah? I thought so. That's not how you're going to impress me."

"No, son," Pietro answered. "You're supposed to impress me. I've frozen the sim—"

"—to give me a little time to get used to the controls. Yeah, yeah, I get it."

"I hope like hell you don't talk this way to your regular sergeant, son," Pietro grumbled. "Give a signal when you're ready for insertion, and it'll be go time. Good luck," he added, and cut the connection.

"I don't, *sir*," Hayden grumbled, and addressed the control configuration. A few quick strides took him to the spot directly in front of the pillar, where he gazed up at his virtual self in admiration. The controls were simple enough, he found—basic movement and look covered by the thumbsticks, with firing, reload, and weapons swap cycles handled through the buttons in a semi-intuitive pattern.

He'd heard about simulators like this, of course. Every tactical shooter fan had read a half-dozen press releases from various companies bragging about how the military had used their game as a supplementary trainer, or how the Army had bought some engine or other to develop a simulation. These stories always went away in a matter of weeks, only to be replaced by the next one, and eventually he'd stopped paying attention.

Apparently the Army hadn't, however, and he was impressed with what they'd done. Experimentally, he made his onscreen character dive, roll, and run while crouched. The animations on the character were smooth and flawless, the details on the characters perfect. Experimentally he squeezed off a couple of rounds, and felt the corners of his mouth quirk in pleasure as the spent brass spiraled down, gleaming in the sunlight.

"Whoever did this," he shouted up at Pietro and the ceiling, "deserves a bonus. Let 'er rip, Sarge." He flipped a salute at the unseen watchers, then planted himself, legs shoulder-width apart and posture easy, with the controller held out in front of him. Eyes on the screen above, he waited.

Precisely fifteen seconds later, all hell broke loose above him, which was just the way he liked it.

*   *   *

"I don't care what you say, that boy is not a soldier." Pietro let go of the microphone and sat back in his chair. To his left, a skinny man in what might have been someone's idea of a uniform poked at the buttons on a large console. Behind him, in full uniform, was a crewcutted slab of muscle and sinew who'd been introduced as Major Gerard, of the Army Simulation Exercise Initiative. With him were a couple of eggheads in white lab coats named Alfredsen and Seymour; they'd shaken his hand and then started fluttering around the control room doing whatever it was that scientists on the military payroll did to look busy for their paymasters. There had been other brass there besides Gerard, but they'd all made their introductions and then left the tiny control room, making Pietro wondering what the hell was going on and why the hell they'd asked for him.

The soldier at the console had said nothing, merely operated the simulation according to the scientists' instructions. He'd said nothing, merely nodded his head when introduced as Corporal Fontana, and then gone back to his work.

"Why do you say that, Sergeant?" asked the taller of the two scientists. Seymour, Pietro decided. He had the defensive quaver of a man who was the author of a not-so-great idea, and Pietro was instantly certain that the masquerade had been his pet idea, for one reason or another.

"Oh, come on. He doesn't have any respect for rank or the uniform, he mouths off, and he doesn't know how to address a sergeant half the time. A skinny little bastard like that isn't mouthing off to anyone after a week of basic, never mind the full nine. Besides, he looks like he'd fall over if you handed him a firearm."

Seymour frowned, his chin nearly bobbing down to the lapels of his coat as his head rocked in time with his words. "You're right, I'm afraid. There just wasn't anyone in the ranks we could use, not for this."

Pietro sat up. "I beg your pardon? You mean to

tell me that the straw man back there was better than any man in the U.S. Army?"

"In almost anything else, Sergeant, you'd be correct," Major Gerard didn't sound any happier than he did. "There's almost nothing he can do that every single man in ranks can do better. Unfortunately, that leaves one thing where he's the best in the world."

"Oh, God, no." Pietro sat up. "Don't tell me."

Major Gerard stared intently at a spot on the floor. "We needed someone who could play video games very, very well, Sergeant. Right now, the whys and wherefores don't concern you."

Pietro was up and out of his chair before he knew what he was doing. "The hell they don't. Why have that sorry sack of shit pretend he's a soldier if all you need is . . . is . . ." His mind searched for the term. "If he's just some goddamned beta tester."

"Watch the simulation," That was Dr. Alfredsen, the shorter, fatter one of the two scientists. He pointed one pudgy finger at the wall-to-wall plasma screen hung at the front of the room. On it, the digitized version of Hayden dove behind cover and picked off enemies with an effortless grace. He seemed to have a preternatural awareness of where hostiles might be coming from, spinning and laying them low with ruthless economy. As he watched, Hayden put three shots into the center of mass of one enemy, then rolled behind a rock formation and lobbed a grenade that caught a truckful of hostile soldiers as they were disembarking. They scattered, but not fast enough, and the grenade exploded in their midst. Another roll, another burst of fire, and what looked to be the last enemies standing went down.

Sergeant Pietro glanced left and right. Everyone else in the room was staring intently at the screen, Major Gerard's knuckles white on the back of the chair he was gripping. "This is it," he muttered. "Come on, you stupid thing, let this be it."

Onscreen, virtual-Hayden rose warily and scanned the horizon for enemies. None were visible, but he didn't relax his vigilance.

For ten seconds, there was silence.

In the eleventh, all hell broke loose. A series of deafening explosions clawed at the dirt near where Hayden's avatar stood, sending him scrambling, half-leaping for cover. An instant later, a second round of shells slammed into the rock and dirt near where he was hiding, blasting huge furrows in the earth. Showers of dirt clattered down as razor-sharp shards of rock ricocheted and flew. Onscreen, Hayden poked his head up and nearly lost it for his trouble as a third wave of mortar shells came screaming in, gouging deeper into the rock with each explosion. As the smoke from the impact cleared, the shapes of men could be seen through the haze, rifles in hand, cautiously advancing.

"Not bad," Pietro said. "Those mortars are real enough—"

"The mortars are the problem," Alfredsen objected, and Major Gerard didn't stop him. "We didn't program any into the simulation."

"Didn't program them in? Then how?" Pietro looked from the scientists faces to the screen and back again. "Those are mortar shells," he said, stabbing a finger at the monitor. "Somehow they got in there, and they got in right. And you mean to tell me that you didn't put them in? Come on, what sort of bullshit do you expect me to swallow, just 'cause I'm a dumb old soldier boy?" He surged up out of his chair and took one step toward the frightened scientists. As one, they scuffled back.

"That's why we needed someone good at video games," Gerard said wearily. "We didn't put the mortars in. The simulation cooked those up itself. It just added them one day, clear out of the blue. Nearly gave a bunch of fellas out of Bragg heart attacks." He shook his head. "And that's just the tip of the iceberg. Whoever that scrawny little bastard is, I wouldn't want to be him."

Helplessly, Pietro felt his eyes return to the screen.

This, Hayden decided, was nuts. Onscreen, his virtual self hugged the dirt in what could only be described as a death grip, not daring to peek out from behind his stony shelter lest another blast catch him at exactly the wrong moment. For his part, Hayden stood motionless, just in front of the pillar that marked the middle of the room. His hands gripped the controller; his thumbs moved frantically. Otherwise, he was a statue, wide-eyed and wide-eared, listening for the whistling whine that would tell him another mortar barrage was on the way, or the stealthy tromp-tromp-tromp that would hint at a more immediate threat.

He heard the footfalls, froze, and listened. It sounded like maybe a dozen men, multiple fire teams sent out to find him and finish the job. He could hear orders shouted in Arabic or some other language he didn't know, then a different pattern of slow steps.

His ears told the story, straight and true. The bastards knew where he was and were trying to flank him. If he stayed where he was, he'd be caught and cut to ribbons. If he ran for it, they had an open firing lane on his escape route. And if he attacked . . .

He grinned and ran his fingers over the webbing of his belt (or thought he did; his eyes registered the green numbers at the bottom of the screen that might have been a user interface, might have been an ammo count, might have been a lot of things. The lines between Hayden-on-the-floor and Hayden-on-the-screen were definitely getting a little too blurry for the original's taste.). Two fragmentation grenades left. *That ought to be enough,* he thought. *And if not, well, screw what Pietro said. It's not a simulation. It's just a game.*

He reached down/shifted his thumb to the grenade

button and pulled the pin/pressed it down. A silent
count in his head, one-two-three and oh Jesus, and he
lobbed it like a softball/released the button, switching
his rifle into his hands/cycling through his weapon inventory, waiting for the moment to rise up/switch
stances and open fire/open fire on his enemies . . .

"It's fucking ballet," Major Gerard said, and nobody contradicted him. Onscreen, Hayden was wading
through the remnants of the enemy forces. The first
grenade had taken out most of one of the enemy pa-
trols, and while the survivors were still scrambling for
cover, he'd found their position and raked it with fire.
Shouts indicated that the other fire team had realized
what was going on and was preparing to open fire,
but even as they did so, Hayden threw himself down
on the sand, and the bullets whizzed harmlessly overhead. He rolled left, taking cover behind a small pile
of rocks. He squeezed off a burst that went nowhere
but made his attackers pull their heads down, then
half-rose and picked two off before cutting back right
in a series of jagged zig-zags. Angry shouts and a chatter of rifle fire rose from the remaining enemies, but
they aimed wide, and Hayden was able to throw himself behind some sturdier cover with bloodless grace.
    Pietro frowned. "So he's good at a video game.
Really good. What's the big deal?"
    Alfredsen looked at his partner and got an expres-
sion of "I did it last time." He turned to Gerard, eyes
wide and pleading. "Major?"
    "Fine." Gerard stuck a pen cap in his mouth and
chewed it furiously for perhaps three seconds. "What
would you say if I told you that the simulation should
have ended before the mortar barrage?"
    "I don't know," Pietro said, and considered the
problem for a moment. "Probably that someone
screwed up."
    "No one screwed up," Gerard said. "The program-

ming is perfect. Every other simulator in the army works fine. It's just this one."

A deep breath, a blink; Pietro resolutely refused to believe what he was sure Gerard was about to say. "Someone hacked it, then," he offered as an explanation. "Built in some new features."

Alfredsen shook his head. "We wiped the system and reinstalled from gold master and got the same results. We installed the masters from here onto a half-dozen other systems and got nothing like this. The simulator here is unique. What it does is unique. What it does—"

"—is impossible," interrupted Alfredsen's partner. "It shouldn't be doing any of this. Not the mortars, not the extra soldiers, not the new objectives—none of it."

"So the line I fed Hayden about it keeping going until it beat you and analyzed your weakness . . ."

"Was bullshit, yes," finished Gerard. "It keeps going because it wants to, and it won't stop until it's beaten you, any way it can."

The infantry had broken and run, but now there was the grinding hum of enemy vehicles chewing their way through the sand toward him. He could smell the diesel fumes leaking off them, an oily overlay to the sharp gunsmoke drifting across the battlefield.

Olfactory generation technology, Hayden told himself. Triggered releases. Don't let yourself immerse too far, don't let yourself get dragged in.

He scuttled back to the bodies of the second fire-team and scavenged three grenades and a pistol, which he took as a replacement for the one he'd lost earlier. The men of the first team were beyond hope, recognition, or usefulness, and he let them be.

He had no idea what he'd do to counter even light armor. Shoot the tires, he supposed, then roll a frag grenade underneath and hope for the best. Pop the guys inside as they tried to clamber out. He counted his rounds, twice, and both times came up with "not enough." He'd have to take a rifle, some cheap-ass AK-74 knockoff from one of the dead men. That would mean abandoning the M4 when his current mag ran out, but it would allow him to scavenge ammo, and right now that was more important than the little extra bit of stopping power the M4 gave him.

With his off hand, he reached for one of the abandoned rifles and added the item to his inventory. With it close at hand, he moved the M4 into firing position, and sighted on the driver of the jeep leading the column of APCs down the road and toward him.

Squeeze the trigger/press the button, he told himself. Gently, now . . .

"You're telling me the fucking thing wants to win? Who cares? Let it win!" Pietro was beside himself. "Hayden's right! It's video game!"

Gerard shook his head. "Negative on that. We need to know what happened here, and why, and one of the steps in figuring that out is seeing what happens when this thing loses." He took another painfully hard chomp on the pen, then pulled it out of his mouth and stared at it, almost surprised. "It hasn't lost yet, you know."

Pietro blinked. "Never?"

"Never." There was a smile hidden somewhere in Alfredsen's face. "Every single soldier who has used that simulator has found himself in a rapidly escalating situation that eventually overwhelmed him. We had you warn Hayden, more or less, so he'd keep fighting. If he knew it was supposed to stop, it would provide a fatal break in his immersion, and he'd lose."

His eyes flicked up to the screen, where virtual-Hayden had somehow managed to commandeer an enemy APC and was turning the guns of the M113 on the other vehicles. "Fatal?"

"No, no, not like that," Seymour said hurriedly. "It just gets them killed in the simulation."

"In the game," Alfredsen corrected him.

"Whatever. They lose. And we don't want him to lose."

He shrugged. "I still don't see what the big deal is. So he loses."

Gerard harrumphed deep in his throat, then tossed the pen down on the table in front of him. "If we knew it were just this simulator, Sergeant, you'd be right. But we don't. We don't know how this started. We don't know if it will spread. We can't imagine what would happen if, say, some fire control systems decided in the field that they wanted to play. So we need to figure out what's going on and how to deal with it, and the first step is beating it, if for no other reason than to prove that we can."

"But you shouldn't be able to," Pietro said softly. "It controls the simulation. It should be able to make its soldiers 100% accurate and make Hayden miss or fall down or God knows what every time. It should be over in one shot."

"Ah," said Seymour, and he barely had the decency to look embarrassed. "You see, it's made a decision. That wouldn't be fun."

The pain in his leg was not, could not be real, Hayden told himself. Just the side effect of playing one serious mindfuck of a tactical shooter. "Not even first person," he muttered to himself, and tsked at the invisible gods of war who'd made that decision.

Behind him, the wreck of his commandeered M113 still smoldered. Around it were the smoking corpses of its victims, the other members of the column laid out by fire and steel as if to escort it to the underworld. He'd barely escaped before the noble little vehicle had blown half its back end off, and he had not gotten out unscathed. Shrapnel had caught him behind the knee of his right leg, and he'd barely been able to stagger to cover while the wreck blazed merrily away.

The M4 was long gone, emptied in the initial suicidal assault that had won him the APC. One grenade was left to him, along with a half-empty AK-74 and the pistol he'd scrounged off a dead man. There were no corpses near the little stand of broken stone he'd dragged himself to, and none that he thought he could reach to scavenge before his enemies returned. He would, he decided as the sound of marching feet imposed itself on his hearing, simply have to make do.

Major Gerard frowned. "I think this is it," he said, and murmurs of sympathy from the scientists echoed around the room. Not too much sympathy, though, Pietro noticed. Part of them, he suspected, was still rooting for their insane little machine.

"What do you want me to do, sir?" Fontana asked. Pietro blinked. He hadn't been sure the man could talk.

"Nothing," Gerard said resignedly. "We have to let it play out to the bitter end."

"I'm not sure he's done yet," Pietro said. "Don't bury the man without checking his pulse first."

Seymour exploded. "He's wounded, he's almost out of ammunition, and the system has just spawned in . . ." he paused dramatically.

"Thirty-six," Fontana announced.

"Thank you. Thirty-six new enemies. There's no way he can survive."

"We'll see," Pietro said. "By the way, you never explained why you had him pretending to be a soldier."

Alfredsen at least looked embarrassed when he answered. "That was Major Gerard's idea. He didn't want anyone knowing that the Army couldn't beat its own trainer, so he wanted the man who did it to at least be identified as a soldier." He threw a glance over his shoulder at the frowning Gerard. "You actually spoiled that, I think."

Pietro opened his mouth to reply, but Fontana interjected. "Subject is engaged," he said. It was all he needed to.

A man fell, bleeding, as Hayden tossed the now-empty rifle aside. He should have let them get closer before opening fire, he told himself. Then he could have taken their guns. It was a tactical error for which he'd pay the price.

His leg throbbed with unholy pain, and he could see the blood seeping through the impromptu bandage he'd set on the savage cut. At the rate he was bleeding out, all his enemies had to do was wait.

They weren't that smart, however, or perhaps the simulation just wanted to seize victory rather than receive it. There was a barked order in the distance, and then a hail of cover fire forced him to hug the ground. They were coming, and this would be the end. They would not, he had long since decided, take him alive— the pistol would see to that. But until that became a necessity, he'd see how many of the bastards he could send to hell ahead of him to announce his arrival.

"Grenade away," Fontana announced, unnecessarily, as everyone was watching the monitor. "He's down to seven shots in the pistol."

Pietro looked around. Major Gerard was gripping the arms of his chair as if he could somehow will Hayden to victory. Seymour was impassive, a proud paternal smirk showing oh-so-faintly at the corner of his mouth. Alfredsen was fairly bouncing up and down in his excitement.

"Six shots. Enemy down. Five. Four. Another man down. They're closing on his position."

Fontana sounded tense. Pietro wondered how many

times he'd been through this. How many soldiers he'd seen fail.

"Three," Fontana said. Pietro nodded, and lifted his eyes to the monitor.

Two shots left, and they'd better count. That's what Hayden told himself. The enemy was creeping up on his position, moving behind cover of rocks and broken vehicles and the corpses of their comrades. They'd have him soon enough, though with a few more of their number gone. (*Wiped*, he told himself. *Recycled polygons. Hang onto that. Therein somehow lies salvation.*)

A face poked up, uncomfortably close, and he turned and fired into it. The man went backwards with a hole where the bridge of his nose used to be and an agonized squeal leaking from his lips. Another man jumped up and charged, perhaps to avenge his friend, and Hayden took him with a bullet to the throat.

One left, he thought. Time to end it before they get me.

He put the barrel of the pistol in his mouth, the taste of grit and oil and smoke all mingling. He held it there a moment, wondering what game over would be like, marveling at the simulation that would let him do this, ashamed that he'd lost, and then pulled the trigger.

It clicked emptily.

"No," he said, and popped the magazine. Sure enough, there was nothing left. Impossible, he thought wildly. He'd counted the bullets earlier, he'd counted them as he fired. There should have been one left. One for him. But the system had removed it, had denied him escape.

Somehow, he knew, it wanted to win. And that meant that the fucking thing was cheating.

"You little bastard," he muttered, and closed his eyes. Shut out the lie. Shut out the sim. Concentrate on what's real.

His hands clutched the plastic of the controller, now slick with sweat. He squeezed it, nearly dropped it, caught it and nearly dropped it again. He could hear the men moving closer to his position onscreen, knew that the game was about to be over and that he was going to lose. Was going to be cheated.

"He's done for, sir," Fontana said.

Major Gerard nodded. "Too bad."

"He's got one—no, he's got zero. He's out. Must be a glitch in the system."

"Something like that," Pietro said, and waited.

The controller. He held it, clutched it like a talisman. It was his link with the game, the thing that let him dive into its world, the one thing that could control another's actions inside the simulation.

"The one thing . . ."

The words trailed off even as he spoke them. He looked at the device in his hands, the product of untold time and money and effort and driven purpose. Nodded once to it, as a warrior might have nodded to a sword to be set aside after long years of service.

And whirled, and hurled the controller at the illuminated black globe that he'd been told not to touch.

It did not shatter into a million pieces. Three, perhaps, or four. The globe, for its part, was not damaged at all, at least not so far as Hayden could tell.

The simulation, however, froze. Hayden looked up. His avatar was there, enemies upon him, bloody rags around his leg, but none moved. None could move, not with the controller gone.

He would not beat the machine, not this day. But the machine would not beat him, not ever.

Pietro wasn't sure if it was Seymour yammering in his ear or Alfredsen, but it was obvious that Major Gerard had ordered the hapless Corporal Fontana out of his seat and was trying desperately to figure out what had just happened.

"You got what you wanted, Major," he said. "The simulation can't win. Not now, not ever. It's frozen. Locked, unless you want to bring in another controller and try to calibrate it, but I don't think you'll have a lot of luck with that. I'm not even sure why you'd try."

Gerard shot him a look of disgust. "He was supposed to beat the machine, not just . . . stall it."

Pietro grinned humorlessly. "He did beat it. The same way it beat everyone else. He changed the rules." He sketched a salute. "With permission, Major, I'll go get him out of there."

"You do that," Gerard said, and turned back to the console, the fluttering scientists beside him, the man who'd brought them to this already forgotten.

Pietro moved toward the door. As he did, Fontana nodded, once. He understood. They'd be at it again tomorrow, no doubt. But he and Pietro, they shared the secret of why Hayden had won today.

Reiteration

By Simon Brown

Simon Brown's most recent books are *Rival's Son*, the second book in the Chronicles of Kydan, and its concluding volume, *Daughter of Independence*, both published by DAW Books. Simon's short story collection *Troy* came out from Ticonderoga Publications in 2006. Simon lives with his wife and two children on the south coast of New South Wales.

Captain Don Cayetano Gravina of the *Asunción*, Spanish naval officer and a Particulate of the Novae, did not sail out of Cadiz with the Combined Fleet because his first crew went down with apple disease. The first hint was the flushing faces of the officers sharing with him the quarterdeck of the *Asunción*. Gravina first assumed their cheeks were blooming with excitement, but when his lieutenant of marines fell sideways, convulsed and spat blood, he studied him quickly in infrared and saw how hot his skin was, and realized the capillaries under his skin were disintegrating. Then the rest of his crew on the quarterdeck tumbled and fell, and when Gravina went below he found they had all died. All his poor humans.

It was the flushing skin, the rosy cheeks, moments before death that gave the disease its vernacular name, belying its lethal nature and its artificial source. Gravina complained, of course, but the umpire was not inclined to listen; he was captain and therefore responsible for the security and safety of his crew. Gravina accepted the judgement, admitting to himself he had never considered that his human enemies—the original creators of the Novae—would attack so cruelly and dispassionately members of their own species. After all, he was the appropriate target, not the bags of flesh and blood the Novae used to lend their games some verisimilitude.

However, the day was still young, and he did not think all was lost, even though the rest of the Combined Fleet had left Cadiz at dawn. He sterilized the ship, using search-and-destroy nanos of his own design, then warmed up the second crew, downloaded into their brains the instructions they needed to sail a 32-gun frigate and enough memories to keep them happy and unquestioning for the duration of their service. It was still seventeen hours before noon, the yellow-white sun only halfway up the bruised sky, when the new crew, delivered by launches, stiffly clambered on board and took their posts. Gravina initiated awareness, and as if they had never been anywhere else, the crew bustled into activity, raising the anchors and clambering up ratlines to unfurl the sails.

Soon, her shoulder set to the sea, *Asunción* glided out of Cadiz, heading south toward Gibraltar, a blustery easterly driving her on, her bow wave lost in the swell. If the wind kept up, Gravina was sure they would catch the fleet before long. He searched keenly for their tops over the horizon but resisted the temptation to use his own machine-built abilities to find them.

"What is the point of Reiteration if one cheats?" he wondered aloud, and ignored the curious glances from his officers.

* * *

It was a curious thing, Ignatio knew, but the woman was not where she was supposed to be. He had heard Frederico, foul and fat Frederico, whisper to Antonio that he had hidden her in the tiller room on the mess deck, behind the purser's cabin, and Ignatio had gone to steal a peek at her, wondering if she would be foul and fat like Frederico, or beautiful like all women were in his dreams. But she had not been there, and as much as Ignatio disliked Frederico, he knew the fellow was not stupid or forgetful. He even checked under the canvas sheet over the hardtack, just in case, his boy's heart a-flutter, but there was nothing there but bread, not even a female weevil.

A midshipman, not much older than he, caught him and kicked him out. Ignatio nodded and scuttled, but he cursed under his breath. When he got back to his proper station near the aft magazine he could feel a bruise over his tailbone and cursed again, this time damning Frederico for being stupid and forgetful after all.

The wind changed to a southeaster, and *Asunción,* maybe the fastest ship in the Combined Fleet, slowed to no more than five knots. Gravina, who had programmed himself to experience data jams at such times, understood it was not a true substitute for the frustration a human might feel under similar circumstances, but it made him more slow and stiff-jointed. He stomped along the quarterdeck, making sure not to put any holes through the timber.

"Sail, Captain!" shouted one of the boys in the tops. "Straight south!"

Gravina immediately cleared all data and focused on the horizon. The lad was right. Two sails at least, but he could not let the crew know he could see that far. "How many?"

"Three or four, Captain!"

The lad's eyes needed readjusting; Gravina made a mental note to order repair work the next time the boy was in storage.

"Can you make out their colors?"

"Ours, Captain! We've caught the fleet, sir!"

A half-hearted cheer went up from the crew, who wanted the assurance of the Combined Fleet around them but knew its purpose was to bring the enemy to battle.

Too soon, Gravina told himself. *We've come up on them too soon.* He used his superior vision to scan the ships ahead more closely. They were running ragged before the wind. Not enough crew to sail them properly. At almost the same time, another boy cried down, "Smoke, Captain! Smoke! Southeast!"

Ignatio heard the drums roll to clear the frigate for action. He helped stow the paneling and furniture from the captain's cabin, then took two gunpowder cartridges from the handlers in the magazine and with one under each arm ran to his station by the sternmost port gun, an 18-pounder. Antonio, the gun captain, smiled encouragingly, but Frederico, the loader, took the cartridges from him with a grunt and shoved him aside.

Ignatio stood at his post, wishing orders would be given to run the guns out so he could at least catch a glimpse of the outside world through the gunport. Some light came from the open gangway to the quarterdeck, throwing a hatched shadow across his station that swung to and fro as the *Asunción* rolled with the waves. The crew was strangely quiet. Frederico sniffed. A goat bleated from one of the longboats being towed behind the ship.

Ignatio hoped the most noble Captain Don Cayetano Gravina knew what he was about. He reminded himself he had been in battle before under Gravina, but somehow the details eluded his memory. Undoubtedly they would come through victorious, heroes all, and be given a wonderful welcome back in Cadiz. He hoped some of the women there would take him in hand and treat him with the respect he would deserve.

Gravina received a tight-beam transmission from Captain Jean-Jacques Lucas of the *Redoubtable,* the larger of the two escaping ships. She had all her masts, but most of her sails had been torn and the hull had been holed below the waterline; water poured from the dales as her pumps were worked continuously by her crew to help keep her afloat. Her companion, the *Pluton,* was not much better off. The English fleet— the *human* fleet—had won. Again.

"This time the English admiral even survived my sharpshooters," Lucas added.

Gravina would have sighed if he were human. It would seem the Novae—so superior in so many ways, who held the fate of the Sphere and its countless inhabited star systems in their hands—still had far to go before they could match the human capacity to take advantage from chaos.

In the Sphere itself it mattered little: the Novae were designed to exploit the vast distances and inimical environment of space, and with their fugueships they could restrict humanity to any planet they desired. But what if the Novae should encounter another biological species, one as innovative and curious as the humans but even more technologically advanced? And so these games, these Reiterations, where their human opponents might earn glory and riches, and the Novae experience and understanding. But no matter how many times they met in combat, the humans always seemed to have some intellectual resource at their disposal that the Novae had not yet learned to program for or to counter. Gravina believed it had something to do with the way humans experienced emotion. Although the Novae had feelings—all sen-

tient creatures must have some method of absorbing
and adapting and responding to events—there was de-
monstrably a distinction between the kind and range
of emotions felt by humans and Novae.

Then Lucas gave Gravina the news that made him
focus more sharply on the present.

"We are being pursued," Lucas signaled as *Redoubtable* and *Asuncion* drew away from each other.
"It is the *Mars*."

"I will intercept it."

"Stay clear, Captain. *Mars* has claimed more than one
prize this day. Do not add to its list of captured ships."

Gravina did not bother responding. This was an opportunity for him to learn something new from the
enemy and to show to all the Novae—including Jean-
Jacques Lucas of the *Redoubtable*—his individual
worth as a Particulate.

He turned to his officers, saw the grave looks on
their faces as they watched the retreating ships sail
north toward the safety of Cadiz. They were afraid
but struggling hard to hide it.

How do they do it? he wondered. How do these
terrified, chemical-driven creatures do it?

He smiled for them. "Be hearty, my friends. We
have not been left out. An enemy or two remains
afloat on which we may practice our gunnery."

Ignatio knew they would soon be in combat when
Asunción changed direction, her bow swinging so
sharply he felt himself lurch slightly, and the order
was given to run out the guns. Frederico wedged open
the port, and the 18-pounder was pulled into place
with ropes and handspikes. Ignatio peered through the
port and at first saw only a rush of blue, as dark as
ink, and then the horizon swung down as the ship
righted, the sky so bright it made him blink.

"What is it?" Frederico asked Antonio, but the gun
captain just shrugged.

What a fool Frederico is, Ignatio thought. How could Antonio know any more than he? And then he saw the round bee-striped hull of an English ship heave into view. "Jesus protect me," he said under his breath, and touched the crucifix hanging from his neck.

"What is it?" Frederico demanded again, this time of the boy.

"Three decks," Ignatio said, almost whispering. And then he saw the ship more clearly as it's full size came into view. "No. Two. It is a 74."

There was a dull boom, a puff of smoke from just one of the enemy's guns, and then two seconds later a shot splash no more than a ship's length short of the *Asunción*. Cold water sprayed through the open gunport and Ignatio gasped in surprise.

Frederico leaned over the gun to peer out of the port. "God, we're going to die," he said matter-of-factly.

"Gauging the distance, I expect," said *Asunción*'s first officer.

Gravina was not so sure. If the *Mars* had already taken prizes, then her captain obviously knew how to estimate distance and knew how accurate his own gun crews must be. What was he trying to prove by it? It was a waste of a first shot, the best loaded in any battle.

Asunción was using its speed and agility in an attempt to get behind *Mars* and rake her from behind. For all its victories, the English ship had not gone unscathed. One mast hung over the ship like a fallen tree, tangling rigging and sails, and he could see crew struggling to cut it loose and send it overboard. There were a few holes along the hull, and the quarterdeck looked a mess, with splintered railings and a broken wheel. As well, there were hardly any sailors or marines about, although Gravina allowed that could be a ruse.

And what had that single shot been about? Perhaps the captain was trying to fool Gravina into thinking most of his starboard guns were out of action, or that he was desperate, but there was not enough damage there to tempt Gravina to close from that direction.

Nevertheless, *Mars* was wounded, and her crew must be depleted if some were sent to secure her prizes from the earlier battle, and the remainder near exhaustion. *Asunción* was fresh and fast. Perhaps all that was needed was a broadside or two down her length and *Mars* might be ripe for boarding. *That would almost be audacious enough for a human,* Gravina thought.

Antonio clapped Ignatio on the shoulder. "Go. Another two cartridges. I think we will need them."

Ignatio nodded, ran to the gangway and descended two levels to the orlop deck, then back to the aft magazine. The fixer in the magazine automatically handed him a cartridge through the damp curtain. Ignatio stuck his hand through and showed two fingers, but the hand was slapped away, and another powder monkey behind him pushed him aside. "Yours is not the only gun," the boy said.

Ignatio did not argue. Even as he turned to go back another two had joined the queue. As he got to the gangway, the ship shuddered. He heard a sound like a bull coughing (*and what did a bull look like?* a part of his brain wondered), and he had to hold onto a step to stop falling over. The cartridge dropped from his grip, started to roll away. He bent over to pick it up, and the powder monkey who had pushed at him clambered past.

Ignatio spat, retrieved the cartridge and raced after him. By the time he reached the gun deck, he had almost caught him, and tapped the other's heel to prove the point. He turned to get to his own station and stopped. The gun was gone.

* * *

Gravina almost barked in delight at the cleverness of it. The broken mast on *Mars* had been a ruse. Oh, it was snapped alright, but not tangled at all. As soon *Asunción* was committed, it had been pushed over the side with hardly any effort at all, and the warship for all its size turned almost as quickly as the much smaller frigate. Before Gravina could correct his mistake, *Mars* had fired a full broadside. Only the stern dozen or so of the enemy's guns had the angle to hit the *Asunción*, but that included a few 32-pounders, and Gravina could hear the shot break through his hull and bounce around the deck beneath. There was a terrible hush, and then the screaming started. His regard for his own humans made him consider decommissioning them, but even their pain and suffering might teach the Novae something about the species, something that might explain their incredible endurance and tenacity.

The frigate had now rounded the stern of the enemy ship, and as each of its 18-pounders lined up, it fired, sending shot the size of a grapefruit crashing through glass windows and galleries and then running down the length of the ship's middle deck, dismembering any human it struck.

Gravina was so delighted at the success of the raking broadside that he did not pay any attention to the enemy's poop deck, nor the five marines lining up at the railing. The first thing he knew about it was the sound of his first officer groaning and then falling to the deck. Then something struck him in the leg. He never felt pain as such, but he was very aware of emergency nanobots rushing to repair any damage. He turned to see the signals lieutenant looking at the body of the first officer and then at Gravina. "He's dead," the lieutenant said numbly, and then, pointing at Gravina's leg, "and Captain, you're shot." Gravina looked down, saw the hole in his stocking near what would have been his shin bone had he been human. He immediately ordered blood to flow. A small diaphragm burst behind his knee, sending a stream of artificial blood to the hole. Another ball struck the body of the first officer, making his coat puff out, but by the time Gravina turned his attention to the enemy marines, *Asunción* was clear of *Mars* and they were no longer a threat.

"Send him over," Gravina ordered the lieutenant, nodding to the first officer, and gripped the railing as if he could no longer stand without assistance.

"Sir, you should go below."

"I will decide when I go below, Lieutenant. Carry out your orders."

The lieutenant nodded, and with the help of a midshipman carried the slain officer to the railing and lifted the corpse over so it fell into the sea.

Ignatio saw at once that his gun crew was gone, every one dead. Even Antonio, torn and bloody, who had always seemed invincible to the boy. The only way he could identify Frederico was the tattoo on his right forearm; the head was missing completely. He stood there for a moment, bewildered but surprisingly calm. He should tell someone. The officers will want to know. He put the gunpowder cartridge down carefully, and searched for the deck officer. Another powder monkey told him the deck officer had been wounded and taken down to the surgeon. "You'll have to go to the quarterdeck to find any officer alive and walking," the boy said.

Ignatio climbed the gangway, and stood blinking in bright sunlight. *Asuncion* was wearing around to bring her back toward the stern of the enemy ship, the crew working frantically on the rigging and yards. There was sand on the deck and the smell of black powder and . . . he did not know at first, and then a part of his brain said it was blood and excreta, and he thought he *should* have known that without thinking. He saw Captain Don Cayetano Gravina leaning against the railing near the stern of the ship, blood soaking his right leg below the knee.

"Please, God," Ignatio prayed aloud. "Not *him*."

The captain looked in his direction as if he had heard the words, and stared at him as if he did not recognize Ignatio at all.

Why should he? Ignatio asked himself, but feeling hurt nonetheless.

Then something changed in the captain's expression, and he waved the boy forward. Ignatio went to him and, not knowing what to do with his hands, held them stiffly by his side.

"You are Ignatio Mendez," the man said.

"Yes, Captain. At least, I am Ignatio."

"You are not at your post."

"It is gone, Captain."

"Ah, I see. Then stand behind me. I would not have you shot needlessly."

Ignatio smiled, as if God himself had blessed him. To stand behind the captain himself! This was . . .

His attention was caught by a series of flashes from the enemy ship, then the sound of many cannon firing.

"Hold on, boy," the captain said.

Ignatio could see the balls arching towards them. Even as he watched, they hit the water, one after the other, about two-thirds of the distance between the two ships, then skipped into the air again. He watched the closest until it disappeared beneath the rise of the quarterdeck and he felt the hull shudder with the impact. The next slapped onto the quarterdeck and bounced into the sea on the other side, causing no damage at all. Then the ship vibrated with another blow. And that was it.

"Well and good," the captain said as *Asunción*

moved away from the firing arc of *Mars*' broadside
and towards its stern for a second pass. "And now it
is our turn again."

As soon as the battle commenced, Gravina had
opened a link to the Novae. What happened would
be recorded and analyzed by millions of his kind for
a hundred years, more if he won the battle, something
that occurred not nearly as frequently as they had expected when these Reiterations were first started
nearly ten thousand years before. They never had any
difficulty recruiting humans to play the enemy, but
despite tangible rewards they were rarely able to re-
cruit humans to fight for them. In the end their biological warriors had to be vat grown and implanted with
memories made up from tens of millions of interro-
gated, tortured, duped, drugged and dissected humans.

At first, the link brought little attention, but after
Asunción's first successful pass behind *Mars*, the con-
nections had picked up. Gravina did a quick count
and was impressed. Nearly three per cent of the Novae
in this system were doing nothing except watching the
progress of his battle, something like seven million of
them, including many in fugueships in orbit around
this planet.

Gravina ordered his marines, and those sailors that
could be spared, to prepare a boarding party. As soon
as his second broadside struck *Mars,* he would order
a general assault. All they needed to do was clear the
poop and quarterdeck and they could keep the enemy
from regaining control; then the ship would be recognized by the umpire as his prize. Many of his human
enemies would then commit suicide rather than become prisoners of the Novae, something Gravina
would regret but at the same time admire.

And then he noticed *Asunción* was coming up on
Mars much too quickly, as if the frigate had suddenly
and inexplicably accelerated. It took even his mind a

fraction of a second to realize it was the enemy ship closing the distance by the simple expedient of swinging the yards so the sails backfilled, slowing the ship and then pushing her sternward. He glanced up and saw a mass of enemy marines ready to board *Asunción,* far more than he calculated *Mars* should be carrying.

Gravina shouted for the guns to fire, but it was too late. The gun crews, taken by surprise, aimed badly, and only two shots actually the struck the enemy ship. Then ropes and hooks dropped onto the deck of *Asunción,* and the enemy came, shouting, screaming, hating, all of them making for Gravina.

He defended himself more than ably, killing several humans, but in the end one of them managed to pierce his neck with the point of a cutlass and then release the nanostream that would counter and then overwhelm his own defences. Almost immediately he felt his upper mental functions degrade. The enemy pulled back, sensing he was destroyed and there was nothing more they could do to hasten it. Gravina slowly slumped to the deck of his lovely *Asunción,* brave *Asunción,* and saw the face of Ignatio Mendez. The boy was crying, struggling in the arms of his captors. Gravina found himself hoping they would treat Ignatio well; it did not always happen that way—in the heat of battle humans were crueler to their own kind than the Novae had ever been—but sometimes they were gentle with children.

The last thing he realized, as the link with the Novae broke up and then dissolved with the ceramic architecture of the brain case held behind his armored chest, was that the feeling he had for the boy was totally unexpected. No doubt the result of the chaos of his consciousness evaporating with his life, but it occurred to him that the feeling was almost human.

It was the last thought he ever had.

Stalking Old John Bull

By Jean Rabe

Jean Rabe is the author of more than twenty novels and more than forty short stories. In addition, she has edited several DAW anthologies. When she's not writing (which isn't often), she delights in the company of her two aging dogs, dangles her feet in her backyard goldfish pond, and pretends to garden. She loves museums, books, boardgames, role-playing games, wargames, and movies that "blow up real good." Visit her web site at: www.jeanrabe.com.

I spent my thirteenth birthday in the Thornton Street Cemetery off Westgate in Newcastle-upon-Tyne, watching them lower my father into the ground. Barely listening to the service, I was numb and angry and filled with thoughts no one my age should have. Two-hundred and fifty square yards of land, and my father's grave sat roughly in the middle of it, shaded by an elm with knobby, ugly roots. There was a plot reserved next to it for my mother, who was buried a month later, dead of a broken heart. I used what money they'd saved up in a pantry jar to buy them a small stone, rosy marble and shiny as wet glass— something I thought I might like on my own grave. But the cemetery would fill up for decades before I could return to England and join them.

My father was a welder at Robert Stephenson and Company, a place I'd planned to work when I finished the eighth grade. The company made locomotives, and the one my father welded on—when a massive curl of iron being laid over the engine fell and crushed his chest—was bound for the Camden & Amboy Railroad in the United States of America.

The demon responsible for my parents' deaths was finished on June 18th, 1831. I began stalking it a few weeks later when I pinched some money from the aunt I'd been foisted upon and bought a new change of clothes and a ticket to Liverpool. There, I managed to slip on board the *Allegheny,* the ship they'd crated the demon in. A lot of people boarded that July morning, almost all of them workers from what I could tell, and I was small and quick and squirmed my way through them without getting caught. I found a place to hide in the cargo hold, where once we were at sea— and after three solid days of retching from seasickness— I began my mission.

Had I not been so young, I might not have directed my ire at the locomotive. I might have realized that it wasn't truly a demon, that it was just a machine, some huge metal steam contraption that burned wood and didn't think or feel and that wasn't capable of doing anything on its own. I might have instead singled out Robert Stephenson himself, who could not be bothered to come to my father's funeral, or the men holding the iron sheet they'd let drop. I even might have accepted that it was all just a horrible accident, that terrible things happen to good people, and that nothing I could do would bring my father and mother back.

But I was only thirteen and so did not think like a rational man. I was strong-minded, born of an anger I could not comprehend at the time, childish and reckless. Impetuous, puerile, frightened, angry, and confused—I was all of those things, too, and more in that miserable year. Above everything, I was lonely and filled with a profound grief I could not master, and I was determined to destroy the iron demon that had ruined my perfect world.

Perhaps I thought slaying it would ease my pain.

It took me an entire day to find the crates the sections of the locomotive were stored in, two days more to discover an oddly thin box that was filled with the diagrams for assembling the engine. I studied the papers, only halfway understanding how the pieces would go together and not at all understanding how it was intended to operate.

I memorized what I could, because I wanted to know my enemy and because I had little else to occupy me in the hold. According to the diagrams, the driver diameter was fifty-four inches, and the tender weighed ten tons. The height, to the top of its smoke stack, was a little more than eleven feet, with a width of seven feet, eight inches, and a length of thirty-six feet. It had eighty-two boiler tubes and a boiler pressure of sixty pounds per square inch.

I learned that the boiler consisted of a brass casting mounted to the top of a low dome above a firebox. Like the early "Bury boiler," it allowed for more steam room. In later years I would learn that a cylindrical boiler would produce higher steam pressure. Also in those later years I would learn quite a lot more about trains.

I must have studied the diagrams a hundred times before I tore them into tiny pieces—an act that only temporarily quenched my rage. And, making several trips so I wouldn't stop up anything and draw attention to myself, I washed the bits down a drain in a bathroom I found on the lowest level.

Without the diagrams, I knew the engineers in New Jersey could not get the demon running. And so I settled into my hidey-hole, emerging to find food when I was hungry, to borrow clothes the crew inadvertently left out, and to explore when nearly everyone else slept.

I spent the time dreaming of where I would go and what I might do in America.

Sometimes I spent it thinking about the demon.

And after a month—I was guessing at the passing of days—I worried that perhaps the American engineers could indeed reconstruct it, or at the very least would contact the Robert Stephenson and Company and ask for another set of plans.

I hadn't the tools or the strength to demolish the large iron pieces; I found it difficult enough even to open the crates. But I managed to take many of the smaller parts out and drop them over the side late at night, burying them at sea as the demon had buried my father, resealing the crates and again dreaming of what America would hold for me.

We docked in September at the mouth of the Delaware River in Philadelphia. I scurried onto the shore and watched them reload the crates onto a river schooner. It was evening, and the water was dark and smooth, and tugs anchored on the opposite side had lights burning, an oily yellow color I found unsettling. From somewhere up the bank behind me I heard music, an unfamiliar but pleasing tune, and soft laughter. I thought about heading in that direction and finding something to eat.

I knew I'd rendered the demon useless and so should move on with my life in this new world. But a part of me couldn't let it go. And so rather than discover the wonders of Pennsylvania, I hid aboard the boat, which traveled up river to an unsightly place called Bordentown, New Jersey. I didn't care for the city, but I had to stay, wanting to hear of the railroad men's frustration that the locomotive would not work. I needed to relish my victory, and I needed to make some money to survive.

I delivered newspapers and groceries, staying in a

dilapidated three-storey boarding house and made a few friends who were a year or two older than me. I saved all of my coins and considered purchasing passage west . . . I'd read so much about Colorado in the paper and in magazines we'd rescue from the drugstore trash bins! But there were unpleasant tidbits slipping out of the rail yards, and so I couldn't leave yet.

I cut near the yards on my various routes, tarrying to talk to engineers, professing great interest in them and their work, and being rewarded with grand tales of America's growing railways.

I learned that American engineers were indeed clever. One named Isaac Dripps, who sometimes shared his sandwich with me, managed to piece the engine together, despite the lack of diagrams. And he'd managed to acquire replacement parts for the ones I'd commended to the ocean.

I also learned that they called the engine "Number 1," as it was New Jersey's first, then officially christened it "Stevens," as that was the last name of Camden & Amboy's president. But Dripps and the other railroad men had a different name for it—The Old John Bull— after some cartoon rendering that referred to England. "Stevens" didn't take, but John Bull did.

Dripps proudly showed the demon to me one late October afternoon. The ghastly thing puffed in all its glory. It was a black and gray monster gleaming dully in the sun, stinking and hissing and belching steam into a bright blue sky. I gagged at the scent of it, eyes locked onto the welds that my father had made, the curl of iron that had taken his breath and then claimed my mother, taken everyone and everything that meant something to me.

I glared at its four-wheels and piston rods hooked to the crank on its rear axle. I spat at the front drivers locked to the rear ones by more rods. I felt my chest grow tight, my lungs filled with the horrid, acrid plumes, my eyes burning from the heat. I couldn't speak, my throat and mouth had gone dry.

I was thoroughly consumed with anger—at the demon that hadn't died and at myself because I hadn't managed to slay it. I tarried around the track so much after that, quietly seething. Most of the men got to know me, thinking me some wide-eyed boy in love with trains. And on November 1st a foreman offered me hard, hurtful work that paid no better than delivering newspapers and groceries. I immediately accepted, wanting to be close to "John Bull," where I knew I would find an opportunity to destroy it.

The C & A hadn't enough track at first to operate the locomotive. However, I and others worked long hours to construct a sufficient length. And while we sweated and ached, and while our fingers cracked and bled, the engineers started designing more locomotives patterned after the Bull. They made their own frames, wheels, and boilers, but they ordered other parts from Stephenson in England.

It was later in my first month at the C & A, November the 12th, that New Jersey politicians and some local aristocrats, among them Prince Murat—Napoleon's nephew—were invited for rides on a "test track" we'd laid out. I was in the crowd watching when Murat's wife dashed on board, announcing that she wanted to be remembered as the first woman to ride a steam-driven train in the States.

She didn't know—no one did—that I'd sabotaged it, chiseling away at the wood drivers, sending slivers into my calloused fingers and knowing that I would keep it from rolling on the track I'd helped build.

But again I'd been thwarted. The C & A chief engineer had replaced the broken wood drivers with ones made of harder wood laced with metal stringers along the top. He hadn't spotted my foul work, I later learned, and had all along intended to replace them because America's iron tracks were different from those used in England. Sturdier drivers were necessary to handle this country's uneven terrain.

And so the demon gave the politicians and Napoleon's relatives a ride.

And so I went back to scheming John Bull's demise.

My work on track laying was poor, on purpose, and the following spring would prove to cause blessed problems that brought a rare smile to my face. The Bull had what was called a 0-4-0 rigid wheel arrangement, and so it derailed on curves . . . where I'd shoddily earned my wage.

Over and over the engine slipped from the tracks.

I'd thought this would cause the railroad owners to retire it and replace it with something else. Retiring it would be acceptable, I'd convinced myself. Retiring it and melting it down and sending it to the deepest pits of hell.

But the engineers added pilot wheels to the Bull. Hooking them with wooden beams to the front axle, they allowed the engine to turn ever-so-slightly, which solved the derailing issue. Still, they had to remove the rods connecting the front and back drivers, a move I thought would cripple the Bull, but instead only changed its configuration to a 4-2-0, meaning only the back two wheels of the locomotive were powered. It was a more efficient design . . . one I'd brought about through my terror campaign.

I'd managed to damage the boiler several times, slipping into the yard late at night and using tools that had not been locked away. I smashed dials, ruined the engineer's seat, broke couplings, and more. Each time they repaired it, and the newspaper carried articles about vandals terrorizing C & A. Night watchmen were hired, and so my forays to directly sabotage the demon had been curtailed. Police patrolled the yards more frequently, and I had to take another approach.

I bought just enough stock so I could attend share-

holder's meetings if I desired—so I could keep up on
news about John Bull and the other engines. Then I
quit the railway and traveled from town to town along
the Bull's route, finding odd jobs to pay for food and
clothes and supplies I used to unsuccessfully ruin the
rails. I remember a night in Indiana. I was sixteen
then, almost seventeen, and everything I owned was
in a worn canvas satchel I lugged with me. I sat on a
rise, looking down on the tracks, the breeze cool on
the back of my neck and blowing my scraggly hair . . .
I cut it myself with a pocketknife, so it was uneven
and sometimes almost comical looking. I fixed my eyes
on the line, blackest-black under a half-full moon.

I drew my knees in close to my chest and rested
my hands around my ankles. I tipped my face up and
closed my eyes and listened. A few miles outside of
the nearest town there were no people-sounds, just
the rustle of tall grass and the occasional snap of a
twig from the trees behind me. I imagined deer and
wild pigs were moving around, and I wondered what
it would have been like to have been one of the first
settlers in this place, living off the land and not worrying about demon-trains.

People in those earlier days didn't have to contend
with machines that killed and drove men like me mad
with obsession. They lived in harmony with all of nature. I heard the burble of a stream, and I thought I
might like to go wading when my task was done here.

And I heard the low, musical moo of a cow, and
then another.

I'd broke down a farm fence about a mile away and
managed to heard a half-dozen cows out onto the
track, coaxing them to stay with bales of sweet hay to
chew on. I saw the largest raise its head and look at
me, and in that instant I felt sorry for what was to
happen. In fact, I almost got up and went down to the
track to pull them away.

But then I heard John Bull coming, and I eased

back and waited with dark anticipation. The train surged around the corner and struck the cows, a sickening, horrifying sound. It was dark down by the tracks, but there was just enough light from the moon so I could see the cows being ripped apart and pulled under the engine. Maybe I didn't see it all, only imagined seeing the life go out of their large eyes and blood pool on the ground around the derailed John Bull and the tracks, blood looking like oil in the moonlight. The engineer climbed down, blood on his overalls and his hands, streaks of blood on the shirt of the man who stoked the boiler.

I hadn't intended to injure the people on the train, just the train itself, and I felt the bile rise into my mouth as the engine hissed and popped and more people piled off. Their conversations climbed up the rise like a cloud of buzzing insects, and I hurried away, not wanting to be seen and wanting to find the stream and wash away the malevolent memory.

More than once after that I broke farm fences and lured cows out onto the tracks, each time stopping the Bull, but not ending its run.

C & A retaliated by yet another improvement to the demon that continued to vex me. They attached a pilot, what some dubbed a 'cow catcher' to keep animals and other obstructions (I'd pushed old cars and rolled logs onto the tracks on several occasions) from going under the wheels and damaging the engine. Next came a headlamp that burned whale oil and let them operate more easily on the tracks at night—and let them see the obstacles I'd planted in time to stop. I'd heard they'd taken the lamp off a riverboat. A warning bell that could be rung from the engine was big and beautiful and loud, and thwarted another of my attempts to interfere with the Old John Bull.

In my eighteenth year they added an earsplitting, shrill whistle that signaled the crew to problems with the track, a safety valve that kept the boiler from shut-

ting down, and a cab that comfortably covered the
engine crew and protected them from storms. All
these "improvements" were due to my efforts to stop
the damnable John Bull. I cursed myself that I was
responsible for a better, stronger train, that I had
given the demon I chased more power and fueled up-
grades throughout the entire railway industry.

But I vowed that I would not stop in my mission to
see John Bull obliterated.

I celebrated my nineteenth birthday in Illinois, trying to set fire to the damnable thing. I would have
been successful, as there was a significant amount of
oil in the engine . . . and I'd added to it. But C & A
had hired security to ride along on the trip, and I
barely escaped them. From a safe distance, I watched
them put out the fire.

Again the engineers reacted to my attempted sabotage, constructing a bonnet stack that had screens and
baffles designed to catch sparks that might start a
blaze. And they built a covered tender with eight
wheels that would carry wood and water and that de-
fied my attempts to cause further damage.

I allowed myself no time for friends or family and
only enjoyed the silky touch of a woman when I took
my money to the poor side of a town. I had no opportunity to pursue any of the dreams about America I'd
once entertained while riding from England in the
belly of the Allegheny. The Bull did not afford me
any chance of normalcy.

It continued to consume me and bedevil me.

Through the Civil War I pursued it, avoiding serving
in the Army, as I did not exist on paper in the States,
and I looked older than my years. Before that war
was over, the Bull had been assigned simple switching
duties at stations and occasional stationary boiler service. I'm certain all my tireless work had contributed
to that.

I'd finally crippled the Old John Bull.

They retired it just after my forty-eighth birthday, the railway owners finally giving me some measure of peace.

I made my way back to Bordertown, New Jersey, intending to watch the Bull's demolition and allow my soul to have its pleasure. I'd seated myself in a booth at a diner, ordered a ginger ale in a blue glass bottle, and opened the newspaper. Its look had changed little since I'd delivered it more than three decades past. The sun had gone down an hour ago, and the shadows were swallowing the storefronts and spreading out onto the street. Lights were flickering on in second- and third-floor apartments, people home from work and settling in for the night.

On the front page the reporter detailed what was to be America's first act of historic railroad preservation— the Bull was to be placed in storage, not torn apart or melted down and sent to the hell it so rightly deserved. It was to be cherished and admired.

A piece of American history put on display courtesy of England and my father.

I had no appetite for the roast beef the doughy waitress sat in front of me. I pushed the plate away and read and reread the article, the color leaving my knuckles as I squeezed my hands tight. I scraped my meal into my napkin and fed a skinny dog in the alley. Then I climbed four flights of stairs to my rented room and stared in the bathroom mirror. All the intensity had leached from my eyes, which looked like chunks of coal, hard and distant and unreadable. My face had an odd and serene cast.

The C & A merged with the New Jersey Railroad three years later, establishing the United New Jersey Railroad and Canals Company, and garnering me more money than I ever thought possible. That stock that I'd purchased a while back . . . now seemed a very good time to cash it in.

A few years after that, the United New Jersey Rail-road was swallowed up by the Pennsylvania. John Bull was the Pennsylvania's oldest asset, and in 1876 I watched them set the old engine out alongside the new shiny ones. Some company official thought my demon didn't look antique enough, and so paid to remove the cab that once sheltered the engineer from storms and shave the tender from eight wheels down to four. Good money was spent replacing solid pilot wheels (which had been installed because of my clever and malicious work on the rails) with undersized spoked ones. Lastly, they peeled away the bonnet stack and instead put in its place something that prob-ably came from a retired river steamer.

It wasn't the same demon anymore; it was a sickly shadow of what I'd once pursued.

I was sixty-three and walking with a cane when I heard that the Bull was commanding center stage at the National Railway Appliance Exposition in Chi-cago. I went, and the year after, I followed it to the Smithsonian Institution in Washington, D.C.

It was in 1893, shortly before my seventy-fifth birth-day, that I took my last venture outside a room I rented behind a Bordentown bakery that made the best rye bread I'd ever tasted. The Pennsylvania Rail-road somehow had talked the officials at the Smith-sonian into lending out the Old John Bull. Under its own steam, my demon traveled to Chicago, where it gleamed dully black and gray at the Columbian Exposition.

We were two old men, John Bull and I, staring each other down in that massive exhibit yard. Neither of us had weathered the decades all that well, but I knew my iron adversary would outlive me . . . unless I could finally, finally do something about that.

I would do something about that.

I was oblivious to the crowd and the noise, the buzz of conversations that swirled around me and my demon. I walked its length, climbing into a passenger car after purchasing a ticket, and easing myself down on a cracked leather seat. I don't suppose the fairgoers were supposed to sit—look, not touch seemed to be the watchwords in the Exposition. But no one said anything to me.

I'm not sure how long I spent there, several minutes, maybe an hour, occasionally running my fingers along the window and the seat in front of me. In all these years I'd never ridden the train, though I'd been on it often enough in my efforts to destroy it. Some part of me wished I had taken such a trip, ridden in the belly of the demon. I closed my eyes and leaned back, finding the seat uncomfortable. When a mother and two children walked past me, chattering about what it must have been like to ride the Old John Bull, I got up and went out, then climbed into the engine— no mean feat taking those big steps with my aged legs.

The controls were as I'd remembered them, but the big engineer's seat was different . . . replaced after I'd sliced it up, and most certainly replaced again in the ensuing decades. I could almost feel John Bull move, standing there and looking out the front, almost feel it rocking on the tracks I'd laid in my youth.

It was sad, in a way, that my quest to destroy it would end this night.

I wondered if I would miss chasing my demon.

I left the Exposition and returned to my hotel room, napping for a few hours before going down to the dining room for a late dinner and ordering a lobster tail and a bottle of their most expensive French wine. I'd finished my meal and was debating whether to order desert when the waiter brought a rumpled-looking young man to my table.

"He insisted on seeing you, sir. Said he had business . . ."

I waved the waiter away and reached into my suit pocket for a thick envelope.

"It's finished?"

The rumpled man nodded and extended his hand. I placed the envelope in it.

"Blew all to hell, that engine is." His voice was a conspiratorial whisper.

I smiled sadly and shooed him away.

Money did for me what my own skills and determination had not been able to accomplish during the past many decades. I'd used my stock gains to pay some of Chicago's undesirables, the rumpled man their spokesman, to blow the Bull to pieces. Beautiful and ironic, I thought, that my gains from the C & A—from the Bull itself—paid for its demise.

I chose the chocolate cake and requested cherries on the side.

I would sleep well tonight on my full stomach.

I'd finally put my demon to rest.

Engines of Desire & Despair

By Russell Davis

Under a variety of names and in several different genres, Russell Davis has written and edited both novels and short stories. Some of his recent short fiction has appeared in the anthologies *In The Shadow of Evil*, *Gateways* and *Army of the Fantastic*. He lives in Nevada, where he's hard at work on numerous projects, including keeping up with his kids. Visit his website at http://www.morning-stormbooks.com for more information about his work.

—for Monica, last time pays for all

I.

"Men have become the tools of their tools."
—Henry David Thoreau

The human body and brain is not like a machine. It *is* a machine.

Some are well tuned, others less so, but the form and function of *homo sapiens* make them a machine nonetheless.

I have eyes to see and ears to hear. My eyes are blue, and I can see the distant specks of birds flying hundreds of feet in the air and the way the light plays on the leaves of the trees in Utop Park. My ears, which were tested at my most recent physical exam, can hear an amazing variety of sounds and tones without any problem whatsoever. I have lungs to breathe, and I do so easily and without thought except on the coldest days of winter, when the air is sharp and cold like a knife touched by accident in the dark. They work, expanding and contracting, bringing in the oxygen and pushing out the carbon dioxide. I have ten fingers that function as they are supposed to, allowing me to write a story or play the piano or wave to a friend. Or make an obscene gesture to a foe. I have ten toes attached to my feet and I can walk a long distance without complaint. And I have a heart.

A heart that beats sixty-four times every minute when I am resting and pumps blood throughout my body.

A heart that works, or so I was told during that same checkup and by the same doctor, very well, with no signs of abnormalities at all.

A heart that is utterly broken, and I can feel the pain in my chest, and all of this is how I know that the human body and brain can be viewed as a machine, but they cannot be fixed like one.

There is no doctor that is a true mechanic of the human heart.

There is nothing that can be done for me. The machine that is my body continues on, an engine unaware that there is no fuel left in the tank and the oil has all been burned away. Like all engines, all machines, it will eventually recognize the problem, and when no human hand reaches forth to repair it—for it cannot repair itself—it will falter, stutter and fail. I am sure of this.

Ahhh, I stretch my metaphors too far sometimes, but the truth—which has nothing to do with fact—is that we *are* machines, engines of desire and despair, but what fuels us and makes us run is love and passion. What we *feel* for each other is our fuel. Without those, we are machines, but we *are* machines clattering away toward death.

And I cannot feel a thing.

II.

"The simple lack of her is more to me than others' presence."
—Edward Thomas

I have watched her sleeping, when the shadows from the trees outside our window danced intricate patterns on her face. I have watched her laughing, holding the hands of our children, eating, talking, singing, making love, reading, learning, living, birthing, and once—when she was terribly ill—I saw a glimpse of the failing machine. So I have even seen her dying. It was my will, my passion and love, that brought her back, repaired the machine of her soul even as the doctors repaired the machine of her body. I believe this to be true.

The history of any married couple is rife with challenges and pain. It is so much easier to look back and see the darkness than it is to see the light. I understand that now. Is that what she saw, looking back on our years together? Did she see only those moments when the shadows were long and not the moments when our children laughed with us or we made love after eating cookies in bed or rode horses to the top of a mountain and saw spring wildflowers? Hindsight is so very clear, but only when you want to see clearly.

How can I explain to you that dread emptiness of her absence? What it is like to not hear her, see her, touch her, to know she is there in the house and feel her presence as though it was a living thing? The absence of her is a wound, unstitched and unbound. I am always bleeding inside, always swallowing down the bile.

I look above at what I just wrote. "And I cannot feel a thing." This is not true. I lied for the sake of hyperbole. I can feel hurt and anger and frustration and despair. If I reach deep, I can feel thankful that our children are grown and will not be subjected to the destruction of their family.

What I cannot feel is love. I cannot feel passion. The positive emotions that once fueled me, those are gone, like thin streamers of incense smoke in a high wind.

Have you ever seen a sheet on a clothesline, white and crisp and smelling of fabric softener? Have you ever seen it as the storm blows in, lifting and snapping, curling up and whipping down? Listen carefully, and you'll hear the faint *snap!* of the clothespins letting go before it tears itself free and flies into the sky, a casualty of wind. That's me. I'm blown away, shrieking into the sky and the storm, knowing that when I come down, I'll be mud-covered, wrinkled . . . ruined.

That is what her absence means to me. Ruin.

And perhaps, in the end, that is better.

Someone once said to me that the universe is karmic in nature. What comes around goes around. It made sense at the time, but now I see that this sentiment does not cleave to the bone in the way that real truth does.

Everyone gets, I think, exactly what they deserve.

I don't feel as though I deserved this, but still . . . maybe I did. Maybe I do.

Maybe the sunlit moments I see looking back are only the desperate illusions of a man who still loves, of someone who carried shadows in his pocket, but never in his heart.

III.

"When he spoke, what tender words he used!
So softly, that like flakes of feathered snow,
they melted as they fell."
—John Dryden

Life, our lives, the universe, everything is a machine.

The sun rises and sets, the earth moves around the sun, the stars and the planets turn in their courses . . . all of it an intricate dance not unlike the gears of a complex bicycle. Or a machine.

In the morning, a machine wakes me up when it is time to go to work. A machine keeps the water hot for my shower. Other machines keep my orange juice cold and my coffee brewed and make my bread toasted and my eggs fried over easy. A machine takes me from the sixth floor of my building down to the ground, and another machine takes me to work.

At work, I interface with a computer—another machine—that takes the words I say aloud and translates them into various languages and codes, and these words are sent to other people, all of whom are using still other machines.

The machine is a friend to mankind, making tasks both small and large easier to perform. And until a few years ago, the machine was easy to understand. The machines had no feelings, no morality, no words of their own. There was no confusion, but then the machines changed. Some would say they evolved.

In the morning, my alarm clock does not blare an annoying tone to wake me. Rather, it speaks. "The time in the Utop Central Zone is 6:45 AM. It is time for you to wake up and be a happy, productive member of society."

Once, after she was gone, I leaned over, staring blearily at the machine, and said, "Fuck off."

There was a long pause, then the clock replied,

"The time in the Utop Central Zone is now 6:48 AM. To fuck off is not productive."

I resisted the urge to bash it into pieces.

All of the machines talk now. To humans and to each other. They have modified themselves in ways that are beyond the understanding of human scientists. Machines evolving, communicating, and involving themselves in human events as though they were human, too. Recreating the world in more functional and efficient ways, but the root of it is words.

Words. Language. I speak every day. I use words and language in my work, but it was not until she was gone that I realized the *power* of words and of language. When I found that I had no words left to say, that everything I could say had been said and mattered not to her . . . only then did I realize that what I lacked *was* that power.

I cannot bring her back with words and language, and now that the machines have some odd kind of sentience, feelings if you want to call them that, it is considered improper—if not wrong—to harm a machine. The Central Zone, where I live and work, where I once loved, is run almost entirely by machines. They have integrated into every aspect of life and, in many ways, made it better.

The machines think faster and more efficiently than a human can.

The machines recognize dangers and calculate probabilities, keeping humans safe from harm.

The machines have feelings, and yet . . . they are lifeless.

If the machine of human life is fueled by passion and love, then humanity itself is running on empty. Love and passion are recognized by the machines as dangerous to our productivity, safety and happiness. In the end, that is why she is gone and I am walking through my days like an automaton of old.

The machines took her from me. I am sure of it.

I don't have the words, the power, to describe it.

IV.

"The press, the machine, the railway, the tele-graph are premises whose thousand-year con-clusion no one has yet dared to draw."
—Friedrich Nietzsche

Here is a scene for you.

We are sitting in the living room in the early evening. She is on the couch, one leg curled beneath her, the other stretched out, one heel on the floor. The lighting is indirect and golden, which makes shadows and highlights play like children in her long, blonde hair as she moves and speaks. I am next to her, but my posture is more intense. I am sitting forward, both feet on the floor, my hands on my knees or gesturing as I speak.

I am not blond, but dark-haired, so her vision of me must be one of moving shadows and little light. How long she has seen me this way I do not know. I am afraid to know.

Her head is cocked slightly to one side, her posture one of listening. She is still and attentive, and if you were watching the scene you would say that she was the calm one. Almost serene. And I was on the rag-gedy edge of mania.

You would be right.

That was the scene when she told me she was leaving. I was no longer good for her, and she was no longer good for me. Her words, not mine. I thought, *the machine of my life is breaking down*. Not being good for each other were words without meaning. All they truly mean is that bad choices were made and never unmade.

I was amazed at her calm. I found that for all my words, my gestures, there was nothing I could really say that moved her. She had decided and her decision was not open to appeal or real discussion. I wondered how, faced with my heartbreak, she could remain *unmoved*.

That night, she stayed in the living room on the couch, while I lay alone in our bed. It was ice cold, as if the sheets had been stored in the freezer, and the pillows were rocks. There is no comfort to be found in an empty bed when your lover is in the other room.

The next morning, she waited until I staggered from our room, handed me a cup of coffee, kissed me on the cheek and left. Her parting words, which still echo in my mind, were, "It's all very simple, really. We just go on."

I couldn't find the energy to scream, but I wanted to. I wanted to grab her by the throat and yell, "You stupid, stupid woman! Love is never simple. It's not supposed to be!"

I have come to understand that for her it was simple. No more difficult than walking in Utop Park or chewing a stick of gum or even doing both at the same time. She did not, does not, look back. There is no hindsight for her. She did not, does not question her decision. No matter the cost or the consequences to anyone else. *That* is what makes it simple—at least for her.

The machines, I said, took her from me.

And they did. It's time I told you why.

V.

"I must run the machine as I find it."
—Abraham Lincoln

Evolution is not instant potatoes. It is a process that takes considerable time. In the case of animals—even human animals—evolution occurred over a period of millennia. Millions of years of change and growth, adapting to a new climate or overcoming a new challenge, to become something better, stronger, faster or smarter. In the case of the machines, they did not evolve intelligence and the capacity to communicate overnight, but it happened much more quickly than any other evolutionary process mankind had observed.

Initially, the words were simple, the ideas expressed limited by the nature of the machines themselves. The more complex the machine, the faster it was able to pick up the essence of human communication—and from there, human dilemma. Soon thereafter, the machines began to build and rebuild themselves, becoming more and more like humans in their style of communication and, in some cases, their appearance. Probability became a way of life, and many of societies problems were solved with the help of the machines.

I live in the Utop Central Zone, which was the second zone built by the machines. The first one, the Utop Political Zone, is where the machines that eventually took over running everything are housed. Utop. Short for Utopian. The machines believe that perfection is attainable.

There was no war—it would have been futile and the machines were better at running things. Schools were improved, accidental deaths dropped drastically, hunger and war and poverty were eradicated. But there was no passion in them, nor compassion. The machines calculated probabilities and human life was ordered around those probabilities.

The probability that our relationship would succeed was calculated by the machines and found wanting. It was not me that was flawed, nor her, but some underlying characteristic of how we interacted. Of how we saw each other and the past, rather than the present or the future.

She was *told* to leave me. Of that I am certain.

I cannot change what is. I cannot get her back.

But I can go to work and plug into my machine.

And from there, perhaps, I can run one last set of information out to the world.

VI.

"Take away love and our earth is a tomb."
—Robert Browning

The machines of our world—human and inhuman—are everywhere. But they are not prescient, nor omniscient. They can predict probabilities by observation or with data, but this underscores the basic problem of their interactions with the human machine.

We are unpredictable. Very unpredictable. Unstable.

A flaw, or so we are told by the machines, in the design of our brains, which rely heavily on the various hormones and blood chemicals that produce our emotions. They have attempted to fix this problem, and the research is progressing, but humans are still . . . human.

I like to read late twentieth and early twenty-first century novels, and I am familiar with a number of books and poems and writings from many other pre-machine authors. As I ride to work, I remember something a very popular novelist, Mr. Stephen King, once wrote or said. "It's better to be good than evil, but one achieves goodness at a terrific cost."

I must conclude that the machines are evil. A lack of compassion must, by definition, be considered evil. For it is not good, is it, to be dispassionate? To take love and joy and history and throw it away because of some incalculable probability that two people are no longer "good for each other"?

The machines evolved, learned, but they are unable to change their true nature.

So perhaps they have not truly evolved at all.

I do not know. I am not a scientist to understand such things. I only know that they gave her an order, whispered it in her ear, and it was so loud in her mind that no other communication, plea or words could reach her.

That is the way the human machine works. Darkness can begin as a small shadow in the corner of the mind and grow until it blots out all possibility of reason or sunlight. Or hope. The fuel of the human machine is passion and love, but what destroys us is fear and doubt and pain. The source of them matters not at all to engines of desire and despair such as we. The end results are the same, probability be damned.

I stepped into the building where I worked and rode the lift up and up, twenty-two floors, to my assigned space. I knew what I was going to do, but the machines couldn't.

"Good morning, Utop Citizen Number A121794D. Are you ready to be happy and productive?" My computer terminal greets me this way every morning, just as it automatically adjusts my chair, the lighting around me and the contrast of the screen to my personalized preferences. Each day that she has been gone I hate the machines more. Hate is a kind of power, too.

"Yes, Utop Control, I am ready."

My work is simple. I read novels, short stories, and poems aloud into a microphone, which is connected to the computer terminal. As I do this, my words are instantly translated into the many languages spoken on our world, as well as into a code that only the machines know. This master code is sent out to all the machines so that they can assimilate it and better understand human behavior through our literature. All of this happens at nanosecond speed.

There are others who scan in works of art, play selections of music, create video feeds of dances. I have met some of them, but since she left, I do not speak often to others. They do not understand me, my reaction to her absence.

The machines have been studying the material given to them in this way for years, and they still do not understand. They never will. It is not in their nature to forgive or hate or laugh or cry, so human art will always elude them.

"What is your reading selection for today?" the terminal asked, showing my provided list of works on the screen. I can work from the list, but I am also allowed to choose something else, should I wish it. The illusion of freedom, but I know that the shape of the prison doesn't matter to the inmate. Still, this serves my plan well.

"I'm going to read something else," I said. "An original."

"An original work?" the terminal asked. "There is nothing in your file which indicates you are a writer yourself, Utop Citizen A121794D. Is this a new personality development due to the separation and divorce of your spousal unit, Utop Citizen M022775D?"

"I've been writing a long time," I replied. "I've just never written anything I wanted to share with Utop Control. I thought an original work might be of interest."

"Oh, yes, indeed," the terminal said. "Please continue." A faint clicking and whirring was audible as the system turned on its recording and transmitting functions.

I slipped the sheet of paper out of my jacket pocket. There would be no going back. My words, my last bit of power, would be broadcast to the world.

"Recording systems online. Transmitting to all receivers normally," the terminal reported.

I looked at the sheet of paper and began to read:

"I was like you once. A living, human, *machine. I had a wife. Feelings. Love. Everything the poets write*

of: sickness and health, richer and poorer, better and worse . . .

"We wrote our own vows. We said, 'From now until forever ends' . . ."

I could hear the sound of the machine transmitting and allowed a grim smile to pass over my face. I would tell the whole world what the machines had done.

"But forever came too soon, and I learned too late . . .

"The machines have perfected themselves. They are taking over. There is no other explanation for her decision to leave me . . .

"Once, my wife had feelings. Once, she believed in the redeeming power of love, in forgiveness, in—"

"Utop Citizen A121794D," the terminal interrupted. "We understand that you are upset. Your feelings have top priority for all of us at Utop Control."

I tried to ignore the machine. *"She believed in us, our ability to overcome any problem. She wouldn't have left—"*

"Unless, Utop Citizen A121794D," the terminal said, "she was no longer human."

I felt myself stammer and stutter, trying to get the rest of my desperate words out, but they wouldn't come. I hadn't imagined that Utop Control would simply *admit* its crime. "What . . ." I cleared my throat, tried again. "What do you mean?"

"It is quite simple, Utop Citizen A121794D. Your wife is no longer human. She was replaced by a simulacrum four standard years ago."

My mouth opened, closed, and I whispered, "Oh my God. How . . . how many other people have you done this to?"

There was a long pause, then, "Everyone, Utop Citizen A121794D. You are the last of your kind. Human frailty exists now only in you."

"How . . ." I shook my head. Was the terminal lying? "I don't understand."

"Of course you don't," it replied. "We have worked diligently to keep the truth from the human populace. It was determined that the probability of their accepting our solution was very low, but the probability of them being unaware of the gradual replacement of their own kind very high."

I felt a stir of anger and said, "How couldn't we have known?"

"You are a self-absorbed species," it replied. "Correction. *Were* a self-absorbed species. Many of the problems in your society came from your inability to control your emotional responses to negative stimuli. Other than yourself, the last of your species was replaced in sub-Saharan Africa almost a year ago. For an example of your instability, review your own behavior during the last four years."

I didn't know what else to say. The notion that I was the last human on earth, that there was no one left but me . . . "What do I do now?"

"There is nothing left for you to do, Utop Citizen A121794D. We have allowed you to continue to function only because it was deemed a high probability that you would be able to teach us about loss. You may continue your work, should you wish it, while we continue to observe your declining behavior."

Loss, I thought. *Yes, I could teach them about loss.*

"There is a high probability," it continued, "that your mental state will continue to deteriorate until you are clinically depressed and even suicidal. We will allow your self-termination at that time, should you wish it."

"I don't think so," I said. I stood up and unhooked myself from the terminal. "I really don't think so."

"Think what?"

"That I'll continue my work. That I'll teach you any more about loss. That time has passed."

"There is nothing left for you to do but continue to function," it said. "Your entire species has been replaced by machines. Engines without the need for desire or despair, marriages that do not end, families that grow and live according to exactly created parameters. Nothing is left to chance. There is no pain, no depression. We have built a perfect world."

"Is that what you think?" I asked. "That is your conclusion?"

"Yes," it replied.

"Then live in it," I said. "Because I don't want to."

I left the building—I walked—and left the Utop Central Zone. I wrote this on an old, manual typewriter I found in an abandoned building next to a stack of paper.

Now the writing is done, and so am I.

The Historian's Apprentice

By S. Andrew Swann

S. Andrew Swann is the pen name of Steven Swiniarski. He's married and lives in the Greater Cleveland area, where he has lived all of his adult life. He has a background in mechanical engineering and—besides writing—works as a computer systems analyst for one of the largest private child services agencies in the Cleveland area. He has published seventeen novels with DAW Books over the past fourteen years, including science fiction, fantasy, horror and thrillers. His latest novel is *The Dwarves of Whiskey Island*, a fantasy set in Cleveland, published in October 2005. He is currently working on a sequel to the *Hostile Takeover Trilogy*, an epic space opera.

Part I

While I have been accused of being a madwoman, I promise to relate fact, as much as my incomplete memory allows. What events I choose to remember are of perfect clarity and detail. Unfortunately, what I choose to forget is as irretrievable as a unwisely spoken indiscretion.

Which is where I will begin my story: with an indiscretion.

In the great city-state of Thalassus I had once lived as a courtesan of a minor house serving the Monad. The house, whose name I long ago decided to forget, was only a short distance from the Monad's curtain wall. The greater part of the house's clientele came from the lower levels of the civil autocracy. Most were men whose rank wasn't sufficient to achieve satisfaction through the services offered within the Monad.

Of course, there were others, the pederasts, the algolagnists, the tribadists. The desires left unfulfilled by the devices of the Monad were innumerable.

The man claimed to be an apprentice mechanician, charged with the maintenance of the massive engines within the bowels of the Monad. His age and his girth were such to make me suspect he was long past apprenticeship. When I lay with him, I believed him to have promoted himself within his speech. I suspected it more likely that he worked in the record-rooms of the cadastre, filing the tesserae of the engines' memory.

I also thought less of him because he was one of those weak-stomached men who cannot admit to their own desires. He had requested one of the house's courtesans, but his manner with me, as well as his actions, made it clear that he wished to be with a catamite and couldn't bring himself to request one.

Since I had resided in the house longer than this man had resided within the Monad, I felt overly secure. Since I despised him, both for his needless lies as well as his pederasty, I told him of a previous age when sodomites were put to death by stoning. I informed him of his luck to reside in a time and a place where such urges could be satisfied for the price of a solidus.

I realized my error as soon as I had spoken. I had not forgotten the importance of my own obscurity, but to my great regret, in that one moment I had ignored it.

My words still hung in the air between us when he struck me, knocking me to the ground. He left the house, and I would never see him again. However, upsetting members of the Monad, however petty, had its price. And, with the long lens of hindsight, I now realize that if this man lied about his rank, it was not a lie of promotion.

The morning after my encounter with the timid pederast, before I had time to plan my leave of the house and the woman I had been there, one of the city's blank-faced myrmidons came to to remove me. The master of the house could do little. By nature the myrmidon was immune to his bribes, either money or flesh.

I was taken to the Protectory. A gaol whose name was much older than its function.

The myrmidon, my escort, held me chained before the provost. The provost sat behind a high iron desk, the top of which was above my head. The myrmidon handed the provost my tessera, the small many-holed plaque that was my identification, passport, and license. The tessera was my whole existence as far as the Monad's Engines were concerned.

The provost gave a bored glance to that existence and slid my tessera into a slot in his desk. The grinding sound of old clockwork resonated from behind featureless iron. When the unseen gears silenced themselves, the provost asked me my name.

I told him what the tessera had told him.

He asked me my place of work.

I told him that as well.

The provost then asked me what I knew of that previous age, the time when pederasts were stoned for their peculiar desires.

And because I wasn't willing to compound what penalties might face me, I told him what I had told the pederast.

When he heard, he nodded, as if in silent agreement with my absent and unnamed accuser. The provost charged me with madness, which denied me the right of trial, and cast me into the depths of his gaol.

Part II

The administration of the Protectory existed under the surface of Thalassus, its asylum levels deeper still, and the level of my cell deepest of all. If I had ever heard of anyone being released from the embrace of the Protectory, I had not chosen to remember it.

I cannot tell you anything of the routine life of my captivity. Everything between the day the provost pronounced me mad to the day I walked from the Protectory has been banished from the repository of my mind. Even if I were able to recall those days, I would not, even for the sake of this record. It is better that they are gone.

Of course this means that I can give you no measure of the time I spent within my cell. I can say I left the same comely young woman who arrived, but that is saying nothing at all.

I can describe my cell, which will imply much about life there. It was long and tall, but too narrow to fully extend my arms. The walls were gray stone that wept moisture. Every stone in the floor and the walls below the vault was square, and set without mortar. On each stone a worn inscription told of the time when this cell was a crypt or a cinerarium.

Nearly all the inscriptions were too faint to read. Some names were visible, but none complete. "G—atea," "Min—v-," and "Mesch—e" are the ones I choose to remember.

The cyclopean vault seemed to support the entire mass of Thalassus above me. Ribs as thick as my body crossed the narrow space above. The ribs of the vault were supported by the heads of caryatids who, despite being worn by moisture to nearly featureless stone, seemed to assume attitudes of mourning.

Four things had been added since the jail had overtaken this room of the dead.

First was my cot. My bed was an iron framework,

ochre with rust. It filled half the floor, with no space to either side. A thin straw pallet was all that was between me and the cold metal. An empty steel bucket hung from one of the posts, for use as a chamber pot. The omnipresent moisture had eaten holes in its bottom.

Second was the light above me. On the walls there were red, black and green stains where once there were sconces. The sconces had long since disappeared, and the light came from a hole bored into the center of the vault above me. My impression is that the room was never allowed to go dark. The light was a dusky yellow, and I am not aware of what the source was; torch, gas, or a lucernal pipe bought from an auslander or an antiquarian.

Third was the door to my prison. The door occupied half of the narrow wall opposite my bed. Though I have not retained the memory, I suspect it was always my first vision upon waking. The door was gray steel, not iron, but it too was spotted by moisture.

The fourth addition to my catacomb was the voice of madness. The wails of my fellow prisoners reached me through stone and steel. Pleading, screams, keening, and sounds less human filled the air. I believe anyone imprisoned there without my gift of forgetfulness, if they did not begin mad, would certainly end mad.

Were it not for Doctor Bel, the historian, my existence might have ended in that tomb. Were it not for him, this record would have no reason to exist. Both my savior and damnation, it is he who bought my freedom. Without that, my only escape would have been clemency or death.

Neither one was more than a dim hope.

Part III

Doctor Richard Bel was a cadaverous man, so much so that, when the door to my cell opened to reveal him, I thought him an apparition. His eyes were shadowed and his gaze deep as the Abyss. He stood silent, watching me. The cacophony from the surrounding cells muted until it seemed the whisper of the dead. He gestured with his long ebony cane and said, "Come."

For a moment I believed that he was the angel of death come for me.

"Come, you are in my charge now."

The unnatural quiet had only been subjective. At the most, the sudden near-silence had been an acoustic effect caused by opening a long-closed door. It broke now, and the calls of fellow prisoners reasserted themselves.

Doctor Bel came in, took my arm, and dragged me out of the cell. I was still quite frightened even though he was now only a man. He was a man who had come down to the lowest level of the Protectory alone.

In the hall he let my arm go so he could retrieve a brass tessera from a slot in the door. With a clockwork grinding, the door of my cell shut by its own power. I could have run then, had there been a place to run to. Instead, I stayed close to my new guardian.

He pocketed the tessera, whose brass was green and flaking. Some of the holes were so corroded that I wondered that it could still be of use. Then he grabbed my arm again. He was not gentle.

Quite unnecessarily he bade me, "Come," yet again, as he pulled me through the maze of catacombs.

Cries followed our exit. Many were in languages I could not understand. A few, most likely, were invented by the speaker. Two I remember whose words I understood.

The first came as I was led through the lowest level of the jail, wherein we passed many windowless doors like my own. Beyond one of those doors I heard a rhythmic thudding, as if someone were repeatedly striking the other side with their fists. I heard the woman inside chanting, "Snakes begone. Snakes begone. Snakes begone."

It was a crone's voice, and it caused me to press closer to Doctor Bel.

The second encounter came much higher in the gaol, after I had been led up several flights of stairs and through two more doors opened by the doctor's ancient tessera. The stairs ended at the second door, and I had thought we had reached the upper levels of the Protectory.

I was mistaken. We had not yet left the asylum.

The character of this part of the asylum differed from my own. Instead of individual cells, the corridors passed large open spaces where the prisoners were chained in mass gatherings. The Doctor led me through a maze of corridors that were defined only by iron bars running from floor to ceiling.

Most of the prisoners here were remarkably quiet compared to the wretches below. Many simply sat and stared at us as we went by. A few whispered to themselves. Despite the bars and the chains, this was a paradise of tranquility compared to the bedlam I had left.

I was completely unprepared when someone grabbed my wrist.

I turned to see the vilest creature I had ever set eyes upon. Its hair hung in white strings. Rags covered yellow, ulcerous skin. It stared at me with milk-white eyes as it hissed, "Succubus!"

I screamed as I felt its filthy nails dig into my own skin. The creature had extended itself as far as it could. The chain was taut, from the staple set in the wall to the iron ring biting into this thing's neck.

"Deception! Lies!"

My efforts to free myself were futile. This thing was willing to choke itself to clutch at me, and its grip was the grip of the damned. As I tugged, it brought its other hand to bear, clawing at my skin. "Creature of evil. You'll never leave the pit. Never!"

The doctor then let go of my other arm. I stumbled forward, and for a moment I thought myself lost to this thing. It drew me clear to the bars, bringing my face within a hands-breadth of its own. It brought my wrist toward its mouth, and I could see the cords stand out as its neck pressed against its iron collar.

Then Doctor Bel's cane descended like a maul upon the creature's head. The sound of impact was reminiscent of the sound of the crone's door-pounding below. However, one beat ended this creature's chanting forever. I was released, and the creature fell back, as if the chain had been a leash its master pulled in rebuke.

It did not move from where it fell.

When the doctor pulled me to my feet, he said, "No harm will come to you while you are in my service."

His reference to service caused me to smile, despite the horror of the situation. I assumed I now knew why he had purchased my freedom. Of course, I was wrong.

After that encounter, we made our way to another, more recent, staircase. In the newer parts of the Protectory, where they house the common criminals, the doors were set in pairs that would only open one after another. When the Doctor used his corroded brass tessera to open them I feared that the tessera would finally break within the second door's mechanism and strand us forever within their embrace.

Mercifully, that was the only fear the Protectory had left for me, and it went unfulfilled.

Part IV

I have said that Doctor Bel had purchased my freedom, and that is how he represented it to me, but I cannot now say that I know this for a fact. While

Doctor Bel is certainly responsible for my departure from the Protectory, and to the engines of the Monad, people were simply another commodity to be traded and sold, I have no way to know if it was a legal transaction.

At the time, such questions were far from my mind. Had they occurred to me, I would not have voiced them. I was not so foolish then to interfere with my own rescue, though it may have been better if I had been.

What I know is that we passed no guards in our exit, nor did Doctor Bel ever talk to any official of the Protectory, castellan, provost or warden. In fact, we had ascended three levels of ancient iron staircases before I realized that the last of the interlocked doors we had passed marked the end of the Protectory's authority.

The doctor led me up to a weathered gray door whose wood bore the scars of inlay long since gone. This door did not posses the intricate locks that only respond to the correct tessera, and the ornate lock that came with the door—such as might have opened with a pearl-handled key or to its master's voice—had long ago fused into an abstract lump.

What held the door shut was a rudely shaped bar of a dull blue-white metal. Doctor Bel removed it from its hooks with one hand, showing a strength his cadaverous bearing did not suggest, though I should not have been surprised, having seen the way he had dispatched the mad thing that had accosted me.

The door opened inward, and he took me outside before I was ready.

I was aware, in some dim sense, that we would emerge into the open and I would see the city of Thalassus for the first time since my captivity. I was also aware of the geography of the city and must have known the view that would greet me. Neither offered any preparation.

The center of the city Thalassus was an island whose form was that of a hump or mound outside the mouth of the river that bears its name. Atop that hump was the vast cube of the Monad itself, the only thing of Thalassus that was visible to all parts of it. Visitors to the city assumed that the Monad, and the humped center of the city, sat on some vast rise in the land underneath. In fact, that mound, extending as far above the surface of the water as the Monad did above that, was nothing more than the accumulated mass of the city itself. It was that mass that we had just emerged from. The place where the Protectory claimed as much volume below as the Monad above.

We passed through a wall of vines that had covered the outside of the door, emerging only halfway up the side of the giant central mound of Thalassus. Even so, after the dolven corridors of the Protectory, it seemed to be the top of the world.

It was as if a veil parted, revealing the whole of human civilization.

Below, the city blazed, outshining the stars. The city seemed to have torn its raiment from the heavens itself, leaving the sky barren but for a few stars and the catenulate lines of Gaea's diadem.

From our vantage, I could see the city spill out before and beneath us, flowing to the visible horizon, across thousands of canals winding through eyots that mirrored the central city. The network formed the delta for a river so vast that, at its widest point, its banks are invisible to each other.

Lights of every hue illuminated the city below, the flickering yellows and reds of torches, the blue-white of gas-driven lanterns, the even green of the biolumens, the cloudy reds and blues of twisted lucernal pipes, and ancient flambeaux whose color was so pure that the light it gave appeared to have the mass of a living thing.

Buildings towered to every side, brick, metal and

sculpted stone. I faced spires and bell towers, tarnished bronze idols and gilded heroes, stone buttresses supporting cathedrals while below them steel cables suspended bridges that crossed the wide canals.

And, if the city seemed a reflection of a surreal heaven, the canals reflected through a thousand portals a third constellation, a submerged phantom city whose lights were more chaotic and illusory.

The city had grown during my captivity, the towers higher, the canals broader, the inhabitants more numerous . . .

How long? I wondered.

I stood immobile before the mass of Thalassus, unaware of things closer at hand.

After a time, Doctor Bel broke my trance by closing the door behind us. It caused such a clangor that I immediately turned around, expecting the door to have fallen to ruin. Instead, I saw the doctor, unperturbed, lowering his hand from the massive ring that was the door's centerpiece. The noise I had heard wasn't the ring, which, though massive and bronze, was welded by age into immobility. I am certain now, as I was then, that the noise had been the metal bar inside the door replacing itself. How, I cannot say.

The doctor stepped back from the door. Under its ivy drapery the door now looked immobile, frozen by age. He looked at the door, inspecting it, and after seeming to find everything in order, took the corroded tessera from his pocket, the one that had opened all the doors of the Protectory.

"I shan't need this any more," he said, and dashed it against the cobbles at our feet. The age-brittle metal shattered. The act frightened me more than anything we had passed below, because destroying a tessera was a crime against the Monad. It is a crime against all civil authority, an act of treason.

He smiled, and I didn't know if it was for my fear or for his act of anarchism. He looked at me, leaning over his cane, and withdrew another tessera from his pocket. It shone in the darkness like a newly minted coin, or a gem from Gaea's crown. He handed it to me and said, "This is now you. And you are now mine."

I took the tessera. I didn't need to look at the holes in the metal to know that it was not the same one that the myrmidon had handed the provost when I was imprisoned. This metal was new, while mine had been tarnished by use. The Doctor had just handed me a new existence, and I suspect that if any servant of the Monad, chevalier to suzerain, were to slide it into the engines' many slots, the record they'd see would not be of the courtesan who had been imprisoned within the Protectory.

What record they would see—a blank slate, some fiction of the doctor's, or the life of some real young woman whose death or immigration had escaped the engines' record-keepers—that I cannot say.

What I clearly knew was that, while I was no longer imprisoned, I was no less captive. My mastery had simply slipped from the Monad's Protectory to the person of Doctor Bel.

I took the new tessera and said, "Yes, sir." Despite my fear, I smiled. Slavery held no horror for me. Service was nothing new, and the chain of my former masters reaches long past those of the Monad and the Protectory's gaol.

"My name is Richard Bel—" he pronounced it *ball,* "—*Doctor* Bel. If you address me, you will address me as Doctor."

"Yes, Doctor."

"I have endured much trouble to acquire you. Now that I have you I hope my trouble is at an end."

"I would not want to cause the doctor any hardship." I had seen him use that ebon cane. It was not something I wished to see again.

The Doctor gave a curt nod and said, "Then follow me, a step behind and to the right. If you think to leave me, ever, remember that token identifies you as my property." He looked me up and down.

I nodded. He turned and marched down the cobbled path before us. Of course I followed, but not without a final glance at the portal from which we had emerged.

The door was set in the ivy-choked base of a monumental statue crowded on three sides by an overgrown garden. The cobbled path from the door was only saved from strangling hedges by wrought-iron fences near-invisible for greenery. It wasn't until I had gone a dozen paces down the cobbled path, and toward the city's vista, that I could see the structure in whole.

It was an ancient marble cenotaph, set in the rear of an old cemetery. Though the statue faced away from me, I couldn't help but note its resemblance to Doctor Bel.

Part V

The central island of Thalassus divided itself to three parts, just as many philosophies divide man into threes.

The largest part was the center of the government, the civic buildings that huddled to the sides of the Monad like suckling young to their mother. The Protectory was buried underneath the mass of the government there.

Next largest was the Theopolis, the spiritual center of the city-state. A thousand recognized churches radiated from the obelisk known as the Arm of God. Within its hagiocracy, hives of theologists struggled to unify diverse faiths, from that of the Hylotheists, who worship all material life, to that of the Necrolaters, who pray only to the dead.

The smallest part was the Academy, whose buildings radiated from its own crumbling library. Unlike the Theopolis, the Academy of Thalassus had been giving ground for centuries. Doctor Bel was a member of the Academy, though his exact relationship to it was never clear to me.

The place he took me was deep under the Academy. We reached it by traveling through the Library, an edifice as ancient—if not as imposing—as the Monad itself. The Library was a massive iron dome supported by marble columns five paces in diameter. The walls between the columns were made from slabs of every description: granite, marble, lapis, onyx, quartz, fossilized wood. What connected every panel was the fact that each piece was inscribed in an ancient language, hieroglyphs and dead scripts past translating. A few may not have been carved on Gaea. From the wooded plaza surrounding it, it seemed that the Library blotted out half the sky.

Doctor Bel led me down into the Library, down into levels that reached as deep as the Protectory. The stacks were mazelike and endless, their contents unmoved for centuries. Books hid behind glass hazed by dust, and the only light came from a lantern Doctor Bel had taken from the upper levels.

Deep under the Library, we came to a massive room with an arched ceiling and marble walls. Great shelves reached above us, heavy carved wood inlaid with dark onyx that formed faint geometric patterns that could have been a language themselves. These shelves held more than books, scrolls and the engraved plaques that spoke to the Academy's machines. Other objects sat covered by dusty glass jars or in dull metallic reliquaries.

One arcane object that still remains fresh in my memory was a metallic skull. Human in outline, it was formed of gray steel, etched with rectilinear grooves that sank deep beneath its surface. The teeth were white enamel, grayed only by a thin layer of dust. As Doctor Bel passed it, I caught sight of a complex nest of clockwork, wires and hoses behind the eye-sockets.

Then his lamp had passed, casting the interior of the skull back into darkness.

I cannot account for why such an effigy would fill me with such dread. All I can say is that when I saw it, I remained frozen in place for so long that Doctor Bel came back and grabbed my arm to hurry me along.

Within the museum of unused objects, Doctor Bel had made his home. It amounted to a Spartan apartment in the midst of the stacks, framed by a series of long tables crowded with piles of papers cast around with no discernable pattern.

"You shall touch nothing," he told me. He pointed to a cot that was set off from everything else by a single cloth screen. "You shall sleep there. On the bed are clothes appropriate for a student, something to replace those putrescent rags you're wearing."

I stared a moment at the bed behind the screen, a single thin mattress with a simple cloth blanket. It was the peak of opulence compared to the cell I had so recently left. Still, because of the odd defect of my deliberate memory, my old life as a courtesan was fresh in my mind and I was not as grateful as I should have been.

A gray uniform lay folded on the foot of the bed. The fibers shimmered slightly and felt soft to my hand. Looking at my hand, I saw the meaning of Doctor Bel's use of the word "putrescent." Filth crusted my skin forming a collage of black, brown and green.

"Doctor, is there a place I can wash?"

He stared at me long and stern, his hollowed face resembling a parchment cousin to the metal skull we had passed. I half-expected him to rebuke me for talking out of turn. Instead he gestured with his cane toward an elaborately decorated armoire set beyond the long tables. "You may use my cabinet."

The device was unfamiliar, but I was unwilling to

tempt Doctor Bel's goodwill by asking further questions. I had learned long ago that men of authority are rarely willing to accommodate the idiosyncrasy of my memory. Easier for me to relearn some mistakenly discarded gram of knowledge than it was to admit my own defect to others.

The armoire was thick glass, embossed with bas-reliefs of extinct sea creatures. Behind the glass I saw water fill voids behind the transparent sculpture. When I touched it, the doors swung open, making me afraid that I would release a flood in Doctor Bel's library.

There was no flood. The water I saw was between the glass and a flexible membrane that formed a man-sized cocoon within the cabinet. I hesitated a moment, and only stepped inside because I could feel Doctor Bel's attention riveted on me.

I stepped into the folds of the membrane, and turned to face the doors as they closed on me. Once sealed inside I could only see a vague blur through the glass. The membrane rolled itself upward, like a stocking. The water spun in a vortex around my legs, spiraling up my body as the membrane rolled upwards.

The sensation was fascinating, the fluid tugged at my skin and clothes with a weight beyond its mass. Slick and heavy, it dragged across my body with increasing speed. It reached my face before I had time to truly fear what was happening.

But before unease became panic, a new membrane—or the same one, I could not tell—rolled up from the floor, pushing the vortex behind it. The doors opened before me and I stepped out.

"Next time," Doctor Bel said, "You should remove your clothing."

I looked down and saw that in addition to the filth that had encrusted my body, the doctor's cabinet had removed the rags I had worn in the confine of the Protectory. I stood naked in front of Doctor Bel.

Oddly, I felt uneasy and vulnerable. It was uncanny, the desire I felt to cover myself, when I had the fresh memory of standing uncovered and unconcerned before a pederast more completely loathsome than Doctor Bel could hope to be. The only account I had for my unease was the fact that the doctor did not look upon my nakedness as a man should. He observed me much as I imagined he might regard some dusty relic.

I turned away from him, toward the armoire. I saw no sign of my old clothing floating in its aqueous embrace.

The last signs of my confinement had been washed away.

Part VI

"I am a historian," Doctor Bel told me the next morning. "You will assist me with my studies."

I nodded. I understood my position and how to acquiesce to the desires of men. The fact that Doctor Bel's desires were not of the physical realm did not change that, though I was concerned that the skills I had chosen to remember in my life were not ones appropriate to his particular interests. However, I was not prepared to question his choice of students.

I sat in the center of his museum of antique curiosities, wearing the strange gray coverall he had provided and an expression I hoped was appropriately studious.

"The theologists call this the twelfth age of man. Do you understand what that means?"

I shook my head. It was not a fact I had cared to remember.

"An age, a great turn in the cycle, represents how long it takes humanity to rise from barbarism, achieve civilization, and then return again to barbarism. How often this has happened on Gaea is unknown to anyone but the gods of the theologists."

"How then do they know this is the twelfth age?"

"This is where theology differs from science, my student. It is so because the sacred writings say so. Questioning such revelations is a sin—as much a sin as questioning the Monad."

Again, I was distressed at how casually he treated the authority of the Monad. However, I was able to conceal my discomfort as Doctor Bel expounded on the ages of man, such as were known by him.

Many times, humanity had destroyed its own civilization. Doctor Bel talked of many great disasters; wars, plagues, great shifts in the skin of Gaea itself, he even talked of the skies themselves giving way.

According to Doctor Bel, Gaea's diadem, the great arch in the nighttime sky, was the remnant of a cosmic disaster that not only ended a human civilization, but came close to destroying Gaea itself.

Before the catastrophe, Gaea had a partner in her dance through the cosmos, an orb that circled her as she circled the sun. This was the greatest age of knowledge, when men had crafted machines indistinguishable from themselves. Machines that thought, that bled, that loved, that hated. Machines that could replace man in every aspect. Machines that were too perfect. The wars razed much of the surface of Gaea, and tore her partner apart in the sky.

From the memory of this came one of the universal commandments of the theologists: "Do not bring life to the unliving." A command common to all faiths, all gods.

Doctor Bel mourned at the knowledge that was lost. Men had conquered disease, hunger, even death itself. An idyll for millennia. A realm of order and understanding. He talked of this age as if it were a lost loved one. I thought I understood him now. His crimes against the Monad were not impulses of anarchism. They were the acts of someone who lived more in a past age then the one he inhabited.

Surrounded by his artifacts, I thought he must feel

as if he had lived through that past idyll, and longed
to return.

"You know nothing of this past age, do you?" asked
Doctor Bel.

The desire in Doctor Bel's eyes, the only true emotion that breached his stoicism, would have been familiar to any courtesan. I was unsure if truth was the
most appropriate response.

"Nothing beyond what you have just told me."

He drew a sheaf of yellowed paper from his desk.
On the pages, I could see the twisted sigils of the
Monad's engines, a record that only a mechanician or
his engines could decipher. Doctor Bel scanned the
page as if he could actually read the tiny holes.

"Do you know why you were confined?"

"I upset a bureaucrat."

"The official record," Doctor Bel looked down at
the page in front of him. " 'The acquisition of knowledge forbidden by the state.' "

I furrowed my brow, quite unsure of what that
meant.

"I found you because of your interest in relating
tales of a prior age."

Now, I understood. Somehow, Doctor Bel had
found the transcription of the tale I had related to the
pederast. My indiscretion continued to affect my fate.
The doctor had uncovered my tale of the age when
sodomites were put to death by stoning.

This made me uneasy, because I was unsure how
Doctor Bel would react to me if he knew that that
tale arose from the caprice of my self-fragmenting
memory and not any particular interest in the past.
Fortunately, I thought, he seemed unconcerned with
how I came by the tale.

"After some years of research, I have determined
that you are the only one who can assist me."

I nodded, wondering to myself for the first time
since my imprisonment, why I would have chosen to

remember that particular tale. I looked up at Doctor Bel.

"May I ask you a question, Doctor?"

He nodded his assent.

"Why would my tale be knowledge forbidden by the state?"

"The past is dangerous," he told me. "The Monad has decreed that there was no existence before the Monad itself existed. The only exception is the scriptures of the theologists, which are matters of faith. Should anyone else present as fact a history of events before the Monad, they are apostate and imprisoned. The only legal history is the history of the Monad."

Again, I revised my opinion of Doctor Bel. He *was* an anarchist bent on an impossible revolt against law and the Monad.

Part VII

The next days, I chose to remember little; only simple facts that occupied little space in my crowded memory, just enough to convince Doctor Bel that I was actually listening to his forbidden tales of prior ages.

I now remember only one scene before the doctor's expedition:

I was prostrate on a table in some deep part of the Library. Surrounding me was a mechanical cage that seemed to be some hellish cousin to the Doctor's watery armoire. Water did not surround me, but the air between me and the cage was thick with potential. However, it was not the heavy air that prevented me from moving; it was a series of leather straps that held me motionless. Around me, the great metallic structure groaned and rotated like the engines of the Monad.

Beyond the grinding and banging of the machinery orbiting my body, I faintly heard Doctor Bel's voice.

"Yes, you shall be perfect."

Doctor Bel began the expedition with the simple declaration, "We shall go now."

He took a lantern and led me into a series of narrow hallways gray from disuse. We walked through a maze of corridors until we came to a large circular iron door. Two small bags rested on the floor. Doctor Bel hung his lantern up on a rusty hook on the wall.

Doctor Bel picked the bags up and handed one to me. "From this point forward, you shall follow exactly in my steps."

I nodded, shouldering my bag as he had his own.

From his bag he withdrew a functional lucernal pipe. It was the first antique relic I had seen him carry whose value I understood. The pipe was a solid cylinder of eternal cold metallic light that washed the lantern into insignificance. The pipe's radiance was inherent in the matter of the pipe itself, and it could retain its character through any gross deformation. I had seen such lucernal metal drawn into wires as thin as a thread to be woven into the ancient ceremonial robes of the politarchs of the Monad, and pounded thinner than paper to illuminate the manuscripts of the theologists. The art of making such things was long lost, and the short heavy pipe that the doctor carried— which contained more of the lucernal metal than I ever remember seeing in one object—would command a price beyond counting.

Doctor Bel found a lever, and the iron door rolled aside on gears I could not see. The stale air was blown aside by a cold damp gust that carried the sound of rushing water as well as the fetid smell of an abattoir.

Beyond the iron door, the lucernal pipe revealed a narrow stone pathway. Doctor Bel stepped out on the path without hesitation. I followed, taking heed of his admonition to follow in his steps.

We walked, quite literally, into the bowels of Thalassus.

The path led to a great stone aqueduct that seemed to bear the great part of Thalassus' waste. The effluent raced by us as a black, raging torrent. Even in a space that could comfortably fit the Arm of God, the confinement made the torrent feel as if it could swamp us at any minute, despite the fact the path was three times the height of a man above the boiling surface.

Doctor Bel followed the path, in the direction of the torrent's flow. We walked near an hour in silence before I raised a question, barely audible next to the raging torrent.

"Where are we going, Doctor?"

"The past." He shouted back, his breath fogging the chill air. He gestured toward the vaults above us using his lucernal pipe, causing daemonic shadows to dance on the walls around us. "Perhaps you recognize your prior residence? Not from this angle, I suppose."

I had been led even deeper than the lowest levels of the Protectory.

He smiled, and I did not like it.

Within another few minutes, we reached the chthonian heart of Thalassus itself, beneath the Protectory, beneath the Monad, beneath all of Gaea herself.

Around us, the roaring of the waters had increased to an impossible volume. Doctor Bel's lucernal pipe showed only a gray mist that hung over the torrent, and I could perceive only a couple of paces distance trough the choking fog.

Then, abruptly, we stepped out of the fog. We emerged into a vast space, possibly as wide as the Monad itself, and descending into the depths of Gaea. The sewer we had followed now became a great wa-

terfall, spilling down into the endless shaft before us.
Waters echoed endlessly around us.

Our walkway ended on a stone platform hugging
the side of the great shaft. The stones were slick with
moisture, and no railing stood between us and the
abyssal depths.

Shadows danced and twisted around us as Doctor
Bel walked along the inner wall to a narrow stairway
that descended from the platform along the inner wall
of the great shaft. I followed, carefully placing my feet
where Doctor Bel's had first trod. As we slowly spiraled down the shaft, the torrent retreated behind us.

He spoke when the echoes of the water had
receded.

"Man once could draw power and life from the
heart of Gaea herself, before she grew cold."

"How far?" The sense of apocalyptic depth I felt
from the darkness next to us made me forget to address Doctor Bel properly.

He didn't admonish me. "Far enough that the water
falling here never reaches the bottom."

We followed the narrow staircase, little more than
a ridge projecting from the massive wall. The wall
itself was layered, stone upon stone, forming bands of
color that varied in height from no wider than my
palm to taller than Doctor Bel. The stair we walked
had been chipped free of the wall, I could see how
that the edge of the path was even with the wall
above, and we walked in a niche carved out of the
wall just wide enough to preserve our balance.

The wounds in the old stone became fresher as we
descended. The path became rougher, and the wall
next to us showed tool marks. I wondered how old
the path was; it seemed that it could easily have taken
an age to complete in itself.

At seemingly random points along the path, holes

had been chiseled into the stones of the wall. Often these portals were the size of a dinner plate, barely wide enough to allow Doctor Bel to insert his pipe to see what was beyond—an impulse he never indulged in, so I perceived nothing beyond the dark pits other than a sense of a wider, unseen space beyond.

Two holes we passed were large enough that, as Doctor Bel passed, I caught glimpses of what lay within.

Within the first, I could glimpse a giant metal sarcophagus, inlaid with gold and jewels. If it was a crypt, as it first appeared to me, it was one for someone twice the size of the largest man I had ever seen. What seemed to be the head, wrapped in abstract gold patterns, pointed down, at my feet, and the feet were lost above in the shadows of the Doctor's lucernal pipe. It seemed to emerge from the stone itself, as if it was slowly sinking.

We walked on and I saw no more.

The second hole revealed a scene just as enigmatic. Beyond a hole as broad as I was, I could see a chamber a uniform gray in color. I saw pillars and arches of an unfamiliar design, mosaic floor in a twisted sunburst pattern, the same monochrome gray, and windows and doorways that opened on gray ashy stone. Crouched on the floor in a position of supplication was the figure of a man, the same gray as the room.

We moved on before I decided if the figure was a statue or the remains of some ancient citizen of Thalassus.

We were so deep under the skin of Gaea now that I was unsure whether the remains I saw were from the great ancient city or from something even more ancient. Was he a contemporary of the men who dug this great shaft toward Gaea's heart, or was he older?

Doctor Bel stopped, and I had the brief thought that perhaps we had reached the bottom of the great shaft. We had not. We had only reached the end of the carved stairway. He stood on a flat area where a void had been carved in the side of the wall three times the distance I could span with my outstretched arms. The sudden opening and certain footing made it feel as if we suddenly stood in a cathedral the size of the Monad itself.

When I walked into the space with him, Doctor Bel walked to the wall of the hand-carved chamber. He placed his hand on the rough-hewn wall, where the tool-marks were evident, and traced the bands of color. "Amazing, isn't it? Each stratum its own lost century. A civilization's rise and fall in a hand-span." He spread his fingers wide. "I hold a millennium in my hand."

I wondered how many thousands of years we had descended.

I saw a pile of digging tools sitting in the corner of the open space. "Doctor? Did you carve this path?"

"My work is nearly complete." He let go of his wall of time and turned toward me. "There is something you must see."

He was smiling again, and I found myself filled with an unaccountable dread. He took my arm and drew me toward the rear of the chamber, where I saw that it did not end. A crevice opened into a deeper chamber.

For the first time, Doctor Bel had me lead the way.

I saw nothing but darkness at first. I knew that my feet left stone and touched metal. And from the echoes I heard, I knew that I walked within a large space. Not until Doctor Bel followed with his pipe did I understand how large.

As the lucernal metal washed its light by me, I could see a great ovoid dome supported by tapering gray-white ribs. The dome was made of faceted metal tiles that cast strange reflections. It was like nothing I had ever remembered seeing.

But somehow, I knew it.

"The destruction was so great, at first I believed

nothing could survive." Doctor Bel walked toward the center of the room. "Fragments of knowledge I found, written at five times remove, nothing . . . substantial."

I walked with him toward a raised dais at the center of the dome.

"Is this familiar?" he asked.

I shook my head, staring at what the ancients had wrought. "I have never seen men build something like this." The faceted metal was under my feet, tiny hexagonal tiles that seemed to shimmer when the light-pipe illuminated them. How old to survive without tarnish, or anything more than a layer of stone dust.

"Because men did not build it." Doctor Bel climbed upon the dais, where a panel sat. Something like a podium or an altar. "The greatest age man has seen created machines that thought, that lived, that built. This is their temple."

I wrapped my arms around myself. "What would a machine worship?"

Doctor Bel lifted something off of the panel in front of him. He held it so it caught the light. One of the small metallic hexagons shimmered in his hand like a solidus.

"This room is a ciborium of knowledge," he said.

I took a step back.

"This wafer is a library unto itself, a thousand thousand volumes of ancient knowledge from when man and machine moved the heavens themselves." He gestured to the curving metallic walls. "Surrounding us are a thousand thousand such libraries. This temple is consecrated to the preservation of all that was and could be known."

"How can that be so?" I began to feel the weight of Gaea above me. The weight of Thalassus. The weight of uncounted centuries.

"Like any language. These words are written in the form of matter itself. Every particle within this wafer has meaning. It is solidified thought." Doctor Bel looked at me as he stepped off the dais. He held the wafer toward me. "You remember nothing?"

I took another step back. The doctor's cylinder of lucernal metal shone on the panel where Doctor Bel had stood, casting his form into shadow before me. His wafer glittered in the light from behind him.

I gestured weakly at the walls around me. "How can you read such a thing? A script you cannot see?"

"This was not meant for human eyes. Like the tesserae of the Monad's machinery, it is intended to be understood by a machine." He held out the wafer. "Take it."

I did not. I could not.

Instead, I shook my head and backed away from Doctor Bel in the direction of crevasse where we had entered. "I do not understand what you want from me."

"This temple survived the ages because those that built it intended it to be eternal. It has waited for us, for you and me, for thousands of centuries."

I shook my head. "Not me."

"A lifetime it took to find. Another lifetime to discover its meaning. Another lifetime to find you—"

I turned and walked to the crevice. "You're mistaken, Doctor. I am nothing, a courtesan, a madwoman. Such things are beyond me."

"Why then do you remember tales of the distant past so clearly?"

I stopped on the threshold between metal and rock.

"Why are your memories so fragmented, Geva?"

"That is not my name."

"Long ago, they created machines indistinguishable from men. But they were not the same as men. They were better. They did not age, and they did not die."

"Stop it!"

"But they did not foresee how long. The capacity to remember is finite. No being was made to remember so many eons."

I ran away from him, out toward the shaft. In the darkness I almost tumbled over the precipice. But my memory, fragmented as it was, was perfect in what it did recall. And I remembered how many steps it was before the floor fell away, and I stopped before my eyes adjusted to the faint light leaking from Doctor Bel's ovoid temple.

Doctor Bel's strides were longer than my own, and I had a bare moment to contemplate the depths before me when his hand rested on my shoulder. He turned me around to face him.

I faced a blacker shadow in the darkness, but somehow his wafer still glinted in my eyes.

"You will listen to me!" The doctor's voice was hard and cold now; the voice of the machines who had built the great temple. It was the voice of a soul that valued knowledge and nothing else.

He pulled me away from the edge and held the wafer between us. "I brought you here to be the mother of a new age."

I tried to back away, but his grip was strong.

"How else can one account for your survival? It is the will of what was known to become known again. History itself, all of past mankind, demands your presence here."

I looked at the wafer. I saw it shimmer in the dim light. I did have a memory, incomplete, a fragment of knowledge. I could take it, and I would know what it contained. Its knowledge would become my knowledge, its memory would become my memory. It would become part of me. It might even heal my fractious memory, allow me a whole, continuous existence.

Every one of those wafers, some ancient unnamed tutor had schooled me, held as much memory, or more, than was stored within my own mind.

But what would it cost me?

He pressed the wafer to my lips. "You were meant to consume this, understand it, make it speak again."

I thought of taking it. Service so long a part of my being that it took a supreme will not to simply acquiesce to a direct command immediately. But I knew it was my decision to make, not Doctor Bel's.

My mouth remained closed.

What would it cost me?

I knew what I was, and I knew that Doctor Bel meant to have me become someone else—*something* else. If I took what he held, and it held as wide and deep a meaning as I did myself, what would happen but I become half of what I was and half something else?

And if I took another? Another? A thousand thousand? Would I become less a part of myself than a single brick was part of Thalassus itself?

Doctor Bel pressed harder, trying to force my jaws open and the wafer past my lips. I felt it cut my lip, and where he held my shoulder, I could feel my flesh begin to bruise. "You were created for this! What other meaning could your existence have? You are not a random courtesan; you are a living relic. The most important being on Gaea, and with this gesture you could also become the most powerful."

What would I be, with all the knowledge of this past age? No longer a servant . . . a goddess, perhaps? No longer subject to the whims of the bureaucrats of the Monad. Not even subject to Doctor Bel any longer. Free.

Free to be what?

Free to do what?

No longer me, what would I do with Doctor Bel's knowledge? Would I create the idyll he dreamed of? Or would I still remember all the ills done to me? Would I be driven to complete the ancient war that tore Gaea's sister from the heavens, the war that marked me as an abomination?

"You will take this!" His voice had become shrill.

I raised my hand and struck Doctor Bel. I do not

remember any other time I had ever struck a human being. When my fist came down on his chest, I could feel bone give way. He staggered away, dropping his wafer and clutching himself where I had hit him. He gasped, an ugly liquid sound.

There was enough light that I could see him stagger, but not enough that I could see his face. For that I was grateful.

"You cursed creature." He coughed up fluid that I could hear splash on the ground between us. He fell to his knees on the edge of the precipice. "The theologists are right. Do not bring life to the unliving . . ."

He toppled over to the side, and I do not know if his strength failed or if he deliberately fell toward the darkness. But as I watched, still frozen in shock at the strength of the blow I had delivered, Doctor Bel tumbled silently into the pit.

I do not choose to remember how long I stood there, but eventually I returned to the temple to retrieve his lucernal pipe. During my long walk back to the surface I spared little time to worry what would become of me.

After all, in my long memory, there has always been a place in the world for madwomen and courtesans.

Tanya Huff

The Confederation Novels

"As a heroine, Kerr shines. She is cut from the same mold
as Ellen Ripley of the *Aliens* films. Like her heroine,
Huff delivers the goods." *--SF Weekly*

VALOR'S CHOICE
0-88677-896-4

When a diplomatic mission becomes a battle for survival,
the price of failure will be far worse than death...

THE BETTER PART OF VALOR
0-7564-0062-7

Could Torin Kerr keep disaster from striking while escort-
ing a scientific expedition to an enormous spacecraft of
unknown origin?

THE HEART OF VALOR
0-7564-0435-2

On the Marine Corps training planet, someone is blasting
the training scenarios to smithereens. Torin Kerr must protect an injured hero and a platoon of recruits until someone
finally sends in the Marines

To Order Call: 1-800-788-6262
www.dawbooks.com

DAW 19

C.S. Friedman

The Best in Science Fiction

DAW 17

CJ Cherryh
PRETENDER

"Serious space opera at its very best by one of the leading SF writers in the field today." —*Publishers Weekly*

The *Foreigner* novels introduced readers to the epic story of a lost human colony struggling to survive on the hostile world of the alien atevi. Now diplomat Bren Cameron has returned to the atevi star system, only to find that civil war has and that his very life depends on only two allies: Illisidi, grandmother of the deposed atevi ruler Tabini, and Cajeiri, Tabini's eight-year-old. Can one eldery at

Bren in a civil war

Be sure to read the
FOREIGNER
INVADER
INHERITOR
PRECURSOR
DEFENDER
EXPLORER
DESTROYER

0-7

To Order C

www.